SWEPT IN
TYCOON'S ORLD

CARA COLTER

ADDING UP TO FAMILY

MARIE FERRARELLA

MILLS & BOON

First Published in Great Britain 2018
by Mills & Boon, an imprint of HarperCollinsPublishers,
1 London Bridge Street, London, SE1 9GF

ISBN: 978-0-263-26517-0

0818

This book is produced from independently certified FSC™ paper to ensure responsible forest management.

For more information visit: www.harpercollins.co.uk/green

Printed and bound in Spain
by CPI, Barcelona

SWEPT INTO THE TYCOON'S WORLD

CARA COLTER

To Kymber,
the man my daughter has given her heart to.

CHAPTER ONE

"WHO IS THAT?" Chelsea's whisper was breathless.

Bree Evans shot her young assistant an exasperated look. "You've got to stop it. We were asked at the briefing not to gawk at the celebrities. It's part of our agreement to provide sample products and a display for this event. To be strictly professional. No staring. No autographs. No—"

Chelsea, unaware, or uncaring, that she was jeopardizing Bree's big break, was not paying the least bit of attention to her boss. Instead she was standing completely frozen, a neatly gift-wrapped box of Kookies for All Occasions' Love Bites in her hand. Bree followed her gaze, looking toward the outside door that led into the foyer area of the concert hall, where they were setting up.

Oh, no.

"Who *is* that?" Chelsea whispered again.

Oh, no. Had she said it out loud?

He was everything Bree remembered, only more. She had not seen him, in person, anyway, for six years. Though it hardly seemed possible, in that time his *presence* had multiplied. He had lost any hint of boyish slenderness, and the gorgeous lines of his face had settled into maturity. His dark brown hair, which she remembered as untamed, touching his collar and sweeping across his forehead, was now cut short and neatly groomed, as befit his position.

"It's Brand Wallace," Bree said carefully. She positioned herself with her back to the doorway he was coming through. Her heart was beating way too fast. Good grief. Her palms were sweating.

"Like in *Braveheart*?" Chelsea gasped.

"That was Mel Gibson," Bree explained with what was left of her patience. "Gibson *played* the part of William Wallace—he *wasn't* William Wallace."

Still, even though she didn't want to, Bree understood why Brand would make her young assistant think of brave hearts. There was something about him, and always had been—a way of moving with supreme grace and confidence that suggested a warrior, a man who was certain in his own strength and courage and capabilities.

Chelsea was still totally distracted. "I have never seen a more stunning example of the male of the species. Never."

Despite ordering herself not to, Bree slid another careful look at the doorway. She had to give Chelsea that. Brand Wallace was a stunning example of the male species!

He'd stopped just inside the double glass doors, his head tilted toward Shelley Grove, organizer of the Stars Come Out at Night, a charity gala to help fund the construction of a new wing for Children's Hospital.

Shelley had her hand cozily on his arm and was beaming up at him. He was steel, and women were magnets drawn to him.

Though the room was beginning to fill with well-known celebrities, many of whom were in Vancouver—"Hollywood North," as it was sometimes called—filming television series and movies, he stood out from all of them.

Even surrounded by some of the world's most dazzling people, there was something about him that was electric. It sizzled in the air around him, sensual and compelling.

He was in a sports jacket that, by the cut, hang and fit, was obviously designer. It showed the breadth of his shoulders, the power in him. White shirt—no doubt silk—and no tie. The shirt was tucked into dark jeans that clung to the hard lines of his thighs.

He was as fit and muscular, as outdoorsy-looking, as he had been when he'd worked as a summer student for her dad's landscaping company.

Brand made the extremely famous actor, who was standing a short distance away from him, look small and very, very ordinary.

"I'm sure I know who he is," Chelsea said, her tone mulling. "I've seen him in something. *Warriors of the New Age?* No, I know all of them. Maybe that new series. You know the one? Where the lady time-travels and the gorgeous guy—"

"He's not an actor," Bree said. "Chelsea, please put the cookies out. We only have twenty minutes until the official start time and I—"

She had to what? Leave, obviously. Before he saw her.

"But I know who he is," Chelsea said. "I'm sure of it." She unwillingly turned back to emptying the cookie-filled boxes, her body angled sideways so she could keep casting glances his way.

"You probably saw him on the cover of *City* magazine," Bree said. "That's why you feel as if you know who he is. Could you put a row of Devilishly Decadent at the end of the display?"

"Brand Wallace," Chelsea announced, way too loudly. "The billionaire! You're right! *City* had him on the cover. I couldn't turn around without seeing that glorious face on every newsstand! I don't usually buy it, but I did. He founded an internet start-up company that went insane with success—"

Bree shot a look to the doorway. Apparently he had heard Chelsea yelling his name like a teenager who had spotted her rock-star idol. He was casting a curious look in their direction.

Bree did not want him to see her. She particularly did not want him to see her in her Kookies outfit. She and Chelsea were both wearing the uniforms she had designed, and Chelsea had sewn. Until precisely three minutes ago, she had been proud of how she had branded her company.

Kookies sold deliciously old-fashioned cookies with a twist: unexpected flavors inside them, and each different type claimed to hold its own spells.

And so the outfits she and Chelsea wore were part sexy witch, part trustworthy grandmother. They both had on granny glasses, berets shaped like giant cookies, and their aprons—over short black skirts and plain white blouses—had photos of her cookies printed on them, quilted to make them look three-dimensional. It was all so darn *cute*.

Somehow she did not want the man her father had convinced to escort her to her senior prom to see her as cute. Or kooky. She certainly did not want him to see her with a giant cookie on her head!

In fact, she did not want Brand Wallace to see her at all. He belonged to another time and another place. A time when she had still believed in magic. A place that had felt as if her world would always be safe.

She shot another glance at the doorway. He was still looking in their direction—she could see he was trying to extricate himself from the conversation with Shelley.

"He's coming this way," Chelsea sighed. "How's my hair?"

Out of the corner of her eye, Bree saw Chelsea flicking her hair. She also saw there was an emergency exit just a little behind and to the left of their table. For some reason, it felt imperative to get out of there. And out of the apron. And the beret. Especially the beret.

It was trying to remove both at once that proved dangerous. She was twisting the apron over her head and taking off the beret with it, when, too late, she saw the corner of a box of Little Surprise cookies that was jutting out from under her display table. At the last second she tried to get her foot over it and failed.

The toe of her shoe caught on the box, and it caught the leg of the table, which folded. Apron and beret twisted around her neck, she had to make a split-second decision whether to save the cookies or herself. The cookies, which represented so much hard work, and her future—being invited to participate in this event was a huge coup for her company—won.

She dove under a cascade of Spells Gone Wrong boxes, which fell on her, one by one, until she was very nearly buried in them.

Really, it was a slow-motion and silent disaster, except for the fact she had managed to break the fall of the delicate cookies.

The incident probably would have gone completely unnoticed if Chelsea had not started shrieking dramatically.

And then he was there, moving the avalanche of boxes gently out of the way to reveal Bree underneath them. He held out a hand to her.

"Miss, are you—"

He stopped. He stared at her.

She blinked where she was lying on the floor, covered in boxes, and remembered. She remembered his eyes, the glorious deep brown of them, warm as dark-roasted coffee. She remembered that very same tilt of his mouth, something faintly sardonic and unconsciously sexy in it.

She remembered the *feeling* of his gaze on her, and a forbidden warmth unfolded in her that made her feel boneless.

"Bree?" he said, astounded.

She heard Chelsea's cluck of astonishment.

"Breanna Evans," he said slowly, softly, his voice a growl of pure sensuality that scraped the nape of her neck. And then his hand, strong and heated, closed around hers and he pulled her to her feet, the cookie boxes, which she had sacrificed her escape to save, scattering. His grasp was unintentionally powerful, and it carried her right into the hard length of him. She had been right. The shirt was silk. For a stunned moment she rested there, feeling his heat and the pure heady male energy of him heating the silk to a warm, liquid glow. Feeling what she had felt all those years ago.

As if the world was full of magical possibilities.

She put both hands on the broadness of his chest, and shoved away from him before he could feel her heart, beating against him, too quickly, like a fallen sparrow held in a hand.

"Brand," she said, she hoped pleasantly. "How are you?"

He studied her without answering.

She straightened the twisted apron. Where was the beret? It was kind of stuck in the neckline of the apron and she yanked it out, and then shoved it in the oversize front pocket, where it created an unattractive bulge.

"You're all grown up," he said, in a way that made her blush crimson.

"Yes," she said, stiffly, "People do tend to do that. Grow up."

She ordered herself not to look at his lips. She looked. They were a line of pure sexy. The night of her prom she had hoped for a good-night kiss.

But he hadn't thought she was grown up then.

Did it mean anything that he saw her as grown up now?

Of course it did not! Chances of her tasting those lips were just as remote now as they had been then. He was a billionaire, looking supersuave and sophisticated, and she was a cookie vendor in a bulging apron. She nearly snorted at the absurdity of it.

And the absurdity that she would still even *think* of what those lips would taste like.

But she excused her momentary lapse in discipline. There wasn't a woman in the entire room who wasn't thinking of that! Chelsea's interest, from the first moment she had laid eyes on him, had made it clear Brand Wallace's sex appeal was as potent as ever.

"You know each other?" Chelsea asked, her voice a miffed squeak, as if Bree had kept state secrets from her.

"I was Bree's first date," he said softly.

Oh! He could have said anything. He could have said he was a summer student who had worked for her father. But oh, no, he had to bring *that* up.

"I don't recall you being my *first* date," she said. "I'd had others before you." Freddy Michelson had bought her a box lunch at a fifth-grade auction. That counted. Why did he think he'd been her first date?

No doubt her well-meaning father had told Brand that his bookish, introverted daughter had not been asked to her senior prom. Or anywhere else for that matter.

She could have felt annoyed at her father spilling her secrets, but no, she felt, as she always did, that stab of loss and longing for the father who had always acted as if she was his princess, and had always tried to order a world for her befitting of that sentiment.

"Your first date?" Chelsea squealed, as if Bree had not just denied that claim.

Bree shot Brand a look. He grinned at her, unrepentant, the university student who had worked for her father during school breaks. The young man on whom she had developed such a bad crush.

She turned quickly to the fallen table, and tried to snap the fallen leg back up. It was obstinate in its refusal to click into place.

"Let me," Brand said.

"Must I?"

"You must," Chelsea said, but Bree struggled with the table leg a bit longer, just long enough to pinch her hand in the hinge mechanism. She was careful not to wince, shoving her hand quickly in her apron pocket.

"Here," he said, an order this time, not an offer. Bree gave in, and stepped back to watch him snap the leg into place with aggravating ease.

"Thanks," Bree said, hoping her voice was not laced with a bit of resentment. Of course, everything he touched just fell into place. Everything she touched? Not so much.

"Is your hand okay?"

Did he have to notice every little thing?

"Fine."

"Can I look?"

"No," Bree said.

"Yes," Chelsea breathed.

Bree gave Chelsea her very best if-looks-could-kill glare, but Chelsea remained too enamored with this unexpected turn of events to heed Bree's warning.

"Show him your hand," she insisted in an undertone.

To refuse now would just prolong the discomfort of the incident, so Bree held out her hand. "See? It's nothing."

He took it carefully, and she felt the jolt of his touch for the second time in as many minutes. He examined the pinch mark between her thumb and pointer, and for a stunning moment it felt as if he might lift her tiny wound to his lips.

She held her breath. Somewhere in the back of her mind she heard Chelsea's sigh of pure delight.

Of course, one of the most powerful men in Vancouver did not lift her hand to his lips. He let it go.

"Quite a welt," he said. "But I think you're going to live."

Feeling a sense of abject emptiness after he'd withdrawn his hand, Bree turned her attention to the boxes of cookies scattered all over the floor, and began to pick them up. He crouched beside her, picking them up, too.

"Please don't," she said.

"Thank you for your help," Chelsea said firmly, clearly coaching her boss how to behave around an extraordinary man.

"I can get them," Bree said.

But Brand stayed on the floor beside her, reading the labels out loud with deep amusement. His shoulder was nearly brushing hers. An intoxicating scent, like the forest after rain, tingled her nostrils.

"'Little Surprises,'" he said, reading the boxes. "'Love Bites. Devilishly Decadent. Spells Gone Wrong.' These are priceless," he said.

His appreciation seemed genuine, but she now felt the same about her cookie names as she had just felt about the apron and the beret. She felt *cute* rather than *clever.* She wished she had come up with an organic makeup line, like the woman at the booth set up across the foyer from her.

"Bree, are these your creations?"

"Yes, Kookies is my company."

"I like it all. The packaging. The names. I'm glad you ended up doing something unusual. I always wondered if it would come true."

The fact that he had wondered about her, at all, knocked down her defenses a bit.

She stared at him. "If what would come true?"

"That night, at your prom. Don't you remember?"

She remembered all kinds of things about that night. She remembered how his hand felt on her elbow, and how his same forest-fresh scent had enveloped her, and how every time he threw back his head and laughed her heart skipped a beat. She remembered dancing a slow dance with him. And she remembered that she, school bookworm and official geek, had been the envy of every other girl in the room. She remembered, when the evening had ended, leaning toward him, her lips puckered, her eyes closed, and him putting her away.

"Do I remember what?" she asked, her voice far more choked than she would have liked it to be!

"They gave out all those titles in a little mock ceremony partway through the dance. Most likely to succeed. Mostly likely to become prime minister. You don't remember that?"

"No."

"Most likely to become a rodeo clown, most likely to win the Golden Armpit for bad acting."

"Those weren't categories!"

"Just checking to make sure you were paying attention."

As if anyone would *not* pay attention to him. His grin widened, making him seem less *billionaire* and more *charming boy from her past.*

She remembered this about him, too—an ability to put people at ease. That night of the prom, gauche and starstruck, she had wondered if it was possible to die from pure nerves. He had teased her lightly, engaged her, made himself an easy person to be with.

Which was probably why she had screwed up the nerve to humiliate herself by offering him her lips at the end of the evening.

"Now that I've jarred your memory, do you remember what your title was?"

"I hardly remember anything about that night." This was not a lie. She remembered everything about *him*, but the other details of the night? Her dress and the snacks and the band and anyone else she had danced with had never really registered.

"Most likely to live happily ever after. That was the title they bestowed on you."

The worst possible thing happened. Not only was she here on the floor, picking up her mess with the most devastatingly attractive man she had ever met, in a silly apron, with her hair scraped back in a dumb bun and granny glasses perched on her nose, but now she was also going to disgrace herself by bursting into tears.

CHAPTER TWO

No!

Bree Evans was not going to cry in front of Brand Wallace. She had a broken dream or two, but so what? Who didn't?

She bit the inside of her cheek, hard. She made herself smile.

"Of course they did," she said. "Happily-Ever-After. Look. Here's the proof." She bought a moment away from the intense gaze of his eyes on her face. She picked through the boxes of cookies.

There they were, the favorite kooky cookie for when she supplied weddings. She opened a box and pulled a cookie from its wrapping.

Shortbread infused with strawberries and champagne.

She passed it to him, and he took a quizzical bite.

"There you go," Bree said, and hoped he could not hear the tight, close-to-tears note in her voice. "Happily-Ever-After."

She watched as his eyes closed with pleasure. He was distracted, as she had hoped.

When he opened his eyes again, he smiled at her.

"That is one of the oddest—and tastiest—combinations of flavors I've ever experienced. Ambrosia."

"Thank you. I'll tuck that away for a new cookie name."

But then she saw she might not have distracted him quite as completely as she hoped, because he was watching her way too closely. She felt as if his eyes locked on the faint quiver of her lip.

"My company has an event coming up, a charity ball in support of this same goal, to raise funds for the new wing of Children's. Do you think I could get you to supply some of these?"

Bree's mouth fell open.

"Of course," Chelsea said smoothly.

"I'm sure they will be planning some kind of midnight snack or party favor," Brand said. "Have you a card? I'll give it to my event planner, and she'll be in touch."

Being around him was a roller-coaster ride, Bree thought, as she turned, flustered, to get him her business card. For a stunning moment she had thought he was showing interest in her. He'd quickly doused that by saying his event planner would be in touch.

This kind of opportunity was exactly why she was at this event, Bree reminded herself firmly, turning with a bright, hopefully professional, smile to give him the card.

He slipped the card into his inside jacket pocket, and popped the rest of the cookie into his mouth. It drew her attention, unfortunately, to the rather sensuous curve of his lips as he chewed.

"Do you want to go for a quick coffee?" he asked her.

A roller-coaster ride!

The invitation seemed to take him by surprise as much as it did her.

"R-right now?" she stammered. "Things are just about to begin. See? People are going through to the auditorium. The program said Crystal Silvers is going to sing first."

"I don't care about that."

One of the most sought-after performers in the Western world, and he didn't care about that? He cared more about having coffee with her?

This was dangerous territory indeed.

Bree gestured helplessly at her display. "Oh, I couldn't possibly—"

"You're going for coffee," insisted Chelsea, who had never had a stubborn moment in her life—she was certainly changing things up tonight. Her tone was firm, brooking no argument.

"No." Bree aimed her best who-is-the-boss-here? look at her assistant.

Chelsea ignored it. "Go, I can handle this."

"No, I—"

"Go!" Chelsea said, and then, under her breath, she added, "Live dangerously, for Pete's sake."

"Unless your husband would object," Brand said smoothly.

Chelsea snorted in a most unflattering way.

Brand's gaze slid to Bree's ring finger. She wanted to hide it behind her back as if its nakedness heralded some kind of failure.

"Boyfriend, then."

Chelsea rolled her eyes. "She doesn't have a boyfriend."

She was as oblivious to the daggered look Bree gave her as she had been to the who-is-the-boss-here? look.

"The last guy she met on e-Us was a loser."

Since Chelsea was so adept at ignoring Bree's looks, dancing happily with insubordination, Bree managed to step hard on her foot before she could elaborate on the e-Us thing. Chelsea gave her a sulky look, but clamped her mouth shut.

Even so, damage had been done. Bree could see him registering what e-Us was.

One thing that was obvious about someone like Brand Wallace? He'd never been on a site like e-Us in his life.

"We'll just go around the corner," he said persuasively. "Two old friends catching up."

"Old friends," Chelsea breathed. "Do *you* have, uh, a significant other, Mr. Wallace?"

"Does my dog count?"

Chelsea gave Bree a not-so-subtle nudge on her shoulder.

"I don't think—" Bree began.

"I'm interested in your business. You'll be back in half an hour," he assured Bree. "The first set will have hardly started. These things never go off quite on time."

Meaning he was very familiar with *these things*. Big surprise.

"I'll have you back before intermission."

"I bet he won't stick you with the bill, either," Chelsea said helpfully, sidling out of the way before Bree could get her foot again.

The firm line of his mouth registered disapproval as he registered that morsel of information about the sad state of Bree's dating life.

"Your young assistant looks more than capable of finishing the setup here." His voice was suave.

Chelsea preened. "More than capable," she said, and flipped her hair.

It would seem churlish to refuse. It would seem like she was *afraid* of him, and life and surprises and the very thing she tried to bake into all her cookies.

Magic.

It was that magical thinking that always got her in trouble, Bree reminded herself. He had mentioned business. She was not in a position to turn down this kind of connection to the business world.

"All right," she said, resigned. "A quick coffee."

Bree came face-to-face with her truth. She was terrified of believing in good things.

And terrified especially to believe in the happily-ever-after that men like him had made women like her yearn for since the beginning of time.

"For goodness sake," Chelsea said in an undertone, "lose the apron. And do something with your hair."

She ran a hand through it, and followed Brand, tilting her chin at him when he held the door open for her.

It was a beautiful spring evening in Vancouver, and Bree was aware her senses felt oddly heightened. The air smelled good from a recent rain, and plump crystal droplets fell from the blossom-laden branches of the ornamental cherry trees that lined the sidewalk.

There were two coffee places around the corner from the concert hall, and Bree liked it that Brand chose the independent shop, Perks, rather than the one that was part of a big chain.

It was cozy inside, with mismatched sofas and scarred old tables with brightly painted chairs clustered around them. It smelled heavenly, of coffee and exotic spices.

"Have you been here before?" he asked her.

"Just to introduce them to Kookies. They passed."

"Fools."

Brand said it with such genuine indignation. It was going to be hard to keep her defenses about her. But she had known that when she was trying to refuse his invitation.

"Thank you for saying so. But it wasn't personal. They already had a contract with someone."

"Humph."

She had managed to get rid of her apron, but remembered Chelsea's instruction to do something with her hair. "If you'll excuse me for just a sec, I'll go freshen up."

"What can I get you?"

She was going to say hot chocolate; coffee was out at this time of evening. But in the spirit of living dangerously and allowing life to astonish her, she didn't. "Surprise me," she said.

"Oh. That sounds fun."

Somehow, she was not at all sure he was talking about beverage selection! She excused herself hastily before he could see the blush moving up her neck.

She found the washroom, slipped inside and looked at herself in the mirror. What she saw was so ordinary as to be discouraging. Her light brown hair, average at the best of times, was pulled into a tight bun—even worse. She had gone very light on the makeup, so faint freckles stood out on her nose. She had on no lipstick, and she had worn glasses tonight instead of her contacts. A wholesome, old-fashioned look was exactly what she wanted when she was behind the table giving out cookie samples.

To have coffee with an old crush—who could coax a blush out of her with a turn of phrase—not so much!

She pulled her hair out of the bun. It fell, stick-straight, to her shoulders. She rummaged in her purse for a brush and added a touch of lip gloss.

It was an improvement, but she was aware she still felt very ordinary, the kind of workaday girl who was virtually invisible.

"Not in his league," she told herself. But then she saw the plus side of that: she could just relax. It was just old friends catching up, after all. Nothing would ever come of it, except maybe a beneficial business connection.

She went back out into the main room. He had chosen two love seats facing each other with a round coffee table in between. She walked over and sat opposite him.

"You've let your hair down," Brand said.

Physically, not figuratively, despite her intention to relax. She hoped he didn't think she had done it to impress him.

"More comfortable," she said.

"I always liked the color of your hair. It reminds me of sand on a sun-warmed beach."

He had remembered the color of her hair? She gawked at him. *Sand on a sun-warmed beach?*

Do not gawk at the celebrities, she ordered herself. *And do not take it personally*, she also ordered herself. It was obvious he knew his way around women. He had found her one redeeming feature and flattered her about it. And it had worked some terrible magic on her. She could feel her nerves humming so hard it felt as though her skin was vibrating.

"I always considered it mousy brown," she said.

"That is ridiculous."

If she wasn't careful, she was going to gawk again. Probably with her mouth hanging open.

Thankfully, the beverages were delivered. Two steaming cups were set in front of them. She took hers, blew on it gently so as not to blow a blob of foam right onto his forehead and took a sip.

"What is this?" she asked, delighted.

"So I did manage to surprise! You've never had it before?"

"No."

"It's a chai latte. Spiced sweet tea with steamed milk. You like?"

"Wonderful. I can taste the tea, which is so ordinary, but then the spices and the mound of sugar-crusted foam raise it to a new level."

Suddenly she wondered why he had picked it for her. And she found herself looking at *ordinary* in a different light.

"And what are you having?" she asked him.

"Coffee, black."

"Given the variety on the menu, that seems unadventurous."

"I save my adventuring for other arenas."

She was going to blush again! No, she was not. She would not give him the satisfaction.

"You have had some great adventures in business," she said, pleased that she did not miss a beat. "I've been reading about you, Brand," she said. "You've done so well."

"Ah, the *City* article. I had no idea that magazine was so widely read."

Bree doubted it had been before they featured him on the cover!

"I must say I didn't treasure anonymity nearly enough when I had it. Everyone suddenly knows who I am. It's a little disconcerting. But thank you. The success part seems to be luck and timing. I jumped on an opportunity."

"My dad loved the quote—'opportunity meets preparation.' He always thought very highly of you. He admired your work ethic. He was fond of saying, 'That young man is going places.'"

"He used to say the same thing to me. When not another person in the world was. I feel as if he was the first person who truly believed in me. That goes a long way in a young man's life, especially one with no father figure. I don't think I ever had a chance to tell him that. What his faith in me meant. I regret it, but I'm glad I've been given this opportunity to tell you."

It became evident to her this was why he'd invited her for coffee. It was an opportunity to tell her what her father had meant to him.

It was lovely.

So, why did she feel faintly resentful—as if she was a chai latte that had just been demoted to a very ordinary cup of Earl Gray?

He watched her now over the rim of his coffee cup. "I called several times after your dad died. I spoke to your mother. Did she tell you?"

"Yes, she said you had called and asked after me."

"One day I called and the number was out of service. I dropped by the house and it was empty. For sale, if I recall."

Bree took a sip of her drink, and let the spicy aroma

fill her nostrils and warm the back of her throat before she replied. "I left for college. My mother felt lonely in the house, so she sold it quite quickly. Then she remarried and moved to San Francisco."

"Is she happy?"

"Yes, very." She did not say it seemed her mother had moved on to happiness with unseemly swiftness. Bree had felt so abandoned. Of course, there was nothing like feeling abandoned to leave a young woman looking for love in all the wrong places.

"What did you take? In college?"

Heartbreak 101.

"I took a culinary program. I'm afraid I didn't finish."

He cocked his head at her. "That doesn't seem like you, somehow."

She cocked her head back at him. "Doesn't it?" she asked, deliberately unforthcoming, and letting him know that really, he knew very little about her, past or present.

"In some ways, you are very changed," he told her.

For a moment, she felt panicked, as if the sad ending of the pregnancy that had forced her to leave school was written all over her. She hoped her face was schooled into calmness, and she made herself release her stranglehold on her mug.

He *still* made her nervous.

"Your confidence in high heels for one thing."

Relief swept through her at his amused reference to her clumsiness on the night of the prom.

"Oh, geez, you must have had bruises on your arm the next day. I should have practiced. I clung onto you most of the night."

"And I thought you were just trying to feel my manly biceps."

Despite herself, she giggled.

"It was a really nice thing for you to do," she said. "To take the boss' dateless daughter to her senior prom. I don't think I thanked you. Of course, it didn't occur to me until later that it probably wasn't your idea."

"It wasn't," he confessed. "I didn't date girls like you."

"Girls like me?"

"Smart," he said. "Sweet."

Not quite as smart as anyone had thought.

"I bet you still don't," she said wryly.

"I'm more the superficial type."

He made her laugh. It was as simple as that.

"So," he said, leaning forward and looking at her intently, "tell me how you have passed the last years. For some reason, I would have pictured you the type who would be happily married by now. Two children. A golden-retriever puppy and an apple tree in the front yard."

Happily-ever-after.

She could feel that same emotion claw at her throat. It was exactly the life she had wanted, the dream that had made her so vulnerable.

He had her pegged. Well, you didn't rise as fast in the business world as he did without an ability to read people with some accuracy.

There was no sense denying it even if it was not in vogue.

"That is my type. Exactly," she said. She heard the catch in her voice, the pure wistfulness of it.

"It's what you come from, too. I can see that you would gravitate back to that. Your family was so..."

He hesitated, lost for words.

"Perfect," she said, finishing his thought.

"That's certainly how it seemed to me. Coming from one that was less than perfect, I looked at the decency of your dad and the way he treated you and your mom, and it did seem like an ideal world."

One she had tried to replicate way too soon after the passing of her father, with a kind of desperation to be loved like that again, to create that family unit.

It was only now, years after her miscarriage, that she was beginning to tiptoe back into the world of dating, looking again to the dream of happily-ever-after. So far, it had been a disaster.

"Are you, Bree? Happy?"

She hesitated a moment too long, and his brow furrowed at her.

"Tell me," he commanded.

Ridiculous that she would tell him about her happiness, or lack there of. He had worked for her father a long time ago, and somehow been persuaded to take the hopeless daughter to her prom. They were hardly friends. Barely acquaintances.

"Deliriously," she lied brightly. "My little company builds a bit each day. It's fun and it's rewarding."

"Hmmm," he said, a trifle skeptically. "Tell me, Bree, what do you do for fun?"

The question caught her off guard. She could feel herself fumbling for an answer. What could she say? Especially to someone like him, who moved in the sophisticated circles of wealth and power?

She couldn't very well say that she had all the Harry

Potter books and reread them regularly, with her ancient cat, Oliver, leaving drool pools on her lap. That after Chelsea, seamstress extraordinaire, had showed her how, she had individually quilted each of the cookies on her aprons. That she was addicted to home-renovation shows, especially ones hosted by couples, who had everything, it seemed, that she had ever dreamed of. That she trolled Pinterest features about homes: welcome signs, and window boxes, and baby rooms.

It would sound pathetic.

Was it pathetic?

"My business takes an inordinate amount of time," she said when her silence had become way too long.

"So you don't have fun?"

"Maybe I consider developing new cookie recipes fun!"

"Look, my business takes a lot of time, too. But I still make time for fun things."

Just then a man came over and squatted on the floor beside her. He stuck out his hand. "Miss Evans? I'm the manager here. Mr. Wallace leads me to understand you have a line of cookies. We'd love to try them. Have you got a minute?"

She looked over the manager's shoulder at Brand. He was smiling. He nodded encouragingly at her.

"Yes, I have a minute," she said. The manager got up and sat beside her. She started to tell him about Kookies.

When she looked over at Brand, he was gone. The love seat across from her was empty.

No goodbye.

But at least he hadn't stuck her with the bill.

Fifteen minutes later, she left Perks. They were going to give Kookies a trial term of six months.

She walked back to the concert hall. Outside the door, before going in, Bree debated only for a full five seconds before she pulled out Brand's business card with his phone number and called him.

"Hello?"

She had been expecting it to go to voice mail, since she thought he was probably now in the front row for the Crystal Silvers performance. But there was no background noise.

"I was expecting to leave a message," she said.

"Bree. What an unexpected pleasure."

"I was rehearsing my message!"

"Okay, just pretend this is my voice mail."

"All right. Hello, Brand. Thank you for a pleasant evening and for buying me coffee. I wanted you to know Perks is going to try my cookies for a trial period."

"Excellent!"

"Voice mail does not respond," she reminded him primly.

"Oh, yeah. Forgive me. Continue."

She took a deep breath. "Thank you, but you didn't have to use your influence for me."

"Of course I didn't *have* to. But what exactly would be the point of having influence if you didn't use it to help others?"

And then he was gone, no goodbye again. She contemplated the kind of man that would make a statement like that.

This was what her father had always seen: the decency of Brand Wallace, a guy who could be trusted to do the right thing, even with a starry-eyed eighteen-year-old girl, desperate to be kissed.

His innate decency made her feel shivery with

longing. He appeared to be the polar opposite of Paul Weston, the college professor who had taken what was left of her heart after the death of her father and run it through the meat grinder.

But it would be a form of pure craziness to think that a woman like her could ever have a man like Brand Wallace.

On the other hand, who had ever looked at her hair before and seen sun-kissed sand?

She went in the doors, and could hear the music blasting out of the auditorium. Chelsea, looking a little worse for wear, was behind a completely rummaged-over sample table, dancing enthusiastically by herself to the loud music spilling out into the foyer. She danced salsa competitively and managed to look ultrasexy even in the cookie apron and beret.

She stopped when she saw Bree coming toward her. Sadly, it did not appear her sudden cessation of movement was because it had occurred to her it might be inappropriate that the table in front of her was badly in need of straightening.

"Did you have wine?" Chelsea demanded.

"No, I had a chai latte." Bree decided, then and there, she probably would never have one again. Those smoky, spicy exotic flavors would remind her of a surprisingly pleasant evening—and forbidden longings—for as long as she lived.

"Oh, you're all glowy."

Bree was pretty sure *glowy* was not a word, not that she wanted to argue the point.

"What has happened to the table?" Bree asked, not wanting to encourage an interrogation from Chelsea. "It's a mess."

"Oh! About ten minutes before Crystal Silvers started to sing, the people just started to pour through the front door. They were on me like the barbarian hordes. Just grabbing things, ripping open boxes, uninvited. I have tidied, you know. There were wrappers all over the place. Anyway, somehow samples made it back to the lady herself. She sent out an assistant to tell me she loved our cookies, to expect a big order for her birthday blowout."

It was more than Bree had hoped for! So why did she feel curiously flat about it?

If that came through, along with the extra business from Perks, there would be no time for thinking about happily-ever-after, or lack thereof, as the case might be.

Thank goodness.

"Oh, there goes the glowy look," Chelsea said. "The frown line is back. Miss Worry rides again."

Bree deliberately relaxed her forehead. She hadn't even realized until tonight she was endangering her chances of aging gracefully because of her perpetual frown. Despite the fact she knew better than to encourage Chelsea, she could not stop herself from asking.

"What color would you say my hair was?"

Chelsea regarded Bree's hair, flummoxed, clearly thinking this was a trick question that she was not going to answer correctly.

"Brown?" she finally ventured.

Bree nodded sadly. "Just as I thought."

CHAPTER THREE

You didn't have to use your influence for me.

After Brand had disconnected the phone and put it back in his pocket, he made his way through the rain-glittered streets. He had decided to walk home. Going back to the gala after being with Bree Evans would have felt like getting dumped onto an eight-lane freeway after being on a quiet path through the country.

Despite her new proficiency with high heels, and the way she filled out her trim white blouse, she was still sweet and smart. Definitely adorable. Totally earnest.

And completely refreshing.

Those words—*you didn't have to use your influence for me*—just reinforced all those impressions of her.

Everybody wanted him to use his influence for them. Even the manager at Perks had approached him, not the other way around. He'd recognized him from that blasted *City* article.

Brand came to his house, and stood back for a second, gazing at it through the walkway opening in the neatly trimmed hedge. His architect had called it colonial, a saltbox, and, thankfully, it was less ostentatious than most of the mansions on his street.

Inside, Beau, who seemed to be largely telepathic,

had figured out he was home, and gave a deep woof of welcome.

When people asked why he'd gone with a single-family house instead of a superglamorous condo, he said he'd purchased the Shaughnessy heritage home because it was close to his office tower in downtown Vancouver, his golf course and the VanDusen Botanical Garden.

That seemed much easier than admitting he had purchased the house because he thought his dog would prefer having a tree-shaded backyard to a condo balcony.

He opened the front door he never locked. Anyone with the nerve to try and get by his one-hundred-and-thirty-pound bullmastiff deserved a chance to grab what they could before dying.

The dog nearly knocked him over with his enthusiastic greeting, and Brand went down on his knees and put his arms around him. They wrestled playfully for a few minutes, until Brand pushed away Beau, stood up and brushed off his clothes.

"You stink."

The dog sighed with pleasure.

"I met a woman tonight, Beau," he told the dog. "More terrifying than you."

Beau cocked his head at him, interested.

"And that was before she laughed."

Since the events of this evening were about the furthest thing from what he had expected when he'd headed out the door, it occurred to him that life was indeed full of little surprises. He had the renegade—and entirely uncomfortable—thought that maybe her cookies held predictions in them after all.

And he had eaten that one.

Happily-Ever-After.

But one lesson he had carried from his hardscrabble childhood, left far behind, was an important one.

Fairy tales belonged to other people. People like her.

Except, from the stricken look on her face when he'd asked her about her happily-ever-after, somehow her great ending had evaded her. Or she thought it had. She was way too young to have given up on a dream.

And it was none of his business why it had, or why she had given up hope on it, but he felt curiously invested—as if that night he had taken her to the prom, he had made a promise to her father, a man who had been so good to him, that he would look out for her.

Brand also felt, irrationally perhaps, that he had given Bree a dream he couldn't have and she had let him down.

She was, in many ways other than just the high heels, very different. All grown up, as he had noted earlier. Her hair had been very long, but now, once she had let it down, he'd noticed it was shoulder-length and very stylishly cut. She used makeup well, and it made her cheekbones stand out, high and fine. She hadn't had on lipstick when he'd first seen her, but when she had sat down across from him at the coffee shop, her lips had the faintest pink-tinged gloss on them, shining just enough to make a man's eyes linger there for a moment.

And yet her eyes, huge and brown with no makeup at all, were almost exactly, hauntingly, as he remembered them—owlish and earnest, behind spectacles.

Almost, because now there was a new layer there. Sorrow. For her father, of course, but maybe something deeper, too.

She had pegged it. He'd never dated a girl like her before her prom, and to be honest, never had again.

"And I'm not about to start now," he told the dog. He took off his jacket and threw it in a heap on the floor, then undid his shirt and took off his shoes and socks. He padded barefoot through his house.

The architect had kept the outer footprint of the house, as the historical society demanded, but the inside had been stripped to the bones and rebuilt in a way that honored the home's roots, yet still had a clean, modern aesthetic.

The kitchen was no exception. Except for the Elvis cookie jar in the center of a huge granite island, his kitchen was a modern mecca of stainless steel and white cabinets, photo-shoot ready.

The designer had convinced him to go with a commercial kitchen, both for resale value and for ease of catering large events at his home. So far, there had been no large events at his home. As good as it sounded on paper, he didn't like the idea of boisterous gatherings in *his* space. Home, for him, was a landing strip between business trips, one that was intensely private. It was what it had never been when he was growing up—a place of quiet and predictability.

The cookie jar was stuffed with Girl Guide cookies. Brand shared a fondness for them with his dog, but he wondered if his enjoyment was now compromised for all time after sampling Bree's wares. Not feeling ready to admit to that, Brand passed on the cookies, grabbed a beer from a fridge that could have stocked a cruise ship for a month and went to the media room.

The media room was bachelor heaven: deep reclining leather seats, set up theater style, and a wall-to-wall television set with surround sound. There were Elvis posters on every wall. He flopped into one of the chairs, while Beau took up guard in his dog bed at his feet. He turned on the TV set, and let the comforting rumble of sound fill the room. He flipped through to the hockey game that had been recorded in his absence.

"This is the life," he told Beau, a little too forcefully.

Beau moaned, and he was aware of an echo, as if this room, filled with everything any man could ever want, was empty.

Bree had done that, made him aware of emptiness, in one single encounter.

If there was one thing Brand was really good at, in the business world and wherever else it mattered, it was heeding the subtle first tingles of a warning.

She was the kind of woman that would require more of a man.

No doubt most men would find her quite terrifying. That included him.

So, he knew what he had to do. Nothing. Absolutely nothing. Disengage. He'd already done way too much. In a moment of madness he'd actually given her his phone number. She had already shown she wasn't afraid to use it.

Or maybe she had been afraid, and used it anyway, which was much, much worse.

See? That's the kind of woman she was. Simple things could become complicated way too fast.

He thought of the new layer of sadness in her eyes. Was that from the death of her dad, or had something else happened to her? He thought of her trying to get that business off the ground by herself. He thought of her not having an answer about having fun. He thought of her assistant letting it slip that Bree was on a dating site, and was meeting losers who stiffed her with the bill. He thought about how good her father had been to him.

He took her business card out of his pocket. It was a well-done card. Glossy. Colorful. Professional. Memorable. Kookies for all occasions. Her number was already in his phone, because she had called him.

He took a deep breath, scrolled through to her information and added it to his contact information. He hesitated and pressed the green phone symbol.

She wouldn't answer. She was in the middle of—

"Hello?" Her voice was breathless.

He had the renegade thought he would like to make her breathless in quite a different way. It nearly made him end the call, because what the hell did a thought like that have to do with honoring her father by helping her out a bit? But there was no placing an anonymous call these days, so he sucked it up.

"Can't get the taste of your cookies out of my head," he said.

Funny that thinking about taste made a vision of her lips pop into his mind.

"I try to warn people," she said. "Spells and enchantment."

He thought of her lips again! That must be it. He was spellbound. Now would be a great time to tell her he had pocket-dialed.

"Aside from my charity function, I thought we should talk about the possibility of you supplying my office staff room. And meetings."

She was silent.

"Bree?"

"It's very kind, but—"

There was suddenly a great deal of noise.

"I'm sorry," she said, "it's intermission. I'm going to have to—"

"Meet with me next week."

"Um—"

Geez! He was offering her a huge opportunity here. What was the problem? While the rest of the world was yapping at his heels wanting things from him, she was resistant—the lone exception.

"I'll be in the office all day Wednesday," he said smoothly, "if you want to drop by and we'll figure out the details."

Again there was hesitation, and then she asked, "Around ten a.m.?"

"Perfect. My office is—"

"I know. It's in the article."

"The *damn* article," he said.

She rewarded him with that laugh, soft, like a brook gurgling over rocks. "Okay. Wednesday at ten. Dear Lord."

"What?"

"Crystal Silvers is walking toward me. Good grief. She hardly has any clothes on."

And then she was gone. Brand stared at his phone. "Beau?"

The dog lifted his head and gave him a watery-eyed look.

"You're an expert on all things stinky. I stink at relationships, right?"

The dog laid his head back down with a groan as if there was no point in having bothered him with such a self-evident question.

"That's what I thought. I'm putting on my big-brother shirt."

He remembered the refreshing innocence about her. Crystal Silvers had been walking toward her, the chance of a lifetime, possibly, and she focused on the no-clothes-on part.

Innocent in a world that was fast. Old-fashioned in a world that could be slick. Real in a world that distracted with shock.

So, she needed a bit of coaching. His offer to get her under contract to supply his office was perfect. Of course, he could have left the details up to his office manager, but this way he would be able to check up on her a little bit, and make sure some great business opportunities came her way. And maybe, subtly, move her in the direction of happiness, which she so richly deserved.

"Not that I'm any expert on happily-ever-after," he muttered.

The dog wagged his stump of a tail in approval. One thing that both Brand and Beau knew was that Brand was not cut out for relationships. Brand's father had abandoned him and his mother. At six he had become the man of the family. He'd been there for his mom, and he still was, but he was pretty damn sure that his father's genetics ran strong through his blood.

"Ask Wendy," he said out loud.

The dog's tail stopped thumping, no doubt a coincidence, but still Beau and Wendy had never seen eye-to-eye. It had been okay when Brand was just seeing her, as he had been exclusively for two years.

But then, she'd moved in. You thought you knew a person until they took down your Elvis posters and replaced them with original works of abstract art. He'd had to rescue the cookie jar from the garbage. People as svelte as Wendy did not let cookies touch their lips.

Within twenty-four hours, she was planning a Christmas extravaganza. Here. In their home. In their private space. She thought they could easily host two hundred people!

Thankfully, in short order, Beau had chewed through the sofa she had brought with her, a ridiculous antique thing that wasn't even comfortable. Next on the menu had been three pairs of her shoes, imported from Italy. For dessert, Beau had eaten her Gucci wallet, with her credit cards in it. All that had been left was three gooey strands of leather and one slimy half of her Gold card.

She had said, "It's the dog or me."

He'd paid for the wallet and shoes and sofa, and chosen the dog. But in his heart he knew it wasn't really about the dog. It was about being unsuitable for the kind of cozy domestic future she was envisioning. It had all been great when he could pick her up at her house, and take her out to dinner or a function, without her cosmetics and hair products all over his bathroom counter.

Something in him had already been itching to move on, three days after she'd moved in. He was pretty sure he would have got out of it, one way or another, way before the Christmas extravaganza, just as his father had done.

After Wendy's departure from his home and his life, Brand put the Elvis posters back up. The Elvis memorabilia had been his mother's pride and joy. Her suite in the seniors home had not been able to accommodate even a fraction of her collection. Always emotionally fragile, she'd gone into hysterics trying to decide what she could keep and what she could part with.

Another reason for a rather large house in Shaughnessy.

Okay, it wasn't the most pragmatic reason to buy a house. But when he picked up his mother on Sunday afternoons and brought her to his home, she was so happy to see it. Somehow, having them around him, reminded him of exactly what he came from. And that might be the most important lesson not to forget.

As if on cue, his phone went off—it was the quacking ringtone he reserved for his mom, a private joke between them. He glanced at the clock. Late. He could feel himself tensing ever so slightly.

"Hi, Mom."

"There was a movie tonight," she told him. "*Abracadabra.* Have you seen it?"

"No, I heard it was good, though. Tell me about it." The tension left him as her happy voice described the movie.

It was, Bree told herself firmly as she glanced at her wavering image in the polished steel elevator cage that was whisking her up to the forty-third floor, a second chance to make a first impression. Technically, her third chance, if she counted the prom.

Even though she was going to pitch a cookie contract to Brand's office, there was no cookie beret today and no quilted apron.

Something in his voice when he had called her offering her the contract had given her pause. It was why she had hesitated. Did he consider her a charity that would benefit from his generosity? It was as if he had relegated her to a perpetual little-sister position in his life. No doubt he had done the same the night of the prom! No wonder he had refused her lips that night. Not that she was offering her lips today. Or even letting her mind wander in that direction.

No, today, Breanna Evans was erasing *cute* from his impression of her, erasing a cookie beret and a quilted apron. Today, she was going to be one-hundred-percent professional. Polished. Pure business.

And grown up!

Even the night of the gala, when he had pronounced her all grown up, it seemed to her now, in retrospect, it was something said to a thirteen-year-old that you had last seen when she was ten.

Toward this goal, Bree had dug deep into her resources and purchased a stunning deep red, bordering on burgundy, Chloë Angus hooded cloak to wear over her one and only business suit, a nondescript pantsuit in a color that might be best described as oatmeal. The cloak made her hair, piled up on top of her head in an ultrasophisticated look, seem like sun-kissed sand.

Then, to compound the insanity, she had bought a matching pair of heels. The shoes made her look quite a bit taller than she really was, and hopefully, more powerful, somehow, like a busy CEO. She wasn't quite as graceful in them as she wanted to be, but she wasn't planning on running a marathon wearing them, either—she just wanted to make a crucial impression.

The one to erase all other impressions.

"CEO," she muttered to herself in the elevator, and then more firmly said, "Chief executive officer. Who got a contract to provide Crystal Silvers with five thousand cookies for her birthday blow-out? You! That's who!"

She hoped the elevator didn't have security cameras that recorded sound. A security guard somewhere would be having a good laugh at her expense.

She was carrying two large, rectangular white bakery boxes of cookie samples, which she always took, as a gift, when she was pitching an office contract. Unfortunately, the samples would not fit into a briefcase. Or maybe that was fortunate: who knows what kind of money she would have spent on that power item?

The elevator stopped. Despite her pep talk to herself, her heart fell to the pointy toes of her new red shoes. She considered just riding back down. She felt overcome by nerves, despite all the money she had spent trying to shore up her confidence with the beautiful, subtle raven-imprinted cloak.

But when the doors whispered open on the penthouse floor of one of Vancouver's most exclusive downtown office towers, Bree took a deep breath and forced herself to be brave. The world did not reward cowardice after all!

She stepped out into a gorgeous foyer, and her feet sank into a deep carpet. Hard surfaces would have been so much better for the heels! The lighting was low, and she noted two white leather sofas facing each other. Beyond them was a receptionist desk, currently empty of a receptionist, in some kind of exotic wood. On the far wall, to the right of the elevator, a stone wall had water trickling down its face, and was embossed with shining, wet gold letters that announced she was at the right place, BSW Solutions.

It looked like a solid wall behind the receptionist's desk, but then a sliver of light appeared in it, and Bree realized there was a door hidden in the wall. It pushed open a little more, swinging out into the room.

And then it was flung back with such force that the door hit the wall. Bree took a startled step back just as a monster shot out the door and galloped toward her! Her surprised mind grappled with the fact it was a dog. Not just any dog, but the largest one she had ever seen. He was brindle-colored with a head the size of a pumpkin. He was dragging a leash, and slobber was flying from his mouth as he covered the distance between them in three gigantic bounds.

Was he going to jump on her? Her own safety was not as paramount in her mind as the new cloak and her cookies.

She let out a little shriek and took a step back. Her heel caught in the extravagant pile of the carpet, and she lost her footing and dropped the cookies. She windmilled her arms, trying to stay upright, but to no avail.

She fell on the floor and closed her eyes tightly, resigned to being killed by a beast in the luxurious foyer of Brand Wallace's business. Why did nothing ever go quite as she planned it?

After a full second of anticipating her imminent death, nothing happened.

She opened an eye and sat up. The beast had skidded to a stop, and as she watched he nudged open the lid of a box and began to gobble up three dozen or so Spells Gone Wrong cookies.

"Beau!" The tone commanded the dog's complete respect. He sat immediately at attention, eyes on his master, his cookie-encrusted muzzle the only evidence he had done anything untoward.

"Bree. Oh, my God, I'm so sorry."

Brand was standing over her, his forehead puckered with concern, his eyes on her face. He reached down to her and his hand, strong and warm, closed around hers. He pulled her up and then he just stared at her, as if he'd never seen her before. Somehow, he forgot to let go of her hand.

He was dressed casually, far more so than he had been the night of the gala. He was wearing a jacket over a T-shirt, faded jeans and a nice pair of leather loafers with tassels on them.

The stunned look on his face made the Chloë Angus cloak and the shoes worth every penny of the investment.

"Are you okay?" he growled.

"Yes, I think so. Just in a bit of shock. You don't expect, er, *that* in an office like this."

"No, I know. I apologize. It's unforgivable, really."

"Brand," she said firmly, "I could tell you a thing or two about unforgivable, and believe me—" she looked at the dog, comic in his contriteness "—he doesn't even register."

She was shocked she had said that, as if she was ready to share confidences from her sordid past with him, which she most certainly was not. His hand was still holding hers. That was the problem. She had just been attacked by a monster beast, but her hand in his made her feel safe and protected.

And about as far from a CEO as you could get!

"Are you sure you're all right?"

"Positive, though I do think we have to stop meeting like this."

He realized he was still holding her hand. He looked down at their joined hands with surprise, and then let go abruptly. He looked at his hand. He looked at her hair, and lifted his hand as if he was going to touch the scattered tendrils of what was left of her lovely upsweep. Then he looked at her cloak. It seemed as if he was debating whether or not he should be brushing her off, and then thought better of it. He jammed his hands in his pockets. Bree actually found herself smiling, and then chortling.

She could tell it took a lot to rattle Mr. Brand Wallace, but he was rattled now.

"This is not a laughing matter," he told her sternly, and then looked to the dog. "Bad dog."

The dog flinched at the reprimand, but then turned a repentant gaze to Bree. His stub of a tail thumped hopefully.

"It's okay," she told the dog. He came out of his seated position. His whole monstrous back end wiggled.

"It's not!" Brand said. The dog sat back down.

Just then a breathless girl came out the door that both the dog and Brand had come through.

"Mr. Wallace, I'm so sorry. He's never done that before! I was just bringing him in off the terrace, when he bolted. I just wasn't expecting it. One minute I had the leash, and the next I didn't."

Brand looked really annoyed, despite the explanation. "Jennifer, he knocked over our guest."

"No—no, he didn't," Bree said quickly. "He startled me and I took a step backward. I fell over all on my own."

The girl was close to tears. It was obvious she had a bad case of hero worship for her boss and felt far more terrible that she had let him down than that their guest had taken a spill in the main foyer.

"I'm so sorry," Jennifer said tremulously.

"I take the blame," Bree said, still smiling. She picked up the open, and now empty, box of cookies and held it up. Spells Gone Wrong was clearly written across the lid. "Things always go off the rails whenever I make them. When it's combined with Little Surprises, watch out!"

"Oh," Jennifer said knowingly. "Cookies."

"That dog could not have possibly smelled cookies through that door," Brand said. "It's impossible."

He looked hard at his young employee, and seemed to realize she needed forgiveness. Nothing could be changed now. Unfortunately, Bree's sense of him being somehow safe in a stormy world intensified when his tone softened as he addressed the girl.

"Cookies are his weakness. I'm afraid I give him the odd one. Keep a firmer hold on him next time, Jenn."

Jenn heard the *next time* and beamed. "He likes the vanilla Girl Guide cookies," she told Bree. "Mr. Wallace has a closet full of them for the days he brings Beau to work with him."

The girl's attitude reminded Bree so much of Chelsea being altogether too revealing about Bree's personal life that she laughed out loud. Brand—one of the most successful men in Vancouver's business community—owned the world's ugliest dog. And brought him to work with him. And fed him Girl Guide cookies.

"He probably won't eat Girl Guide cookies ever again now," Brand said woefully, looking at the empty box and the dog's cookie-encrusted muzzle.

"I'll take him, Mr. Wallace."

"No, it's okay, I've got him now. If you could look after this mess I'd appreciate it." He stooped and picked up the leash, though it was probably entirely unnecessary. The dog was stuck to him like glue, as he leaned into his leg.

The dog made a moaning noise, as the mashed cookies were packed up, and Bree looked at him. He gave her a woebegone look that she could not resist. She got down on one knee in front of him.

“Don’t touch him,” Brand warned, too late. “He stinks.”

But she already had the dog’s big, wrinkly face between her hands. “Did you call him Beau?”

“He mostly answers to ‘bad dog,’” Brand offered, “but sometimes I call him Beau.”

“Beau,” she said softly. “You are not a bad dog. You have one of the most beautiful souls I’ve ever seen.”

The dog regarded her thoughtfully, and then his big, ugly chops spread into an unmistakable grin. His big tongue whipped out and removed most of her makeup before she could move her face away. She laughed, and stood back up, while wiping at her face with a corner of her brand-new cloak.

She stopped, aware Brand was staring at her.

“What?” she said.

He was looking at her with the oddest look.

As if he had found a treasure he had waited his whole life to find. A woman lived for a look like that.

CHAPTER FOUR

BUT THEN HE spoiled it all when he said, "You look just like Little Red Riding Hood."

Just the look she was going for! Should she tell him he looked just like the Big Bad Wolf? Before she could, he spoke again.

"I've provided the wolf, I'm afraid. Beau usually doesn't like people."

Hmmm, he thought the dog was the wolf.

"Not that he's nasty or anything," Brand continued, "just colossally indifferent."

That look she thought she had seen was gone from his face and, in fact, Bree wondered if it wasn't her ever fertile imagination going into overdrive. She'd thought she had made a breakthrough in being perceived as an adult woman, but he was seeing a character out of a fairy tale!

"Let me show you around," Brand said, then led her to the door and held it open for her. Beau sat as she passed.

"Look at him," Brand said, "anxious to prove he's the perfect gentleman, and *not* the Big Bad Wolf."

As she went by him, Bree had the impression that Brand was uncomfortable, as if he knew, in that split second, he had revealed something he didn't want to reveal, and was now covering his tracks as quickly as possible.

If his intention was to distract, the room she found herself in certainly did that!

It was like nothing she had ever seen before.

It was a huge open space, scattered with deep fabric chairs that could have been mistaken for boulders, if people were not sunk so deeply into them. A cat was curled up in one young lady's lap.

Bree shot Beau a look, but he was looking off into the distance, regally indifferent to the cat.

"The cat and him sorted things out a long time ago," Brand said. "He's terrified."

"People bring their pets to work?" she asked, astounded. It was one thing for the boss to bring his dog on occasion, but it was startling to see the cat.

Brand nodded. She noticed a colorful hammock was suspended by ropes from the arched wooden beams of the ceiling, and a bearded fellow swung gently, as he tossed a beanbag in the air above his head and caught it. At the far end of the room the whole wall was covered in the colorful footholds and handholds of a climbing wall. There was a ball pit, of all things, filled to overflowing with bright yellow and red and blue balls. Music, a flute she thought, flooded the area.

A guy walked by them in bare feet. "Hiya, boss. Beau."

The dog, as Brand had predicted, was indifferent to the greeting. Brand took her elbow and guided her through the rock chairs and past the hammock bed hanging in the middle of the room.

He ushered her into his office and dropped Beau's

leash. The dog padded across the floor to a large doggie bed.

The office was beautiful and expansive. Floor-to-ceiling windows looked out over the cityscape, and beyond that she could see the ocean and mountains, still white-capped at this time of year. A gorgeous desk, possibly rosewood, with deep chairs in front of it, anchored the room, but off to one side two love seats faced each other over a glass-and-steel coffee table.

"This seems like the only conventional space on the whole floor," she said. "Except, of course, for Beau, who is, um, hardly conventional."

The dog did several circles on the bed, then with a happy sigh, laid down.

"What on earth is his breeding?" she asked. "I think the floor shook when he settled!"

"He's part bullmastiff. And part rhinoceros. I've held off on letting the world know there was a successful interspecies breeding. He's introverted. I don't think he could handle the attention."

"I can clearly see he's introverted," she laughed.

"I suspect you smell overwhelmingly of cookies. He really is introverted, as I said, largely indifferent to people, with the exception of me. Have a seat." He gestured to the love seats, rather than the seats in front of his desk. "Can I get you something?"

"No, thanks." She sank into the masculine, distressed leather, and Brand took a seat on the identical one across from her. "Is that a Lalique?" she said of the vase on the coffee table between them.

"A leak?" he said, and looked around puzzled.

"The vase."

Then she saw he was teasing her. His eyes sparkled with devilment.

"Yeah, their Midnight Blue collection. According to my designer, an investment." He rolled his eyes.

She knew she should be entirely professional, and just get down to business, but as always, he had a gift for putting her at ease. Curiosity overwhelmed her. "Tell me about that space out there. I have never seen anything like it."

"The thing about a business like mine is you can't just go with one idea. You have to be looking for the next one, and the next one after that. You have to be continually evolving and you have to be light-years ahead of the competition and the copycats.

"I'm good at business," Brand said, "and maybe even great at it. But I'm not strong in creativity, and I don't have top-of-the-line tech skills. And so I want to attract the best and brightest computer and creative working minds in the business. And I want to keep them. I've researched what makes a happy and productive workplace, and it's evolving it. That guy in the hammock, tossing the beanbag? His name's Kevin. He had an idea that made the company ten million dollars last year. He is one guy I make sure to talk to every single day."

"That's a lot of cookies," she said with a gulp. "The article—correction, the damn article—never said how it all began."

She still felt nervous, and a little off balance. But, of course, here she sat, Little Red Riding Hood, hair in shambles, her makeup licked off and her cloak askew. It would be good if she could get him talking until her wits came back!

"I had an idea a few years back—kind of Uber meets

Facebook, only in real time. I was traveling overseas for the company I worked for at the time. I was in Copenhagen and had a couple of hours on my hands. I thought, I wonder if I could find a pick-up game of hockey anywhere?"

She couldn't help herself. She laughed.

"What's so funny?"

"It's just so Canadian. And so *guy* somehow."

He smiled. That smile! So charming. So sexy! He leaned forward. His gift, or one of his gifts, was that he could make anyone feel as if they were the only person in the world that mattered to him.

"I know. A more sophisticated guy probably would have been checking out the museums and art galleries and restaurants. But I'd been on airplanes and in meetings for three days and I just wanted to blow off some steam and get very physical."

She felt her admiration for him grow even more. Because, really? If a guy like him wanted to get physical… She had to wrestle the blush that was threatening back down her throat.

Instead, her tone completely professional, she said, "It seems ironic that this hugely successful company came out of a desire to play hockey."

"I know, there is a bit of a bizarre element to it. Even more so because I was in no way unhappy with what I was doing. Loved my company. Loved the job. But this idea wouldn't let me go."

She actually had a general idea, from the magazine article, exactly where his thought of playing hockey in Denmark had taken him, but she was enjoying hearing about the birth of his company from him, directly and in detail.

"Intents was born. I liked how the name said one thing, but if you said it out loud it sounded like another—intense.

"The premise is you find yourself in a strange city, or country, but you like playing hockey or you like rock climbing or you like going to the opera or you like playing chess. An app shows you where to find those activities, and also people nearby who might be available to do them with you. You've been security-checked, they've been security-checked. It's all totally free. The pop-up ads on the website and app pay for it."

"It's quite brilliant," she said.

"Thanks, I'm proud of it. One of the things that surprised me, but is very satisfying, is how deep, lasting friendships come out of these connections sometimes. It's simply a great way to meet people who like the same things as you. We've had several weddings as a result."

"That isn't a dig at me meeting a guy on e-Us is it?"

"Who stiffed you with the bill," he reminded her.

"Thank you, Chelsea," she said. They both laughed, but when the laughter died, he was looking at her intently.

"What did you mean when you said you could tell me a thing or two about unforgivable?" he asked softly.

"Wh-what?" she stammered.

"When I said the dog knocking you over was unforgivable, you said—"

"I know what I said. A slip." She was *not* telling him. She clamped her mouth firmly shut and folded her arms over her chest. "Let's talk about cookies," she said brightly.

"I don't think you should be meeting people on e-Us," he said.

"Really?" she said. He did not appear to hear the coolness in her tone. "That's the accepted way of meeting people in this day and age."

"Well, it sucks."

She thought back over the majority of her experiences on e-Us. He had her there. "How would you suggest meeting people?"

"You like books? Go to a bookstore and tap some guy on the shoulder. Ask him what he's reading."

"That seems very forward. And maybe even dangerous."

"Unless he's in the memoirs-of-serial-killers section, you're probably okay," he said drily. "Geez, meeting a complete stranger, whose profile you've seen on the internet, is better somehow?"

"It's always in a public place. For a cup of coffee. Not very different than what we did the other night."

"I am not a complete stranger! I'm sure you knew, from our former acquaintance, I wasn't going to wait outside in the parking lot and club you over the head. Or follow you home. And I'm sure you knew I wasn't going to stiff you with the bill."

"Thank you, again, Chelsea."

"Not that I've been on one of them—"

She'd guessed right on that account!

"But it seems to me the problem with dating sites would be you can't get a read for people, the way you do when you meet them in person. The site is filtering all the facts. Even the picture can be a lie, can't it?"

She would certainly not admit that her last date had looked at least ten years older than he had in his profile picture.

"Plus there's the problem of sitting across from

someone you barely know in a coffee shop. How does that not end up feeling awkward? Like an interview?"

She hated it that he, who had never been on a dating site, was picking up the weaknesses of the system.

Why was it that this meeting, which was supposed to be an interview of sorts, did not feel like one at all?

"If you'd seen that guy in the bookstore, your little hinky sense would have told you—jerk. Something about the way he was standing, or the hole in his jeans, or the kind of book he was reading."

"Especially if he was in the serial-killer section!"

"More subtle. *How to Get Your Internet for Free, Collecting Coupons for Dummies.*"

She had the awful thought this was why she was really here. Despite her every effort to be the consummate professional, to correct those first impressions, here they were again.

With him feeling some kind of obligation to take care of her!

She had to get this back on track. The encounter with the dog had literally knocked down her defenses!

"All right," she said brightly. "I'll get the Intents app on my phone. Next time I'm in Denmark, I'll meet some fellow Harry Potter fans. I'll probably end up marrying one."

Harry Potter? Had she really said Harry Potter? She, who wanted to appear so grown up?

"Is that guy on the hammock out there single?" she said in a rush to correct impressions. "Maybe, on my way out, I'll just stop and ask him what he's throwing around. Is he single?"

"He is," Brand said drily, "but you have to speak Klingon to interest him."

"Klingon," she repeated, playing along. "I could learn. How often would I have to watch *Star Wars* to pick it up?"

"*Star Trek.* A mistake I'm okay with. Kevin? Not so much."

He was smiling. As if he found her intensely amusing! And here she was playing along with him. Well, enough was enough!

"Is that why I'm really here? Not to sell you cookies, but so that you can give me unsolicited advice about my personal life?"

CHAPTER FIVE

BREE KNEW SHE should stop right there, but she didn't.

"Despite playing the role at my senior prom, you are not my big brother!"

"You're right," Brand said. "I'm sorry. I've overstepped. I was acting like your protector, and—"

So, she *had* guessed right. She was here out of some form of sympathy. Support for the old boss' daughter. Okay, just the tiniest bit of weakness unfolded in her when he said *protector* like that. Oh! To have a protector such as him! She felt as if she had been on her own, with no one to lean on, for so long.

But, no! She was not giving in to that weakness. She was here to correct that very impression. That somehow she needed something that only he could give her.

She knew she was never going to be able to dislodge that first impression, not even if she went out and bought four hundred Chloë Angus capes. It was set in his mind. He was always going to see her as a hopelessly naive young girl. Nothing she had done today, from tripping over carpets to kissing dogs, had corrected that impression. Even the fact that she was sophisticated enough to recognize a Lalique had gone completely over his head!

Brand Wallace was buying her cookies, entering a business arrangement with her, out of pity! Out of some misguided desire to help her.

Suddenly she knew one way to correct his impression of her. To make him realize he didn't know her at all. The boldness it required stole her breath. It made her realize maybe her impressions of *herself* also needed a bit of tweaking.

She got up. She felt like a soldier going into battle. Her heart was beating so hard that surely he could see it hammering, right beneath the cloak. Some sort of momentum carried her across to his sofa. A granite determination overtook her as she sank into the seat beside him.

She could hear the frantic roar of her own heart in her ears.

She leaned closer to him, put both hands on either side of his face and drew him to her. Her heart went still. A great and surprising calm overtook her.

His cheeks, beneath her fingertips, were ever so slightly whisker-roughened, as if she was touching sandpaper. His scent was pine and rain and man. His eyes were the deepest brown she had ever seen, and the devilment in them had been replaced by surprise. And understandable wariness.

He was a man not accustomed to being caught off balance, and she had put him off balance. He was a man accustomed to calling the shots, and right now, in this surprising instant, she was calling the shots.

If she dared.

She saw it in his eyes that he knew what was coming, but was not sure she had the nerve.

She hesitated for one moment at the edge of the cliff,

terrified of the dizzying height she stood at. And then she jumped.

And felt the exquisite and glorious freedom of free-fall. She kissed him. She kissed him hard, and she kissed him passionately. She kissed him until neither of them could breathe. She kissed him until any resistance from him melted and his hands were tangled in her hair and he was kissing her back, his delicious lips nuzzling her own, exploring her own, claiming her as his own.

She lost the point of the exercise. Somewhere, she lost herself. Her world became so small, only this: his lips, the taste of them and the texture of them and the suppleness of them and the force of them. Her world became so large, only this: the stars in the sky, and the birds in the trees and the rivers flowing endlessly to the sea. All the mysteries were in this one small thing.

It seemed it might go on forever. There was that word, *forever*, that beautiful, enticing, enigmatic word from fairy tales.

But then the whole love seat seemed to groan, and his lips left hers.

"Beau!"

The dog had hefted himself up on the couch, and inserted his bulk gingerly between them. His huge tongue was flattened across the whole of Brand's cheek, slurping upward in slow motion.

With an impatient shove, he put the dog off the couch and wiped at his soggy cheek with the sleeve of his jacket.

Before she could lean back in and offer her lips again, Brand leaped off the love seat. He stared down at her. He ran a hand through his hair. He paced away from her.

"Harry Potter fans of the world, beware," he muttered. "What the hell was that about?"

Bree made herself sit up straight. She took a deep breath. She adjusted her cloak. She touched her hair. Her upsweep was now totally unswept.

Still, she made her voice firm. "I am not some cute child who has showed up at your office selling cookies, like a Girl Guide going door-to-door," she said.

"Okay, I think you've made that point."

"And I am not the gauche girl who was so innocent you could not risk a kiss good-night after her senior prom."

He swore under his breath. He was looking at her way too closely. "Have you been nursing that little grievance all these years?"

"No!"

"I think you're lying," he said softly.

"Well, you don't know anything about me."

He touched his lips. "That's true," he conceded.

Suddenly, she was mortified. She had just kissed Brand Wallace! What would he think she *was* selling? She thought of apologizing, and then she thought better of it.

Okay, it might not have been the most professional thing she had ever done, but really? From the look on his face, he was never going to think of her as a child again!

And really? She felt alive, and powerful. She felt she was practically sizzling with energy and life and passion.

"Now," she said, "are we ready to talk business?"

Under his breath, he said something that sounded

like a word a sailor might say. He looked downright wary. That was better!

"I'm not sure we're done discussing *that*."

"We are," she said firmly.

"If you didn't think of it for six years, where did that come from?"

"It's Spells Gone Wrong," she said, lifting a shoulder. "Again. Deadly, in combination with Little Surprises."

"You must have brought some Devilishly Decadent, too," Brand said drily.

He remembered the names of her cookies! *Stay on track*, Bree ordered herself.

"You're right, I must swear off delivering that particular combination of cookies. And speaking of cookies, how many people are in your office? I usually recommend starting with two cookies per person per day. Initially, I'll send quite a variety, but I'll give you a voting sheet to put on the coffee table. Then I'll start sending what people like best. If I was going to guess for this office? Earth Muffin. Vegan cookies…"

Brand watched Bree. She seemed composed enough after what happened, but if he was going to guess? She probably didn't usually talk this much.

Still, as she detailed her ordering and billing procedures, he noticed that, despite the rather shocking interchange that had just occurred between them, she had a really good business head on her shoulders. Nothing *kooky* about that part of her.

This whole fiasco was his own fault.

He'd been rattled since the first moment when he'd found her on the floor. His sense of not being in control had deepened when he had seen how she had reacted to the dog licking off her makeup.

No shrieking. No hysterics.

And she hadn't been putting it on to impress him, either. She genuinely loved animals.

But nobody loved Beau!

Except him.

This suddenly felt like one of the scariest moments of his life: she looked like Little Red Riding Hood, and kissed like a house on fire. She wove spells into her cookies. And she could see the souls of dogs.

He had known she was going to kiss him. He'd known it as soon as she sank down on the couch beside him.

He'd known and yet, he had not moved. He'd been caught in some spell of curiosity and enchantment.

He had to get her out of here, and out of his life. She was right. Absolutely right. She was totally grown up. One-hundred-percent pure woman. She'd proven that beyond a shadow of a doubt. There was nothing brotherly about the way he was feeling about her.

"Okay," he said abruptly. "Where do I sign?"

"I'll email you a contract with the terms we've just discussed."

City magazine would love to see him now. The man they'd declared to be the businessman of the decade was going to be emailed a contract and he had not the slightest idea what was in it, or what they had just discussed.

He forced himself to focus on her. A mistake. Her hair was scattered around her face. She was glowing. Her lips looked faintly bruised. She looked more like a woman who had just had some loving laid on her than one who had just made a great sale.

"Cookie delivery will start on Monday," Bree said, a complete professional *now.* "The cookies have a shelf life, not refrigerated, of six days. I like to leave them only for a maximum of three. My delivery guy will change out any older cookies when he comes midweek. We donate them to a kitchen that feeds the homeless. Is that okay with you?"

"Fine," he said.

She stood up. "Thank you for your business, Brand." For a moment, her in-charge businesswoman persona faded. She took her hand out of her cloak, looked at it and looked at him as if she was considering offering it.

He could feel himself holding his breath. He really did not want to risk the temptation touching her again would no doubt create!

Thankfully, she saw his hesitation, tucked her hand back under her cloak and went out the door. He was aware, as it whispered shut behind her, that he was exceedingly tense.

He deliberately rolled back his shoulders, shrugged them up to his ears, then let them slide back down. He shot his dog a dirty look.

"Traitor."

Beau opened one eye and thumped his tail a few times. If he could talk Brand was pretty sure he'd say, "Look, buddy, we both kissed her. How is it I'm the traitor?"

"What did I just order, anyway?"

Bree rode the elevator down. "CEO of the century!" she told her reflection. Despite things going slightly off the rails—well, a lot off the rails if it came to that—it was a great contract.

She was not going to think about that kiss! Or the taste of him. Or the way he had looked after she had kissed him. Baffled and off-kilter and aware of her in a whole new way!

She was not going to think about what strange madness had overtaken her. She suspected he was right.

It was comeuppance for his rejection of her lips all those years ago. She probably had thought of it way more than she should have. Well, now she knew. She knew what he tasted like. She knew she could make him see her as a woman, not a child. She knew and she could put that all behind her.

She was not thinking of that anymore. He could be the worst possible kind of distraction. She was going to keep him at arm's length. She didn't have to see him again, and she was not going to indulge the little swoop of loss she felt right in her tummy at the thought of not seeing him again.

She was thinking of her business. How could she be in close proximity to those lips and still think about her business? So, proximity was out.

Between this, the new Perks contract and her special order for Crystal Silvers, Kookies for All Occasions was in the best shape it had been in since she had started the company.

Her phone vibrated in her pocket just as she exited the office building.

It was Chelsea, and she was talking loudly and rapidly, on the verge of hysteria. Bree had to hold her phone away from her ear.

"Chelsea, slow down. What happened?"

The story came out, bit by disjointed bit. When Bree understood completely, she froze in shock. But this is what she should have remembered about life: for her, good things were followed by disaster.

Since her father had died, it seemed that lesson got hammered home again and again. She had fallen in love with Paul, head-over-heels in love, shamelessly blinded by what she had felt for him. It had been, she thought, the best thing that ever happened to her.

The pregnancy had shown her his true colors. She had been shocked by how, underneath all that charm, he was self-centered and mean-spirited. He had accused her of doing it on purpose! Paul had seemed like the most romantic of men, but it had really been nothing more than manipulation of a vulnerable, very young and hopelessly naive woman. His abandonment had been complete and immediate.

That's what she knew about unforgivable!

Still, there had been the pregnancy, acting as a beautiful buffer to complete heartbreak. Of course she had been afraid. Of course her life had been disrupted. But underneath all that had been a little hum of joy that walked with her, a constant, through her days.

A baby. Her baby, growing beneath her heart. She sang it lullabies of pure love. She talked to it of hopes and fears.

But her joy stopped abruptly with the miscarriage, and never, if she thought about it, ever really came back. Not completely.

"I am not thinking about that right now!" she said fiercely, out loud, not caring who sent wary glances her way.

No, she was not going to pathetically catalog her heartbreaks and disappointments because of the blow Chelsea had just delivered.

She was harnessing the energy of her visit with Brand. The aliveness of it. The powerful surging energy, a sense of not being able to do anything wrong.

"I am the CEO of the century," Bree reminded herself. "I've been given a problem. A big one, but there is no point in crying over spilt milk. I need to find a solution, not fold up my tent and creep into the night!"

But forty-eight hours later, exhausted and broken, she admitted defeat.

With what was left of her strength she called his number. For some reason, it felt as if it was going to be her hardest call and so she made it first.

"Bree! I've been waiting for that contract."

She had steeled herself to sound only businesslike. Did he have to sound so happy to hear from her?

"I'm sorry."

"Bree?"

"There isn't going to be a contract."

"Are you crying?"

"No."

"Not because of what happened here, I hope."

"I am not crying." But she was. Still, he couldn't see her, red-faced and snotty-nosed, the antithesis of the woman she had been two days ago.

So, he was still thinking of that kiss. Well, so was she. The taste of his lips—and the surprising boldness that she was capable of—was one of the few things that had sustained her through forty-eight hours of hell.

"*If* I was crying it would have nothing to do with what happened there."

"What's wrong?"

She found herself unable to speak.

"You *are* crying, aren't you? Where are you?" he asked.

"I'm at my apartment."

"I'm coming over."

"No, I—"

"Give me the address."

Oh, the temptation. There it was again, that foolish weakness, not wanting to be so alone with it all. To just lean on someone else, even for a little while.

"There's been a…situation, and I need to shut the company down temporarily." She had planned to tell him she hoped perhaps she would be up and running again in a few months, but she knew she could not keep control, so she quickly ended the call. "Goodbye, Brand. It was nice connecting with you again. Thank you for the opportunity."

"Bree—"

She disconnected.

She looked at herself. Of course he couldn't come over. Her whole apartment was smaller than his office. It was three o'clock in the afternoon and she was still in her pajamas. Her hair was tied up on top of her head with a neon orange shoelace. Her eyes were puffy. She wandered into the kitchen and opened the fridge. There was nothing in it. Well, a bottle of unopened wine, left over from a girls' night several weeks ago.

She could not have a drink. That was no way to deal with sorrow. It would be the beginning of the end.

Defiant of the bleak future the wine promised, she took the bottle out of the fridge. It wasn't even good wine. An Australian screw-top. If she ordered a pizza, it would be okay to have a glass. Lots of people—grown-ups—had a glass of wine with their pizza.

It might be a good idea to eat something, come to

think of it. Chocolate ice cream and the broken cookies she'd brought home could not sustain her forever. Plus, she was out of the ice-cream part of the equation. She called for a pizza, and took the wine into her tiny living room. Her cat, Oliver, was in her favorite chair, so she took the less comfortable couch.

She poured a glass of wine and eyed it. Red. She didn't even like red wine. It generally gave her a headache. She closed her eyes without sampling the wine.

The doorbell rang. Had she fallen asleep? She glanced at the clock. Only a few minutes had passed.

The pizza place was just down the street, but that was fast, even for them. She looked at her disheveled state: Oliver-approved pajamas with cats on them, furry slippers that looked like monster feet, her hair uncombed, her face unwashed.

She didn't owe an explanation to the pizza-delivery boy! He probably saw it all. Wasn't there even a commercial about that? Where a guy goes to the door in his underwear to get his pizza? Still, she found herself formulating a story about the flu as she opened the door.

The shock was so great, she tried to close it again.

CHAPTER SIX

"GET YOUR FOOT out of my door," Bree said. She shoved hard on the door. She felt like a mouse trying to move a mule.

"No."

"What are you doing here? I never gave you my address." Having failed to shut the door, she tucked herself behind it and peeked out at him. This was worse than being seen in her Kookies apron and beret. She was an absolute mess.

He, of course, was not. A mess. Or anything close to it. He was supremely put together in a light blue button-down shirt, dark chinos, boots, a black leather jacket and a scarf. She thought one man in a thousand could wear a scarf well. Naturally, he would be that one.

"I work with the world's best computer geeks," Brand said smoothly. "Your address, to them? Child's play. A great big yawn. Not even a challenge. Had it in my hand forty seconds after I asked for it."

"I'm not sure if that is completely ethical," she said crisply, from her station behind the door.

He cocked his head at her. "I'm not sure it is, either," he said thoughtfully. "But you should think of how easy it was next time you are arranging to meet a stranger on e-Us."

"How did you get in the front door of the building?"

He blinked at her twice, slowly, demonstrating his hypnotic charm. "This is a face that inspires trust, particularly in a little old lady trying to manage an unruly beagle and a bag of groceries at the same time."

"Mrs. Murphy," she said, annoyed. "Why are you here, Brand?"

And why did he have to look so good? Strong, and put-together, and sure of himself, the kind of guy a woman in a weakened state might want to throw herself at.

"I wanted to make sure you were okay."

"Well," she said, "you can clearly see I'm okay."

"You're hiding behind a door. How do I know if you're okay? Maybe one of your computer dates hit you over the head with a club."

She stepped out from behind the door. "See?"

He looked her up and down. He looked insultingly unconvinced about her okayness. He stared at her feet for a long time before he looked up again.

"You look as if you've been crying," he said softly.

"I have the flu, sick to my stomach, cold symptoms, runny nose, puffy eyes. You know," she said, relieved she had prepared an excuse for the pizza-delivery boy.

Who chose that minute to get off the elevator, in his distinctive red ball cap and shirt, and come to her apartment door.

"Your front-door security clearly sucks," Brand noted in an undertone.

"Medium, everything on it, double anchovies?" the delivery boy asked cheerfully.

Brand raised an eyebrow at her. “Flu food?”

She glared at him and turned to get her wallet out of her pint-size kitchen. When she returned the pizza boy was gone, and Brand was inside, holding the box, her door shut firmly behind him.

“Really? Double anchovy?” he asked.

“My weakness.”

“Mine, too.”

She searched his face for the lie and found none.

“Can we share it?” he asked. He was grinning that boyish grin, the same one that had, no doubt, sucked Mrs. Murphy into letting him into the building. Bree found herself as helpless as Mrs. Murphy. Who on earth could resist this overpowering charm?

“Since you paid for it, would it seem churlish to refuse?”

“Yes.”

“You didn’t have to come.”

“No, I didn’t. What can I say? I find a damsel in distress irresistible.”

Somehow, with Brand, there was no point telling him he did not have to do the decent thing.

“I seriously doubt there is one thing about me that is irresistible at the moment,” she said as she led him through to the tiny living room. Oliver gave him a disdainful look and curled into a tighter ball, which left them the option of sharing a too-small couch. Brand sat down on it.

“I should go get dressed. I’m at my worst.”

“Well, I’ve already seen it, so I wouldn’t get too twisted. It’s not as if I can unsee it.”

She flopped down on the couch beside him. “The

old 'no point shutting the barn door after the horse is out,' eh? That bad?"

He slid her a look. "Kind of adorable."

"Adorable," she said glumly. He was ready for his *GQ* cover and she was adorable. "Like a Pomeranian puppy?"

"More like a Yorkie. It's the furry-feet slippers. And the bow in your hair. You know how Yorkies wear those little bows on their heads?"

She reached up and yanked the shoelace out of her hair.

He sighed. "The adorable factor just went down, oh, maybe five points."

Don't indulge him, she ordered herself. "On what scale?"

"Out of a hundred. Being a perfect hundred before and now minus the five points."

"If I take off the pajamas?"

He went very still.

"I didn't mean it like that." She gave him a good hard punch in the arm.

He held his arm and made a face of exaggerated pain. "Oh. Okay. I just couldn't be sure. Because of that kiss—"

She punched him again. "Don't ever mention that to me again!"

"Bossy. Another five points off. And ten for each time you hit me in the arm."

"I should be a rottweiler pretty soon then. I can only hope. People respect rottweilers," she muttered, though inwardly she was greatly enjoying his banter. Only because it was proving a distraction from the last few days, which had been so without lightness of any kind.

"You have the feet for a rottweiler," he suggested.

She kicked off the slippers.

"Minus two for losing the slippers. Cute feet, though. Are your toenails lime-green? Plus twenty."

"With flowers." She held one up for him to inspect.

"Impressive. Plus twenty-five."

"It's not really my style, but Chelsea wants to work in a spa someday, once she gives up salsa dancing. Her toes are always showing for competitions, so she's very good at nail polishes. Still, she likes to practice on other people, namely me. I don't let her touch my fingernails, though, just the parts of me that usually don't show!"

He eyed the glass of wine, the bottle beside it. "For someone a little inhibited it seems like it might be a bit early for that," he said.

"Too early for anchovies?" She grabbed her wineglass. She took a defiant sip. Inhibited? Who had kissed whom?

"You better tell me what's going on." His shoulder was touching hers. Warmth radiated through his jacket. The leather was soft and supple, and if expense had a smell, the scent coming off the jacket would be it. Brand put the pizza box on the hassock and opened it.

She set down her wine and took the piece of pizza he offered. There was no way to eat an everything-on-it with any kind of decorum, but it was too late to make a good impression now, anyway. She was suddenly starving.

Come to think of it, she was all done making impressions. She took a huge bite of the pizza and chewing it gave her a few moments to put her thoughts together.

"You can see from the size of this place, I wasn't making cookies here." She kept her voice firm. "I rented space in a commercial kitchen. It burned to the ground two days ago, just as I was leaving your office, actually. Chelsea was there. I don't want to say Chelsea burned it to the ground, but she does get distracted practicing her routines while the cookies bake. There's some talk of a lawsuit. The building owner advised me to retain a lawyer."

"Ouch."

"Do you know what that costs?"

"Unfortunately."

"If that wasn't bad enough, I lost all my stock and some of my equipment and inventory. Insurance will cover some of the stock and inventory—unless Chelsea is found liable. Then I would have to sue her personally, which I don't think I could do, under any circumstances, even if she was practicing salsa dancing and got distracted and caught the kitchen on fire. She's so upset already."

"Do you have another wineglass?"

"Kitchen cupboard beside the range."

He got up and she watched him go. His shoulders practically touched either side of the galley-kitchen door frame. Her place was small, and now it seemed smaller, as if he was filling it—not just the floor space, but the air. He would leave, but still be here. She would breathe him in forever. She might have to move. On top of everything else.

She sighed heavily. Brand came back with a coffee mug instead of a wineglass. He poured himself some wine. He sampled it cautiously. "Not as bad as I thought it would be."

"My story?"

"No, that's worse than I thought it would be. The

wine's pretty good, though I'm just drinking this to keep you from downing the whole bottle yourself. Not that you don't have reason, but I don't want to see you get drunk. Lose your inhibitions—"

She cocked her fist at him.

"I wasn't going to mention the thing that must not be mentioned." His eyes went to her lips, and stayed there for a heated second until he looked away.

Had he deliberately paraphrased a very famous line from a series of books she had admitted, in an unguarded moment, to liking? Did that mean he had read them?

Possibly just seen the movies, which was way more resistible.

"A gentleman until the end," she said wryly.

"I try," he said.

"This is one of those surreal moments," she decided. "Here I am in my hobbit-sized apartment with a view of the side of the building next door, serving cheap wine in a coffee mug to the man being lauded by *City* magazine as the billionaire businessman of the decade."

"Don't forget the furry-feet slippers and the shoelace," he said, beautifully unimpressed with himself.

"This could only happen to me."

"You're probably right. Cheers."

"Cheers," she said. They rapped their glasses together.

"I like your hobbit-sized place," he said. "It's homey."

"Humble."

"Don't worry about it, Bree. I'm not really a gentleman."

"What? Of course you are!"

He wagged his eyebrows fiendishly at her, but there

was something in his voice when he spoke again. "I'm just a pretender at the genteel life. What I come from makes this place look like a palace."

"Really?" But then she remembered something he had said the night of the gala. He had said her family looked perfect, particularly to someone who came from one that was not. He had mentioned he had no father figure.

He nodded.

Suddenly, she *needed* to know. She needed to know something deeper about him, needed to know he could be vulnerable, too.

"Tell me about that," she insisted softly.

He hesitated. She thought he might distract with charm. But he didn't. After a long moment, he spoke.

"My dad left my mom and I when I was six." His voice had a roughness around the edge of it that it did not normally have. "My mom was ill. We lived in places smaller than shoeboxes. On one memorable occasion, we lived in a car for three days. Sometimes we went to McDonald's and stole creamers because she didn't have money for milk. She would have considered this wine champagne."

Somehow his revealing this part of himself was the most extraordinary of gifts. This was authentic, the edge of raw pain in his voice was real. That he had found her worthy of entrusting with this secret part of himself felt like the best thing that had happened to her in a long time.

Maybe even better than that kiss. Well, maybe not.

The moment of feeling he trusted her was extraordinarily brief. "I don't know why I said that," he said with a regretful shake of his head.

"You can trust me with it," she said softly.

"Thanks," he replied, but his tone was clipped.

She had questions, but assumed from the growl in his voice and his use of the past tense when talking about the champagne, that his mother was dead, and that it still caused him pain to think about it.

"Did my dad know how things were for you?" she asked.

He looked like he was very annoyed by the fact she was continuing the conversation, but after a moment he answered.

"Not all the details, but he knew I was shouldering a lot of responsibility. He helped me apply for scholarships at college. He wrote me letters of endorsement. I think he paid me more than I was worth when I worked for him. Your dad was one decent guy, Bree."

"So are you."

He lifted a shoulder.

"I think that's why you're such a decent guy," she said softly. "You know firsthand what it's like to have it tough."

Maybe it was the wrong thing to say, because a veil went down completely in his eyes, as if he regretted sharing the confidence as much as she welcomed it.

"We'll save my tales of woe for a different day," he said smoothly. "Right now I want to hear the rest of yours."

She would have liked to talk about him some more, but she could clearly see he had said all he was going to say for one day. She appreciated his confidence and did not want to appear to pry. So, she took a fortifying gulp of her wine before launching into the rest of the story.

"I thought I could rent another kitchen, but I've been

unable to find a suitable space in my price range. I'm behind on orders. You can see I can't work out of here. I'm going to have to cancel the Crystal Silvers contract. And Perks. I'm going to have to let Chelsea go, and she's already a mess, poor kid. I know I will eventually get back on my feet, but for now—" Despite that fortifying gulp of wine her voice cracked.

"For now, I'm done," she choked out. She finished her wine in one long pull. When she went to refill, he took the bottle and put it out of her reach, beside him on the floor.

"Bree, I might be able to help you out."

So, here they were again. He was going to help her out. He still felt as if he owed her dad a debt of gratitude.

But she didn't want to fight it anymore. She was so tired. She just wanted to sink into his strength. To let him take care of her. To let him rescue her from her life. There were worse things than letting a super successful man—who had a good heart and was decent to boot—look after you, take your troubles away.

Okay, so she had taken ten giant steps back from the woman in the beautiful cloak and high heels that she had been just two short days ago. She might never see that woman again, she realized sadly. The cloak was probably going to have to go to a consignment store. She couldn't in good conscience take it back. The dog had slobbered on it.

"You probably have a team of lawyers," she said. "Thank you."

"Wasn't even thinking of the legal aspects of your dilemma, but yes, I'll run your liability issues by my legal eagles."

"What were you thinking about?"

"A place for you to work."

"I appreciate you wanting to help, but believe me," she said, "I've already tried everything. I even hoped maybe I could rent a restaurant kitchen, after hours, work all night if I had to, but I just couldn't turn anything up. Again, it's the budget. And I don't want you to offer to rent me a kitchen over my budget, because the cookie business can't sustain that. It's still a business, not a charity, and if I can't run it in the black—"

"Bree, be quiet."

She sighed. Was he hearing her?

"I have a kitchen," he said softly. "In your price range. I have a commercial kitchen. That's completely empty. And available. That no one ever uses."

"Yeah, as if that would be in my price range."

"It's in your price range."

"You don't even know what my price range is. It's laughably small."

"The kitchen is free."

"Are you kidding me?" She could not keep the skepticism out of her voice. "I would have to hate you forever if you rented a kitchen for me, and then told me it was free out of some kind of misguided—"

"I would never lie to you like that. Never. And I would never risk having you hate me forever."

She could feel herself falling toward the most frightening thing of all: hope. She searched his face. She could see the innate trustworthiness of him. She felt that hope flutter to reluctant life in her chest.

"If you're kidding me, I'll have to kill you. You know that, don't you?"

"I understand completely. I mean, it's just theoretical, because I have a kitchen, but how would you go about killing me?"

"I'd have to think about it," she said regally.

"Because I'm quite big, and you're quite small. It's not like I would just stand there, with my arms open, saying, 'okay, kill me now.' And to be honest, you don't seem very threatening. I think it may be the slippers you took off a while ago that ruin your killer image."

"Maybe those slippers shoot…things. Like in a James Bond movie."

"You'd have to be more specific to convince me. Bullets? Darts? Cookies?"

She loved this bantering back and forth, but she had to know.

"Brand, please do not keep me in suspense another moment! We can discuss your potential demise another time. Tell me about the kitchen! No one *has* a kitchen, just sitting around, at their disposal."

"Well, I do."

Don't get your hopes up, she told herself. She was crying. She couldn't help it. "Where is it? Brand, I need to start right away. I'm so far behind. If I work night and day I might be able to get the Crystal Silvers birthday cookies done. Maybe."

"You'll get them done," he said, with such absolute confidence in her that she cried harder.

"How can I thank you? Where is it?"

"It's at my house."

Her heart dropped, and the tears of relief stopped. She tried not to replace them with the despairing, hopeless kind.

She took a deep breath, and did her best not to sound

too skeptical. But she'd already resigned herself to it. It was too good to be true.

"You have a commercial kitchen in your house? No one has a commercial kitchen in their house. Why would a bachelor have a commercial kitchen in his house?"

"When I bought the house, I renovated it, top to bottom. The designer told me a commercial kitchen was an investment. She said the kind of house I have is where large functions are catered."

Of course he'd have that kind of house. Brand was a billionaire. Still, Bree was a little awestruck all the same.

"I gave my poor designer a pretty hard time about that kitchen. She just kept insisting that someday I'd be really glad I had it. And you know what?"

"What?" Bree breathed.

"She was absolutely right."

His voice was soft and strong at the same time, the voice of a man who could make someone believe, all over again, even when they knew better, that magic was part of the fabric of life, that miracles happened all the time.

That when you had totally given up, when you had no hope left, life could surprise you all over again with how good it could be.

CHAPTER SEVEN

BREE EVANS WAS in his house.

Brand recognized, on the danger scale, the needle was edging toward the top of the red zone.

Because she was so very complex. Adorable. But smart. An astute businesswoman. The daughter of a man who had helped him. A woman whose kiss he could not get out of his head.

He'd confided in her that he'd once lived in a car. No one but his mother knew that about his life. What kind of moment of ridiculous weakness had that been?

Brand watched her race around his kitchen, nearly beside herself with excitement, and it felt as if every ounce of that danger he had invited into his life was worthwhile.

She stopped at the Elvis cookie jar. She took out a cookie and examined it as if she had found a bug.

"Beau's?" she said.

"He does have a weakness. Despite what Jenn said, I restrict him to one or two a week. He mostly gets dog biscuits, which he only tolerates."

"When I get caught up, I'll try making something for him that's healthier and that he'll love." She put the cookie back in the jar, and examined the jar itself. "Somehow I didn't figure you for an Elvis kind of guy."

The less she figured out about him, the better. Especially now that he had given her hints. Especially now that she was under his roof. Making herself at home.

No, that wasn't quite right. She wasn't making herself at home, she was making it feel like home.

Without even trying. She was making it feel like home even *before* she tried baking cookies for his dog.

"What exactly would you consider an Elvis kind of guy?" he asked, intrigued despite himself.

"Sleazily oversexed?"

"Elvis?" he said, with pretended hurt. "That's slanderous. You have enough legal problems without slandering the King."

"I think e-Us matched me with him once. Complete with the sweaty scarf." She shuddered delicately.

"Okay, here's the deal. I said the kitchen was free, but it's not."

"Don't do this to me," she moaned.

"No more e-Us. That's the price."

"Deal," she said, way too fast.

He eyed her suspiciously.

"I've got my sights set on Kevin."

"I hope you don't."

"I do," she said and whipped her phone out of her back pocket. "Look. There's an app that teaches you to speak Klingon."

He saw she was teasing him. Or he was pretty sure she was teasing him. But she did know about the app.

"I'm going to be way too busy to have a social life," she declared happily.

Why was he happy, too? What did he care about her social life or lack thereof?

She was dashing around the kitchen again, opening drawers, looking in cupboards. She ran reverent hands over one of the ovens. "A steam oven. I could not have dreamed."

She opened it up. "You've never used this," she said with faint accusation.

"How do you know?"

"The racks have cardboard on the corners."

"Oh."

"Three ovens," she whispered, looking around. "Have you used any of them? Oh!" she squealed, before he had a chance to answer. "Look at this!"

He came over to see what was causing such excitement. She had changed out of her pajamas, and put her hair up with a band. He liked the shoestring better, not that he wanted her to know he'd noticed. She was wearing snug jeans and a white top.

She was bent over a lower cabinet looking inside it. He could look at that particular sight for a long time, but it made him feel like an oversexed Elvis so he made himself focus on what she was looking at. Something huge and ugly and red was in his cupboard.

"What is that?" he asked, astounded.

"It's in your kitchen. You don't know?" She tossed an amused look over her shoulder.

"See that thing over there?" he said, and pointed. "It's called a microwave. I know that. And the fridge. I've used the coffeemaker a couple of times."

"That explains why it's so clean in here."

Actually, a cleaning staff kept it clean in here, but it seemed so pretentious to say it, that he didn't.

"Well, this—" she tugged, and the whole shelf slid out and began to rise "—is a stand mixer. Sometimes called a batch mixer."

He was so startled at it moving by itself that he took a step back. He actually took her shoulders and moved her back, too.

The monstrous apparatus rose silently and then stopped at counter level.

"If it moves toward you, run," he whispered.

He loved her giggle. She sounded like Goldie Hawn.

"It's not dangerous," she assured him. She reached out as if she was going to pet it.

He grabbed her hand. "Don't touch. I think it may be HAL."

"HAL?"

She had to ask. He wouldn't break it to her just yet that she didn't have a hope with Kevin. He didn't care about her and Kevin. Shoot. He cared about her and Kevin. And her and some guy who had stiffed her for coffee. And her and the sleazy oversexed guy with the scarf. He was still holding her hand. He dropped it like it was hot.

"2001: A Space Odyssey."

She was all over that ugly red space alien piece of machinery. "I'm not familiar with it."

Kiss Kevin goodbye.

"It's a movie. Old. Sci-fi."

"Hmmm, you don't look like a sci-fi kind of guy."

Or an Elvis kind of guy. He was going to ask her how she knew a sci-fi guy from one who wasn't, but she'd probably dated one.

Instead he said, "I'm not really a sci-fi guy, but when you work with the geek squad, you pick up on what they consider to be the essentials of life. Consider it like being immersed in a continuous episode of *The Big Bang Theory*."

She was very focused on the apparatus in front of her but laughed at his joke. She was obviously very familiar with the ugly red space alien. Was she caressing the damn thing?

Don't ask. "What kind of guy would you say I am?" he asked.

"The best kind," she said with a smile. "The kind with a commercial kitchen *and* a stand mixer."

"I have other sterling qualities."

"Where's your bedroom?"

His jaw dropped. He, who considered himself virtually unshakable, felt like he was turning the same color as the darned mixer.

"That's not what I meant," he said. His voice sounded like a squeak.

She actually turned her attention away from the attractions of the mixer and stared at him. And then her eyes widened. And then she giggled, that funny little Goldie Hawn giggle. And then the giggle deepened into something even better. She laughed. She laughed until she doubled over from it. She laughed until the tears were squirting out her eyes.

"Oh, my God, Brand."

"What's so damn funny?"

"I wasn't suggesting you had sterling qualities in the bedroom. Not that you don't. I mean maybe you do."

Her laughter dried up, just like that. Now they were both standing there with faces as red as the mixer.

"I'm going to be trying to catch up on my orders." She was speaking very fast, her words tumbling over one another. “I need to call Chelsea. We’ll probably work all night. I wanted to know where your bedroom was so we wouldn’t disturb you. So I know how quiet I need to be. We usually work with music. And equipment like this—” she patted that mixer with disturbing affection again “—is quite loud.”

“Oh.” He said. “That’s a relief.” Well, kind of a disappointment, but mostly a relief.

She actually looked faintly hurt. “Yes, isn’t it?”

“My bedroom’s a long way away. Play anything you want. As loud as you want.”

“Do you have a favorite Elvis song?”

The soundtrack of his childhood. He could tell from which one was playing when he walked through the door after school how his Mom was going to be that evening. Or maybe more accurately, who she was going to be.

He could have never told Wendy about that. Had never wanted to.

And yet, at this precise moment, there was an ache to tell Bree. It felt as if he would die of loneliness if he didn’t tell her.

But he didn’t.

Instead, he forced his tone to be smooth and light, and answered, “Must I pick only one? Impossible. Yours?”

She didn’t hesitate. “‘I Can’t Help—’”

She stopped. She stared at him. She stammered, “Uh, I can’t think of one. ‘Jailhouse Rock’ maybe.”

He should tell her never to take up poker. She was a terrible liar.

They were definitely in the danger zone right now, right this instant. He could feel the chemistry between them. The needle was edging up into red. He’d made a mistake inviting her into his space. He could clearly see that.

"Don't worry about disturbing me at all," he said. "I was just going to pack a bag, anyway."

"You were?"

"Yes, I have a business trip. We're opening a new physical location. Bali." He hadn't been planning on going to the opening until thirty seconds ago. Suddenly it felt imperative to put a world of oceans between them.

"Bali," she said.

He thought of her in Bali. Carefree. He wondered if she'd ever snorkeled. Or surfed. That was where he had learned to do both. He felt an unfortunate curiosity about what she would look like in a bikini.

"Okay," he said, hastily "if you've got everything you need, I'll go pack."

"Yes," she said formally. "I've taken enough of your time."

He moved away from her, edging toward the door. Edging back toward the world where he controlled everything. Where there were surprises, of course there were, but in a way, even though they were surprises, they were predictable kind of surprises. Like deciding to go to Bali on a moment's notice.

Nothing that made his heart do what it was doing right now.

Thank goodness!

"Yes, you do that," she said, as insultingly eager to get rid of him as he was to go. "Go to pack. Do I need a key? To get in and out? I'll need to go for supplies."

He started to say he didn't lock it. But suddenly he didn't want his house unlocked with him away and her coming in and out. What if she was coming in with her arms full of groceries and there was an intruder, already inside? Or what if she was inside making a bunch of noise, so much noise she might not hear an intruder? Beau would be left at the office while he was away. Should he leave him here with her instead? To protect her?

No. The dog would probably compromise the health standards of the kitchen. There was a keypad on the front door that Brand had never used. He was going to have to figure it out. He'd call one of his technical geniuses.

It occurred to him he'd never thought he had anything of value in here. It was valuable stuff, but he recognized, right this minute, he had no attachment to any of it.

It felt as if Bree Evans was the only valuable thing in his world.

Her and Beau.

Beau could look after himself.

"I have to get going," he said again. He could hear the desperation in his own voice. He was pretty sure there was a line of sweat breaking out over his top lip.

She waltzed over to him. She looked as if she was going to kiss him again. He backed away from her rapidly.

"Make yourself at home while I'm away," Brand said. "If you need a break there's a media room through that door. The freezer has microwavable stuff in it, if you get sick of eating cookies. There are guest bedrooms upstairs if you need a snooze. There's four, no, five powder rooms, so take your pick."

There was that look again, as if she might kiss him. He backed away from her even more rapidly. As unmanly as it was, he was practically running from her.

"Thank you," she called after him, as he went through the door to the hallway.

Her voice sounded as if it had laughter in it. Minx. She *liked* making him uncomfortable.

And he liked making her laugh. In fact, Brand was very aware that a man could live to make her laugh, to wipe the worry lines from her forehead, to erase the sorrow from her eyes…

A better man than him, he reminded himself. One without baggage, a ragtag excuse for a family, a number of failed forays into the relationship department, his only serious one, Wendy, having failed quite colossally.

Bali, he told himself. That should take his mind off her. Sand and surf and work. Lots and lots of work.

Work. It had always been the place he escaped. It was a world where a person could apply their mind to problems and make them dissolve. It was a world where the challenges were not personal, where they had no emotion attached to them. It was a world he could lose himself in, shut out any little thing that bothered him or caused him distress or discomfort.

The only thing was, he'd never been aware before that he used it to escape the nebulous unsolvable kind of problems that popped up when you became attached to another person.

He waited until he was out of the house to slide his phone from his pocket. He punched in the familiar number. He got her answering message.

"Hi, Mom, I'm going to be away for a couple of days. I'll video-call you tonight on your phone."

His mother loved that feature on her phone. "It's just like being on *The Jetsons*," she'd say with wonder every single time he called.

CHAPTER EIGHT

BREE CAME AWAKE with a start and a little shriek.

"Sorry, I didn't mean to startle you."

His voice wrapped around her in the darkness and made her feel safe.

"Brand?" she asked sleepily. In what context would she be waking up to Brand? It was a dream, obviously, a delightful dream that she never wanted to end.

"I had no idea you were in here," he said, softly, his voice like the touch of a silk scarf across the back of her neck.

She remembered, slowly, she was in one of the deep recliner chairs in his media room. She had helped herself to one of the Icelandic wool blankets artfully placed in a huge basket in one of the corners.

"What time is it?" You could never tell in the media room, because, unlike the kitchen, which was saturated in light from the banks of windows, light had been deliberately blocked out of this room.

"Eight."

"In the morning?" she asked, shocked.

"Yeah."

"Are you just getting home?"

"Yeah. I was going to unwind from the trip in here for a bit, but I'll—"

"No—no, of course you can unwind in your own home. Chelsea and I finished late. It was about two in the morning. I should have gone home," she said, suddenly embarrassed. "I was just going to sit here for a moment, but I made the mistake of reclining the chair. So comfy! I hope I didn't leave the ovens on." She sniffed the air. "I wouldn't want to burn down two kitchens."

"There's nothing burning. The house smells incredible, though. You could bottle that smell. Make a fortune."

Her eyes were adjusting to the dark. He was still dressed for the tropics in light pants and a sports shirt. He looked so yummy, ever so slightly travel-rumpled, his hair not quite as crisply groomed as normal, his cheeks and chin dark with whisker stubble.

She remembered she had on the white-net baking cap, and she tried to remove it as surreptitiously as possible and stuff it in the pocket of her chef's jacket. Why did he always have to catch her at her worst?

"How was Bali?"

He didn't answer.

"Not what you hoped?" she asked. "Did something go wrong?"

"No, not really. I'm just a bit off. Time difference." He moved by her, took the deep chair next to hers and pushed it back into full recline. "Anything new in the fire investigation?"

Bree cast Brand a glance out of the corner of her eye. His hands were folded over his stomach and he was looking at the ceiling. It had been a week since she'd seen him. Was he deliberately avoiding talking about himself?

"Chelsea's a mess. She's been interviewed twice, and they've intimidated her horribly."

"Does she have a lawyer?"

"On what I pay her?"

"Would you let me look after it?"

A terrible tenderness unfolded in her at the weariness etched into the lines of his handsome face.

Of course she felt tender toward him! He had saved her business. He had given her a place to work that was beyond her wildest dreams. Now he was offering to help Chelsea.

"Thank you," she said, feeling any defenses she had left against him crumbling as she accepted his gift with the graciousness it deserved. "You should go to bed."

"You should, too."

Together. She knew the renegade thought proved she was not just feeling tender toward him because of her business or his offer to help Chelsea.

"I think I'm awake for the day," she said hastily, to move the talk and her still dream-weakened thoughts away from the topic of beds.

"Yes, me, too. The worst thing I could do this morning is indulge my desire to sleep. I need to force myself back on to this time."

It reminded her, no matter how tender she felt toward him, that her feelings had to remain her closely guarded secret. They were from different worlds. He was a man accustomed to dealing with jet lag, business trips to Bali and beyond. She made cookies for a living.

"How did the cookies go?" he asked, as if he could read her mind. He asked it as though he really cared, damn him, and as if there was not a huge gap in their socioeconomic circumstances.

"We're completely caught up. All my regular orders are done. Perks got their first order. Chelsea took the

Crystal Silvers order to the airport last night when we finished."

"You've been busy," he said.

"Yes, my poor cat has been feeling neglected." Now why had she said that? Add crazy cat lady to cookie maker! Besides, it wasn't true. Her neighbor, an elderly lady, loved Oliver and had liked nothing more than taking the cat while Bree put in these long hours.

"I guess you probably feel the same about Beau? Will you pick him up and bring him home today?"

"I'll probably banish him while the baking is going on. I think your health standard would be compromised by his presence."

"Aw, poor guy."

"Not really. He's used to me being away. He's got a pretty nice setup at the office, too. There's people working there all the time."

"Your office runs all the time?"

"It's that creative-brain thing. Lots of my people say they work best at night. I just go with it. The office is open twenty-four hours. I let them keep track of their own time."

"You need more cookies if you're running twenty-four hours," she said. "Your office is next on the list. I've been filling orders in between the Crystal Silvers special order, and I'm caught up. Your office will be going into the rotation starting on Monday."

"You haven't sent me a contract yet," he said. His voice was husky with sleepiness.

She wouldn't tell him this just yet, because he was sure to reject it, but she wasn't sending him a contract. She was baking his office cookies for free, for the rest of her life. And cookies for Beau, too, as soon as she figured out a dog-friendly recipe.

His chest was starting to rise and fall.

"You can bring Beau home," she said. "I'll be taking the next two days off."

She realized she wanted to stay here forever, feeling warm and safe and oddly happy. She forced herself to throw back the blanket and get up. "Can I bring you anything before I leave?"

"Sure. A Love Bite and a Decadent."

He remembered things. That was the nature of being a businessman, remembering details about people and their businesses. Still, she felt inordinately pleased that he remembered the names of her cookies.

Then he added, "And with anyone else, a decadent love bite would mean something quite different than it does with you. Just saying."

She laughed, a bit uneasily. There it was again, between them, teasing, which was wonderful, but it was teasing with some finely held tension, like a shiver when you went outside on a cold day. "I'll be right back."

But he got up and followed her into the kitchen.

"I don't want to go to sleep," Brand insisted. "I know from past experience what giving in to that temptation does. It can take weeks to get back to normal if you don't force yourself back into a regular daily schedule right away."

Morning light was streaming in the kitchen windows. In the brightness, he still looked tired, and also sexily roguish with that hint of whisker shadow on his face. She could see his skin had picked up a faint golden glow from the sun.

She felt something tingle along her spine. There was something about the way he was looking at her that could give that expression, about giving in to temptation, many meanings. They had been apart for a week. It had not cooled the way she felt about him. It had intensified it.

Did he feel the same way? Or was it all just banter to him? He would be good at flirting, probably with no awareness of how good he was at it. In one sentence of that *City* article they had called him Vancouver's most eligible bachelor.

"Wow," he said, looking around. "If there's a heaven this is what it looks and smells like."

She looked around and saw what he saw. His kitchen was, indeed, a beautiful sight. It was bright and clean, with clearly defined workstations. But the best sight of all—well, besides him—was those big clearly labeled rectangular bakery boxes, stacked up on racks in the center island. Cookies all boxed up and ready to go to their various destinations and drop-off points.

"I'm interested in what brought you to filling up your life with cookies," he said as she handed him the two flavors he had requested. Their fingertips brushed. Something electrical, like static, leaped between them.

It was probably from the Icelandic wool!

"I don't usually recommend these for breakfast," she said, as if she could chase away the electricity, and the helpless feeling it gave her, with stern words.

"Ah, well, its suppertime in Bali." He popped a whole cookie in his mouth—no easy task—then closed his eyes and chewed contentedly.

"They aren't healthy for supper, either!"

Though watching him, a memory tickled the back of her mind.

"My dad used to eat them for supper sometimes," she said softly, then added thoughtfully, "I guess that's the *why* of cookies. I got an Easy-Bake Oven for Christmas when I was six, and was soon tired of the limitations of it. I graduated to the big-girl oven and started baking cookies for my dad. If there were cookies, warm out of the oven, when he got home, he'd get so excited. He'd gobble them down for supper. He'd do impressions of the Cookie Monster until my mother and I were in hysterics, rolling on the floor, begging him to stop. Of course, it just egged him on.

"The base dough for those cookies you are eating right now is the recipe I kept working on as a kid. It still changes slightly from time to time. For instance, last year, I started adding a bit of coffee to it."

"Good business," Brand said, opening his eyes and regarding her. "Coffee and chocolate, highly addictive."

"I never gave that a thought."

"You wouldn't," he said.

If he was going to insist on seeing her as an innocent, she was going to have to kiss him again.

No! She could never kiss him again. Because it made her long for things she could not have.

He was so far out of her league it wasn't even funny.

"I haven't just been making cookies. I've been looking for another kitchen. I can't impose on you forever. I think I've got a line on one. It sounds as if it might be available for the beginning of the month. Beau can come home."

"Sheesh, stop feeling guilty about Beau."

"I've displaced him. And you, too."

"This is pretty normal for me. To travel. To be away for long periods."

"Do you ever stay still?" she asked quietly. "Do you ever just kick back and enjoy your beautiful home?"

"Oh, sure," he said. "I wind down here. You've seen the media room. It's perfect for football and a beer."

"That's not actually what I meant," she said.

"Oh? What did you mean?"

"I meant…" She tried to think of how to put it. "I meant a fire in the fireplace. And a turkey in the oven. A Christmas tree."

"It's May!" he said.

"I'm not explaining it very well." She was *not* explaining it very well, but she also suspected he was being deliberately obtuse.

"No, you're not."

"It's not about Christmas. It's about a feeling. Of being *home*."

"Cue the *Little House on the Prairie* music," he said sarcastically.

But, in actual fact, she already knew this about him: his space lacked a sense of being a home. It was as if the house had spoken to her while he'd been away, divulged some of his secrets.

It was a beautiful house, like the houses you saw in magazines. She had taken advantage of his invitation and in his absence she had napped in one of the gorgeous upstairs bedrooms. She had found excuses to inspect all the powder rooms.

Everything was perfect, as perfect and as high-end as the kitchen would have you predict it would be. There were beautiful original art pieces, priceless hand-knotted rugs, painted silk wallpapers, incredible one-of-a-kind light fixtures and the aforementioned hand-knitted Icelandic throws. There were collectibles from many different countries, artfully worked into the décor. The furniture was all stunning. There were gorgeous scenes all over the house, as if they were waiting for a photographer. A desk with a leather-bound journal open and a pen beside it in an alcove under an upstairs window. A fireplace in the formal living room with the fire laid, as if all you had to do was strike a match. There were two vases of spring fresh tulips on a long dining room table that looked as if it had never been eaten at. There were fresh rosebuds in all the guest bedrooms, and a bucket full of delicately blushing pink peonies in the landing of the grand staircase.

And yet, as almost overwhelmingly beautiful as everything was, and despite how busy and how exhausted Bree was, she thought that his house felt empty. Staff came in, to clean and change flowers, but that just made it feel even more like a house that was being beautifully staged to sell, rather than a house anyone lived in.

There was no sign of his entertaining female guests, either. There was no second toothbrush, no tubes of mascara left out, no feminine shoes in the front coat closet, no chick flicks in his enormous collection of movies, no yogurt or diet soda in his fridge.

She felt as if the house cried for the feminine touches that would have made it a home and for children screaming and running up and down the halls and leaving messes everywhere. It felt as if the house longed for laughter, love, energy. It felt as if the house wanted to be filled up with the smells of people living in it: roast beef in the oven, crisp Yorkshire puddings erupting out of baking tins.

It was the saddest thing she could think of: a house that had never had cookies baked in it, or at least not while he had lived here. She could tell none of the three ovens had ever been used. The state-of-the-art appliances all sparkled prettily, but, like the stoves, she would put money on whether or not they had ever been turned on until she came along.

And even now, it was the scent of cookie *production*, not cookies, that had welcomed him back from his trip.

That is what she was very aware of. It was a house.

Not a home. A place to crash and watch a football game and drink a beer.

Instead of making her feel awed by his success, the house had made her feel the acute loneliness of it. She understood perfectly why he would not spend a great deal of time here, or be eager to come "home" to it.

The only room she truly liked was the media room, with its deep, ugly chairs, and its stinky dog bed, and its gaudy Elvis posters and its faint smell of old popcorn.

Underneath Brand's sarcastic tone—"cue the *Little House on the Prairie* music"—Bree heard the faintest thing: a longing, a wistfulness.

All of a sudden she knew she wasn't leaving right away, even though that would be the smartest thing to do, even though her cat had suffered enough neglect this week.

If she wanted to protect her poor heart, and she did, she should already be halfway out that door.

But suddenly, it was not all about her. Suddenly, she was aware that was not how she had been raised. She was almost ashamed of the self-centeredness that wanted her to protect herself when she had the most precious gift to give this man who had done so much for her.

She had discovered what she could give him. This man who had saved her business, casually, as if it meant nothing, as if life was a game of Monopoly and he had a pocket full of save-a-business-for-free cards.

She wanted to repay him. But how did you repay a man who had everything? You gave him the one thing he had never had.

She could give him something he had missed. She knew from the small snippets of his childhood that he had confided in her about—living in a car for three days, for goodness sake—that it was unlikely his home had held normal activities, like baking cookies.

Giving him cookies for life was not enough. Besides, they were material. He could buy warehouses full of cookies. Her cookies, or someone else's. She'd been in this business long enough to know competition was stiff and rapidly growing. Hers was not the only company that produced a delicious, meticulously made product.

So, she could give Brand the experience of *making* cookies. A piece of a missing childhood. A magic piece. A sense of what that place called *home* could feel like.

"Have you ever made cookies?" she asked him.

"No, never." He confirmed what she had already guessed, but he looked wary.

"Let's change that. Right now."

"No, you're tired. Go home."

But she wasn't going to go home. Now that she had figured out the gift she could give him, it felt imperative to do it now. Maybe because he was tired, his defenses were down a little bit.

Because really? Under normal circumstances what billionaire was going to spend a morning baking cookies?

But he cocked his head at her, reluctantly interested. He lifted a shoulder in assent.

"Do I need one of those?" he asked, gesturing at her chef's jacket.

"Only if you're worried about your shirt." She shrugged out of her own. "We're not baking commercially right now. We're making a single batch of my original-recipe chocolate-chip cookies. For you."

"Do they have magic in them?" he asked softly.

"Oh, I hope so," she responded, just as softly. And then, she moved away from the intensity building between them. She moved, instead, over to her iPod station.

"Want some music?" she asked.

"Sure."

She found an Elvis Presley hits playlist and started it, then glanced back at him. "What?"

"Maybe not Elvis this morning."

There was something in his face, guarded and yet vulnerable. There was some secret about him and Elvis he was not yet willing to divulge.

Yet. The word suggested her subconscious was already looking to a future her rational mind knew was not possible.

She changed the setting to random. She supposed, if he listened, her music selection was going to say as much about her as his house did about him.

Romantic. Hope-filled. Longing for love.

"Okay," she said brightly, hoping to distract him from the telling messages of her music choices. "Let's start. Cookies 101."

"Do I have to touch HAL? I don't think I can touch HAL."

She giggled at his pretended fear of the mixer. "I was thinking something a little more old-fashioned. A big bowl. A wooden spoon, some basic ingredients. And my secrets."

"I want to know your secrets," he said huskily, "especially if they involve a wooden spoon."

He was tired. She was tired. They had to tread very carefully here, so she ignored his playful, suggestive innuendo, even as she filed it away. *He's seeing me as a grown-up. You don't say things like that to someone you think of as a kid.*

"Secret number one, coming right up." She went to the fridge, reached in and held the tinfoil packet out to him with showmanship.

"Butter," he said. He lifted his eyebrows at her. How could a man say so much without saying a single word?

"Stop it!"

"I never said anything."

"I know. That's a special talent, being so bad without saying a word."

One eyebrow stayed up as the other went down. It was a very sexy look.

"You're being very wicked," she said sternly.

"Yes, I am," he said, not a bit contrite. "I think people usually use oil, but butter might—"

"You need to stop it." The protest was token. Again, she felt a little tingle. He was definitely seeing her as a woman! That decision to show him some magic was having consequences much more dangerous than she could have imagined. She didn't feel anything like a Girl Guide doing a good deed!

She wondered exactly what she had let herself in for.

And the truth was she couldn't wait to find out!

"There is no wickedness in cookie making," she told him sternly.

"Yes, ma'am, no wickedness in cookie making." He repeated it dutifully. The way he said *wickedness*, with so much heat, could melt an iceberg!

"Butter, real butter, no imitations, is the number-one secret to making good cookies," she said primly, as if his teasing was not making her feel alive and happy. She could feel the laughter bubbling up inside of her. Of course, if she laughed, there would be no stopping him. She had not anticipated this particular problem when she had thought of giving the gift of some childhood magic to a fully grown man.

She had to ignore his sexiness. If she didn't, she would teach him nothing about home, and underscore his ability to distract. She had wanted it to be fun, yes, but she could not succumb to his charm, or fun was going to take an unexpected turn that had nothing to do with her original motivation in extending this invitation.

"You need to pay attention." She said it out loud to herself, a reminder to stay focused on cookies and not the dark tangle of his lashes, the sensual curve of his bottom lip, the way his light pants clung to the large muscles of his thighs.

"Will there be a test?" he asked solemnly.

Focusing hard, she unwrapped the butter from its tin-foil and put it in a small bowl. Her fingers felt clumsy under his gaze, as if she had dipped them in glue that had hardened. She turned from him and softened the butter in the microwave. "Thirty seconds," she told him, "just enough for it to slide out."

"Slide out," he repeated as if he was being an obedient student, which he was not! He made the words sound like something out of the *Kama Sutra*!

She shoved the two-cup measure at him. "One of white sugar, two of brown."

She cast a glance at him a minute later after the room had descended into total silence. His tongue was caught between his teeth. His focus was intense.

"You're not measuring gunpowder."

"You're the one who stripped all the fun out of it already."

"I did not."

"I'm surprised you didn't tell me I can't use the word *stripped*. As well as not speaking of anything wicked."

"For heaven's sake, I am not a complete stick-in-the-mud!"

"Okay. When's the last time you had fun, since you brought it up?"

"This *is* fun for me."

"But you are not a complete stick-in-the-mud," he said sadly. "An example of fun that has nothing to do with cookies. Tell me the last thing that made you laugh."

The last things that had made her laugh all involved him. Nearly. "I bought a laser pointer. My cat chases the red dot."

He was silent.

"Obsessively."

He remained silent.

"It's much funnier than you think."

"You need to get out more."

Her sense of deep gratitude to him, and of wanting to give him a gift, was dissipating quite rapidly.

"We can't all spend our lives frolicking on beaches, turning that lovely shade of gold that you are right now."

"You do look a little pale," he said, regarding her solemnly. "Jailhouse pallor. Chained to the kitchen too long. You need to get outside."

"Thank you. If you could measure the brown—"

"If you did frolic on a beach, would it be in a bikini or a one-piece?"

CHAPTER NINE

SHOOT, BRAND THOUGHT. There it was, out of his mouth. The whole time he'd been in Bali he'd wondered that. Bikini or one-piece? Bali had not been quite the escape that he had hoped for. Now, here he was in the kitchen with Bree, being as wicked as baking cookies allowed, and somehow the question had just popped out of his mouth.

Bree's mouth fell open. She looked flustered.

Well, who could blame her? He was tired. He should have never agreed to the cookie-making session.

He knew what it was really about. She had seen something in him, sensed something in this house. A longing. A vulnerability. He was going to distract her from her quest.

Which was what? To know the real him?

That, yes, but more. She was determined to show him something he had missed.

Her motivations, he was one-hundred-percent positive, were nothing but altruistic. He should have never let it slip about living in the car, about his childhood being less than ideal, because she was busy filling in the gaps now. The problem was, once you had been shown something like that, didn't you then ache for it forever?

He did not want to be thinking of the word *forever* anywhere in the vicinity of her.

"Why don't you guess?" she suggested, her cheeks pink.

His distractions, he was pleased to see, were working. He had entirely removed the focus from himself.

"I'm going to guess a one-piece—"

"That's correct."

"When it should be a bikini."

"Four eggs," she said, a little too loudly. She held up a device in her hand. "This is a handheld electric mixer. Think of it as HAL's little sister. We're going to whip the butter."

"Look, if you don't want any wickedness you can't talk about whips."

She put her hands on her hips. "I hope you aren't that kind of guy, Brand Wallace." Sternly, she handed him the electric beaters. "Put them in the butter and sugar and turn them on. That should drown out the sound of your voice."

"I'm offended," he said, though he was not. In the least.

"Aside from butter, this is the secret to making really, really good cookies."

"Good whipping?" he said innocently.

She pinched her lips together. It didn't help one little bit. The laughter gurgled out past her closed lips.

He'd totally succeeded in distracting her from the topic of himself.

And he had totally failed to protect himself.

Because her laughter was a balm to a life that suddenly came face-to-face with the emptiness of all his accomplishments and all his stuff. He had somehow missed the most important thing of all.

Connection.

She laughed until she doubled over, until tears ran down her face.

It made him realize he knew secrets about her, too, that she probably did not want him to know.

Despite her laughter right now, there was some sadness in her that would not let her go, that had not been in her when he had escorted her to her prom. She had been shy, yes, and awkward, yes, but almost filled to the brim with an innocent confidence life would be good to her. He wondered, not for the first time, what might have happened to her.

Don't go there, he ordered himself. *Keep it light. You don't want to go deep with her. You'll be drowning in the pools of light that are her incredible eyes before you even know you're in trouble.*

That was the whole problem, wasn't it? He wasn't that kind of guy, there was nothing twisted or kinky about him. Not even close. But he was not the kind of guy that a girl like her needed, either. As long as both of them were playing by the same rules, as long as both of them remembered that.

"All I am is the kind of guy who likes to make a pretty girl blush."

"I'm not blushing." She was trying to stop laughing. She was blushing with the intensity of a house on fire. She had unbent herself and was cracking eggs into the cookie mixture as if her life depended on it. "Keep, er, mixing it."

As he mixed, she slowly added flour and other ingredients. She was standing close to him, and he could look down on her hair, her gorgeous sunshine-on-sand hair. Would it get lighter if she frolicked on a beach?

The dough began to take on the texture of thick peanut butter.

It was such a blatant lie, about her blushing, that he laughed. Her face, from laughter and racy undertones to the conversation, was nearly as red as the stand mixer.

"And I'm not that pretty, either," she said quietly.

"What? What the hell?" His own laughter died. So did his resolution not to go there, to her secrets, to her sadness, to some place that had stolen the confidence that had just begun to bloom in her when he had taken her to her prom, a lifetime ago.

"I'm not," she said firmly.

"What would make you say something like that?"

"Maybe I'm adorable, like a Yorkie," she said. "But I know I'm not the greatest. All those guys—the ones I meet on e-Us? They never call me back. Not even the Elvis look-alike."

"That's impossible," he said grimly.

"I have an affliction."

Good grief! "An affliction? Like you're dying or something?" He could not believe how his heart stopped in his chest.

"Oh, for Pete's sake," she said. She actually flicked a piece of cookie batter at him. "Of course I'm not dying."

He tried not to let his relief show. He scraped the dough off his shirt and licked his finger. He was aware of her eyes on him. He took his time licking his finger. The dough was delicious.

"The affliction?" he reminded her, not allowing himself to be distracted by the deliciousness of the dough, as difficult as that was.

"Even growing up," she said slowly, "I knew exactly what I wanted. It was so ordinary and old-fashioned. My girlfriends wanted to be doctors and lawyers, writers and scientists. Oh, sure, they wanted to get married, and have families, but it was like an afterthought. I'll win the Pulitzer Prize, *then* I'll have a baby.

"But my happiest moments were when my family was together, raking leaves, or sitting beside the fire on a cold night, all reading our books. I loved plain moments—arguing over whether it was really a word in Scrabble, or my dad trying to explain football to me, yet again."

It was that *thing* that he had worried about. That she was painting pictures of all the things he had never had, and it could create an ache in him that would never ease.

"I felt safe and cherished—"

Things he had never felt, except maybe with Beau. He was pretty sure that made him, the guy who had been named businessman of the decade, and who had just returned to his beautiful home from a business trip in Bali, pathetic. But this was not about him.

"And that's all I ever wanted for my future. To feel that way, forever."

"And?" He had to force himself to ask the question, because she was taking him on a journey that he did not have a map for. He did not like journeys without maps.

"When my dad died I wanted it even *more*."

"That seems pretty natural."

"I can't *make* it happen." Now that she had started, it felt like the floodgates were wide open. "I'm plagued by first-date anxiety so strong I never get a second one."

"You're getting a terrifying look on your face," he told her, and it was true.

"A terrifying look?" she asked, all innocence.

"As in you want a first date that leads to a second date, and then a third one."

"And?"

"And then wedding bells and babies."

He hadn't thought she could blush any deeper than when he'd been teasing her while whipping the cookies, but she could.

"I had no idea I was so transparent!"

"Believe me, on the transparency scale? You are a perfect ten."

"My only perfect ten," she said glumly.

"That's not true."

"Anyway, I can't help it if my dreams are written all over me. It seems deceitful to not let it be known upfront what your end goal is. I mean why lead someone to believe I'm into casual—"

The fiery burn moving up her cheeks increased, if that was possible. No wonder her kitchens caught fire. She managed to avoid using the word *sex*.

"Casual relationships when nothing could be further from the truth."

"It seems to me if that dream is what you really wanted, you'd already have it because not all guys are as terrified by such dreams as me."

"Well, as I told you, I have an affliction."

"That wasn't it?" he asked. "Wanting babies and weddings and forever?"

She scowled at him. "No."

"Okay, give. About the affliction."

"I get nervous," she confessed.

"Who doesn't get nervous on a first date? That's hardly an affliction."

She sighed.

"I guess you better give me an example."

"I blurt out dumb things. I sweat in my dress. I've steamed up my glasses, and gotten dust under my contact lenses. I've spilled my wine. And dribbled food down my front. Once, I broke a tooth and I had to find an emergency dental clinic. And he didn't even help me.

"It's like I have that terrible affliction like the one golfers get. Where they start whiffing or flubbing or whatever it's called, and once they start thinking about it, they can't get over it. It just gets worse and worse and worse."

She had been focusing hard on the cookie dough. She looked up at him. Her eyes were wide and earnest.

He could feel his lips twitching. Anyone who did business with him, or worked with him on a regular basis, knew it was not a good thing.

But she, innocent that she was, looked puzzled. "Are you laughing at me?"

"Laughing? No! I'm feeling really annoyed with you." The truth was, he wanted to kiss the living daylights out of her, because she had so badly lost who she really was and had painted herself into such a corner of self-deceit.

"What? Why?"

"Because you are believing this line of crap that you are telling yourself. And you know what I'd like to know? What's really going on? What's really made you so afraid of your own happiness?"

He inserted a word between *your* and *happiness* that was the universal song of displeasure and that meant "I am dead serious. Do not try and snow me."

CHAPTER TEN

BREE STARED AT BRAND. How had things gone so terribly off the rails? She was supposed to be helping *him*. She had entered his kitchen with the naivety of a Girl Guide thinking she was doing her good deed for the day.

How had he turned things around like this?

And how could it possibly feel as if she *had* to tell him, as if to carry this burden alone for one more second would be to be crushed under the weight of it?

How could it possibly feel as if he had unlocked some secret that she had hidden, even from herself? That somehow she was so afraid she was sabotaging her own dreams?

Could that be true? She grabbed a bag of chocolate chips and began to dump them in the bowl. She should have passed him the wooden spoon, but she felt the need to blow off the energy building in her. She started to mash those chips into the cookie dough, when really it should have been a nice, gentle blending motion.

"It was a man," Brand said softly.

She risked a glance at him. He was regarding her with narrowed eyes, flashing dangerously now, with something that was not mischief. He took the spoon from her and began to pummel the cookie dough with barely leashed aggravation.

"How could you know that?" she whispered.

"I can tell by looking at you," he said. "Some evil bastard broke your heart."

You could never, ever forget this about Brand, not even when you were baking cookies, that he was a keen observer, that he saw things that would remain hidden to those not quite as astute.

Don't tell him, she begged herself. And yet, it felt that if she told him, if she finally said these dreadful things out loud, she would be free in some way. She would solve a puzzle that had mystified her. He already knew anyway. He had guessed it.

"As you know, my dad died shortly after my prom," she said tiredly. "I had already been accepted at college, and I knew he would want me to go.

"But I was extremely vulnerable. I was grieving. My mom had already moved on, already made a decision to sell our house, all of which shocked me and left me with a sense of my whole world disintegrating. I had never spent time away from home before, or lived on my own. One of my professors took an interest in me. It doesn't take a psychiatrist to know I was trying desperately to replace my father's love with the affection of this older man.

"I actually was so naive that I thought my father was in heaven looking after me, that he had sent me this man to ease my broken heart."

Bree had been focusing intently on the cookie dough, but some small sound coming from Brand made her glance up.

The fury in his face might have been a frightening thing if it was directed at her. But it was not.

"Go on," Brand said tersely.

"I found out how much I really meant to him when I discovered I was pregnant."

Brand groaned, a growl of fury and frustration so pure it was almost animal-like. But his voice was soft when he said, "Aw, Bree."

"Even though the pregnancy was the end of my love affair, and I felt I had to leave school so as never to see Paul again, I was happy about the baby. It made me feel not quite so alone in the world. It made me feel as if I had purpose and meaning.

"And then," she whispered, "the baby was gone, too. I miscarried."

She felt his arms go around her. Ever so gently, Brand turned her into his chest. He held her hard and tight. He held her as if there was one solid thing in the world for her to hold onto. He held her in a way that made her finally let go.

At first it was a small hiccup. And then a sob. And then the floodgates opened, and she leaned hard into his strength and his warmth and his acceptance.

"When you told me you knew a thing or two about unforgivable, that day Beau knocked you over, you were right. Really right. And I'm so sorry you had to experience something like that."

That he remembered something she had said, almost casually, days and days ago, released something more in her.

Brand stroked her hair and her back, and whispered to her over and over again, gentle words of pure compassion.

"Let it go, sweetheart. That's my girl. Get it all out."

And she did. She cried until she was exhausted from it, until there was not a tear left, until surely a different man would have given up holding her a long time ago.

But, no, Brand Wallace stood there like a rock—her rock, immovable in his utter strength.

And when the tears finally did stop, Bree felt something she had not felt for a long, long time.

She felt utterly at peace with herself.

"Thank you for listening," she said. "You've given me some things to think about, self-sabotage for one."

She pulled away from him. His summer shirt had a big splotch on the front of it. She turned to the big bowl of cookie dough. "I think we should just throw this out. I don't think tears make a good secret ingredient."

"I disagree completely," he said. "I think healing is the secret ingredient. Let's bake them and see what happens."

And so, side by side, they scooped dough onto the sheets. She had done it millions of times, and so her cookies were uniform and all the same size.

His were haphazard heaps that made her smile. He made big cookies and small ones and lopsided ones, and she found herself loving all those imperfections. And loving being with him. Was it because she had shared her most secret of secrets that she felt so connected to him? So safe? So comfortable?

But not just comfortable. Aware. Maybe even aware in a way she had not allowed herself to be aware since Paul.

Of Brand's masculinity, in contrast to her femininity. Of his physical size and strength in comparison to herself, of how she had fit against him, of how he smelled, and of his energy.

They put in the cookies to bake, and there was quiet between them as they cleaned up the kitchen, but it was in no way uncomfortable. In fact it was quite lovely, something Bree was aware she had not felt for a long, long time.

It was exactly the gift she had intended to give him, but as was the way with most gifts, she received it herself. Bree had a sense of being home after a long journey away.

The timer rang on the cookies, and she pulled them out of the oven and then she and Brand filled a plate with cookies so warm that chocolate was oozing out of them. Without speaking about it, they both knew where to go, and they retreated to side-by-side chairs in his media room.

She nibbled on one cookie, aware it was his enjoyment that made it the best batch of cookies she had ever made. He ate every one of those cookies they had put on the plate.

And she hoped he was right, that the strange ingredient—tears—had put healing in them. Because just as he had seen so clearly that there was something broken in her, she also saw that in him.

Maybe what had just happened had strengthened some bond between them. Maybe he would share confidences with her, too.

But he fell asleep with crumbs from the last cookie still in his hand. She brushed them away from him and placed the soft wool blanket, the one that she had used earlier, on him.

She tucked it around him, and took advantage of the

fact he was sleeping to study him: the sweep of thick lashes on his cheek, the strong nose, the full lips gently parted, his hair, dark as those melted chocolate chips, just touching his forehead. There was something soft in his face that made her realize how guarded he was most of the time.

All that boyish charm hid something deeper. Something he didn't want anyone to see.

But she had seen it. And as he had said in her apartment that day, it was impossible to "unsee" it now.

He was a man who had absolutely everything. Every material gift that it was possible to own, he owned.

He owned cars, and art pieces and a beautiful house in one of the most exclusive neighborhoods in the world.

And yet, the most precious things of all had evaded him. Children screaming up the staircases, and the Scrabble board open on a table, with a misspelled word on it. Heaps of leaves to leap in, and tying the Christmas tree to the roof with string so it wouldn't fall off. The smell of dinner in the oven, or cookies, the little arguments over whether the toilet-paper roll should unroll over or under. All the simple, complex, wonderful things that went into a home and a family he had missed.

Knowing this with her soul, Bree felt something for him so deep and so stirring that it made her want to weep all over again.

She bent over him, touched his warm, rough cheek, and then followed where her fingertips had been with her lips.

She knew exactly what was happening to her.

It was like the words of that tender Elvis song had crept around her from the first moment she had walked in this house and seen the kitchen where he used the microwave and didn't even know he had a stand mixer, or steam oven or what either of them were, for that matter.

"What exactly does that song say?" she whispered, "That only a fool would rush in?"

She laughed at herself. That's exactly what it was. Foolishness. Foolish to feel the posters staring down at her. She wasn't rushing at all.

Still, she couldn't stop herself from finishing the first line of the beautiful, haunting song.

Her voice a husky whisper, she sang the words softly, as if it was a lullaby to the sleeping man.

Her voice fell into utter stillness.

And she recognized the truth of it. She was falling in love with him. Or maybe, more accurately, had never fallen out.

She had loved him as a girl. Oh, it had been an innocent love, based on his looks and his physique, and his charm, but still, that wild crush on him had been her first experience with love outside of her family. That night that he had walked into the gala, and she had tried to leave before he even saw her, hadn't she sensed the danger of him?

Hadn't some part of her known that despite the dating sites, despite going through the motions of wanting love, she hadn't really? She hadn't felt brave enough for it. Hadn't she known as soon as she'd laid eyes on him, he would be the one that would call it from her, that need to be brave, to engage love again, to risk its slings and arrows?

She gazed at him a little longer, and then turned rapidly on her heel, and nearly ran from the room and from his house, and from the hard hammering of her own heart.

Once home, Bree busied herself with laundry and the multitude of other things that had gotten stacked up while she had been trying to get her cookie orders caught up. She was also trying, unsuccessfully, to win back the affection of her neglected cat with his favorite game, but his chasing of the red light seemed desolate at best.

Her phone rang. She stared at the caller ID. There was that hammering in her heart again!

"Hello?" She hoped she didn't sound breathless.

"You sound out of breath. What am I getting you from?"

She tucked the laser pointer behind a plant, as if he could see it, as if it was evidence of a life that had gotten too staid, too safe.

"I was just coming up from the apartment-building laundry room with a basket," she said. Okay. Fifteen minutes ago. She was *not* still out of breath from that. "I take the stairs. My version of a StairMaster."

She was talking to a billionaire about basement-laundry facilities and stairs. He probably hadn't done his own laundry in years.

"You weren't supposed to let me fall asleep," Brand chided her. His voice was so natural, as if this was the most natural thing in the world, his calling her.

She felt something in her relax, just a bit. She thought of baking cookies with him, and the way his face had looked when he was sleeping.

Okay. He was a brilliant businessman. He was a billionaire. He was also still just Brand.

"I know you have your own formula for dealing with

jet lag, but you just looked so tired. I didn't have the heart to wake you up."

"I have chocolate around my lips."

She giggled, even though she did not want to be thinking about his lips.

"I was thinking about what you said about taking a couple of days off," Brand said. "Are you going to spend them doing laundry?"

"Possibly," she said cautiously. She tried to think of something more exciting that she could tell him she was doing with her days off, but she was coming up blank. The sound of his voice was having that effect on her.

"Look, when I've been under a lot of stress, or I've been really busy—or if I'm fighting jet lag—I like to go kayaking. It grounds me."

"Oh," she said. Just when she was thinking she could dismiss his billionaire status, he had to show her the difference in their worlds. Basement laundry. Trying to get your cat to play. Jet lag. Kayaking.

"Have you ever done it?" he asked.

"No," she said, a little tightly.

"Would you like to?"

She had to sit down. Was Brand Wallace asking her on a date? And then it hit her. No, not a date.

More of the same. Poor girl. Had an affair. Ended up pregnant. Left school. Life in ruins. Needs looking after. Needs bolstering. It was so far from how she wanted him to feel that she could have screamed. Instead she bit down hard on her lip.

"Are you there?" he asked.

"Are you asking me because you feel sorry for me?" she finally asked.

"Yeah," he said, "I am."

She didn't know what to say to that. Well, besides no, she couldn't go on a date with him on that basis, because it wasn't really a date. She wasn't even sure what it was.

"There I was in Bali while you were slaving away over cookies. I've been thinking about your jailhouse pallor."

"Oh, brother," she said. She had been so far off the mark it wasn't even funny. He wasn't thinking about her confidence at all. Well, maybe it was still a little funny. Or maybe not. Here she was thinking she was falling in love, and he was thinking about jailhouse pallor.

"It's making me feel guilty about the trip to Bali. I hate feeling guilty."

"I thought maybe you were asking me because you felt sorry for me," she said. "After I confided in you about what happened to me in college."

"Weird," he said.

"In what way?"

"That you would think I would perceive you as weak, because of that. The opposite is true. I find you very brave."

"Me?"

"Yes, you. You don't see yourself as brave?"

"No, not really." Bree had never, not even once, thought of herself as brave. Though she supposed maybe it did take a certain amount of bravery to wear that silly cookie beret and her quilted apron!

"That's how I see you," he said firmly. "It takes a lot of guts to start a business, especially after your dreams have pretty much had the crap kicked out of them. You picked yourself up, you dusted yourself off, you started again."

So, he had heard everything she had said to him, and

instead of making him see her as weak and foolish, a girl who had let her heart get her in a world of trouble, he saw it in a completely different light.

"You have what it takes, Bree, you have what it takes to make your business whatever you want it to be."

"Thanks."

"But you have to take care of yourself, too. You have to know how to intersperse hard work with fun and time away from your business."

So, it wasn't really a date then. More like a mentorship. She should say no, shouldn't she? Just on principle? Just because, in their minds, it was obvious they were moving the relationship in different directions?

"Hey, I don't ask just anybody to go sea kayaking. It's not for the faint of heart."

Another very good reason to say no. She was not sure Brand had mentioned the *sea* part of kayaking when he had first mentioned it. Kayaks were very small boats, weren't they? In a sea that could roil up, cold and dangerous, in a second? In channels shared with huge ships and creatures of the deep?

"In fact," Brand said, "I've never asked anyone to go with me before."

"You haven't?"

"It's kind of my sanctuary out there. A deep and private pleasure. But also, amazing stress relief. Which is why I'm asking you. I know you've been under enormous stress, with the fire, and catching up on those orders."

Bree listened to what he wasn't saying.

It struck her that, despite the "mentorship" spin on this, he was nervous about asking her. She was almost positive about that: the gorgeous, self-confident, successful Brand Wallace was nervous about asking her to do something with him.

Suddenly, the whole "unknown" of it, the adventure of it—not just of sea kayaking, but of getting to know Brand better—was completely irresistible.

Something had been healed in her when she told him her most completely guarded secrets, when her tears had fallen like a secret ingredient into those cookies.

And this is what it was: for a long time, despite going through the motions, despite going on the dating sites, despite saying something different, she had been saying no to life instead of yes.

And suddenly she just wanted to say yes, even though it sounded faintly terrifying. But she wanted to be brave again, even if it ended in heartache, to embrace whatever life, in all its magnificence, offered her.

More, she wanted to trust someone again.

None of which she said to him. To Brand, as casually as she could, as if a billionaire invited her to go kayaking with him every day, Bree said, "That sounds fun. Sure."

CHAPTER ELEVEN

BREE HAD TO look up online what to wear for kayaking and it was only then that she realized she knew nothing about what she had let herself in for. Was she going to be paddling her own kayak? She hoped not! Most sites recommended a few lessons before you went out on your own, particularly so you would know what to do if you capsized.

Capsized? In ocean water in May? She checked what the temperature of the water would be. Forty-six degrees Fahrenheit. Not a death sentence, but still, even if you were wearing the recommended clothing it would be simply awful. Wouldn't it? Unless Brand saved her…

Given her investment in the cloak, she couldn't really justify buying an outfit made specifically for kayaking, so she was pleased with the look she managed to assemble: cotton leggings, a T-shirt topped with an oversize wool sweater and a light jacket.

Brand was already at the English Bay parking lot they had agreed to meet at when she got there. He was single-handedly sliding a slender kayak from the roof rack of the vehicle.

Bree paused for a moment, just watching him, the play of muscle, the ease with which he handled himself, before she got out of her vehicle. He was gorgeous and rugged-looking in multi-pocketed outdoor pants and a hooded jacket.

As she approached him, she was welcomed with a smile that made her feel like her heart was a flower opening up to the sun after a long rain.

After they greeted each other, she studied the kayak.

"It has two holes in it," she noted. "I thought you said you usually go by yourself?"

He slid her a look. "I didn't figure you for the jealous type."

"It's dating the Elvis guy," she admitted. "It's given me a suspicious mind."

He threw back his head and laughed. She knew, with sudden delight, it was going to be that kind of day—laughter-filled and fun. His laughter was a sound that eased some of the nervousness in her, caused both by trying something new and more one-on-one time with the billionaire.

"By myself is relative, I guess," Brand said, answering her question. "Beau usually takes the front hole, which, by the way, is generally referred to as a cockpit."

The idea of that big dog in the kayak with him made her laugh, too. She'd been nervous, but now with the sun on her face, and the smell of the sea in the air, and Brand smiling at her, and handling the kayak with easy strength, she could feel her confidence rising.

He took her cell phone and keys and put them in a waterproof bag.

"We aren't going to get wet, are we?" she said, and her confidence dipped a little.

"It's Vancouver. It could start raining anytime."

"I didn't mean that."

"I know you didn't. I am seriously hoping we are not going to get wet. But we'll put these on just in case."

Bree was glad she had not purchased an expensive outfit when he handed her an ugly yellow life vest, which made about as much fashion statement as wearing a neon marshmallow!

He came and helped her when her zipper stuck.

"Is this Beau's, too?" she said, blinking up at him as he leaned in close to her to unstick the zipper.

"Believe me, you'd smell it if it was."

And they were laughing again, even as she became aware that what she smelled was him: a delicious scent, deeply masculine, outdoorsy, clean.

He picked up the kayak and swung it up over his head, part of it resting on his back.

"I can help," she offered.

"Don't worry. I'm used to doing it by myself." She took the paddles and followed him down to the water's edge, admiring his strength and the broadness of his shoulders, the ease of long practice that made what he was doing seem natural to him.

He set down the kayak and pushed it into the water, but just a bit.

"Okay, get in. Straddle it, feet on both sides, paddle in the middle, push it along until you can step in to that front cockpit."

Before she knew it, she was in the kayak, and she hadn't even gotten her feet wet, though she had worn light canvas sneakers just in case. When she wiggled a bit to get comfortable, the kayak rocked, despite him steadying the back of it.

But then he shoved it hard, and got in the back cockpit in one easy motion. The vessel seemed to stabilize with his weight, and they glided off the beach.

"We'll do a fairly short paddle today," he said, "Just to get you used of it."

He was saying that as if there might be more excursions!

"Don't feel like you have to paddle with me. Rest if you start getting tired. And don't be shy to tell me if you've had enough."

And then he went over some of the rudiments of steering and paddling together. They practiced stopping, turning and reversing direction a few times. It was fun! She hated to admit how right he had been about her life not having enough fun in it.

Maybe this wasn't a date. She wasn't quite sure about how to define this outing, but whatever it was it was so much better than anything that had ever happened on e-Us. Going for coffee suddenly seemed like the most ridiculous way to get to know a person! And meeting someone at the bookstore hardly seemed better.

Because this was getting to know a person: learning to paddle together, watching in awe as eagles soared and fish jumped, laughing when she accidentally splashed him and then laughing harder when she did it again on purpose.

The setting was glorious and kayaking seemed very simple, but she suspected he was doing most of the work. Before she knew it, they were gliding effortlessly through the stillness of the dark water toward the mouth of the bay.

Tell him when she had had enough? Really, it felt as if she could never get enough of this.

It occurred to her, once they were way out in the water, that she had him exactly where she wanted him.

Because she could finally ask him questions he could not get away from. She could, maybe, find out where all this was going. Was this a date? Was this delightful little outing going to lead to something else?

Don't be terrifying, Bree warned herself. *No wedding bells or babies.*

They paused to rest off the shore by Stanley Park. She was breathing hard, and her arms and shoulders ached, but in the nicest way. Not too far off was the hum of traffic, and she could see people walking and biking the Seawall, but she had a sense of it being deeply quiet. The kayak rocked ever so gently on the sea. He passed her a bottle of water.

"Do you like it?" he asked. "Kayaking?"

"Love it." She took a deep sip of her water. "Brand, why don't you have friends who are, um, women?"

He took a sudden interest in something on the shoreline. "Is that a deer?"

She squinted where he was pointing. "I think it's a branch."

"Oh."

"How come?" she said, refusing to be distracted. She might never have him in a boat again!

"What makes you think I don't?" he said, raising an eyebrow at her.

"Your house told me."

"What? How?"

"A million ways. No forgotten umbrella. No makeup around. No *The Lucky One* or *Dirty Dancing* or *The Notebook* in your movie collection."

"Did you go in my bedroom?"

"Of course not! I didn't have to to know you basically live out of three rooms. I bet your bedroom is a man cave, too."

"You're right," he said with a shrug. "The house is a masculine haven inhabited by Beau and me."

"I'm trying to get the *why* no significant other." *When you're obviously so irresistible.*

"I'm busy," he said uncomfortably.

She waited, not commenting. As she had hoped, there was no place to run from the question.

"I had a girlfriend. We saw each other for two years. We weren't engaged, though I think she wanted to be. We actually, ah, tried living together. She moved in. And she moved out again. Three days later."

"What happened?" she asked in horror. Three days? Was something horribly wrong with him? Three days?

"Beau."

"What?"

"He ate some of her stuff. Like her sofa. She gave me an ultimatum. Dog or me."

She knew she shouldn't laugh. She knew she shouldn't. But she giggled. "She knew you had a dog, obviously, before she moved in."

"Yeah, she just hadn't had to live with him before."

"Fantasy meets reality?" She would do well to remember this. He was the kind of man a woman might build a fantasy around.

But for two years? His ex hadn't known after two years how much that dog meant to him? She could actually say to him "dog or me" and think she was going to win that one?

Bree felt she knew Brand better than that after just this tiny bit of time!

"She took down the Elvis posters. She didn't even ask."

"Actually, since you mention it, I'm curious about the Elvis thing. I don't get the impression you like Elvis much."

"Actually, I know it really wasn't about Beau or the Elvis posters," he said carefully.

She was looking over her shoulder at him. Unless she was mistaken, he was deliberately not telling her how he felt about Elvis. He had the cookie jar, yes, and the posters, but when she had put on Elvis music that morning he had arrived home from Bali, she was almost positive he had flinched.

"So what's it really about then?"

"I'm not cut out for it. The whole domestic-bliss thing. I wanted to be, but I'm not. We'd been dating two years. It was fine when we both had our own spaces, but as soon as she moved in I felt suffocated by her. A two-year relationship in ruins, and I was so happy to see her marching out of my house, I was practically dancing. I don't know what that says about me."

"That she wasn't the right woman?" Bree suggested mildly.

"I don't think that's it. I think it's more that I'm not the right guy. Maybe I'm just like my old man. No staying power. When the fun stops, I'm gone."

This brutal self-assessment surprised her so much it put her off the trail of how he really felt about Elvis.

"I don't believe that," she said firmly. "I've seen how you treat people. Not just me, but your employees. Chelsea told me your lawyer who called her has hired his own fire investigator. She's practically a stranger to you, and you did that for her. You're a good, good man, Brand Wallace."

"Aw, shucks," he said with mild sarcasm, clearly trying to brush off the compliment.

"No, I mean it."

"Does this mean you've forgiven me for not kissing you at your senior prom?"

"That was part of being a good man, wasn't it?"

"Yeah, I guess."

"I think we should have a do-over."

"What?"

She could not believe this was her, but one thing she was learning was you only came this way once. Why not take chances? Why not go after what you wanted? Why not take a risk?

She was falling in love with him. She knew that. Even today, it felt as if it was deepening around them. The level of comfort, of connection, of companionship.

And something was definitely brewing on a deeper level, too.

Awareness.

A wanting.

To taste him again. To know him in a different way.

In a way, his choosing kayaking was the safest thing he could have done. There was a whole boat in between them! No cuddling was possible. No physical contact. The closest she could come to touching him was splashing him!

Was she just going to let him relegate her to friend-I-can-decompress-with position? Was she constantly going to be the one *helped*? No, for once in her life she was taking a chance. She was going to put it all on the line.

"Your company's charity ball is coming up," she said.

"Did the organizer get in touch? Are you making cookies for it?"

"Yes, for the midnight lunch, plus four-cookie boxes for party favors, though that's not why I mentioned it."

He waited. She glanced over his shoulder at him.

She took a deep breath. "I'd like to go."

He dipped his paddle in, setting them in motion, trying to move away from it. "Of course you are welcome to go!"

"Not as the cookie caterer."

The strength of his stroke carried them a long ways out into the stillness of the water.

"With you," she told him firmly.

She could feel the bravery in her. She could feel a shift in her perception. She wasn't the hapless, heartbroken woman pleading for people to choose her on the internet, desperate for a first date, never mind a second one.

She just wasn't that person anymore. Maybe just speaking about what had happened to her with Brand had clarified something in her.

Helped her make a vow.

No more being a victim. Not of men. Not of life. Not of circumstances.

She was going to take the helm. She was going to steer. She was going to move in the direction she wanted to, not wait for someone else to move her. Instead of waiting passively for something to happen, she was going to take charge of her own life,

She wasn't waiting, hope-filled, for something to happen to her. She was making it happen.

He didn't answer. His paddle entered the water and pulled the kayak forward with such force Bree wondered if she had ever been helping paddle at all. He looked wary of her invitation.

As well he should, she thought happily, as well he should! Because she was changing right before his eyes. It might not have hit him yet, but what she was really asking him was did he want to explore what was going on between them in a new way? Did he want to move forward?

Yes or no.

As simple as that.

But, of course, she should know by now, nothing in her life was ever simple. Because as that question hung there in the air between them, as she explored the meaning of bravery in this brand-new and infinitely exciting way, out of the corner of her eye, she caught a movement.

She swung her head toward the ripple in the water maybe a hundred feet to the left of the bow of the kayak.

The ripple became larger. A huge round back, black and shiny as a freshly tarred road, rose out of the water.

Her heart felt as if it might beat out of her chest. A mountain was shoving its way out of the gray endlessness of the ocean, way, way too close to them. The powerful movement was rocking the kayak. They were in very real danger of being capsized by a whale!

CHAPTER TWELVE

THE KILLER WHALE swam beside them, its ripples rocking the small kayak. Thankfully, it quickly outdistanced them. It blew out its top spout, a geyser of water droplets making a rainbow in the air. And then the whale's terrific bulk lifted out of the water. The grace, in a creature so large, was astounding. It shot up in the air, a cork released from a bottle. And then it crashed back down with such force that they were sprayed with water, and the kayak rocked more violently, before settling into stillness.

Brand had never seen a whale that close, not in all his years of being on the water.

Bree turned and looked at him. When the whale had first begun to surface, she had gone dead quiet and utterly still. He had been able to read the tension in her posture.

But now, all of that was gone. She was radiant as she turned her wide eyes to him.

"Oh!" she breathed. "Oh! That was the most amazing thing I have ever experienced."

His male ego wanted to remind her that she had just kissed him, only days ago. Certainly for him that kiss had been as earth-rocking as the breaching of the whale.

The whale had distracted her from her invitation to him. On the surface, it seemed as if maybe she was asking him to go to the charity ball. With him.

But, of course, with her, there was another layer to it.

Bree was asking him to define what was going on between them. He'd known, as soon as he had to escape to Bali to get away from her pull, what it was.

He was in the danger zone.

And maybe it was already too late to fix that, to escape it, to change it to something else.

The way she was looking at him now, her face so radiant, a person so capable of wonder, after all that had happened to her, it asked him about the nature of bravery.

It asked him if he could be a better man.

It asked him if he could stand the loneliness of going back to a life that didn't have her in it.

He was not a man used to being terrified, and yet really, he was aware that had been there since the moment he had rescued her from under that cascade of her own cookies at the Stars Come Out at Night gala.

That she would ask more of him. That she would require more of him than anyone had ever required before.

That she would hold out to him the most enticing gift of all: an ability to hope for things he had given up on a long time ago.

There was a possibility he was constitutionally unsuited to the world he saw shining in her eyes like a beacon calling a weary soldier home.

But he had warned her of that. He had tried to tell her.

And this was what she was trying to tell him: she

was not the innocent girl he'd escorted to her prom any longer.

She was a woman, capable of making her own choices, capable of embracing all the risks of the unknown.

Love. The greatest unknown of all.

Love, that capricious vixen who called you in, then shattered you on the rocks.

Somehow, he could not see being shattered on the rocks with Bree. Her eyes were warm, everything about her was genuine.

She wasn't going to hurt him.

And so he said, "Sure, let's go to my charity ball together."

He said it casually, as if it was not every bit as thrilling and as terrifying as that whale breaching the water beside them had been. Saying it was a lift of his shoulder that said "no big deal," as if he had not just stepped off a cliff, and was waiting to see if the parachute would open.

And the parachute was her.

Despite a paddle against a slight current coming back in to English Bay, Bree was brimming over with energy. Life felt the way it had not felt in so long.

Exciting and ripe with potential.

"I'm famished," she said, when they had pulled the kayak up the beach and hoisted it onto his roof rack. "Should we go grab a bite?"

This was the new bold her! Taking chances. Asking Brand to spend yet more time with her. He was going to say—

"Sure. What did you have in mind?"

"I love that Hot Diggity food truck."

"Hot Diggity?"

"Hot dogs. If you give me back my phone, I'll check their schedule and see where they are today."

He was smirking as he handed her the phone. "You know, I can afford a little better than a hot dog."

"You probably can. I'm buying."

"No, you're not."

"Look, Brand, if it's going to be a relationship of equals, you have to let me do my bit, too."

The word *relationship* word wavered in the air between them, like a wave of heat shimmering off hot pavement.

"Did you actually get stiffed for the coffee with the e-Us loser, or did you offer to buy it?" he asked.

"Different lifetime," she said, scrolling through her phone. "I've moved on. You should, too. He's on Robson Street today, by the art gallery."

"The guy who stiffed you for coffee?" Brand asked, surprised.

She glanced at him and saw he was teasing her. Warmth unfurled in her like a flag. "Parking won't be fun."

"My office has some spots down there, if you don't object to that on some principle of equality. We could travel together."

She certainly wasn't going to object to that part.

And so Bree found herself in the deep and luxurious leather passenger seat, enjoying his confidence as he maneuvered his oversize vehicle through downtown traffic. He turned on his CD player. No Elvis. Light classical.

He parked in a private stall in a private lot and they walked the short distance to Hot Diggity. He didn't put up too much of a fight about letting her pay, and just as she had hoped, he fell in love with the hot dogs.

By the time he drove her back out to English Bay, the sun was setting, and both conversation and silence felt comfortable between them. He had an old blanket in the car, and they sat together on it, shoulders touching, until there was no light left.

"My turn to supply food tomorrow night," he said as he walked her to her car. "Meet me at my office around six?"

"Okay."

For a moment he hesitated. For a moment she hesitated.

And then his arms were around her, and he pulled her into him, kissed her soundly on the lips and let her go. They stood there, studying each other with a kind of wonder.

"I don't remember when I've had such a perfect day," she confessed.

"I don't know when I have, either."

"Are you scared?" she asked softly.

"Terrified," he answered.

"Me, too."

"The good kind of terrified, like when a very large whale breaches beside a very small vessel."

And then he kissed her again, harder this time. "Get in your car," he said huskily, "before I invite you home with me. And it wouldn't be to make cookies."

She got in her car. She felt so intoxicated with lust she didn't know how she would drive. Somehow she managed to get home. And somehow she managed to get through the next day until it was time to be at his office.

* * *

It was much emptier than the last time she had seen it, but just the same, Beau came barreling through the door. This time she wasn't so shocked to see him. In fact, she felt delighted. And glad she had opted for slender-fitting jeans that could stand up to him. The rose-colored silk blouse, however, didn't fare so well!

Brand came through the door. "Beau! I don't know what it is about him and you. He managed to give me the slip and was through that door before I knew you'd arrived."

"What did you have planned for dinner? Do I have to change?" she asked.

Brand's eyes moved to the wet splotch on her breast. "Uh—"

"That's a yes."

"Well, we're eating in."

"Here?" she said, surprised.

"Yeah, I thought we'd have dinner and then I'd show you the climbing wall. And the ball pit."

She giggled.

"I have extra shirts here."

"Why not?" she said.

His office was dark, except for candles that burned on the coffee table between the love seats. As the sun went down, the Vancouver skyline was lighting up outside his windows.

She could see the table had been set. And that food was already there. For a guy who claimed to be hopeless at relationships, he seemed to be doing just fine at romance!

"Here," he said. He went into a large cabinet that

turned out to be a wardrobe and passed her a shirt. "Powder room is through there."

The powder room was exquisite and luxurious. She put on the men's shirt. It was clean and crisp, way too large, and for some absurd reason it made her feel sexier than hell.

She came out, his shirt to her knees, with her own soiled shirt balled up in her hand.

"Give that to me. I'll put it in the basket that gets sent out to the cleaners."

"Don't be sil—"

He gave her a look. She passed him her blouse.

"In any other context, me getting you out of your blouse might be kind of fun." He raised that delightfully wicked eyebrow. Then her smile died. She had the feeling he found her as sexy in his shirt as she felt!

"Have a seat," he said. "I took the liberty of ordering from one of my favorite places."

He poured her a glass of wine, and she looked at the plate before her. It held a salad, and she took her fork and took a tentative taste. The salad had greens, but also tomatoes, avocado and crab. It was exquisite, of course!

"Well?" he asked.

It was so endearing that he was anxious that she be pleased. Really, it was like something out of a dream.

"It's not Hot Diggity," she said thoughtfully, "but it's passably good. The bouquet of the balsamic vinegar is lovely."

And then they were laughing together, and as always, when they laughed together everything else fell away.

The rest of the menu was just as exquisite as the salad, as they dined on grilled quail, served with tiny roasted potatoes, and fresh green beans in a lime butter sauce.

"This is so good," Bree said.

"This is what happens when a man doesn't use his own kitchen," Brand told her. "He figures out where to get the best takeout in the city."

The dog, who had been sitting quietly, moaned softly.

"He knows we're done. I won't let him beg at the table, but I always give him a little something after."

Brand opened a bag from the same restaurant, removed a container and went over to a huge bowl.

"What's he getting?" Bree said as she came over and stood beside him.

"Same thing as us. Deboned."

For a moment, she felt extremely awkward and out of place. She was with a man who thought nothing of feeding his dog deboned quail from one of Vancouver's finest restaurants.

He turned back to her. "You want dessert now? Or do you want to try the climbing wall?"

"Definitely the climbing wall!"

There seemed to be no other people in the office tonight, and they had the "play" equipment to themselves. Beau came with them, and Brand threw one of his toys in the ball pit. The big dog leaped in and soon balls were flying everywhere as he searched joyously for his toy.

The awkwardness was gone, just like that. Brand knew how to have fun!

He helped her strap on a harness, and gave her a few tips for her first attempt at the wall. He put on his own harness, though it was obvious he did not need one. With the confidence and agility of a billy goat he topped the wall in about twenty seconds. From his perch up there, he called tips down to her.

"Oh," she cried as, just when she thought she had gotten the hang of it, she fell. But the harness took her weight easily. He was beside her in a second, showing her how to get back onto the wall, or lower herself to the floor and start again. She lost her hold several times, which was good, because she also totally lost her fear. The harness caught her and swung her gently each time.

They spent the rest of the evening finding different ways up the wall. Like the kayaking, it proved to be a terrific way to get to know each other. It involved communication, but not that interview-style intensity that Brand had pointed out was a flaw of the online dating world.

Beau finally captured his toy and abandoned the pit to go chew on it.

Since muscles she did not even know she had were aching, Bree was glad when Brand suggested they take over the pit. Following his example, she let herself fall in over the side, arms spread wide. The balls caught her and cushioned her, and she shrieked with delight, just lying there. Brand swam the backstroke and then dove into the colorful sea of balls. Bree joined him, until she was laughing so hard her stomach ached from it.

They retreated back to his office and had coffee and crème brûlée for dessert.

And then he walked her home, through quiet Vancouver streets, one hand in hers and the other holding Beau's leash.

Bree felt so happy. She thought they probably looked just like one of those couples she had always envied, out with their dog on an evening walk.

He insisted on seeing her right to her apartment door.

"I'd invite you in," she said, "but I don't think Oliver is ready to meet Beau."

"I'm sure he's quite jealous of all the time you've spent away. And now, after arriving with the scent of a strange dog on you, the slathering beast is right on his doorstep."

"I'm not worried. Oliver's forgiveness can be purchased with a new toy," Bree said, and pulled a bright purple mouse from her purse. "Voilà!"

They both laughed when Beau made a try for the toy.

"Plus, Oliver has selected my neighbor as a suitable slave in my absence. She spoils him atrociously. She's recently lost her husband, and I think she and the cat are both loving the relationship."

Of course, Oliver was not ready to meet Beau, but really that was just a convenient excuse not to invite Brand in. It wasn't the real reason, and she suspected he knew it, too. There was something lovely unfolding between them. It felt new and fragile. To move things to a physical plane too soon would bring a layer of complication to what was going on between them that she knew she was not ready for.

He seemed to feel the same way. He kissed her on the lips. It was a beautiful kiss. Welcoming and tender. Brand seemed to recognize exactly where she was at, because he pulled away and looked at her with a kind of respect and reverence that she had never experienced before.

"I usually take Beau for a really long walk in the morning," he said. "Are you game?"

"Absolutely."

And so they began to tangle their lives together in lovely ways: walking the dog, grabbing a bite to eat, watching a movie at his place, cooking dinner at hers. One memorable afternoon, they opened the Klingon-dictionary app on her phone, and they sat out in his backyard in the spring sunshine trying out phrases until they were both rolling on the ground laughing, with Beau leaping joyously between them.

A commercial kitchen space opened up for her, and she moved out of his kitchen. In a way she was sad to be leaving it, because it was so beautiful and she had felt so at home there, but in a way she was happy that their business interests were separating.

They did such ordinary things, but they did things that reflected his wealth and status as well. He took her on a helicopter tour of Vancouver, he rented a yacht for a day, complete with a chef, and he flew them on a private jet one night for a play in San Francisco, where they met Bree's mother and her husband.

It was a beautiful evening.

Her mother looked at her, when they had a moment alone together in the theater powder room, and hugged her hard.

"I know you thought I moved on too quickly from your dad," she said. "But when you love someone the way I loved him, the thought of not having love in your life is unbearable. Of course, every love is different. What Mike and I have is not the same as what your father and I shared. And yet, it is lovely, too. So lovely."

And then she added softly, "But you know that now, don't you, my dear Bree? That a life without love is unbearable?"

Bree thought, just as her mother, she had probably known that all along. Life without love was unbearable. It had made her such easy prey for a bad person. And then it had made her back off of love altogether.

But her mother was so right, that life without love was like crossing an endless desert, thirsty for water you could not find.

Her mother confirmed what Bree already knew in her heart. She was not going down that road again. She felt like a completely different person than the girl she had been before.

"Brand is such a good man," her mother said. "Your father always knew that about him. I have a feeling he'd be extraordinarily pleased right now."

But, for all that, for all that Bree got to experience lifestyles of the rich and famous, it seemed to be the small and ordinary things that had taken on a shine, that made Bree feel alive and engaged and as if happiness was a ball of light in her stomach that glowed ever more strongly outward.

Everyone noticed it. Her clients, Chelsea, her neighbors, her girlfriends.

When Brand went away on business trips, she stayed at his place and looked after Beau, who had completely stolen her heart. Oliver began to come along, and soon ruled Beau with an iron paw.

Brand would always bring her back small, enchanting gifts—a crystal butterfly from Sweden, an exquisite wooden carving from Thailand, a soapstone polar bear from the Canadian north. They even had a tradition: as soon as he came home, they baked cookies together, sometimes in her tiny apartment kitchen, sometimes in his state-of-the-art kitchen.

By the time of the charity ball, they had been seeing each other for a month. Bree was certain of how she felt. She was certain it was not an infatuation, certain where she wanted it to go, certain of Brand's place in her future.

Everything she had known the night she had heard that song in her head—"Can't Help Falling in Love"—was confirmed.

And so Bree decided to find a dress for that charity ball that would tell him all that as much as words ever could.

That would tell him beyond a shadow of a doubt that she was ready for whatever came next.

CHAPTER THIRTEEN

"I CAN'T FIND the right dress," Bree wailed to Chelsea a week later as they were locking up the new kitchen for the day. "Time's running out. I can't go to Brand's charity ball looking like the very same person I was at my high-school prom. And yet everything I've tried on does exactly that. It makes me feel as if I'm a kid pretending to be a grown-up."

"We could remake one of my salsa costumes," Chelsea said. "It would be easy."

Bree had attended a number of Chelsea's dance competitions. She made all her own outfits. "Chelsea, I don't know. Your outfits are gorgeous, but kind of over-the-top sexy."

"You just said you wanted to be sexy."

"Yes, but—"

"I have a red one. Red always makes men sit up and take notice. It's short, but I could add some layers to it. We're almost the same size. I think it would look phenomenal on you. Come home with me right now, we'll try it. You have nothing to lose."

That was true. She had nothing to lose. It was not as if she had found the right dress anywhere else. Plus, the price was right.

Chelsea lived in a cute little basement suite not very far from the new kitchen. It was an easy walk, and they went in.

Bree stopped. There was a large pair of men's sneakers at the door.

"Oh," Chelsea said with a blush, "Reed left those here."

"Reed?" Bree asked. She looked at her young assistant closely. She had been so wrapped up in herself that she hadn't notice a different kind of sparkle about Chelsea. Who was now blushing pink.

"He's the fire investigator our side hired."

Meaning the one *Brand* had hired.

"Don't look at me like that. Of course, he can't get involved with me while he's doing an investigation."

Which, of course, begged the question, why his shoes would be there, but Chelsea looked so pretty and so flustered that Bree didn't have the heart to pursue it.

Chelsea, eager to change the subject, brought out the dress, still in its dry-cleaning wrapper.

Bree took off the wrapper. The dress slid into her hands, surprisingly cool, since it looked so hot, like flames.

"Put it on," Chelsea insisted, and Bree went through to her tiny bathroom.

"No underwear," Chelsea shouted.

Good grief! Still, Bree put the dress on, then turned to face herself in the full-length mirror on the back of the door.

"Cripes," she said, astounded.

The dress fit her like a glove. The top was pure red, with tiny spaghetti straps at the shoulders. The neckline plunged to a narrow waist, where it took on the color of flame, leaf-like layers of fabric in colors of orange and yellow and several shades of red.

"Come out," Chelsea said.

"I'm scared to," Bree answered back, but then opened the door and stepped out. Chelsea's eyes widened.

"It's all wrong," Bree said at the very same time Chelsea said, "It's so right."

"It's too short."

"I knew that. But I've got lots of that fabric, and an idea how I can make it floor-length."

"And the neckline is too—"

"Shush. One little stitch. Here, I'll get a pin and show you."

That single pin changed everything.

And then Chelsea was at her feet, pinning and tucking and pinning some more. "This is just to give you an idea. It will be way more sophisticated. Fall leaves, until you move, and then each piece of fabric will move differently and catch the light differently. It will change from fall leaves to flame."

Finally, Chelsea was satisfied and told Bree she could go back into the bathroom, the location of the only full-length mirror in her tiny apartment.

Bree was almost afraid to look. She turned to the mirror with her eyes closed. Slowly, she opened them, and when she did, her heart beat double time. The dress was incredible, with its beautiful silk leaves falling to the floor, dancing around her. Just as Chelsea had promised, when she moved, the light caught the fabric and turned it to flame.

Chelsea managed to squeeze through the door to join Bree. "These outfits are made to celebrate the female form," she said, "and to move all on their own. It's really a seduction."

A seduction? Bree gulped. Was she ready for that?

She realized it wasn't Brand who had looked at her like a child pretending to be an adult, but that that was the role she had cast herself in.

And suddenly she felt so completely adult, she could feel herself stepping over some imaginary line that separated a girl from a woman.

Oh, yeah, she felt so ready for that! These weeks of keeping each other at arm's length, of only sharing chaste kisses, the longing building to something almost unbearable…

Chelsea moved in behind her and scooped up her hair. It made Bree's neck look long and elegant, and her eyes look huge, dark and startled, like those of a doe.

"I don't know how I can thank you," Bree said.

"Oh, Bree, you already have. You have had faith in me in the face of evidence you should not have. I know you think there's a possibility I set the kitchen on fire. Thank you for not suing me."

"That's ridiculous. The suing part."

"But not the catching-the-kitchen-on-fire part?" Chelsea said with wry self-recognition. And then they were laughing, and Bree felt as if she had been given many gifts.

A man she loved, and the sister she never had.

"It will be ready before the ball," Chelsea promised. "And you will be the most ravishing woman Mr. Brand Wallace has ever laid eyes on."

Bree slipped out of the dress and came back into the main area in her ordinary-girl clothes. But Chelsea wasn't finished with her yet.

"I'm just going to show you a few moves," she said. "Subtle, but sexy as hell."

Bree's eyes got very wide as Chelsea demonstrated exactly what she meant!

* * *

The night of the ball arrived and if Bree had had another outfit suitable to go change into before Brand arrived, she probably would have. She felt nervous and naked. Who did she think she was? she wondered. Julia Roberts?

She, indeed, looked like a movie star—red-carpet ready, which was, as Chelsea had assured her, a very good thing.

Tonight was as close as Vancouver got to a red-carpet event!

But as soon as Bree opened the door, and saw the look on Brand's face, she was happy—almost deliriously so—that she had not lost her nerve about the dress.

Because Brand looked like a man slain. His mouth fell open, and his eyes darkened with heady desire and drank her in with a kind of thirst that could never be quenched.

"You look absolutely stunning," he said, his voice hoarse.

He reached for her and kissed her on the cheek, put her away from himself and stared. "It seems not so long ago you were telling me how ordinary you were," he said.

She realized, with a shiver of pure appreciation, this was true. Being with him, feeling cherished by him, had made her feel beautiful and confident in a way she never, ever had before. He took her hand and walked her outside her building.

A long, sleek, white limo waited, the uniformed driver holding open the door for them. He tipped his hat to her, and called her "Miss."

Sinking into the luxurious leather and having Brand pour her some champagne into a flute was the beginning of a night out of a fairy tale. She floated through every minute of it. The entrance, chatting with people, nursing a drink and, finally, what she had been waiting for her whole life.

The thing she had got the tiniest taste of the night of her prom, a taste that had left her wanting. She danced with Brand.

Not as a child, dancing with the man who had been talked into escorting her to her prom.

But as a woman who knew exactly what she wanted. It was an evening out of a dream. His eyes never left her. Every move he made was subtly sensual, welcoming her in a different way. Brand was so comfortable with himself, and with his body, and it made her more comfortable with her own newfound sexy side.

She demonstrated some of the moves Chelsea had shown her. They had exactly the right effect on him, making his eyes darken and his hands linger on the curves of her back and hip.

They laughed. They teased each other. They danced and their hands touched each other, as if they could not get enough.

Despite the fact there were so many beautiful people there, in gorgeous clothes and jewelry, moving in amazing ways, it felt as if the ballroom belonged to them and them alone. Their eyes rarely left each other. Even when they spoke to other people, it was as if they were in a bubble that really held only them.

Bree had that first glass of champagne, and then one more, not enough to be making her feel as intoxicated as she did.

The evening went both too quickly and too slowly, because she was anticipating the moment they were alone.

So, here they were, seemingly only a breath after he had picked her up, facing the last dance of the evening.

Bree was stunned when she heard the opening notes of the Elvis song "Can't Help Falling in Love." Had he requested it? She didn't think so.

It was the universe conspiring.

His hand found the small of her back and he pulled him in to her. They might have been the only two people in the room.

She put her head back so that she could look up into his beautiful face, so beloved to her now.

The last bars of the song melted over top of them and then the music ended, but what was flowing between them did not. He lowered his head. He took her lips. She reached up, almost on tiptoes, and returned his kiss. It was as if they were in the room alone together.

The heat was scorching.

"Do you mind taking a miss on the midnight buffet?" he whispered in her ear.

"No," she said, trembling.

His hand found the small of her back. Nodding here and there, he propelled her through the crowd. Suddenly they were out on a wet street, the rain refreshingly cool on her scorching skin.

And then they were in the back of the limo.

He stared straight ahead. So did she. She knew if they even glanced at one another, the chauffer was going to get much more of a show than he'd bargained for.

They tumbled out of the limo when it stopped at her apartment, almost running to the building's entrance.

To a passerby it might have seemed they did not want to get wet.

But there was urgency between them now. To open the last chapter, to go to the place between them that had not yet been mapped.

That exquisite new country of pure discovery.

"Security cameras?" he whispered in the elevator.

"No."

He was on her. He had her backed against the wall of the elevator, his hands around her back, crushing her to him, her hands twined around his neck, pulling his lips to her own.

By the time the elevator door opened, they were both gasping with need, with red-hot desire. They tumbled from the elevator. Thank God, at this time of night, her hallway was abandoned.

With great effort, nearly dumping the contents of her tiny evening bag on the floor, she found her key. Her hands were shaking so badly she could not make the lock work.

He reached by her and took the key, inserted and twisted it.

The door fell open.

She stared at him.

He stared at her.

"Are you sure?" he growled.

"Yes," she whispered, and then stronger, because she had never been more sure of anything, she repeated, "Yes!"

CHAPTER FOURTEEN

THEY WERE IN the kitchen, their coats wet puddles of fabric on the floor. He lifted her onto the counter and, with her legs wrapped around him, she tasted him as if she could never get enough. Hungry. Starving.

All grown up. So filled with passion she was trembling with it. She could feel him trembling, too. He rubbed his whisker-roughened cheek down the delicate skin of her neck, as her nails dug into the broadness of his back.

His lips found hers again, no gentleness in them now, no tenderness.

He was a warrior conquering, he was taking what he wanted. But she was no captive, except maybe of her own heart's longings, because she met his savage taking of her lips with an answer of her own that was bold and uninhibited.

The woman in her explored the man in him—she tasted it, and touched it, and rode the enormous energy of it. It sizzled and hissed between them like a fire out of control. She was pulled toward the heat of it, helpless as a moth to a flame, sure to be scorched and yet unable to move away from what was happening between them.

His hands went to her hair. It tumbled out of its knot

and scattered wildly around her shoulders. He kissed the low-cut space in her dress, between her breasts, and she moaned with desire, lifted his questing lips to her own and took them again.

And then a sound.

An insistent sound.

The quacking of a duck.

Stunned, she realized it was coming from him. She realized it was some kind of ringtone. Bree was even more stunned when Brand took his phone out of his pocket and answered it.

Bree had never heard that ringtone come from his phone before. In fact, he rarely answered or looked at his phone when they were together.

But now he took it, his features set in grim lines. He held up a finger to her, answered and went out the door of her apartment.

He came back in seconds later. "I'm sorry," he said, running a hand through his hair. "I've got an emergency. I have to leave."

"An emergency?" she whispered, feeling shattered by her own longing, by the fact what was happening between them had not been so sacred that the phone could be ignored.

"An urgent family matter."

She stared at him, trying to figure out the incongruity of using a quack tone for an emergency. And yet, there was no doubting the gravity of the situation. His face, so familiar to her, was completely closed, set in the ferocious, impenetrable lines of a warrior called to action.

"What family?" she stuttered.

"My mother."

She tried to absorb that. All this time together, and except for the odd reference to a bad childhood, she had not even been aware his mother was still alive. In fact, the afternoon that he had arrived at her apartment shortly after the kitchen fire, she was positive he had *implied* his mother was deceased. She felt the shock of him blocking that part of his life from her.

"I have to go."

But her sense of loss and recrimination needed to be put aside for the time being. He looked so shattered. He looked as if, whatever this was, he should not be alone with it.

"I'm coming with you."

He started to shake his head, but she could see he was rattled, that he both wanted her support and didn't. She scrambled off the counter and went and changed quickly, her evening as a princess as over as if she was Cinderella, midnight had come and she had turned back into the ordinary girl she really was.

His steps were long and urgent as he shepherded Bree outside. In their rush to get into her apartment, he had forgotten to dismiss the limo, and it idled at the curb waiting for him. Now, they got in and he gave his own address. There they switched to one of his own cars, ignoring the soulful sounds of Beau, from inside the house, crying that he knew they were home.

The car Brand chose from his six-bay garage was an Italian four-door Maserati, but it might as well have been a pumpkin for how the magic had drained from the evening. He was silent and grim, barely acknowledging her as he scrolled through his phone, looking something up with urgency.

And then they were driving through the seediest part

of Vancouver, streets lined with dilapidated buildings with people huddled in the doorways.

He stopped in front of one. It was a no-parking zone, but he ignored that. A sandwich board announced Tonight and Tonight Only, Elvis Impersonations.

He was storming through the door, Bree hard on his heels.

The room was dark, and had only a smattering of people sitting at tables. It smelled bad, of smoke and spilled beer.

The stage was illuminated, though, and an Elvis gyrated across it, belting out "Hound Dog."

He *did* remind Bree of that horrible man she had met on e-Us.

She looked at Brand, arms folded across his chest, as he scanned the tables. The performance, the club and the Elvis impersonators sitting around waiting for their turns might have been funny in an absurd way, particularly coming from the ball to this, but it was not funny. Bree glanced at Brand's face. She was not sure she had ever seen such terrible torment in one person's expression before in her life.

He spotted something and moved across the dark room. Bree, not sure what to do, or what exactly was going on, followed.

Brand slid into a chair at a table occupied by a lovely woman with gray hair. She turned and smiled at him, put her arm on his sleeve, then turned back to the music, rapt. Brand, though he hardly seemed to know Bree was there, pulled out the chair beside him and nodded at it. Bree took it.

The song ended with blessed abruptness, as if someone, having suffered quite enough, had pulled the plug on the karaoke machine.

"I'm glad you called me, Mom," Brand said quietly into the sudden silence.

Mom.

"I was trying to get up my nerve to go on," his mother said, and then, her voice sad, she added, "But it's not me anymore, is it?"

"Maybe not," he said gently.

"But don't throw out my posters just yet!"

Her posters. All this time, Brand could have told Bree, but nothing. Not a single word, even though there had been opportunities.

"Hello," his mother said softly, noticing Bree. "I'm Diana. I used to do a great Elvis impression."

Almost shyly she took a bag out from under the table and spilled its contents out for Bree to see. She fingered the white, metal-studded fabric almost lovingly.

"I was good, wasn't I, Brand?" she asked, her tone wistful.

"Yeah, Mom," he said. "You were good."

Bree's mind felt tumultuous as snippets of conversations came back to her. *Somehow I didn't figure you for an Elvis kind of guy. What's your favorite Elvis song? Must I pick only one? Impossible.*

"Bree," Brand said, his flinty eyes intent on her face, "meet my mother."

Bree looked to him, and then to the woman. She extended her hand. "Mrs. Wallace?" she said uncertainly. "My pleasure. Bree Evans."

"Diana."

Lively eyes, dark like his, scanned her face, a certain shrewdness in them. "I suppose I should go home now?"

"I think that's a good idea, Mom."

They left and he put his mother in the front seat, and Bree took the back. They drove through the city in complete silence to a lovely building, which, even in all its loveliness, was clearly some sort of institution.

"I'll call you a cab," Brand said grimly.

"I'll wait," Bree said, just as grimly.

He looked as if he might argue, but his mother got out of the car, and looked as if she might be considering going anywhere but in. The weariness on his face was heartbreaking, and he just lifted a shoulder, got out, put his hand on his mother's shoulder and guided her to the main door.

It was nearly an hour before he came out.

His face was gray with exhaustion. He slid into the seat beside her.

"I'm sorry I took so long," he said. "She was quite agitated. I stayed with her for a while until she settled. It's an assisted-living place, not a jail. My mother's bipolar, with schizophrenic tendencies."

He sounded like a doctor, clinical, rhyming off facts.

"The medication takes away her upswing, and the voices. She misses both. She can be very good at hiding the fact she isn't taking her medication. I probably should have picked up on it."

Bree heard self-recrimination there. He'd been too involved with her. It had distracted him.

"I'll drive you home now. There was no need for you to wait." They drove away.

She knew he had no intention of coming in, that the moment was gone, possibly forever.

She knew he was tired. But it still had to be said. "You don't think we have things to discuss?"

"Must we?"

"Yes. Why didn't you tell me, Brand? Why didn't you trust me with this?"

He was silent. They pulled up in front of her building. He nodded to the door, as if he expected her just to get out!

"You let me believe your mother was dead."

He looked truly astonished by that. "What?"

"That day at my apartment, when we were drinking the cheap wine, you said she would have considered it champagne. *Would have.* Past tense."

"Because she doesn't drink anymore, not because she's dead!"

"All this time you could have said something. Anything. That day in the kayak, I asked you about you and Elvis, I said I got the impression you didn't like Elvis that much. Some might say a perfect segue for you to tell me about your mom. But no. Nothing. Not a word."

"Pardon me for not revealing all my secrets to you." His voice was cold.

"But I revealed all mine to you, Brand," she reminded him softly. "I told you about my baby. I shared my deepest loss with you. I trusted you with it."

She thought this reminder of her own vulnerability would soften him, but his silence was cold. It made her more grimly determined to have her say.

"It's not that your mother is ill that hurts," she told him. Her tone was quiet, but she was not sure she had ever felt so angry. "It's that you didn't trust me to do the right thing with it. To be the right person."

Again, he was silent for a long time, and when he turned to her, her heart stopped beating, and her breath stopped the steady rise and fall of life. What she saw in his eyes was an unfathomable coldness. Cruelty.

She saw everything had changed. She saw he would not see her again.

"No," he said harshly, "I didn't trust you with it. Goodbye, Bree."

Stunned, she got out of the car. In a moment of fury, she slammed the door so hard his car rocked. Still, he did not squeal away. She wished he would have. Instead, he waited to make sure she got to the door. She kept her shoulders straight, her spine proud, as she put in her door code. It was as he drove away that she dissolved, and let the first tears fall.

All this time, she realized, she had given more and more and more trust to him.

And he had given her none in return. He had not even trusted her to be understanding about his mother's fragile, broken condition.

Had he not known her at all?

"All men are rotten," she decided furiously. "All of them!"

Brand drove away after he saw Bree was safely inside her building. He felt sick for what he had just said to her, that he didn't trust her with it.

The truth was, he had not trusted himself with it.

He had allowed himself to be distracted from the truth of his life, to pretend that he could have what other people had.

He had allowed that dangerous thing called hope to creep into his world.

This is what Brand had managed to avoid facing after the enchantment of the last month—that he brought a long and horrible history with him, running down his line from two sides. A selfish man who had such a cold heart he had abandoned his wife and, worse, his son.

And then his mother, his poor long-suffering mother, who would sometimes get better for long periods of time, only to fall back into her delusions, an intensifying of her obsession with Elvis usually providing the first red flag that she had abandoned her medication, that she missed the "ups" and missed the "voices."

But this time, he hadn't noticed. He'd been too busy. Selfish and cold, just like his father.

This is what he knew for sure.

He loved Bree Evans with a love that nearly took his breath away. He loved how funny she was and how brave. He loved how she made the most ordinary of things shine as if they were lit from within. He loved the wonder in her face when he invited her into a world where money could buy anything, and her equal wonder over a dog romping joyously through a mud puddle. He loved her loyalty and her creativity and how smart and how inventive she was. He loved how she had hope.

This is what he'd forgotten that day he had decided that she could not hurt him. This is what he had so selfishly put aside: that he could hurt her. That's what he had forgotten in that totally self-centered moment of *wanting* what he had seen shining in her.

All the things he had never had: a safe harbor, future children laughing.

She deserved those things. The truth was this: both conditions his mother had could be inherited. If he had either, they would have shown up by now. But that did not make his children safe.

Is that what his father had thought, when he walked

away and never come back? That he could barely deal with one person with mental-health issues? What if his son had those issues, too?

Brand could not bear it if he was the one who crushed in Bree, for all time, those things that mattered so much to her. How could he create the kind of home she'd enjoyed as a child? How would he learn those skills when he had never experienced the security and stability of a good home? Nothing in living in a car, and stealing creamers from fast-food restaurants, and walking in the door, listening to see what Elvis song his mother had on so he could judge her mood, had prepared him for the kind of life Bree desired so desperately and deserved so richly.

Really, the most loving thing he could ever do for her? He had just done it.

He had said goodbye. Not just for tonight. Forever. It had felt as if he was ripping his own heart out saying that to her, keeping his face cold and cruel in the light of her hurt and her wanting and her hope. Especially her hope.

As he drove away through the rain-filled night, it felt as if he had entered a pit of impenetrable blackness such as he had never known before, and in a way he welcomed it, like a man facing his absolute reality and coming home to the place he'd always known that he belonged.

CHAPTER FIFTEEN

BREE WOKE UP the morning after the ball knowing exactly how Cinderella had felt. She had *almost* had it all. And then, at the ring of a clock at midnight—or the quack of a phone, as the case might be—it had been snatched away from her. She was lying in her bed waiting for that familiar despair to creep over her, to steal her breath and her strength and her desire to get up.

Instead, as she was lying there, scanning her feelings, she was pleasantly surprised that she didn't feel despair at all. She felt really, really angry.

"All men are rotten," she repeated to herself. She liked it. It would be her new mantra!

She got up and looked in the mirror in her bathroom. Her eyes were ringed with black from last night's cry, but as she washed up, she was aware she was done crying, and that she had something very important to do.

She dressed in slim-fitting jeans and a plain cotton blouse, and then threw her beautiful new cloak over top. She filled up Oliver's water and food dishes, then she put on sneakers to drive, but put her red stilettos in the backseat.

And then she drove. She thought she would have second thoughts on the long drive, lose her courage or her nerve, but neither happened. If anything, her confidence grew. She had a sense that this was something she should have done a long, long time ago.

She drove through the familiar campus. It was summer session, but there was still lots of life. She noticed the girls, in particular, looking so carefree, so filled with hope for their futures.

She had been that girl once. She had *allowed* Paul Weston to steal that from her. But here was the part that filled her with shame: had her silence allowed him to steal it from other young women, as well?

The new her parked in the spot reserved for visiting VIPs, and she changed shoes. The new Bree walked right by the president of the university's stammering secretary, knocked briefly on his door and went in.

He looked up, surprised, and she let the door swing shut behind her.

Twenty minutes later, with assurances of a complete investigation, she strode across the campus in her heels. She felt like a warrior: she could feel the absolute confidence shimmering around her, like a crackle of electricity in the air before a coming storm.

Men stopped and stared at her as if she was the most ravishing woman they had ever seen. Some of them ventured a smile. Women seemed to know she was on a mission for all of them, because they smiled at her as though they recognized her, or recognized something in her that they liked.

She didn't even hesitate at the familiar steps of the culinary arts building. The heels did not even slow her down.

She went in and stopped by the lecture hall.

And there he was. She could see him through the small rectangular glass frame that looked in to the hall.

He was dressed as he always had been: a tweedy jacket and rumpled pants. Today he was sporting an ascot. She could clearly see he was wearing the costume of a distracted, artsy college professor.

She took a deep breath and opened the door. All eyes were on her as she went down the sloping aisle, past the rows of theater-style seats, up the three stairs to the raised dais he stood on.

"Paul, do you remember me?" she asked, her voice loud and clear.

His eyes wide, the man who had haunted her nightmares looked at her. His mouth opened, then closed, opened again.

"Bree," he said, "I'm in the middle of—"

She saw what she had never seen as his eyes shifted away from hers. The weakness and the cowardice, a man who had used his position and power to feed his own sick needs.

"I don't care what you're in the middle of," she said, and she turned to face his students. She took a deep breath, and began.

"I want to tell you about a young girl, who sat right where you are sitting now," she said. There was no hesitation and no fear. "Her father had just died."

"Bree." His voice was plaintive.

"Paul, sit down and shut up."

He stared at her. He scuttled over to a chair and sat down.

She finished her story. For a moment, there was shocked silence. For a moment, she wondered if she had done the right thing. And then one lone, brave young woman stood. Bree could see tears running down her face. She began to clap. And then another rose, and another. The young women were the first, but the young men followed. She turned to look at Paul. His chair was empty.

And then she was surrounded in a sea of caring.

Strangers who felt as if they were not strangers at all were hugging her, some of the girls were telling her about the creepy moves Paul had put on them.

Bree realized she felt as if she was leaving her body, as if she had floated way up above herself and was looking down at the woman in the stiletto heels and the red cape, and seeing her for what she was.

Brave enough, finally, to be worthy of the gift called love.

Days later, she did not feel quite so brave. She felt worn down from emotion, and her devastating sense of loss. Her mantra was not strong enough to carry her, and didn't even seem true anymore.

How did "all men are rotten" fit into being worthy of the gift that was love? It didn't. Her father had not been rotten. And Brand was not rotten, either.

He was human.

She thought of the look in Brand's eyes the last night she had seen him. She had mistaken it for coldness and cruelty and rejection.

But now, having seen Paul Weston again, she was very aware of what those things looked like. And Brand had none of them in him. None.

What she had seen in his eyes was the lonely bleakness of a man who thought he had to protect her, even if that meant from himself.

Bree realized she had to use all this newfound bravery to go into his dark world and bring him to safety. She had to be brave enough to go after him. To go after Brand, a man who had only ever used his position and his power for good. A man who was as worthy of her as she was of him.

He just didn't know it yet.

But when she called his cell, there was no answer. When she called his office, she was told he was not available.

The new Bree put on her bravery cloak, and went downtown. She had a cookie contract after all. There was no reason not to drop by his office!

For once, there was a receptionist at the front desk in that luxurious front foyer. No joyous dog came bounding out the door.

"I need to see Mr. Wallace," Bree said.

The receptionist looked at her, and obviously recognized her. Bree had been a bit of a fixture for the past month. Was there the faint pity of one not unfamiliar with the heartsick trying to get through to her boss in her tone?

"I'm afraid he's out of the country at the moment. I'll tell him you called by?"

"Out of the country? But when will he be back?"

"I'm not at liberty to say that."

Bree wanted to leap across the desk, place her hands around that skinny throat and squeeze an answer from her. What country? How long would he be gone?

"I think he's going to be away for some time," the receptionist said, and now she looked genuinely sad.

"Where's Beau?"

"He's out of the country, too."

Bree felt a wave of relief. "Thank goodness," she murmured. Beau, the only one he trusted completely with his heart, was with him.

She turned to leave. The door that separated the office space from the front entrance swung open.

A young man walked out. She recognized him from his beard, and from her first day here, when he had been swinging on that hammock, throwing a beanbag in the air.

It niggled her memory. *He is one guy I make sure to talk to every single day.*

"Kevin?" she said.

He turned and looked at her absently.

She racked her memory for the afternoon that she and Brand had practiced phrases out of the Klingon language, laughing until they could laugh no more.

Klingons, Brand had told her gravely, did not have greetings per se, but still she drew a phrase from her memory.

She tentatively tried out the crazy sounding mix of consonants and vowels. She must have done something right.

Kevin brightened instantly. He responded with the same mix.

Literally, it meant "what do you want?"

"I want to take you for coffee," she said. The receptionist had been watching the whole interchange. When Bree glanced back at her, she had ducked her head, but she was smiling.

CHAPTER SIXTEEN

It was a life out of a dream, Brand told himself, as he shook seawater from his hair and tucked his surfboard under his arm.

He had his dog, he had the ocean. He had spectacular sunsets, and day after day of sunshine. The palm trees were swaying gently in a tropical breeze. Up the beach was a cottage, completely open-air, with state-of-the-art electronics, so he could check in with the office and talk to his mother.

Unfortunately, the sand was everywhere, golden and unending.

And it was the very same color as Bree's hair.

Unfortunately, even though he was having the life out of a dream, it was not a dream he would wish on anyone.

He had never been plagued with loneliness before, and now he awoke with it as his companion and slept with it at night.

Even Beau was aware something was amiss. Instead of following him exuberantly into the water, snapping at waves he could never catch, he laid on shore, watching, lethargic, sadness coming out of every pore and stinky wrinkle.

Except right now, Beau's ears were perked up. His great head was lifted off his paws, and he was staring at the line of palm trees along the edge of the beach.

Suddenly he gave a woof, heaved himself up and began to gallop along the beach toward the trees.

Someone was coming. A woman.

As she got closer, he saw her hair. It couldn't be. But he had thought no one else in the world had hair like that.

He wasn't tormented enough? Out in the middle of nowhere a woman with the same hair was coming toward him? A woman with a colorful wraparound skirt knotted at a slender waist, wearing a black bikini top.

His heart rose as she got closer.

It couldn't be. It was a mirage, a man dying of thirst in the desert imagining the only thing that could save him.

The dog reached her, and she went down on one knee.

There was only one person his dog greeted like that. Brand wanted to run to her, just like the dog, to throw himself in a delirious pile of joy at her feet.

But he could not.

He needed to be strong. Stronger than he had ever been in his life.

For the love of her, for the love of Bree Evans, he needed to be strong.

He forced himself not to go to her. Instead, he wrapped a towel around his waist, dropped down into his hammock, put on his sunglasses and picked up a book.

"Brand?"

He lowered his sunglasses and peered at her over the rim. He pretended surprise, and then irritation.

"What are you doing here? Nobody knows I'm here."

"Kevin does."

"No, he doesn't."

"Well, he's a geek. He traced a telephone ping or something."

"Why would he do that?"

"He'd do anything for a woman who speaks Klingon."

"Which you don't," Brand said with a snort.

"You'd be surprised what love is willing to do to find its way."

Love. He snapped his sunglasses back over his eyes, nestled deeper in his hammock, looked intently at his book. He hoped it wasn't upside down.

"You've wasted your time," he said. "I don't want to see you. Go away."

"I'm not going away."

He hazarded a look at her, frowned and looked away hastily. There was something new in her. A strength, a self-certainty that she had not had before.

He contemplated that. He was falling to pieces here on his desert-island dream world with his dog. And she was…what? Blossoming? Coming into herself?

She was more gorgeous than she had ever been and she'd been plenty gorgeous.

A bikini! That said it all, really. Over a month ago, she'd been a one-piece kind of girl. He glanced at her again. He wanted to touch her hair. It was the *exact* color of the sand. He glared at the book.

"Do you want to know what I've learned over the past few weeks, Brand?"

"Not particularly," he said. He deliberately licked his finger and turned a page of the book.

She shoved the hammock. It rocked wildly and he

thought he was going to get dumped in the sand. He managed to extricate himself and find his feet.

He stood looking down at her. She gazed up at him with those soulful, earnest eyes. Those soulful earnest eyes that had a new layer to them.

Bravery.

The kind of bravery a man who did not feel brave could cling to, like a life raft was going by just as he had resigned himself to drowning.

"Humph," he said, annoyed with himself.

She lifted an eyebrow, as if she could *see* right through him.

"This is what I learned about myself," she said with that quiet new confidence. "I thought love had broken me once. After Paul, after the baby."

Did she have to mention that? It made it hard to be mean to her, to do what needed to be done to drive her away. No, not hard—impossible.

"But now I see that's not true at all. What broke me was an imitation of love. Real love is different."

He stared at her. He could feel himself swimming toward the paddle she was holding out, even as he ordered himself to swim away from her, to choose the loneliness of an endless sea.

"Real love doesn't break people," she said. "Real love is like the love I received from my family. It filled me with hope and it made me a promise that good would always outweigh bad."

"Naive," he growled. But she put her fingers on his lips. Her touch was a balm to his tormented soul. He could not do anything now but listen, even though he knew he was touching the paddle she was holding out.

"Love, genuine love, makes you stronger. It gives you

a belief in yourself and the world. It makes you more authentic, not less."

He was silent, but inwardly he could feel the slow tremble of complete surrender.

"You think," she said softly, "that you will be like your father, but you have already shown in every way that you are in the world that you are not. He ran away from your mother, and responsibility.

"You have embraced those things."

"Speaking of my mother, there's a chance it's genetic—"

"Shh," she said. "You think I don't know that's the fear you've wrestled with your whole life? Brand, you already know so much more about love than you have ever given yourself credit for.

"Love—the kind that sticks with it through the hard stuff—you already know that. That's what has made you who you are. That's what has made me love you so helplessly. So hopelessly."

"Look, I tried this. The love stuff. It's not for me. I warned you. Wendy. Lasted three days, I—"

"Shh." There it was again. Gentle. But a command.

"I'm not saying you aren't scared of love," Bree said. "I'm not saying that at all. Why else would such a smart man pick such a perfectly ill-matched person as Wendy?

"You're scared of it. You've seen the power it has to wound.

"But what I've seen? I've seen the power it has to make a man like you, who is so *good*, so decent, so courageous, despite the wound."

In his mind, he could see himself heaving himself into her lifeboat.

She felt his absolute surrender the moment it happened. Her arms went around him. She held him with astonishing strength. He could feel the strong beat of her heart, and the tenderness of her skin.

"I love you," she said. "And I'm going to love you until my very last breath. I am never, as long as I live, going to stop."

He let those words ease into him, ease past all his defenses, ease over his walls, something warm and fluid, that could not be stopped by something so small as one man's desire to shield others from the possible pain of this force.

"What about my children?" he asked, and he could hear the anguish in his own voice.

And she could hear it, too.

"What blessings they will be to the world," she said quietly. "What blessings our children—loved and accepted for all their strengths and all their flaws—will be to the world."

He took her face between both his hands and searched it for any trace of fear, for any trace of a lie.

But he saw what he had always seen in her face, even when she was a young girl going to her senior prom.

He saw that her gift to the world was hope.

Belief.

A tremendous unshakable conviction.

And that conviction was that love would always win. It was even stronger in her now than it had been then, when she was a young girl who had never had one bad thing happen to her.

Now, she had had bad things happen to her. She had suffered tremendous losses.

And still, she stood before him, unshakable in her faith, stronger than ever.

The word came from somewhere deep within him. It was his soul recognizing what she had held out to him. It was his soul yearning for a place to rest, for a place he had never had.

It was his soul, his heart, his mind, his whole being accepting the invitation she had held out to him.

To be brave.

To step into the unknown.

To have hope.

To believe.

To embrace the greatest force in the entire universe—love.

"Yes," he whispered to each of those things, and then, his voice stronger, to her he said, "Yes."

And then stronger still, even though this time it was just within himself, it felt as if he was shouting it to the earth and the waves and the trees, and the stars, shouting it with all the joy and strength it deserved—yes.

CHAPTER SEVENTEEN

THE GARDEN LOOKED the way it had always meant to look. Pails of white flowers—begonias, Brand vaguely thought—flanked the back steps, and peeked out from every shaded corner of his backyard.

The house looked different. Every window was open and so were the French doors. Analytically, he knew the house had not changed. It was the same color, there had been no renovations.

And yet, everything felt different, as if the house was happy, and as if its happiness was spilling out those open doors and windows.

The clatter of people busy in the kitchen and a shout of laughter reached him.

His back garden was filled with chairs with white satin bows on them, and people milled around, filling the space with color and energy and laughter and a shared belief in happy endings.

Given Vancouver's weather, it was a miracle it was not raining today, but there you had it.

Brand was a man who had come to believe in miracles.

Bree could have had the wedding anywhere. In a different country, on a beach, in the best hotel in Vancouver, but she had looked surprised when he had asked her where she would like to become his wife.

"At home, of course," she said. "That's where your mom will be most comfortable, and then Beau can be part of our celebration, too. Even Oliver can be part of our day."

Sure enough, Oliver was peeping sourly out from under one of those pails of begonias. They had been adjusting the cat to his new home for several weeks now. He had taken to it—and to bossing around Beau—with a kind of regal disdain that Brand had learned meant he was almost deliriously happy.

He considered that word. Home. In the last few months, his house had been transformed into a home. Bree had not moved in. She had wanted to. He had refused her. And he had refused her desire to seal their relationship physically as well.

He had almost given in to that temptation the night of his company's charity ball. Now, he sometimes wondered about that. If the intervention hadn't been divine.

Because that was not what he wanted with Bree.

He wanted to be the man she deserved, the man her father had always expected he would be. A man who would cherish her and treat her with complete honor, always.

So, here he was, minutes before his wedding, contemplating the nature of miracles and divine intervention. He was a changed man from what he had been just a few months ago.

Then, he had mistakenly thought he had everything. Then, he had thought he was wealthy.

"Time to go, buddy."

Chelsea's man, Reed, tapped him on the shoulder.

He and Bree had become so close to the other couple, who had begun dating almost as soon as Reed submitted his findings on the fire to the investigating team.

An electrical fire.

No one to blame.

A faulty circuit.

Or a miracle. One that had brought this young couple, obviously made for each other, together.

Just as a last-minute decision to go to that gala had reunited Brand with Bree.

Brand walked up the aisle of chairs to the back of his yard, where a flower-bedecked trellis had been erected. Reed flanked him on his right and Beau padded along beside him, looking as pleased as his wrinkly face would allow. Beau's white ribbon was already somewhat bedraggled.

People began to drift to the chairs.

Brand's mother took her seat in the front row, looking beautiful in a pink two-piece suit that Bree had helped her choose. She radiated the soft glow of wellness. Elvis was banished, for now. Brand dared not hope forever, but there was something about watching Bree with his mother that made his throat close and his eyes sting.

Bree treated his mother with an unfathomable tenderness that his mother reacted to like a parched plant that had needed rain. Brand knew love couldn't heal her, or else his already would have, and yet there was something about the steadiness of Bree's love that brought out the best in his mother, that brought out a side of her he had never seen.

He'd asked Bree once how she loved his mother so completely, and she had seemed so genuinely surprised by the question.

"She's part of you," she had said. "She's part of everything that is best about you—your strength and your decency and your drive. I love her for what she gave you, and I love her for her innate bravery. And I love her for the way she sees the world."

Bree's own mother, came and sat by his, and their hands found each other, two women who knew there was a certain kind of bitter sweetness to saying goodbye to one kind of relationship with their children, and hello to another one.

The music started. No Elvis, there was no sense testing his mother's newfound equilibrium with that.

No, it was the soaring and falling notes of Pachelbel's Canon.

The chatter quieted, and a hush fell over the filled seats, letting the music fill the garden area of the yard.

First, Chelsea came out. She was beautiful in a short aquamarine dress. Brand glanced at Reed beside him, and saw everything he felt for Bree in that other man's face.

Chelsea, like Bree, had come in to herself, and she radiated the quiet confidence of a woman well-loved.

A hush fell over the back garden as Bree stepped out of the house and slowly came down the steps. At her side was her stepfather, Mike.

Brand had to swallow, and then swallow hard again.

He had never seen a woman as beautiful as his soon-to-be wife.

The dress, of course, was exquisite. Her sunshine-on-sand hair was up, and threaded with flowers, her shoulders were bare, and the dress fit tight to her slender form, and then flared out at her waist in a cloud of white that floated around her and behind her.

But it was not the dress that stole the breath from him. Bree was so radiant she put the sun to shame. Everything in the garden faded: the music, the flowers, the guests, their mothers, her stepfather on her arm. Everything faded, until it was just her. Until the whole world was just her.

Coming toward him, with the entire future shining in her clear eyes.

* * * * *

ADDING UP TO FAMILY

MARIE FERRARELLA

To
Patience Smith Bloom,
Congratulations on twenty years
As a fantastic editor.
Here's to the next twenty.
May we see it together.

Prologue

"Please, Celia, you're a mother. You must know what I'm talking about," Bonnie Reynolds implored, obviously attempting to appeal to her longtime friend's maternal instincts. "For the first twelve years of that girl's life, I felt as if I could barely keep up with her. Even her homework assignments were so far beyond my own understanding, I had a headache every time I tried to check it."

Despite the situation that had brought her to Celia, there was pride echoing in Bonnie's voice as she added, "Rebecca whizzed through her studies like it was child's play—at a time when she was little more than a child herself."

Celia Parnell smiled understandingly at the distraught woman sitting opposite her in her Bedford, California, office.

When Bonnie had come in, looking as if she was at her wit's end, Celia had closed the door to her small inner office to ensure privacy. Speaking calmly, she had poured them both a cup of vanilla chai tea. She'd urged the trim brunette to take a seat and tell her exactly what was troubling her.

And just like that, the words poured out of Bonnie like a dam whose retaining wall had suddenly cracked in half.

Listening, Celia nodded. It was a story she was more than a little familiar with.

"Rebecca had a wonderful job, Celia. An absolutely wonderful job—for three years. And then one day she decided to just up and leave it. Just like that." Bonnie snapped her fingers. "Don't get me wrong. When you first offered Rebecca a job with your company, I was grateful. I thought that this—this *wrinkle* was something she needed to work out and then she'd be back to herself again. In the interim, she was still earning money. But, Celia, that girl is *wasting* her potential. You know she is," Bonnie cried, sitting so close to the edge of her chair, she looked as if she was in danger of falling off it if she so much as took in a big breath.

"Breathe, Bonnie," Celia counseled.

"I *am* breathing—and very nearly hyperventilating," the other woman cried, very close to tears now. "Celia, Rebecca graduated from MIT at eighteen. *Eighteen!*" she stressed.

"I remember," Celia replied calmly.

But Bonnie only grew more agitated. "And she did it on a full scholarship, because her father, that rat, ran out on us, leaving me with nothing but debts and no way to pay for anything without working two jobs!

That meant hardly ever seeing Rebecca, and yet she turned out like a gem."

"I know," Celia said, doing her best to continue to sound calm.

She had a feeling that she knew where this was going, but she allowed the other woman to say her piece, hoping that Bonnie would find a way to calm herself down and not be so hopeless about her daughter's current situation. Because if there was anything she'd learned these last few years, it was that no situation was hopeless.

"When she first got that job at the engineering firm—practically the best aerospace firm in the country—I was in seventh heaven. But after three years, the bottom suddenly dropped out for her. Without any warning, Rebecca decided that she was 'burned out.' Burned out," Bonnie repeated, shaking her head. "What does that even *mean*?"

"That she worked so hard, exceeding all expectations for so long, that she wound up exhausting herself," Celia told her friend. "She just needs to recharge her batteries."

"She's been *recharging* now for three years," Bonnie lamented. "My brilliant daughter has been *cleaning houses* for three years," the woman cried, looking at Celia for her understanding.

"I know, Bonnie. I'm the one who writes her paychecks," she replied with a smile.

As if worried that she might have insulted her, Bonnie quickly apologized. "Look, Celia, I meant no disrespect—"

"None taken," she replied serenely.

Bonnie let out a shaky breath, then continued. "But I am afraid—no, terrified—that Rebecca is just going to go on cleaning houses forever. That she's never going to be my Rebecca again."

"There is a possibility that she's happier this way," Celia suggested.

Bonnie looked stunned at the mere suggestion that this could be the case. "No, she's not. I know she's not. And right now, she's so busy cleaning other people's houses that she's not doing anything to put her own life back together again. She lives in a silly little apartment, for heaven's sake."

"How's that again?" Celia asked, slightly confused. She interacted with the young woman under discussion all the time, and from where she stood, Rebecca seemed rather content.

"She's not *dating*," Bonnie complained, verbally underlining the word. "She's cleaning other people's houses and not saving up to buy her own house."

Hiding her amusement, Celia said, "I thought she liked living in an apartment."

Bonnie let out a long sigh. "That's okay for now—but what about later? She's not thinking about later," she complained, clearly irritated with the situation. "Am I making any sense to you?"

"Actually, I think you are. You're not upset that Becky's not working herself into a frazzle in the engineering world. What you're actually upset about is that she's not looking for a husband."

Bonnie pressed her lips together. Hearing it said out loud, she had to admit that it sounded rather old-fashioned, as well as self-centered. But it was still the truth and there was no point in denying it.

After releasing another long, frustrated breath, she

confessed, "I want grandchildren, Celia. Is that such a horrible thing?"

Celia laughed. "No, not at all, Bonnie. Been there, done that. I understand perfectly what you're going through."

The subject was touching on something that she and her two best friends, Maizie and Theresa, had begun doing almost eight years ago. It had started as a spur-of-the-moment undertaking to find a husband for Maizie's daughter, without the young woman suspecting what they were up to. But the venture had turned out to be so successful, all three of them began doing it as a hobby on the side.

The women still maintained their own businesses, but they all agreed that it was matchmaking that afforded them the most satisfaction.

Leaning forward, Celia beamed at the woman. "Bonnie, I think that I just might have a solution for you."

"Oh please, tell me," her friend all but begged. "After waiting three years for this to resolve itself, I'm ready to listen to anything and even make a deal with the devil."

"Luckily," Celia told her with a smile, "it won't have to go that far."

Chapter One

"Mrs. Parnell? This is Steve Holder," the deep male voice on the other end of the phone said.

Celia recognized the name. Steve was one of her sporadic clients, making use of her services whenever he suddenly found himself without a housekeeper. Although she didn't remember all her clients, she remembered the ones who were special, and Steve Holder's case was. A widower, he was struggling to raise a preteen daughter on his own.

And Celia had just been thinking of him.

"Steve," she said with pleasure. "How is everything?"

"Not good, I'm afraid," he replied honestly. "It happened again."

Celia didn't have to guess what he was talking about. The young aerospace engineer wouldn't be calling her just to shoot the breeze or talk aimlessly. He was far too conscientious about how he used his time—and hers—for that.

"I take it that you've had another housekeeper quit?" There was no judgment in Celia's voice, only sympathy. She knew Steve to be a very personable man. Unfortunately, for one reason or another, the housekeepers he employed seemed to have no staying power. She suspected that it had to do with his daughter. Incredibly intelligent, the ten-year-old was becoming increasingly difficult to handle.

She heard Steve sighing as he answered, "Yes."

Since she needed the information to update her files, Celia tactfully asked, "May I ask what happened?"

Steve had to admit that at least this housekeeper, who had lasted longer than the others, had a viable excuse for leaving. "Mrs. Pritchett's daughter just had a baby and Mrs. Pritchett is moving to Seattle to help her take care of the new addition. She already told me that she didn't think she'd be coming back," he added.

"Was it a girl or boy?" Celia asked.

He wasn't a people person and had to pause and think for a minute before he could answer the question. "Girl," he finally said.

"That's lovely," Celia said with genuine feeling. "But that does leave you in an immediate bind, doesn't it, dear?"

He appreciated how direct the woman was. No polite beating around the bush. He restated his position. "Well, I can have you and your company clean my house once every two weeks, and Stevi's going to school right now, but I do need someone to cover the hours when she's home and I'm still at work."

"She's going to school?" Celia repeated, surprised. "But it's summer."

"I know. Stevi's going to summer school. She wanted to take some classes so she could get ahead. It was her idea, not mine," he added quickly, before Mrs. Parnell could accuse him of robbing his daughter of her childhood. He was pleased she wanted to learn, but had to admit that he was really beginning to miss his little "buddy." Stevi had begun to change on him in the last few months.

"My daughter's suddenly gone serious on me, Mrs. Parnell," he confessed. "She doesn't even want to be called 'Stevi' anymore. She's 'Stephanie' now. And I've got this feeling that those fishing trips we used to take might just be a thing of the past."

Steve took his work very seriously. These outings he used to take with his daughter were what he'd looked forward to, a way to wind down. And now it appeared that this might be changing.

"Not necessarily, Steve. Your daughter could just be broadening her base, not shifting her focus," Celia pointed out. "Ten-year-olds have been known to change their minds a great deal at this age."

He could only hope, Steve thought. "Could I talk *you* into becoming my housekeeper?" he asked wistfully.

Steve knew it wasn't possible, but if it were, having the woman as his housekeeper would be an ideal solution.

If he could put in an order for the perfect grandmother, it would be Mrs. Parnell. He was beginning to feel as if he knew his daughter less and less these days, but he was fairly certain that Stevi—Stephanie, he amended—would get along very well with her.

"I would if I could, Steve," Celia answered kindly. "But I'm afraid my company keeps me very busy these days. Otherwise—"

"I know," Steve said, cutting her short. He didn't want the woman feeling that he was serious. "I just thought I'd give it a shot."

Celia knew he was attempting to politely extricate himself from the conversation, but she detected an underlying note of bewilderment and even sadness, now that she listened carefully. She didn't think she remembered ever hearing him sound down before.

"Steve, I wouldn't give up on the idea of finding a decent housekeeper just yet." She recalled the visit she'd had with Bonnie Reynolds the other day. An idea began to form. "I just might have the perfect person for you. Let me get back to you—"

"Wait, there's more," he said, wanting to tell her something before she hung up. "I mean, I do need a housekeeper, but she'll need to be more, as well."

"Oh?" Celia wasn't altogether certain where this conversation was going and if she'd be able to help once it got there. She waited patiently for him to continue.

Steve hesitated. "I don't know how to put this, really."

"Words might be useful, Steve. Just start talking. I'll do my best to try to figure it out," she promised.

An intelligent man, he wasn't accustomed to being out of his element. But he definitely was now. Taking a breath, he started doing exactly as she suggested.

"Well, as you know, it's been Stevi—Stephanie and I for the last six years. Despite the demands of my job, I've been able to manage finding a lot of quality time with my daughter. We've done everything together. Everything from fishing to tea parties to baseball games and 'Aliens and Astronauts'—"

"'Aliens and Astronauts'?" Celia questioned, puzzled. As the grandmother of three, including one teenage boy, she made an effort to keep up on the latest trends in games, but this was a new one.

"It's a video game," Steve explained. "It's Stevi's—Stephanie's favorite. I am having a really hard time remembering to call her that," he complained. "Anyway, suddenly, without any warning, she's switching gears on me."

"By asking you to call her Stephanie," Celia said knowingly.

"That's part of it," Steve admitted. "The other part—the bigger one—is that she suddenly seems to be growing up right in front of my eyes."

"They have a habit of doing that," Celia told him wryly. "I think it might have something to do with the daily watering," she added, tongue in cheek.

Distressed over what was going on in his life, he barely realized she was trying to lighten the mood.

"What I'm trying to get at is that all of a sudden, Stevi's got these questions I don't know the answers to. I mean, I *know* the answers, but I just can't—I just can't..." He trailed off helplessly.

"I understand, Steve," Celia told him kindly. "Your daughter's at a crossroads in her life. It's an admittedly delicate area and sometimes a young girl just needs to talk to another woman, no matter how close she is to her father."

"Yes!" Steve cried, relieved that she understood what he was attempting to clumsily put into words. "I need someone who knows how to cook, who's neat, and most of all, for Stevi—Stephanie's sake, I need someone who is understanding and sympathetic. Someone who my daughter can turn to with all her unanswered questions and be comfortable doing it. I know it's a lot to ask," he confessed with a sigh. "And I don't mean to be putting you on the spot like this. To be honest, I've been considering the possibility of perhaps sending Stevi to boarding school."

"Boarding school?" Celia repeated, surprised. She couldn't think of a worse idea. She had a feeling his daughter would wind up feeling rejected if he did that. "Have you spoken to her about it?"

"No, not yet," he admitted. "But I thought that it might be best for her, all things considered."

Celia wanted to tell him how bad she thought that idea was, but managed to refrain. Instead, she tactfully suggested, "Why don't you hold off on that, Steve? Let me see if I can find someone for you who could fill that bill, before you decide to do anything rash." Realizing that he might think she sounded judgmental, Celia softened her words by saying, "I'm assuming that you really don't want to send Stevi away."

"No," Steve confessed, "I don't. But she needs more than me right now. She's got questions about, well—" he dropped his voice "—bras and boys and the changes her body's going through that I can't figure out how to address without embarrassing both of us. Do you understand what I'm trying to say, Mrs. Parnell?"

"Completely," she assured him. "Do me a favor, Steve. Hold off doing anything permanent for now. Don't start calling any boarding schools just yet. Worst comes to worst, I'll fill in as your housekeeper for a few days and be there for Stevi when she comes home after summer school, so you won't have to worry about her. I'm sure we can resolve this situation to everyone's satisfaction."

She could almost hear the weight falling off Steve's shoulders.

"You are a lifesaver, Mrs. Parnell," he told her with genuine enthusiasm and gratitude.

"It's all part of the service, Steve," Celia replied warmly. "One way or the other, I'll be getting back to you," she promised, before hanging up.

The moment she terminated her call to Steve, she was back on the phone, calling first Maizie Sommers, who was the unofficial leader of their informal group, and then Theresa Manetti.

She informed both women that she needed to have an emergency meeting with them.

"Okay, we're here," Maizie announced, as she and Theresa walked into Celia's house later that afternoon. Because she spent a good deal of her time driving from place to place, Maizie had swung by Theresa's catering business and picked her up before coming to Celia's. Theresa had been making last-minute changes to a menu for an anniversary party that she and her company were catering tomorrow afternoon. "So, what's the big emergency?"

"I need to run something by you," Celia told her friends.

"And you couldn't do this on the phone?" Maizie asked. "Celia, we went over conference calls. Are you still having trouble with that?"

Celia shrugged. "I'd rather see your faces when I talk."

"Uh-oh. Is this something we should be sitting down for?" Theresa asked, taking a seat at the dining room table.

Friends since the third grade, the three women had gone through all life's major events together—weddings, births, deaths—and supported each other through the good times as well as the bad.

"Maybe you had better sit," Celia said. "It's nothing bad," she added quickly. "But this might take me a little time to explain."

Waiting until Maizie was settled, as well, Celia finally sat down and began talking. "You know how one of us is usually approached by either a parent or a friend to find someone for their son or their daughter, or maybe even friend, and then we all sit around this table and brainstorm, trying to find the perfect match for that person?"

Maizie studied her friend, wondering what was behind this. "You're preaching to the choir, Celia. Where are you going with this?"

"Fair enough," Celia agreed. "I could be clearer."

Theresa laughed. "You think?"

"I had a friend," Celia started. "Actually, she's the mother of one of my employees. Anyway, she asked me to find someone for her daughter."

"All right," Maizie said. So far, this sounded no

different than anything they normally undertook. "What's the problem?"

"It's not a problem exactly," she replied. "I actually think that I came up with the perfect person for her..." Her eyes swept over her friends. "I just wanted to run this choice by the two of you before I make the introduction."

"So run it by us," Maizie encouraged, waiting for her to get to the heart of the matter. Celia didn't usually have this much trouble making up her mind.

"He's a single dad and his daughter's at an age where she's starting to ask *those* kind of questions," she said. "He told me that he needs a competent housekeeper, as well as someone to field such questions for him."

"And this employee of yours, you think she's a match for this single dad?" Theresa inquired.

"Well," Celia began cautiously, "he's an aerospace engineer and she graduated MIT at age eighteen."

"Wait a minute. I don't understand," Maizie protested, trying to make sense out of the scenario. "She graduated MIT at eighteen? No offense, Celia, but what is she doing working for you?"

Celia smiled. "I know. It sounds strange, doesn't it?"

"Not if she's in the witness protection program," Maizie quipped.

"She's not. She's just kind of conflicted. When Becky first came to me," Celia said, filling her two friends in, "she said she was looking for something 'different.' She felt burned out and she just wanted something that wasn't mentally taxing to do, something that made her feel as if she'd accomplished something basic and simple at the end of the day." Celia smiled. "Like cleaning a bathroom."

"Well, that's basic and simple, all right," Maizie agreed.

"Anyway, my point is that I think they have a lot in common and could help one another," Celia concluded. Again, she looked from Maizie to Theresa, waiting to get their take on the situation.

"Any red flags?" Maizie murmured.

"Not that I can see," Celia replied honestly. She'd gone over their backgrounds a number of times before Theresa and Maizie had gotten here. "Personally, I think they're made for each other."

"Well, if that's what you think, it's good enough for me," Maizie said. "Theresa?"

She nodded. "We've all gotten good at this," she told her friends. "I trust Celia's judgment."

Maizie totally agreed. "And if she's right, we'll all get the credit," she said with a satisfied chuckle. She put her hand on Celia's shoulder. "Have a little faith in yourself, hon. We do."

"All right, then," Celia declared, getting revved up. "I'll call Steve tomorrow and tell him that I have a housekeeper for him."

Maizie beamed. "It's settled, then," she stated. Then the corners of her mouth curved even more. "You know, ladies, since we all came rushing out here and settled this so quickly, how do you feel about a game of cards?"

"You mean play cards without talking shop?" Celia asked.

"You know, it just might be unique at that," Theresa speculated.

Playing cards had always been their excuse for getting together and brainstorming. Usually one of them would have been approached by a parent, and brought that candidate to the table to be discussed and pondered over until the right match was discovered.

"What will we talk about?" Theresa asked innocently.

Maizie laughed, shaking her head as she took out the deck of cards she always kept in her purse. "We are three intelligent women, each with a thriving business and a whole tribe of grandchildren. If we can't find something to talk about other than the love lives of some strangers, then the world is in a very bad state," she told them.

"Don't forget all those successful matches we've managed to set up and bring together. As I recall, we're batting a hundred," Theresa said.

Maizie smiled at her as she began to shuffle the cards. "A thousand, dear. The correct term for that is that we're batting a thousand."

"But we haven't brought together a thousand matches," Theresa protested.

Maizie sighed as she rolled her eyes. "Never mind, dear. The point is, we've been exceedingly successful, and even if our streak ends today, we still have all those happy matches to point to."

"Why should our streak end?" Theresa asked. "We're very good at what we do. There's no reason to think we can't go on doing this for the foreseeable future."

"You're right," Maizie agreed. "We might very well be doing this for as long as we draw breath." She paused for a second, looking at her friends. "Okay, ladies, no more talking. Let's play cards."

"Right, like that's going to work." Theresa smirked. "If I know you, you'll be talking until the day you're six feet under."

"You think that'll stop her?" Celia asked with a laugh.

"No, you're right," Theresa agreed. "Probably not."

"Play!" Maizie ordered, doing her best to keep a straight face.

Chapter Two

"Stevi?" Steve called up the stairs to his ten-going-on-eleven-year-old daughter, as she was apt to remind him any number of times in a week. "Get a move on. You don't want to be late for class and I don't want to be late to work."

The petite, dark-haired girl frowned as she came down. "Dad, I told you to call me Stephanie," she stated, stepping into the living room. "And I also told you that I'm perfectly able to walk to school. You don't have to risk being late to work just to take me there."

They'd been over this ground a dozen times in the last six weeks, ever since Stevi had decided that she had outgrown practically everything. Next, she'd decide that she'd outgrown him.

"Maybe I *like* taking you to school," Steve told his daughter. "Did you ever think of that?"

A tired, sympathetic look passed over her face. "Dad, I'm growing up," she said wearily. "You're going to have to get used to that."

She hardly looked any older than she had six months ago, or even a year ago, but he knew she was. It was inevitable, just as she maintained.

But he didn't have to like it.

Stifling a sigh, Steve put a hand on her shoulder and hustled his only child out the door. "Don't be in such an all-fired hurry to grow up, *Stephanie*. Enjoy being a kid a little while longer." He closed the door and locked it. "Trust me, it goes by fast."

"I've *been* a kid, Dad," Stephanie pointed out, sounding a great deal older than her actual years. She got into the car on the passenger side and buckled up. "And it's not going by nearly fast enough. At least, it isn't for me."

Steve started up the car. He knew he was losing this argument.

"Well, it is for me," he told her. "Anyway, I wanted to let you know that we're going to be getting another housekeeper. I talked to Mrs. Parnell and she called back this morning to tell me that she has the perfect match for us. She's going to be bringing her by this afternoon, right after I drive you home from school."

Steve stifled another sigh, knowing that his next words were going to be useless, but he said them anyway. "I want you to be on your best behavior, *Stephanie*. That means that I don't want you to do anything to scare this one away, understand?"

"I didn't do anything to scare Mrs. Pritchett away," Stevi protested. "She left us because she was going to be a grandma."

"She left because she had already become a grandmother," Steve corrected, wanting Stevi to get the details right.

She maintained a bored expression on her face. "What's the difference?"

He made it through the next light just before it turned red. He didn't think the topic was worth getting into now. "I'll explain it later."

Stevi sighed, sinking lower in her seat and crossing her arms indignantly. "That's what you always say when you don't want to explain something."

He decided that the best thing for now was to ignore his daughter's rather salient point. "Mrs. Parnell is bringing the new housekeeper by this afternoon—"

"You already said that," Stevi pointed out impatiently.

"And I'm saying it again," he told her. "I've rearranged my schedule so that I can pick you up from school and then we will meet this new housekeeper together."

Stevi raised her small chin, a bantam rooster just itching for a fight. "What if I don't like this one? What if she's like Mrs. Applegate? Or Mrs. Kelly?"

"*Please* like this one," he implored. He was torn between begging and telling his daughter that she *was* going to like the new housekeeper or else. He resigned himself to trying to reason with Stevi—again. "And for your information, there was nothing wrong with Mrs. Applegate *or* Mrs. Kelly."

Stevi sniffed. "They were both jumpy and nervous."

Caught at another red light, he spared his daughter a penetrating glance. "And who made them that way?"

The expression on his daughter's face was nothing short of angelic as she replied, "I don't know."

Right. "I've got a feeling that you do. And never mind them, anyway," he said dismissively. "We've got a chance for a fresh start here, so let's both try to make a go of it." When his daughter made no response, he added, "Please, Stevi? For me?"

"It's *Stephanie*," she stressed pointedly.

"Please, whoever you are," he said through almost clenched teeth, as he pulled up at the school where Stevi was taking summer school classes, "do it for me."

Stevi released a sigh that seemed twice as large as she was. Getting out of the car, she nodded. "Okay, Dad, if it means that much to you, I'll try."

"Do more than try," Steve called after her. "Do."

It was half an order, half a plea, both parts addressed to his daughter's back as she walked away, heading toward the building.

He hoped that this new housekeeper Mrs. Parnell had found came with an infinite supply of patience. Otherwise, he thought glumly as he pulled away, he was going to have to start looking into boarding schools in earnest.

Moving his lunch hour so that he was able to pick Stevi up from summer school, Steve arrived at the school yard to find that most of the cars that had been there earlier were now gone. It was a sure sign that everyone had already picked up their child and gone home. Steve really hated being late, hated the message it sent his daughter: that she was an afterthought, even though that was in no way true.

She was the center of his universe, but he seemed to have lost the ability to get that across to her.

Scanning the immediate area, he saw Stevi standing at the curb, a resigned, somewhat forlorn look on her face.

"I could have walked home," she told him by way of a greeting when he pulled up beside her. "You didn't have to come running back for me."

Leaning over, he opened the door for her, then waited for her to get in. "I didn't run. I drove."

Stevi glared at him in a way that told him he knew what she meant.

There were times when it was really difficult to remember that she was only ten years old. It seemed more like she was ten going on thirty—and he didn't know how to handle either one of those stages.

Not for the first time, he wondered why kids didn't come with instruction manuals.

"Anyway, you forget," he told her, pulling away from the curb, "I had to bring you home so that we could meet the new housekeeper."

"Housekeeper," she repeated in a mocking tone. "You know that you're really getting her so you have someone to watch over me," she accused.

"In part," Steve allowed, unwilling to lie to his daughter. He had always been honest with Stevi, and until a little while ago, that had been enough. It was the reason they had a bond. But these days, it seemed as if nothing was working, and he felt, rightly or wrongly, that it was his fault.

"I don't need to be watched," Stevi informed him indignantly, continuing her thought. "I'm too old to have a babysitter."

"She's a *housekeeper*," Steve stressed. "And her job is to run the household. You just happen to be part of it."

Stevi's face hardened. "She can't tell me what to do," the young girl insisted.

"Stephanie," he began, taking great pains to call her by the name she professed to prefer, "I expect you to be polite to the woman."

"You mean you expect me to do what she says," Stevi corrected.

"What I expect, *Stephanie*, is for you not to give me a headache," he told her, the last of his patience slipping away.

Reaching the house, he left his car parked in the driveway and went inside with his daughter.

When had parenting become so difficult? he wondered. He and Stevi had always gotten along, even right after her mother died. Stevi had been only four and they'd helped one another, supporting each other whenever the other was down and really needed it. Where had all that gone?

He was about to say something else to Stevi when he heard the doorbell ring. It pushed his train of thought into the background. For now, he tabled the rest of what he wanted to say.

"Remember," he warned his daughter in a lowered tone, "be polite."

"Only if she is," Stevi said, just as he opened the door.

He gave his daughter a warning glance before turning to look at Mrs. Parnell and the housekeeper she had brought with her.

Steve found himself tongue-tied, staring at the

woman beside Mrs. Parnell. Although no actual description had been given, for some reason he had expected this latest candidate for housekeeper to be like the others: another middle-aged woman in sensible shoes, with a somewhat expanding waistline and a pasted-on smile that ended before ever reaching her eyes.

Instead, the woman beside Mrs. Parnell was a blue-eyed blonde who might have been twenty-five or so. She was slender and there was nothing sensible about her shoes—or the rest of her, for that matter. She was wearing high heels and looked as if she was about to go out on a date, not a job interview. And since nothing had actually been settled between himself and Mrs. Parnell, that was what this actually was. A job interview.

"Mr. Holder," Celia said, addressing him formally for the sake of the interview, "I'd like you to meet Rebecca Reynolds." Celia smiled broadly at the young woman. There was a great deal of pride in her manner. "Rebecca is one of my best employees."

Steve was still at a loss for words. He knew that Mrs. Parnell had brought the woman here to be a housekeeper, but the more he looked at her, the more she just didn't seem like the type.

When his tongue finally came back to life and reengaged with his brain, he heard himself asking, "You're a cleaning lady?"

Rather than be insulted by the demotion, Becky smiled. "My mother would prefer the term 'maintenance engineer,'" she said with a soft laugh. "But yes, in simple terms, I'm a cleaning lady. Mrs. Parnell said the position you're looking to fill is housekeeper."

"You have any experience?" The question didn't come from Steve, but from his daughter, who was regarding this new woman Mrs. Parnell had brought into her life with a great deal of suspicion.

To Rebecca's credit, Steve noticed that she didn't balk at having his daughter ask her a question.

"Yes, three years' worth," she replied.

"As a housekeeper?" Stevi asked, eyeing her closely as she grilled her.

"Stev—Stephanie," Steve corrected, not wanting his daughter to go off on another tangent, "I'll handle the questions."

"I don't mind answering," Becky told him calmly. "This would actually be my first job as a housekeeper. But that would entail cleaning and cooking, and I can do both. I've done both before."

"You'd also have to watch my daughter..." Steve felt bound to tell her that.

Stevi instantly took offense. "I don't need watching," she declared.

He was about to ask her to go to her room, but the woman interjected before he could send her off.

"No, I'm sure you don't," Becky told the girl. "You don't need someone telling you what to do, do you, Stephanie?" Turning away from her very good-looking, would-be new employer, she focused strictly on the little girl. "You look as if you're perfectly capable of watching out for yourself. I'd just be here in case you needed me," she explained. "It would be more to set your father's mind at ease than anything else."

Stevi said nothing. She continued to study this housekeeping candidate as if trying to make up her mind whether she was being misled, or if this new woman might wind up being an ally.

Finally, Stevi nodded and said to Becky, "I guess that's okay."

"Well, Mr. Holder?" Celia asked, speaking up after quietly watching all three parties interacting with one another. It was easy to see that she was pleased with the way this was going. "Are you willing to give Rebecca a trial run? Say, for about two weeks?" she suggested, observing Steve's face.

"Two weeks," Steve repeated, as he rolled the words over in his mind. He was secretly stunned that it was so easy. Considering the way she'd been acting lately, he thought his daughter would fight this new setup tooth and nail. "Yes, I think I can do that. Two weeks should be enough time to find out if we can all work together," he concluded, giving his daughter a quick side glance.

"What about you, Stephanie?" Becky asked the little girl. "Do two weeks work for you?"

"Me?" Stevi asked, clearly surprised that she was actually being consulted in this decision by the grown-ups. "Um, yes—I guess so," she added, no doubt not wanting to seem too pleased to have her opinion matter.

But she was.

"Then I guess this is settled," Celia declared happily. She turned toward Steve. "Until you decide this isn't working out, I now pronounce you housekeeper and boss."

"And charge," Becky added.

"What's a 'charge'?" Stevi asked, apparently wondering if she should be taking offense.

"You." The warmth of Becky's smile defused any indignation that Stevi was debating harboring.

"I'll walk you to the door, Mrs. Parnell," Steve offered, turning toward the woman. "I've got to get back to work soon, anyway." Once in the entry, he lowered his voice. "Isn't she kind of young to be doing this kind of thing? I thought she'd be..."

"Older?" Celia asked, trying to supply the word he was looking for.

But that wasn't it. "Sturdier," he finally said, glancing over his shoulder at the woman Celia had brought to him.

"Rebecca is very capable, Steve. Trust me," she stated. "She can take care of herself, and you'll find that she's more than equal to the job."

"Of cleaning the house," he said. He had no doubts about that. But he did about another matter. "I was thinking more about Stevi."

"She's more than equal to taking care of your daughter, too," Celia assured him. That was based more on a gut feeling than on anything that could be found in a résumé. But there was something about the way Rebecca conducted herself that told Celia she'd be fully capable of doing so.

But Steve wanted to be convinced. "How do you know that?"

Celia merely smiled at him. "Some things, Steve, you just have to take on faith. Faith and instinct," she added, feeling that he needed something more to hang on to. She wasn't about to tell him about Becky's background; that was hers to reveal. Besides, if she told him that the young woman who had just agreed to clean his house and look after his daughter had a degree from MIT, he either wouldn't believe her or, just possibly, he would be intimidated, thinking that there was something wrong with the woman.

Celia wanted him to get to know Becky and vice versa before that extra piece of information was placed on the table. Because Becky wasn't just a walking brain; first and foremost, she was a person. The kind of person Celia firmly believed Steve Holder needed in his life. As did his daughter.

But that was something all three parties needed to discover for themselves in due time. In this particular case, too much knowledge at the outset equaled too much information to deal with. She wanted everyone to proceed unhampered and learn about each other slowly, at their own pace.

Telling Steve goodbye and that she'd be in touch, Celia smiled to herself as she took her leave.

She didn't want to jinx anything, but had to admit she had a good feeling about this.

Becky's mother was due to be made happy very soon, Celia thought.

Chapter Three

If it wasn't for the fact that he had known Celia for the last five years and trusted her implicitly, Steve might have had some doubts about leaving his daughter with this brand-new housekeeper. But Celia was obviously completely sold on the young woman's capabilities, and he knew for a fact that she carefully vetted everyone who worked for her. So if this young woman was good enough for Celia, well then, she was definitely good enough for him.

Besides, it was either that or send his daughter away to a boarding school. He'd already looked into the matter briefly, reviewing several schools and even selecting the top two that seemed to have a great deal going for them. They were exceptional facilities and each would do well in furthering his daughter's education, but her attending them would mean he wouldn't see Stevi for long periods of time.

So far, the longest he had ever gone without interacting with his daughter was a day and a half, and that was only because she was asleep when he had gotten home that one time and still asleep when he left for work early the next morning.

Stevi hadn't been thrilled to be left in the care of a housekeeper, and he knew she wouldn't be happy about it now. But that was still a lot better than having to send her away altogether.

"So," Steve said to his new employee, as he walked back into the room, "did Mrs. Parnell explain to you that this was a live-in position?"

That surprised Becky, but she managed to recover quickly. "Actually, she didn't. What she did tell me was that she thought this would be a good position for me, and that she wanted you to be the one to explain everything that you require."

Steve took a breath. "So I guess I'd better do so," he muttered. He glanced at his watch. "You'll forgive me if I talk fast, but I have to be at a meeting in less than an hour and traffic at this time of day is usually abysmal."

Becky nodded. "It is that," she agreed. "Just give me the highlights and we can discuss the finer points when you come home tonight."

"The biggest highlight is that I need you to look after Stevi—"

"Stephanie, Dad," his daughter said impatiently. "My name's Stephanie."

"Right." Steve tried again. "I need you to look after *Stephanie*—"

"No, you don't," Stevi corrected once again, clearly pained by the declaration.

For the sake of maintaining the peace, Becky intervened. She smiled, nodding her head. "I understand, Mr. Holder."

A sense of relief washed over Steve. There was a lot being left unsaid, but he needed to go, and this woman he was hiring to run his household seemed to understand that. "Bless you," he murmured to Becky.

"Get to your meeting, Mr. Holder. We'll have plenty of time to talk about the rest of this later."

That was the moment when he knew.

She was perfect, he thought. Absolutely perfect.

But the true test would be if she could last the day with Stevi and not want to run screaming for the hills by nightfall—if not sooner.

Mentally, he crossed his fingers.

"Thank you." Steve fished a business card out of his pocket. "If you need to call me for any reason, any reason at all," he emphasized, "these are the numbers where I can be reached."

Taking the card from him, Becky glanced at it, then raised her eyes to his. "You move around a lot, don't you?" she asked, amused.

It took him a minute to realize she was kidding. "Try the top number first," he said. "It's my cell phone. Okay," he added, already walking toward the door. "Any questions?"

"Just one," Becky told him. Pausing, whether for effect or to gather her thoughts together, she said, "You are coming back tonight, right?"

He seemed taken by surprise that she'd even ask something like that. "Of course."

She met his response with a broad smile. “Then I’m fine.”

Before he had time to rethink at least part of this situation, Stevi spoke up. “But I’m not.”

“We’ll talk about it tonight,” her father promised, and the next minute, he was gone.

Stevi stood there, her back to Becky, staring at the door even after it had closed and her father had left the house.

Left her stranded.

Judging by the way her shoulders slumped, Becky thought, the girl clearly thought she had just been abandoned. She needed to find a way to reassure Stephanie that she was going to be all right. That *they* were going to be all right.

“I’m going to need a lot of help, you know,” Becky began, still addressing Stevi’s back.

“If you feel that way, you shouldn’t have taken the job,” she answered, in a dismissive voice that belonged to someone older than a girl who was almost turning eleven.

But Becky was determined to make an ally out of her. “No, I meant help from you.”

This time Stevi did turn to face her, but she didn’t look friendly.

“Again,” the girl repeated, clearly hostile, “if you feel that way, you shouldn’t have taken the job.”

Rather than argue the point, Becky said gently, “I’m not your enemy, Stephanie.”

In response, Stevi just glared at her, the look on her face loudly proclaiming that she thought differently.

“You know who I feel sorry for?” Becky continued. When Stevi made no response, she went on as if the girl actually had answered, asking who that person was. "Your dad."

Stevi's eyes narrowed, all but shooting daggers at this stranger who had invaded her space. The woman had no business talking about her father, even if he had just deserted her, leaving her at the mercy of this intruder.

"Why?" she practically growled.

"Well, for one thing, because your dad feels totally out of his element, trying to raise an almost-teenage girl," Becky answered.

Loyalty had Stevi coming to her father's defense, even though this woman had voiced something that she'd felt herself more than once, if not exactly in those words. "My dad's not out of his element!"

Becky looked at the young girl closely, as if she was actually able to see beneath the layers of anger and bravado. The whole thing made Stevi nervous, though she did her best to cover that up.

"Truth?" Becky asked her kindly.

Stevi shifted from foot to foot, searching for a comfortable stance. "Well," she finally said, backtracking slightly, "maybe just a little."

And then she straightened her shoulders, as if she suddenly felt that she'd admitted far too much. "How would you know anything about that?" Stevi asked, her very tone challenging this unwanted person traipsing through her home.

"Because I was just like you once," Becky replied knowingly.

Stevi's eyes darkened as she frowned. "Yeah, sure. Just because you're a girl doesn't mean you were anything like me," she retorted angrily.

Becky merely smiled. Stevi's response just confirmed that she was right. "Don't be so sure about that," she murmured.

Stevi fisted her hands on her hips. "Okay, prove it," she challenged. "How were you like me?"

"Well, aside from the fact that I had all sorts of questions about what was happening to my body, questions I couldn't put into words, and even if I could, I think my mother was too embarrassed to answer—"

She could see by the light that came into Stevi's eyes that although she was resisting, Becky had guessed correctly. She continued, confident that there was more to the girl's dilemma than what she had just stated. "—I was also smarter than all the other kids who were my age."

Stevi's eyes widened. She hadn't been expecting that.

Bingo, Becky thought.

"How much smarter?" Stevi asked, eyeing her suspiciously.

"Well, for one thing, I skipped a lot of grades," Becky told her, observing the little girl's face as she made each response.

Stevi cocked her head, as if that would help her judge whether or not this woman was telling her the truth. "How many grades?" she challenged.

This was definitely not a trusting child, Becky thought. But that was all right. Neither had she been at Stevi's age, she recalled. That was because she had endured being teased and ridiculed by kids who were ultimately older than she was and who, scholastically, she had left behind. She remembered being ashamed of how smart she was, thinking of it as a burden and a curse instead of a blessing. She found herself wanting to save Stevi from that.

Becky debated saying anything further to Steve's daughter. When Celia had told her about this job and had mentioned that Stevi was precocious and exceptionally bright, Becky had decided not to mention graduating college at a young age until she'd had a few days to get the girl acclimated to her. But already she was beginning to change her mind.

She wasn't ashamed of the fact that she'd been so young when she'd achieved so many milestones, and she didn't want Stevi to feel ashamed of that, either.

"Most people graduate college when they're twenty-two or twenty-three—" Becky began.

"I know that," Stevi said, cutting in. And then, pressing her lips together, she eyed her with curiosity more than suspicion. "How old were you when you graduated?"

The girl had realized where she was heading with this, Becky thought. Most ten-year-olds wouldn't have. She was right; they had more in common with each other than the little girl thought.

"I was eighteen," Becky stated.

For the first time, Stevi's bravado slipped just a little, allowing the young, vulnerable girl beneath to show through. She looked at this new housekeeper, clearly impressed. "Really?"

"Really," Becky responded.

Stevi fell silent for a moment and Becky thought that maybe she didn't believe her. The look on her face was nothing if not suspicious.

But then, after a moment's hesitation, the girl asked, "Um, did the other kids—the older kids," she clarified. "Did they make fun of you?"

"Some of them did," Becky admitted. "A lot of them, in fact. When I got older, I realized that was because they didn't know what to make of me. Later on, some of them admitted that they felt bad that they couldn't keep up to me, but you know, everyone's different and everyone has a different talent inside of them, a different gift.

"They just needed to concentrate on that instead of being angry at me because I got better grades than they did and I could finish tests faster." Becky paused for a moment, letting the words sink in. When she saw the furrows on Stevi's brow, she decided to delve a little into her life. "Do other kids make fun of you?"

"No!" Stevi answered quickly.

And then, because it was a lie, she relented a little. "Maybe."

Not feeling comfortable with that answer, either, she finally sighed deeply and then grudgingly admitted, "Yes."

Becky nodded. "You realize that they're acting angry at you because that's a lot easier to do than finding fault with themselves."

Stevi regarded her doubtfully. And then, because Becky wasn't backing off, she asked uncertainly, "Really?"

"Really," Becky told her with solemn conviction. "Trust me. Years from now, if any of those kids have a brain in their heads, they're going to realize that they were being very unfair to you, when what they should have been doing was studying harder so that they could get those grades they were so envious of. Or better yet, studying with you and trying to find out just how you were able to manage doing so much better than they did.

"Right now," she continued, "you probably feel like you're all alone, but that's going to change, I promise. And most of all, you're going to be the girl who makes it, who becomes *somebody*, while they, if they don't start changing and actually applying themselves to their schoolwork, are just going to wind up fading into the background, while you do great things."

She could see by Stevi's expression that the girl *wanted* to believe her, but still wasn't sure if she could, or if this was just a lot of talk this new housekeeper was trying to sell her.

"You think so?"

Without a single shred of hesitation, Becky stated, "I know so."

Stevi still wasn't 100 percent sold on what she was saying. "But if you were so smart, how come you're a housekeeper? How come you're not doing something…*bigger*?" she finally said, for lack of a better word to describe what she was trying to get across.

"Well, I wasn't always one," Becky confided. "You know what I was before I decided to take a break and become a housekeeper?"

Confusion and curiosity furrowed the girl's brow again. "No—what?"

Becky smiled. Her past life seemed like a million miles away now. "I was an engineer."

"Really?" Stevi questioned, a little unclear on how the woman she was talking to could have been one and then the other. The two professions seemed light-years apart.

"Really," Becky assured her.

"Can you do that?" Stevi asked. She was thinking about her father. "Can you just stop being an engineer and become a housekeeper?"

"I did," Becky responded.

"But *why* would you do that?" Stevi demanded. Her father was totally dedicated to doing what he did, sometimes to the point of staying at work for long hours and coming home after she'd gone to bed. "Didn't you like being an engineer?"

"In the beginning, I did. Very much so," she told Stevi. "But after a while I decided that maybe the pressure was too much. I found I was always working and that it wasn't fun anymore, not like it used to be. So I decided to take a break for a bit and just smell the roses."

"So is that what you did?" Stevi asked, doing her best to understand what this adult was telling her.

She liked the fact that Becky was talking to her as if she were another grown-up rather than just a little kid. Too many adults treated her as if she couldn't understand things. Her father wasn't like that, but lately, communication between them hadn't been going very well. Like an old train with a faulty wheel, it kept breaking down.

"Did you go smell roses?" she pressed.

"Yes," Becky answered. "I took time to enjoy the things around me."

"And being a housekeeper lets you do that?" Stevi was still somewhat unclear about the concept.

"Well, until now, I'd come to different houses, race around cleaning them up and then go home. This will be my first live-in position. So, like I said earlier, I'm counting on you to help me navigate this whole new career change. I'd like to be the best housekeeper that I can be," she confided. She looked at Stevi. "So, can I count on your help?" she asked, holding out her hand.

Stevi looked at it, and after a moment, she grinned broadly and put her hand into Becky's, shaking it.

"Yes!" she declared, doing her best to sound grown-up. "You can."

Chapter Four

Steve left work early, which was to say that he actually left on time. As usual, there was enough work on his desk to keep him busy until well after seven o'clock, but since things were still up in the air at home, he thought he should be there at a reasonable time—just in case. After all, this was Rebecca's first day with Stevi and he didn't want to take any chances on things going wrong.

If he were being honest, Rebecca was not the only one who was on trial here. He felt as if he and Stevi were on trial, as well. Quite frankly, both sides were scrutinizing and sizing each other up, seeing if they met the other party's standards and vice versa.

As he drove home, he *really* hoped that Stevi was on her best behavior. He loved his daughter to pieces, and at bottom she was a really good kid, but she could be trying at times, and not everyone—obviously—was up to dealing with a half child, half fledgling woman. He had been through three other housekeepers to prove that, and even the last one, who supposedly left because her daughter was having her first child, had never seemed completely comfortable around Stevi and her endless barrage of questions.

And Stevi, he knew, had never really taken to the woman, either.

Finally pulling up into the driveway, Steve released the breath he hadn't even been conscious of holding until this moment. When he'd turned the corner toward his house, he'd seen Rebecca's car parked at the curb. That meant that unless the woman had been so terrorized by Stevi that she'd fled on foot, unable to stand being in the same house with her a second longer, Rebecca Reynolds was still in his house.

There was hope.

The second he opened the front door, even before he walked in, Steve was aware of an exceptionally tempting aroma swirling around him. He felt his taste buds salivating.

"Ste—phanie?" he called out, remembering at the last moment to use his daughter's name of preference. He looked around the empty living room. "Ms. Reynolds?"

Following his nose, he made his way into the kitchen. And that was where he found both his daughter and his new housekeeper.

Becky reacted as if she was expecting him. She looked up in his direction. "Dinner will be on the table in a minute," she promised.

"You made dinner?" he asked. He hadn't expected that. Not yet, anyway.

She noted his surprise. "Isn't that what a housekeeper is supposed to do?"

"Then you're taking the position?" Steve made no attempt to hide how relieved that made him feel.

Becky looked at him, a little bemused at his question. "I thought we already settled that."

He cleared his throat, taking in all the activity in the kitchen. She'd obviously made dinner, but there were no telltale signs of chaos. Every time he cooked, it seemed to generate five or six pots and pans, no matter how small the meal turned out to be.

"Well, we did, but I wanted to leave you the option of changing your mind," he told her. "I mean, in case you felt, after spending some time here, that this wasn't going to work out," he added tactfully, slanting a glance in his daughter's direction. "What are you doing?" he asked, when he realized that Stevi's arms were filled with a couple of dinner plates.

Although he thought of Stevi as precocious and definitely on the brilliant side, she didn't have a domestic bone in her body. He was to blame for that, because he'd never attempted to give her any chores that were remotely domestic in nature. The closest he had ever come to making her do chores was to get her to make her bed, which she reluctantly did. The rest of her room looked as if it was home base for a twister that kept passing through on a regular basis.

"I'm setting the table," Stevi informed him, in a voice that indicated he should have figured that out on his own.

After arranging the plates in the small dining room, Stevi doubled back for the silverware. As he watched her, fascinated, she folded napkins, then placed a knife on each one, on the right side of the plates. She put the forks on the other side.

Becky nodded her approval at Stevi's progress. "Don't forget the glasses," she reminded her.

"I'll do those," Steve instantly volunteered, envisioning a sudden shower of falling shards of glass if his daughter tripped while carrying the glassware.

Becky took everything in but said nothing. Turning off the burners, she drained and then transferred the linguine from a pot to a large serving bowl. She did the same for the beef Stroganoff she'd made, then picked up the first bowl and carried it to the table.

"You made Stroganoff," Steve suddenly realized. He smiled broadly at the dish on the counter.

"Stephanie told me that was your favorite," Becky explained. "I thought it might make a good first meal to serve you."

He had a soft spot in his heart for Stroganoff. It was the first dish that his late wife had made for him after they married, although he had to admit that the scent he'd detected back then was of something burning. It had taken Cindy a while before she got the hang of cooking.

Such was not the problem here.

And then, as he looked again at the table, Steve saw that there were only two places set, not three. He thought it was an oversight on his daughter's part.

"There's one place setting missing, Stephanie," he prompted quietly, not wanting to embarrass her.

"Becky told me to only set two places," she answered defensively.

He turned to look at Becky as she set the second serving bowl in the center of the table. "You're not eating with us?"

"I can't," she told him. "I have to go home and do some packing. When Mrs. Parnell told me about this job, I didn't realize that if I accepted it, I'd be living here," she confessed.

"But you will be back in the morning, right?" he asked uneasily. Now that he'd found someone who was acceptable not only to him, but to Stevi, he didn't want to take a chance on having her change her mind.

Becky smiled. "Right."

Because he had wound up skipping lunch and had basically subsisted on a candy bar he'd gotten out of the vending machine when his stomach's growling became too loud to ignore, he was extremely susceptible to the aroma wafting up at him. In short order, he ladled both linguine and a large serving of beef Stroganoff onto his plate as he talked.

He sat down with his dish. Unable to resist, he took a forkful of linguine and Stroganoff and slid them into his mouth. Whatever he was about to say to Becky instantly slipped his mind as the flavor seized his attention and took him prisoner.

Wow!

This woman really was perfect, he couldn't help thinking.

"We haven't talked salary yet," Steve said, after chewing and swallowing. He didn't want to lose her on that technicality, and all but sighed as the next forkful disappeared between his lips. "Name your price."

Becky laughed, pleased at the compliment he was paying her. "That's actually something for you and Mrs. Parnell to discuss and decide," she told him. "And just so you know," she added, "I had help with the meal."

A touch of disappointment nudged him. "You ordered out?" he asked. Takeout had been the meal of choice for his last housekeeper, and the go-to move for the other two more often than not. He'd begun to think that cooking was a lost art—until now. "This has to be from someplace new," he guessed, because he couldn't remember having his taste buds tantalized this way before.

"No," Becky corrected. "Stephanie and I went grocery shopping together—you hardly have anything in your refrigerator beyond breakfast food," she explained. "And then we cooked together."

"You and Stephanie?" he repeated incredulously. Was she serious?

"Yes."

Only his presence of mind kept his mouth from dropping open. He looked at his daughter in complete astonishment. Stevi had never expressed the slightest interest in cooking before.

"You helped with this?" he asked in amazement.

"She most certainly did," Becky told him. There was a note of pride in her voice that took him by surprise. "If you ask me, I think she's a natural," she concluded, winking at his daughter.

Stevi seemed to beam. For his part, Steve was at a complete loss for words.

He was still speechless minutes later, as Becky left the house.

"So, how did it go?" Celia asked, doing her best to keep the eagerness out of her voice.

Becky had hardly had time to walk into her apartment and lock the door behind her before her cell phone began ringing. Dropping her purse on the floor, she glanced at the caller ID on the phone's screen before she answered. All she had time to say was "Hello" before Celia asked her the all-important question.

"Very well, I think. And you're right," Becky added with a smile as she sat down on her sofa. "His daughter does remind me of me when I was her age."

Celia immediately got to the heart of the matter. "Did you have any trouble getting along with Stephanie?"

Celia wanted to make sure that Becky was happy with this choice. Even if she felt she had brought the right two people together, she didn't want to impose her will on either of them, especially not on a young woman she had grown particularly fond of over the last three years.

"It was a little awkward at first," Becky admitted. She tucked her legs under her. "I think that's because she's had a few less-than-satisfying relationships with the housekeepers her father hired in the past. But it didn't take me much time to get her to open up just a little. More will take a while," Becky freely admitted. "After all, the process does require time, but I feel like we've made a really good start."

"I'm so very glad to hear that," Celia told her. "But to be honest, I also hear something else in your voice."

Becky wasn't sure she understood what the woman was getting at. She didn't want to jump to any conclusions. "Mrs. Parnell, I don't think that I under—"

"I hear some hesitation in your voice, Becky," Celia told her honestly. "Is there anything wrong?"

The woman's concern was gratifying, Becky thought. But she was quick to set her mind at ease. "Oh no, not with them," she assured her employer.

"Well, whatever's wrong is certainly not with you," Celia responded. "But I can tell that there's something bothering you..."

Becky sighed. Since the woman was asking, she didn't try to put her off. That would be lying. "To be honest, it's about my apartment."

"Excuse me?"

"Well, I didn't realize that this was going to be a live-in position," Becky explained. "I understand that for the sake of his daughter, Mr. Holder wants me to be accessible..."

Celia was doing her best to grasp what the problem was. "And you don't want to live in his house?"

"Oh no, it's not that. It would actually make things easier if I lived there. But when I moved into my apartment, I signed this lease, and it has over a year left on it," she explained with a sigh. "Paying for an apartment that I'm not living in seems rather extravagant, but I can't just break the lease, so I'm going to be stuck paying for a place that I'm not really using—"

Celia cut in, relieved that this so-called problem was something she could easily tackle.

"Don't worry about a thing," she assured her. "One of my very dearest friends is in real estate. She can find someone to sublet your apartment faster than you can say 'month-to-month.'"

"Really?" Becky cried, relieved. "Because I'm not sure how long this job is going to last."

"Oh?" Was there something Becky hadn't mentioned yet? From what Celia understood, Steve Holder was hoping this would be a permanent position if Stephanie liked the woman, and it seemed that she did.

Becky did her best to explain. "I mean…well, you might as well know, Mrs. Parnell, that the last time I talked to my mother, I promised her I'd think about going back to engineering."

"I understand, dear," Celia said sympathetically. She did her best not to sound too cheerful. She didn't want Becky to ask any questions and she definitely didn't want her figuring out that this was all part of a plan to make her mother's fondest wish come true. "But while you're thinking about it, you can be there, helping out Mr. Holder, can't you?"

"Oh, absolutely," Becky agreed. *Trust this woman to understand*, she thought. "Mrs. Parnell, you have a daughter, don't you?"

She could hear the smile in the other woman's voice as she answered, "I do indeed."

"If you don't mind my asking, what does she do for a living?"

Celia wanted to know where this was going, but refrained from saying so. Instead, she stated, "She's a private investigator."

“Is that what you wanted for her?” Becky asked.

Truthfully, Celia had to admit that she’d been stunned when Jewel had told her that was what she wanted to do with her life. But she’d kept her misgivings to herself and it had all turned out for the best. Jewel had met her husband because of her work and now they couldn’t be happier.

“What I wanted was for her to be happy, and being a private investigator is what makes her that way,” Celia concluded.

“Your daughter is one very lucky woman,” Becky said with feeling.

Celia laughed. “Could you tell her that? Because there were days when I *know* she didn’t feel that way herself.”

“But she does now, doesn’t she?” Becky asked.

Humor entered Celia’s voice. “It’s touch and go at times. Anyway, we have something important to address right now. You said you were willing to take the position.”

“Yes, I am.”

“And are you happy with that decision?” Celia asked.

“Happy?” Becky repeated, slightly puzzled. To her recollection, Celia had never asked her that question before.

“Yes, happy. Becky, I really don’t want you to feel as if you have no choice here. I want you happy about choosing this position.” Realizing that perhaps she was getting a little too carried away in her sentiment, Celia said, “I want all my people to be glad to be doing what they’re doing and not feel as if they have no choice about the matter.”

"Don't worry," Becky said with a laugh. "I'll let you know if I'm not happy about the job. Mrs. Parnell, you're like a second mother to me. At times, even more understanding about my feelings than my own mother, and yes, I'd take this job even if I wasn't happy about it, because you asked me to. But luckily, this seems to be working out well for both of us. I like the idea that I might be able to help Stephanie feel better about herself and not feel as if she was some sort of a freak of nature because she's bright and actually likes learning things."

"I'm thrilled that this is working out for both of you—and don't forget the dad," Celia reminded her casually. "You'll be like a godsend to him. You'll be fielding questions from Stephanie. The kind of questions that I have the impression make the poor man feel completely out of his element."

"He really seems to love his daughter," Becky mused.

"Oh, he does. He adores the ground she walks on, and until recently, whenever he could get some time off, he'd take Stephanie fishing or they'd go off camping together. He was the picture of a loving, doting father, and there wasn't anything he wouldn't do for that girl. But she's growing up and with that comes a desire to carve out a little space for herself in a world that, sadly, excludes him. I believe you can help them both with that."

"You're giving me a great deal of credit here, Mrs. Parnell," Becky said, feeling as if maybe she couldn't quite live up to those expectations.

"And all of it deserved," Celia assured her with feeling.

Becky sighed. “You realize this means I can’t fail you.”

Celia laughed. “That’s exactly what I’m hoping for, my dear. Exactly what I’m hoping for.”

Chapter Five

The following morning Becky was up and ready several hours before she needed to be. She found herself both eager to get started with this new job and dreading what was ahead at the same time.

This was not unlike the time when, in a bid for normalcy for her, her mother had found a way to send her off to summer camp for several weeks when she was the exact same age as Stevi.

She'd had butterflies in her stomach then, too. Just as she did now.

As she recalled, that hadn't exactly turned out the way her mother—and she, secretly—had hoped that it would. The adventure hadn't ended with her making a ton of friends. Or even a few. She had nothing in common with the kids her age and she couldn't exactly get off on the right footing with the older kids there, either. Both sets regarded her as being if not a freak, then someone who was terminally odd. The problem was she was too old mentally for the first group, too young physically to fit in with the second.

At that point, Becky had resigned herself to being a loner. She'd struggled, but after a while had come to terms with it. Eventually, once she graduated college, she found her own niche. She did it mainly by working like a demon. However, that led to her becoming totally burned out. She'd realized that she needed to do something else with her life while she tried to regroup and find some sort of peace.

It wasn't easy, but she wound up accepting herself, and discovered that once she did that, others did, too. Not in droves, but enough to make her feel that she wasn't the oddity she'd come to believe she was. There was something nice about that.

But now, as she placed a couple of suitcases into her car, those butterflies were back. Not in full force the way they'd been all those other times; just enough to be a wee bit unsettling.

Maybe she shouldn't be doing this, taking on housekeeping responsibilities, she thought as she drove to Steve Holder's house. Maybe she was better off just working for Mrs. Parnell, going in, doing a job and then going home at the end of the day. Simple.

Still, Becky reminded herself, yesterday hadn't been a disaster in any sense of the word. It had turned out to be a success. A minor success, granted, not anywhere close to what she'd accomplished while working in the aerospace program, but still… She had managed to get through to Stephanie and had gotten her to pitch in, making dinner.

Okay, maybe that was a sign that she *should* stick it out, Becky told herself. She'd give this "noble experiment" until the end of the following week, and if she still felt that her presence was helping Stephanie, well then…

She'd give it another week, Becky thought with a small smile. After all, differences usually were made by taking baby steps, not giant leaps.

Becky blinked. She'd arrived at the Holder residence, she realized. How had that happened? She didn't remember getting here.

Taking a deep breath, she parked her car in front of the house, right by the curb. She turned off the engine and then sat there in her vehicle for a moment, hardly moving. She was psyching herself up.

Mrs. Parnell seemed convinced that she could do this. If Mrs. Parnell thought that, then she could. All she had to do was put one foot in front of the other. She could certainly do that.

There was no reason in the world not to have confidence in herself.

She took in a deep breath and then slowly let it out. Then did it again.

"Remember, kids can smell fear," she murmured to herself. "So be fearless. Here I go," she whispered, getting out of the car. "The Fearless Wonder."

It was too bad that along with all the brains she had, she hadn't managed to garner an equal amount of confidence to go with them.

Taking her suitcases from the trunk, she slowly made her way up the driveway, one in each hand. Setting the bags down at the entry, she rang the bell.

The next second, the door swung open, almost scaring her.

The look on Steve Holder's face was that of a man whose faith had suddenly been miraculously renewed. "Oh, thank God you're here," he cried.

In the face of his relief, some of Becky's larger doubts slipped into the background, then faded completely away.

She smiled at him. "Well, you certainly know the right thing to say to make a person feel welcome."

He looked at her, confused. "What? Oh, yes. Of course." In the middle of another emergency, Steve found himself stumbling over his words. And then he noticed the suitcases. "Are these yours? Of course they are," he said, answering his own question before she could. "Let me bring those in for you."

And before she could tell him that she could carry her own bags, she found them being whisked away into the house.

Rather than placing them in a spare bedroom, he put the suitcases down in the living room, as if he hadn't made up his mind where they were going.

At first Becky thought the man was just in a hurry, but another look at his face told her that he was actually distraught.

That, in turn, increased her own confidence. It was as if she felt that she needed to balance out the deficit he was exhibiting, otherwise everything would fall apart.

"Is something wrong, Mr. Holder?" she asked him, concerned.

Steve wanted to tell her that no, everything was fine. But if the woman was anywhere near as intelligent as Mrs. Parnell had told him she was, he knew that she'd be able to see right through any half-hearted attempts to lie to her.

So he didn't.

"It's Stevi," he said, reverting back to the name he'd always been comfortable using. Right now, it seemed that getting his daughter's name right was the least of his problems.

"She doesn't want me living here," Becky guessed. Maybe she should have approached this part of the arrangement at a slower pace, she thought. Maybe she'd be better off spending several days working here before she moved in and spent the night.

But Steve negated her assumption. "No, it's not that," he told her. "As a matter of fact, she had a couple of nice things to say about you after you left last night. She seemed perfectly fine with the idea of you living here with us. It might even seem odd not to, seeing as how all the other housekeepers did."

Becky looked at him, confused again. "Then I don't understand…"

"Neither do I," Steve confessed helplessly. "One minute, we're talking at breakfast and she was telling me about a project she was going to do at school. In the middle of talking, she gets up to go to the bathroom. I didn't think anything of it," he said.

"When she didn't come out, after a while I went and knocked on the door, telling her we were going to be late. That was when she screamed at me to go away. I tried talking to her, but that just made it worse." Steve looked at Becky, a totally befuddled and beleaguered specimen of fatherhood. "I just don't know what I did wrong. If she keeps refusing to come out of the bathroom, I won't be able to get her to her summer school class before I have to be at work."

At a loss, Steve glanced at his watch, the numbers on the dial hardly registering. "I'd take the day off, but I'm supposed to be giving this presentation to management..." He looked in the direction of the bathroom, obviously at a loss as to which path he should be taking.

"What's the school's address?" Becky asked him.

Because the present situation was taking all his attention, he had to think a moment before he could remember and tell her.

Becky nodded. She knew where that was. "Don't worry. I'll take her to school, Mr. Holder."

He looked down the hall again. "You're going to have to get her out of the bathroom first."

She smiled as she nodded again. "I'll do that, too," she promised.

He knew he should just thank her and go, but his conscience had him hesitating. "I don't feel right about leaving you like this," he told her.

"It's all right, Mr. Holder," she assured him. "You have to go. Outer space is waiting for you. And don't worry. I'll take care of Stephanie. She'll be fine."

Steve sighed with relief, but still remained where he was. "I just don't understand why she'd have this sudden meltdown," he confessed. "I know I didn't say anything to get her like this. When she left the table, she looked fine." He peered at Becky in bewilderment. "Why would she just...?"

Becky had a hunch, but for now, she kept it to herself. Out loud, she tried to comfort him by saying, "Teenage girls have mood swings."

Stevi wasn't a teenager. She was still his little girl, his fishing buddy. This was totally out of character with that image. "But she's only ten," he insisted.

According to her birth certificate, Becky thought. But developmentally, it was a different story.

"Stephanie is precocious," she reminded him. "Her ten is someone else's fourteen." She hesitated for a moment, then decided to point out something he probably hadn't considered yet. "A lot of hormones are swimming around, causing havoc at this age."

"Hormones?" Steve repeated, saying the word as if he'd never thought about something like that in connection with his daughter. All this was happening way too fast for him. He wasn't ready to accept it. "She has hormones?"

"We all have hormones, Mr. Holder. Hers are just coming into their own. Now go," Becky urged him. "Leave the home front to me."

Steve really didn't want to go and leave her with all this to deal with, but he was completely out of his element here and he was needed at work. There, at least, the problems that came across his desk had eventual solutions, things he felt equipped to handle. Moreover, they weren't mercurial in nature, as his daughter seemed to be.

He let out another long breath. Becky was right. He needed to go.

"Okay," he agreed. "But if you can't get Stevi to come out—and I don't know why you shouldn't, but I also don't know why she's in there now—I want you to call me. You still have my card, right?"

Becky offered him a patient smile. "Yes, I do."

Steve started to go. He got as far as opening the

front door before he turned around and looked at his new housekeeper. "You sure you don't mind my leaving you with Stevi?"

"It's why you hired me," she reminded him, her voice pleasant and cheerful.

"Yes," he allowed, "but technically, this is your first whole day on the job and I feel like I'm tossing you into the lion's den."

"Not the lion's den," she assured him. "Maybe the large kitten's den…"

She made him smile for a second. He was still uncertain about doing this, but he knew she was right. And he needed to get to work for that presentation, so he left.

The moment he closed the door behind him, Becky turned away and went down the hallway to the bathroom. Oddly enough, the butterflies that had been fluttering in her stomach, threatening to overwhelm her when she had arrived on the job, were completely gone now.

She stood for a moment in front of the bathroom door and then knocked. But before she could say a single word, Stevi shouted from inside the room. "I said *go away*!"

For a little thing, she had a powerfully strong set of lungs, Becky thought.

"Stephanie, it's me. Becky," she added just in case, in her agitated state, the girl didn't recognize her voice.

The fact that it was someone besides her father didn't change anything. *"Go away!"* Stevi shouted. "I want to be *left alone*."

"Well, that's not going to happen," she told the

girl. "Sooner or later, you're going to have to come out and talk to me."

"No, I don't," Stevi cried fiercely. "I don't want to talk to you *or* to Dad. Go away!" she repeated, her voice cracking. "I want you both to leave!"

"Well, you have half your wish. Your dad's gone. He wanted to stay because he's worried about you, but I got him to go to work. So it's just you and me, Stephanie," she told the girl. "Why don't you come out?"

"No!"

Well, she hadn't expected this to be easy, Becky thought. She tried to remember being that age again, and how uncertain she'd felt about things. She needed to make Stevi feel as if they were kindred spirits.

"You know, it's a lot more pleasant out here than it is in there," she coaxed.

"I said *go away*!"

Listening closely, Becky could tell that Stephanie was crying. And she had a feeling she knew why.

She tried again. "You know, you can tell me anything, Stephanie. I was your age once and I know that lots of confusing, scary things are happening to you right now. Your hormones are waking up, making you feel happy one minute, angry the next, confused after that. Meanwhile, your body's going through all these changes and you don't know what to make of any of it."

She paused, hoping to hear any sort of response coming from inside the bathroom, but didn't.

"If you unlock the door and let me in, we could talk. Maybe, if we talk long enough, I could make things less scary for you."

"Please go away," Stevi begged. Her voice was definitely shaky.

"I'm not going to do that, Stephanie," Becky said softly. "I'm going to stay right here until you decide that you want to talk to me." Leaning against the wall, she slid down until she was sitting on the floor. "I'll be right here, outside the bathroom door, until you come out. I've got nowhere else to go."

Becky could almost hear the minutes ticking by. Finally, the bathroom door slowly opened. Stevi was standing in the doorway, looking very small and lost. She'd brushed away tears with the back of her hand, but the telltale stains were still there, bearing silent testimony to her fears.

"I'm dying, Becky," she sobbed.

Becky had gotten to her feet the moment she'd heard the lock being flipped. She wanted to throw her arms around the tearful girl, but held herself in check. She wanted to hear Stevi out first.

What the girl had said struck a chord. Rather than dismiss the idea, she treated it seriously.

"What makes you think you're dying?"

Stevi was trying hard not to tremble. "Because… because…when I went to the bathroom…" She broke down for a second, then collected herself again. "There was all this blood." She looked at her, terrified. "It has to mean that I'm dying."

This time, overwhelmed with compassion, Becky did put her arms protectively around Stevi. It was obvious that no one had ever tried to explain certain basic facts to the girl. "No, darling, you're not dying."

The look on Stevi's face pleaded she be proved wrong as she protested, "But I'm bleeding."

Becky's heart swelled as her arms tightened around the girl. "All that means, sweetheart, is that you're becoming a woman."

"What? I am?" Stevi questioned. She was clearly mystified and just as clearly desperate to believe what this new person in her life was telling her—especially since what she was thinking was awful.

"Absolutely." Giving her another hug, Becky stepped back and looked at the girl's face. "Tell you what. How do you feel about skipping school today?"

Stevi rubbed away more tears with the back of her hand and shrugged, trying hard to appear nonchalant. "Okay, I guess."

"Good. Because you and I are going to go on a field trip," Becky said, coming up with a game plan that would help defuse the situation for Stephanie. "We need to go to the drugstore for some much-needed supplies and then we're going to that bookstore just off Main Street."

"Bookstore?" Stevi echoed, confused. "Why are we going to a bookstore?"

"Because I want to get you a couple of books that'll explain what's going on with your body right now, and they'll probably be able to do it a lot better than I could."

The terrified edge was gone from her voice. "So I'm not going to die?"

"No, you're not. Not for a very long, long time," Becky assured her. "And certainly not right now." With a laugh, she kissed the girl's forehead. "Now let's get you cleaned up and go shopping."

This time Stevi didn't tell her to go away.

Chapter Six

There was no answer.

As he heard the sound of his own voice telling him to leave a message on his home phone, Steve terminated the call.

There was no one home.

What did that mean?

Had Rebecca managed to calm his daughter down and then taken her to school? Or had Stevi, still in the throes of her emotional storm, suddenly run off and Rebecca was out there scouring the neighborhood, looking for her?

But if that was the case, why hadn't Rebecca called him? She'd told him that she had his card with all his contact numbers.

Frowning, he tried calling home again. The phone rang five times and then went to voice mail.

Again.

Frustrated, Steve swallowed a curse. Why hadn't he thought to get Rebecca's cell number before he'd left for work?

"Hey, Holder, we need you back at the meeting," Chris Wallach said, sticking his head into Steve's office after quickly knocking on the door.

Giving up, Steve rose from his desk. He hadn't been able to get his head completely in the game all morning. His thoughts kept going back to the chaotic scene he'd left at home. He'd never seen Stevi like that before and it really worried him. But short of taking off and racing home, there was nothing he could do right now. And if he got there and neither Stevi nor Rebecca was in the house, then what?

He'd never been the kind of person to let his imagination run away with him. Hell, his late wife used to laugh and say that he *had* no imagination apart from working with those numbers he loved so well.

But now here he was, thinking of all sorts of terrible things…

He needed to get back to work, and hoped that would wind up distracting him. Otherwise, he was going to fall prey to some pretty awful thoughts that were only going to grow worse if he couldn't do anything to resolve them.

"Holder?" the other man asked uncertainly, looking at his expression.

"Yeah, I'm coming," Steve muttered, then followed him down the hallway.

"You seem pretty distracted today. Everything okay at home?" Chris asked. He stopped before the elevator, pressing the button on the wall.

Steve shrugged off the words, but then said, "Stevi's acting strange."

"Strange how?" his colleague asked.

Steve hesitated for another moment, debating saying anything. And then, suddenly, the story came pouring out. "We were having breakfast and talking this morning. And then she left the table to go to the bathroom. When she didn't come back, I asked her what was wrong—"

"You talked to her through the door, right?" Chris asked, wanting to get the story straight.

"Of course through the door." He sighed. This was all totally new territory for him and he didn't like it. "That's when she started yelling at me to go away."

Chris gazed at him, concerned. "So, what did you do?"

"Well, that's when the new housekeeper arrived. Rebecca Reynolds," he told the other man, in case that was going to be his next question. "She seemed pretty confident that she could handle it. She all but ushered me out of the house, so I let her take over and I left." He frowned. "But I haven't been able to get anyone at the house."

The elevator arrived and they both got on. Reaching over, Chris pressed the button for the seventh floor. "Stevi goes to summer school, doesn't she?"

"Yes. You think that's where she is?"

"She could be," the man answered. "Tell me one thing—is Stevi going to summer school because she wants to or because she has to?"

Steve knew there were some kids who needed to take a class over because they hadn't done well enough the first time to pass it, but that definitely wasn't Stevi.

"Because she wants to. The kid just loves learning things. Why?"

"I think I figured out what's going on," Chris told him.

"What?" Steve asked, eager to have his mind set at ease.

"The same thing happened with Wendy this year. My wife handled the whole thing," his friend confided proudly.

"So tell me," Steve urged. "What *is* going on?"

Chris gave him a knowing look as he paused for effect. "It's a boy."

Steve frowned, not following. The concept was so foreign to him, he didn't make the connection. "What's a boy?"

"The reason why Stevi's acting out like this," Chris told him. He elaborated, when Steve continued staring at him as if he was talking in some foreign language. "She's probably got a crush on a boy and he's already got a girlfriend, so Stevi's upset." Chris shook his head. "I tell you, it's not a pretty sight when they get upset."

"Boyfriend?" Steve questioned. "Girlfriend?" He shook his own head, rejecting the idea. "We're talking about ten-year-olds here," he insisted.

But Chris wasn't about to be dismissed. "Hey, things are a lot different these days than they were when you and I were that age." And then he paused, remembering. "Although, thinking back, there was this one cute little blonde back then and I—"

Steve cut in, unwilling to listen to any of it. "It's not about a boy, Wallach. I know my kid."

Chris looked at him with pity in his eyes. "You

just *think* you know her, Holder," he said. "It's a boy. I guarantee it."

They'd reached their floor and the doors opened. For the first time, Steve found himself grateful to have to go to a meeting. It terminated his discussion with Chris, which, in his opinion, was going absolutely nowhere.

Steve had a report that was due first thing in the morning. That meant that, by rights, he should be staying in the office, putting in the extra time to get it completed. But since, for once, it wasn't one of those things that had to be placed under lock and key at night, not being deemed classified or, worse yet, top secret, he could take the data home with him so that he could work on the report later tonight. After he assured himself that Stevi was all right.

Putting the necessary papers into his briefcase, Steve made sure he had everything he needed to complete the work at home and then took off.

Today's meeting had run extra long because a heated debate over procedure had erupted, and he had had to stay along with the others until the problem was resolved. That meant he wasn't able to call home again, wasn't able to put his mind at ease. While at work, exercising extreme effort, he had been able to force himself to concentrate on his work and blank out all the unnerving scenarios that kept trying to intrude on his mind.

But the moment he was free and able to leave work, he did. Fast.

It took effort to keep to the speed limits. Every time he missed a light, he cursed, something that, as a rule, he *never* did. He tried to talk himself into believing that

Chris was right, that Stevi had succumbed to the supposed charm of some ten- or eleven-year-old Romeo, but that carried with it its own set of problems. He was better off not thinking at all, but that was a lot easier said than done.

By the time he pulled his four-door sedan into the driveway, he had worked up a full head of steam and was perilously close to exploding. He'd hardly turned off the engine before he jumped out of the car and ran to the front door. Unlocking it, he stormed in, trying to prepare himself even though he didn't really know for what.

The one thing he *wasn't* prepared for was the sound of laughter. It took him a moment to even comprehend what he was hearing.

The laughter was coming from the kitchen.

It was Stevi. He would have recognized her laugh anywhere.

A wave of unfathomable relief washed over him as he followed the sound and found Stevi and the housekeeper working together in the kitchen, giggling over some story that Rebecca was telling.

"And the whole soufflé just fell, forming this abysmal pancake-like *thing*," Becky told Stevi as they finished cleaning up the counter.

"What did you do?" she asked, clearly horrified by the image conjured up of the destroyed soufflé.

"What could we do?" Rebecca asked with a grin. "We ate it. It was pretty good, too," she confided. "Despite its less-than-perfect form. Moral of the story is that not everything turns out the way you plan, but that doesn't mean you should just throw it away. And what wound up being salvaged was better than we thought it was going to be."

"What's the moral about not calling Stevi's father?" Steve interjected from the doorway.

Stevi and Becky turned around together, surprised to find him home so early. Stevi actually looked happy to see him, he thought, although she wound up covering her reaction the next moment, looking sedate and startlingly grown-up.

All the inner fire he'd been dealing with on his drive home had somehow been almost put out by the sound of his daughter's laughter. But he still felt he needed to make a point here, given what he'd gone through these last eight hours.

"But I did call you," Becky told him, confused by his accusation. "Around ten."

The one thing that irritated him more than anything was being lied to. "Oh?" he questioned. "And what did I say?"

"You didn't," Becky told him. "One of those tinny voices they use on some devices came on and told me to leave a message, which I did."

"I saw her do it, Dad," Stevi volunteered solemnly, coming to the woman's defense.

"Did you check your messages?" Becky asked him mildly.

"I did," he responded. "Four times. I didn't get a message," he informed her.

Becky looked extremely apologetic, so much so that he felt guilty accusing her. "I'm so sorry. I should have called again, but I really did believe that I'd called the right number."

"You weren't worried, were you, Dad?" Stevi asked him.

The fact that his daughter even thought to inquire, after the way she'd been behaving these last few weeks, made him feel that maybe, just maybe, things had taken another turn, this time for the better. At least she seemed as if whatever was wrong this morning had either been resolved or at least was no longer an issue.

Rather than dismiss the matter or pretend it hadn't happened, he was honest with her.

"Yes, I was worried," Steve told her. "It's not like I have a spare kid to replace you." A small grin curved his mouth. "I haven't gotten around to building her yet."

Stevi shrugged. "She wouldn't be as good," the girl quipped, tossing her head. "I'm an original."

He laughed then. "That you are," he agreed without hesitation. He looked at the stove, taking in the frying pan. "So what are you up to?"

"Becky's showing me how to make chicken Parmesan," Stevi told him proudly. "There's broccoli, too, but that's not my fault." She made a face. He knew she hated the vegetable. That she was helping to make it was another giant step, as far as he was concerned. "It's supposed to be good for you."

"So I've heard." He looked at the woman he'd been ready to throttle when he'd walked in, and now found himself wanting to embrace in relief because of the transformation he'd just witnessed in his daughter. He wasn't foolish enough to believe he and Stevi were back to their original footing, but felt there was a possibility that he might be able to restore some sort of peace, and he was more than willing to take that.

Dinner looked not only promising, but it smelled good, as well. "Will you be joining us this time?" he asked Becky.

Instead of giving him an answer, she asked a question. "Do you want me to?"

He glanced at Stevi before answering. Happy to be consulted, his daughter bobbed her head up and down, so hard that the ends of her dark hair flew around her face. Her eyes were shining.

Steve turned toward the housekeeper. "Yes, we do," he said.

"Well, then I'll gladly join you," Becky answered. "Dinner is going to take another ten minutes," she estimated.

"I think I can wait," Steve responded. He turned his attention to his daughter. "So, what did you do today—besides give me heart failure?"

"Oh, Dad." Stevi rolled her eyes as if exasperated.

"So what did you do in school?" he asked her.

"I didn't go to school today," Stevi finally responded, looking at him uncertainly, as if she had no idea how he was going to take this. "I played hooky."

Although he was proud of Stevi for being such a good student, there were times he worried that, even at ten, she'd forgotten how to have fun as a kid because she'd become so intent on her studies. To hear her tell him that she had done something so normal, yet so out of character for her, he felt himself filled with a sense of hope.

Throwing his arms around her, he hugged Stevi and spun her around. Then, setting her back on her feet, he pretended to put on a stern face and said, "Don't do that again."

Because she was so well attuned to her father that they were almost always on the same wavelength, Stevi put on a straight face and nodded. "Okay, I won't."

Watching them, Becky could only smile as a warm feeling came over her. It looked as if the storm had been weathered, and maybe it would be smoother sailing from this point on.

She didn't doubt that there might be some rough patches to endure, but for the most part, maybe the worst of it was over.

Steve glanced at the housekeeper. It struck him that the woman hardly looked the part. If he were to guess, he would have pegged her as a model or a fashion designer. She carried herself with grace and confidence. A housekeeper would have been the last career he would have said.

"Could I speak to you for a moment?" Steve asked, lowering his voice.

"Stephanie, why don't you go set the table for dinner? Set it for three," she prompted. It brought a wide smile to the girl's lips.

"Sure," Stevi responded. She hurried to scoop up the plates.

Once Stevi was out of earshot, Becky turned her attention toward Steve. As she waited for him to speak, she took the cutlets out and placed them one by one on a serving platter. "Did you want to ask me something?"

Yes. Why aren't you starting a family of your own? The unbidden thought, coming out of nowhere, took him completely by surprise. He shut it down quickly, determined not to allow it to distract him like that again.

"Yes," he answered, clearing his throat. "About this morning."

She raised her eyes to his innocently. "What about it?"

"Was Stevi carrying on like that, telling me to go away, because of a boy?"

Becky was caught completely off guard by the question. Her eyebrows drew together as she tried to understand where the question had come from. "No, it didn't have anything to do with a boy. Why? Is there a boy in the picture who I should know about?"

"Not that I'm aware of. I just thought that maybe..." Now that he said it out loud, it sounded ludicrous. "Someone at work said his daughter was acting out because she liked this boy and he didn't seem to know she was alive," he explained. "I thought that maybe Stevi..."

"It wasn't about a boy," Becky assured him.

"Then what?"

She was prepared for this and also prepared not to go into detail about it just yet. This was something that Stevi had to get comfortable with first before Steve could be informed. She remembered how she'd felt when it first happened to her. It required some mental adjustment.

"Just hormones," she replied lightly. "Nothing more than that."

The answer seemed to satisfy Steve. Or at least he acted as if it did.

Chapter Seven

"So, what do you think?" Stevi asked. It was obvious that she was trying not to sound as excited as she actually was. She was watching her father as he ate the bite of chicken cutlet he'd just put into his mouth. "It's good, huh? Right?" she stressed, never taking her eyes off him.

If Steve was being honest, he'd admit he barely tasted the chicken. Right now he was experiencing a delayed reaction to the emotional roller coaster he'd been riding and had just now finally managed to get off of.

Relieved and thrilled that Stevi seemed to be not just all right, but *better* than all right, he found himself going through his own modified version of an anxiety attack. When he thought of how things might have turned out, he felt really ill. He wasn't thinking of the tantrum that Stevi had thrown early this morning. Instead, he was thinking about the fact that when he'd called, he hadn't been able to reach anyone.

His blood had run cold.

It reminded him too much of that evening when he hadn't been able to reach Cindy. He hadn't been worried then because it hadn't occurred to him that there was anything to be worried about. It wasn't until a little while later, when he'd been called into his supervisor's office and saw the policeman standing there, that he'd thought something was wrong.

However, he still hadn't thought it would be the kind of "wrong" that would throw his entire life into a tailspin and irreparably change it forever. The only thing he had to hang on to at the time was that Stevi had been home with a neighbor who'd offered to babysit, while Cindy had made her run to the store and walked in on a robbery in progress.

It had taken him months to come to terms with what had happened to his wife. There were times, even now, that he wasn't entirely sure he could move past it.

"Dad?" Stevi said, looking at him with consternation.

Steve blinked, trying to return to his present surroundings. He realized that his daughter was waiting for him to answer her question, but he wasn't really sure what the question had been.

Sensing he'd zoned out, Becky came to his rescue with a hint. "Your daughter's a fast learner, Mr. Holder. She just watched me for a few minutes and then made most of the chicken Parmesan by herself."

Things fell into place. He glanced at her with gratitude, then turned toward Stevi. "It's probably the best chicken Parmesan I've ever had," he told his daughter with enthusiasm.

Stevi gave him an impatient look, as if she saw right through him. "You don't have to go overboard, you know."

"No, I mean it," Steve insisted, this time with even more feeling. "This meal is one of the best I've ever had."

This time, Stevi clearly decided to believe him. Her suspicions appeared to dissolve and she grinned, obviously taking his compliment to heart.

"Really?"

"Really," he responded.

"Well, Becky did help. She showed me what to do," the girl said, apparently feeling it was only fair that she share the credit with the woman.

"Becky?" her father questioned. "You mean Ms. Reynolds, don't you?"

Again Becky came to the rescue, this time on Stevi's side. "It's all right if she calls me Becky," she told him. "It feels more comfortable that way."

He was going to protest that he didn't feel calling the housekeeper by her first name showed the proper respect for her, but he had a feeling he was outnumbered. Besides, right now Stevi was behaving like her old self. He was extremely grateful for that and would have been willing to put up with pretty much anything to have that happen.

"Well, if you don't have any objections," Steve finally allowed, addressing Becky, "I guess that I don't, either."

Pleased, Becky smiled at Stevi and then at the girl's father. "Good. Then I guess that matter's all settled."

"Speaking of settled," Steve said, pushing his empty plate away, "now that dinner's over, I'd better get started on that report I brought home with me."

"Work? Really? You're going to work now?" Stevi asked, appearing totally crestfallen.

The look of disappointment on his daughter's face stopped him in his tracks. He knew that he really needed to get to his report. It was due first thing in the morning. But he couldn't just ignore the look in Stevi's eyes. Not when she was finally coming around.

So rather than just leaving the room, he said, "Well, yes, I was going to. Why?" he asked, even though he knew he should just take advantage of the momentary pause and make a run for it while he could. Instead, he heard himself asking his daughter, "Did you have something else in mind?"

"It's Tuesday," Stevi said, as if that was supposed to explain everything. When it obviously didn't, she sighed dramatically. "There's that show on at eight o'clock, remember? The one with the sharp detective and his daughter..."

"Slater and Daughter," Steve said, supplying the title.

It was a program Stevi wanted to watch because she said it reminded her of the two of them. It had been on for three seasons now, and until recently they had never missed an episode. They'd even watched reruns as if they were brand-new. The "new" Stevi had pretended to lose interest in the show the last couple of months, acting as if she was too old for it.

Steve couldn't pass up watching the show with her tonight, especially since it was only an hour episode and her bedtime came right after that.

"I almost forgot about that," he confessed. "Let's go watch it."

He was rewarded with a huge, almost blinding smile. For however long it lasted, his girl was back and he'd be a fool not to take advantage of that because of work.

Stevi suddenly turned toward Becky as they were going to the family room. "You want to come watch it with us, Becky?"

"I'd love to," she answered, then glanced at Steve. "But won't I be intruding? Isn't this your family time?"

Stevi dismissed the protest. "That's okay. It's a good show. You'll like it."

Becky looked toward Steve again to gauge his take on it, but he seemed more than willing to go along with anything his daughter wanted. That was good enough for her.

"I'll be right there," she promised. "I just want to put the dishes in the sink."

"The sink?" Stevi repeated. Her small brow furrowed as she tried to understand why the housekeeper would want to do something so backward, in her opinion, when she didn't have to. "Don't you like using the dishwasher?"

Becky's explanation was very simple. "I always find it faster and neater to just take care of the dishes as I use them," she told the girl, swiftly rinsing the plates before stacking them in the sink. "And I like the feel of hot soapsuds," she confessed.

After wiping her hands on a towel, she hung it back up on a hook and then happily proclaimed, "Okay, I'm ready."

"Great!" Taking the lead, Stevi headed into the living room.

"You sure I'm not intruding?" Becky asked Steve quietly as she crossed the threshold.

"Intruding?" he repeated incredulously. As far as he was concerned, this woman was officially his new hero. "I've got a feeling that if it wasn't for you, none of this would be happening."

She made no comment on that. Instead, she focused on something else. "How long is that report you're supposed to be doing?" she asked as they walked into the family room.

"I'll be pulling an all-nighter after Stevi goes to bed." And then he smiled, glancing toward his daughter. "But it's well worth it."

Becky had to admit that Steve impressed her. Faced with a report, especially one that sounded this important, a great many other fathers would have begged off, promising to "make it up" to their daughter at some other time.

Yet here he was, about to watch a TV program because his daughter had asked him to. He was in a class by himself.

"You're a good dad," she told him, before crossing the room to the sofa. She sat on one side of Stevi while Steve settled in on the other. Becky had to admit that this all felt exceptionally family-like.

She secretly smiled to herself. Her mother would have taken one look at this and been thrilled to death—of course, it would have been because she'd misread the entire scenario.

It occurred to Becky that she was going to have to tell her mom about this new position she'd taken…

But not yet. The minute she said anything, she would have to start defending her decision, explaining to her mother why she wanted to do this.

She honestly felt she was doing far more good here, helping Steve understand his daughter and find a way to reconnect with her, than she could have done if she'd remained in the engineering company where she'd worked for three years.

She could almost hear her mother's voice saying that she needed to stop focusing on other families and focus on starting one of her own.

Her mom, she knew, thought that these things just magically happened. All you had to do was *want* it to be so and it was. Her mother, bless her, didn't have a clue what it was like out there now. She hadn't been in the dating pool since…well, since forever. Back then, when her mother *had* been dating, things were a great deal different, and far less complicated.

You thought you'd found the right man, Mom, and he left, she thought. Her mother never said a word against him, never even told Becky how she'd felt about being walked out on like that. And the amazing thing was, her mother still believed it was possible for Becky to "find the right man."

Still, all things considered, if this mythical "right man" came along, she wouldn't resist. But until that day happened, she was very happy doing what she was doing.

Especially now, she thought, glancing toward the father and daughter duo.

"Do you like it?" Stevi suddenly asked, turning toward her as a battery of commercials came on.

"Yes, I do," Becky answered honestly.

"What do you like most?" Stevi asked, happy that she agreed.

Becky thought for a moment. "I like the fact that they're both smart. They could have made one of them smart and the other just sweet and simple, but they didn't."

"I like that, too," Stevi piped up, pleased as well as enthusiastic. Turning toward her father, she asked, "You do, too, don't you, Dad?"

"Actually, I do. But then, I'm prejudiced," he confided, looking at her with affection. "I've got a smart daughter."

Stevi rolled her eyes. "Oh, Dad." She looked toward Becky. "He says silly things like that a lot," she confided, embarrassed, and then suddenly came to attention. "Shh! It's starting again," she declared happily, waving both adults into silence.

When the show was over—they watched the coming attractions, as well as the credits rolling by—Steve finally rose to his feet.

"Time for bed, Stephanie," he told her, congratulating himself for remembering at the last moment to use the name his daughter claimed to prefer. "I've really got to get to that report."

"'Kay. See you in the morning," Stevi said. Leaving the family room, she saw that Becky was following, and she frowned. "You don't have to come with me, you know," she told the housekeeper. "I get ready for bed on my own."

"I had a feeling that you did," Becky replied. "I just wanted to tell you good-night."

Stevi paused, looking at her thoughtfully, and then

offered, "You can come with me if you want. That way you can tell me what parts of *Slater and Daughter* you liked best."

"That would be hard to choose," Becky told her as she followed her to her room.

She'd obviously given the right answer because Stevi's eyes gleamed.

"You, too?" the girl cried. "I feel that way, too. But I did like the way, after they solved the case, that you got to see them playing laser tag. It looked like fun."

"Have you and your dad ever played that?" Becky asked.

As Stevi cast off her jeans and her T-shirt, Becky automatically picked the clothing up and folded it without even looking.

"No," Stevi answered. "We talked about doing it a couple of times, but he got really busy at work, so we haven't."

Becky nodded. "Maybe you could bring it up to him, tell him how much you'd like to try that sometime," she suggested.

For just a moment, the pseudo sophisticate vanished and the little girl returned in her place. "You really think I could?"

"Stephanie, I think your dad would give you the moon and stars if he could, so yes, I think that getting him to play laser tag with you isn't all that hard to imagine. You just have to be flexible about when," she advised the girl. "Your dad does seem like he's under an awful lot of pressure."

Finished changing into her pajamas, Stevi walked into the small bathroom to brush her teeth and wash her face before getting into bed.

"Oh, he is. They'd probably work him to death if they could." She paused to look over her shoulder at Becky. "Sometimes I don't think that Dad has any time for me at all."

Becky smiled. "Funny, I think he thinks the same way about you." She didn't want to jeopardize things by sounding judgmental, so she softened her remark by saying, "But then, I've only been here for a day. Maybe I'm wrong."

She could see that she'd caught the girl's attention. "You really think that my dad feels that way?"

Becky gave her a sincere, sympathetic look. "Only one way to find out."

Stevi's eyes lit up as she regarded her new ally. "*You* could ask him."

Becky felt that it was way too early in the game for her to butt in and presume to give advice to Stevi's father.

"I wasn't thinking of my asking your father about that," she told the girl. "If *you* ask him, I know he's not going to say no."

Doubt and hope mingled on Stevi's face. "You think?"

"I guarantee it." Seeing that the girl was getting into bed, Becky took a step closer to the doorway, ready to slip out. She paused for a moment next to the light switch. "You want me to leave the light on?"

"How did you know?" Stevi cried, surprised. "Did Dad say something?"

"Not a word," Becky assured her. "But when I was your age, I had trouble going to sleep unless I left one light on. Usually the lamp by my bed."

"Really?" Stevi looked at her wide-eyed. It was

hard to miss the pleasure in the girl's eyes. "Did you feel like you were behaving like a baby?"

"Nope," Becky replied.

"And your parents said it was okay?" Stevi asked uncertainly.

"My mother was very understanding about it," she stated, adding, "I was lucky."

Stevi was impressed—and full of questions. "How long did that last? You keeping the light on, I mean."

"For a few years," Becky answered. "But you know, sometimes I still leave the light on when I'm a little nervous."

"You do?" Stevi asked, surprised.

"Yes. And there are a lot of worse habits to have. Leaving the light on never hurt anybody," she added with a wink. "I'll see you in the morning."

"Becky," Stevi called after her.

She turned around. "Yes, honey?"

"Thanks," the little girl told her.

"Don't mention it," Becky responded.

She left her smiling.

Chapter Eight

Becky was going to go straight to her new room. She hadn't been able to put anything away yet and she hated being disorganized. However, she felt that she needed to look in on Stevi's father first.

Doubling back, she peered into the room that Steve had turned into his home office.

He was sitting at his desk and seemed so intent on what he was doing, she nearly retreated. But thinking better of it, she knocked softly on the doorjamb. When he raised his head, she felt as if she'd caught him in the middle of a thought.

"Sorry to interrupt. I just wanted to say good-night—and to tell you that I think you did a really nice thing tonight."

Steve seemed bewildered. "What did I do?"

"You made time for your daughter even though you

brought home all this work to do," she said, waving a hand at the stacks of papers that were spread out over his desk. "I know you don't need me to say this," she qualified, hoping he didn't think she was overstepping some employer-employee line, "but that made her very happy."

"Well, it wasn't all one-sided," Steve told his new housekeeper. A nostalgic smile curved the corners of his mouth. "That's the way she always used to be, you know. It was nice having that back, even if it turns out to be just for the evening."

Becky had always felt it was wise to nurture hope. "Maybe this is the beginning of a brand-new wave."

He laughed quietly to himself. "I guess one can only hope."

Becky began to leave, then stopped herself. She needed to make this clear, even if it did make her uncomfortable.

"And I just wanted to tell you again how very sorry I am for the misunderstanding with the phone call. I did think I had the right number," she told him. "I absolutely would have never knowingly made you worry like that."

Steve inclined his head. "Apology accepted," he said graciously. "Consider it behind us." He glanced at his computer. "Now I really—"

Becky didn't let him finish. "I know, I know. You need to work on that report. I was never here," she told him, turning on her heel and hurrying away.

"Oh, but you were," Steve murmured under his breath, watching as she made her exit, his eyes lingering on the way her hips moved as she retreated.

She cut one hell of a figure, both coming and going, he couldn't help thinking.

Back off, pal. Those aren't the kind of thoughts you should be having about your housekeeper.

The last thing he wanted to do was scare her off, especially since, at least for now, Stevi seemed to really like the woman.

Sighing, Steve forced himself to get back to writing the report. After all, it wasn't just going to write itself.

He didn't remember when he finally went to bed. All he knew was that it was late. When he realized that his eyes had shut not once but three separate times, he knew he had to stop. There was still one equation he had to finish, but that could be done in the morning, along with reviewing the report in its entirety. His brain should be clear and fully functioning again by then.

At least he hoped so.

He didn't bother changing for bed, just fell on top of the covers—and asleep—still dressed.

Steve wasn't sure what woke him up. It certainly wasn't his alarm clock, because he hadn't bothered to set it.

And it wasn't Stevi. It had been a long time since his daughter had come tearing into his bedroom, bouncing on his bed while begging him to get up so they could do something really "fun."

It didn't hit him until he'd gotten up and was sitting on the side of his bed, trying to clear the fog out of his brain.

What had woken him up out of his exhausted sleep was the strong smell of coffee—and bacon.

He had to be dreaming.

By the time he'd hurried through his shower and gotten dressed, he'd convinced himself that it was just a dream, a very realistic, vivid dream. He continued to believe that until he opened his door and went out into the hallway.

Rather than dissipate, like every good dream did in the light of day, the smell of freshly brewed coffee and frying bacon just grew stronger.

Curious, Steve went downstairs to investigate.

"Dad's finally up!" Stevi announced when she saw him, making the declaration like an official town crier. Turning toward him, she added, "Becky didn't want to wake you up because she said you needed your sleep, but I said you had to get up so you could get to work. We compromised. She decided to let the smell of bacon and coffee wake you up. And it did!"

"Good plan," Steve said, his eyes meeting Becky's. He decided to take a chance, and kissed his daughter's head. To his amazement—and immense pleasure—Stevi didn't pull away.

And the miracle continues, he thought, taking a seat at the table opposite his daughter.

Becky turned to glance at him over her shoulder. "Stephanie said you like your eggs scrambled, but I can make them any way you want if you'd rather have something else." Finished, she slid the eggs from the pan.

"Something else?" he echoed. He looked down at the plate she set before him. Aside from the scrambled eggs and three strips of bacon, there was also toast, coffee and orange juice. "Am I still dreaming?" he asked his daughter.

"Uh-uh," Stevi answered, shaking her head from side to side in an exaggerated motion.

Wiping her hands on a towel, Becky looked at Stevi's father. She had to ask. "Why would you think you were dreaming?"

The reason for that was simple. "Because we don't have breakfast at the house, other than cereal, unless I make it. Either that, or I stop at the drive-through."

Becky didn't understand. "I thought you said that you'd had housekeepers."

"We did," Steve verified. "Three of them. But none of them was too good in the kitchen, I'm afraid, and they *really* weren't too keen on cooking in the morning. Getting up early to make breakfast and then get Stephanie ready for school required a lot of coordination, I guess," he elaborated. "It turned out to be a lot easier if I just made it." The taste was beginning to register, and he ate with gusto. "This is really good."

Pleased but somewhat embarrassed at the same time, Becky shrugged. "It's just breakfast," she said evasively.

"And it's much appreciated," Steve replied as he made quick work of the meal.

"By the way, you don't have to wolf down your food," Becky told him. "I'm taking Stephanie to summer school today. That'll give you a little extra time to finish eating breakfast at something like a leisurely pace before you leave."

But it was too late; Steve had already cleaned his plate. "Maybe next time. Right now, I've still got an equation to finish," he told her. "I think my brain just froze up last night, but the solution came to me this morning in the shower." He tossed the last words over his shoulder as he started for the den. "I guess I think better wet," he added, sending a wink in his daughter's direction.

Becky picked up all the empty plates and took them to the sink. She ran water over them quickly. "Are you almost ready to go?" she asked Stevi.

"I've just gotta grab my backpack," the girl told her.

Becky nodded. "That'll give me just enough time to wash these, and then I'll be ready, too."

"Becky, could you come in here, please?" Steve called, raising his voice so that it would carry to the kitchen.

"I'll wash the dishes," Stevi volunteered, surprising Becky. When she looked at her quizzically, Stevi explained, "So you can see what Dad wants."

Becky had a strong feeling that she *knew* what Stevi's father wanted. Maybe she shouldn't have done it, she thought, reconsidering her impulsive action.

The light had been left on in Steve's office, so when she'd gotten up this morning and passed by the room, it seemed only natural to go in and shut it off. That was when she'd seen that Steve had left the computer on, as well. There was an equation in the middle of the screen and it was incomplete.

She'd debated leaving it alone, but just couldn't. The incomplete equation seemed to be begging to be completed. So she did.

Now she realized that she should have just shut her eyes and left the room. Maybe Steve didn't like people butting into his work.

Sucking up her courage, she approached the doorway. "Yes?" she asked, hoping that he'd called her in for another reason.

"Did you do this?" Steve asked, turning in his chair and gesturing to the screen.

Although it was very plain what he was talking about, Becky took a stab at playing innocent. "Do what, sir?"

"This equation," Steve said, pointing to it on the monitor. The expression on his face looked as if it had been chiseled out of stone. "Did you solve it?"

Becky debated saying she had no idea what he was talking about, but there was no point in her denying what she'd done. And besides, if she lied, any credibility she had would go out the window.

"I'm sorry. It was just sitting there, waiting to be solved. I wasn't snooping," she quickly told him. "You left the light on, and when I passed the room this morning, I came in to switch it off. But then I saw that you'd left the equation incomplete and, well..." She sighed, embarrassed. "I guess I just couldn't help myself. It won't happen again, Mr. Holder," she promised with feeling. "I know you're within your rights to fire me if you want to, but—"

"Fire her?" Stevi cried indignantly. Uneasy, she'd decided to follow the housekeeper when she didn't immediately return. "You can't fire her, Dad. She's the first good housekeeper we've had since forever, and I *like* her," Stevi informed him, up in arms against the very suggestion that her father was going to let Becky go.

"If you're both done talking, I'd like to say something," Steve told the two of them.

Stevi crossed her arms and narrowed her eyes almost into slits. "What?" she demanded, ready to go another round in defense of the woman she'd taken a liking to, if it had to come down to that.

Steve turned his attention away from his daughter, even as he informed her, "I wanted to ask Rebecca how she came up with this answer." Stunned, he looked quizzically at his housekeeper. This wasn't an equation someone could just pull out of the air. "Most people don't have a clue how to even begin to solve this, much less come up with the right answer. Do you have a degree in aerospace engineering?" he asked in disbelief, fully expecting Becky to say that she didn't.

His mystification didn't originate because she was a woman, or even because she was so young. He was astonished because he was asking this question of his *housekeeper.* If Rebecca was capable of solving a problem like this, then what in the world was she doing working in a job like this?

Becky didn't answer Steve's question immediately. She was afraid that he would think she was lying—or crazy.

But then, finally, because he was waiting, she reluctantly admitted, "Yes, I do."

This was insane, Steve thought. There had to be a mistake—but then, he reminded himself, she'd put down the right answer on the computer screen.

"A degree. From where?"

"Does it matter?" Becky asked, wanting to shrug off the whole thing.

Because she wasn't answering, Steve found his curiosity increasing twofold. "It does to me."

Becky pressed her lips together. “MIT,” she told him softly.

“MIT,” he repeated. “You have an engineering degree from MIT?”

Maybe he didn’t believe her, she thought. As much as she wanted to table the discussion, Becky raised her chin. “Yes.”

It wasn’t the easiest school to get into. Steve knew that for a fact. “You have a degree from MIT,” he stated in surprise.

“Dad, you just said that,” Stevi pointed out impatiently. “Don’t make her feel weird.”

Becky smiled at the girl for being protective, while Steve looked at her in astonishment. He wasn’t sure which surprised him more, that Stevi was coming to the housekeeper’s defense or that his housekeeper was an engineer.

His *very young, very sexy* housekeeper, he thought. That brought up another question. “How old were you when you got your degree?”

Becky looked at the floor. He could easily ask Mrs. Parnell for the information. Taking a breath, she told him. “Eighteen.”

“Eighteen,” he repeated, thunderstruck as he stared at her. “You graduated from MIT at eighteen. What the hell are you doing, working as a housekeeper, if you could easily be working as an engineer?” he asked, flabbergasted.

“Right now I’m taking your daughter to school,” Becky answered. He wasn’t telling her she was fired. Maybe there was still hope. Operating on that, she pushed on. “So if you’ll excuse me, I don’t want to make her late for class." She looked at Stevi. "Are you ready to go?"

"Absolutely!" Stevi declared, sensing that they were making their getaway. "See you, Dad," she called over her shoulder as she hurried out of his office.

Becky knew she was just putting off the inevitable, but maybe, if he had some extra time, it would be enough for him to cool off and rethink his decision about letting her go.

In hindsight, she realized that she shouldn't have tampered with the equation. For all she knew, having her input the answer might have affected something else in the computer. And even if it didn't, he probably didn't like having his work tampered with. He might be one of those men who felt as if his space was invaded if someone else touched his computer. Especially a lowly housekeeper, she thought ruefully.

It was just that, for a fraction of a moment, things that she'd spent years learning all came back to her, seeking an outlet. And it seemed harmless enough, inputting a few numbers to make the equation complete.

You're just too smart for your own good, Rebecca Ann Reynolds. She could almost hear her grandmother's shrill voice.

Her grandmother had told her that more than once when she was growing up. She'd been one of those people who felt girls had to pretend not to be as smart as their male counterparts. That was just the way things were, she'd maintained.

More than once Becky had caught herself thinking that she would have hated to be growing up when her grandmother was a young girl.

But then, it wasn't exactly a picnic being someone

like her, either. Even now she caught herself feeling awkward once in a while. That was why she had decided to turn her back on being an engineer, choosing to do something simple instead. For the most part, her current work was rewarding. It had begun as a temporary solution, but she had begun to think that maybe it was a permanent one.

And then that equation had popped out to taunt her and tempt her. Now she wasn't all that sure *what* she wanted.

Becky fervently hoped she hadn't wound up ruining this new situation for herself by solving that equation for Steve.

Only time would tell. Until then, she was determined that she wasn't going to drive herself crazy worrying about it.

"Don't worry," Stevi told her as she got into the car. "He'll get over it. He's nice that way."

Becky smiled. "I guess we'll add mind reader to your résumé when the time comes."

"Mind reader," the girl said, settling back in her seat. She seemed to roll the words over in her mind, then grinned. "I like that."

"I figured you would," Becky told her with a laugh.

Chapter Nine

Steve hadn't meant to stay so late at work. As it turned out, he didn't pull up into his driveway until almost nine thirty that evening. He expected to find the house quiet. Stevi's bedtime was nine and the housekeepers he'd employed previously all retreated into their room as soon as they could, either to watch some TV program or to do something else they enjoyed.

So when he found Becky in the living room, reading a book, he was surprised on two counts. Because she was there instead of in her room, and because she wasn't holding a tablet or a digital device, but an actual hardcover book.

Did anyone read books anymore? he wondered.

"You're home," she said, putting down the book the minute he came in and greeting him with a warm smile. Rising, she told him, "I'll get out of your way in a second. Dinner's on the stove."

The woman was full of all sorts of surprises. "You left dinner for me?" He'd thought he would grab something cold out of the refrigerator and just call it a night.

"Well, you weren't here to eat it, and I thought you'd prefer it warm to cold, so yes, I left dinner on the stove for you." About to leave the room, she stopped when she took a closer look at him. "Hard day?" she asked.

"Long day," Steve corrected. And then he shrugged philosophically. "No different, really, from any other long day."

She nodded, taking his response to mean that he didn't want to talk about it. That was her cue to leave. "Well, enjoy your dinner," she told him cheerfully as she started toward the stairs again.

"Sit with me while I eat?" Steve suggested hopefully.

"Okay." She hadn't expected him to say that, but suppressed any sign of surprise.

Preceding him, Becky walked into the kitchen and headed straight for the stove. She picked up the covered plate and placed it on the table.

Caught off guard, he shook his head. "I didn't mean I wanted you to serve me."

"Well, since I'm here in the kitchen, I thought I might as well put your dinner on the table." A smile flickered across her lips. "Besides, I think you're probably a lot more tired than I am."

His laugh was a dry one. "You might be right," he allowed.

Taking a seat at the kitchen table, Steve stretched his legs out in front of him. "I feel like someone just sucked out my entire brain."

"Colorful image," she commented. Opening the refrigerator, she asked, "What would you like to drink?"

He picked up his fork and began eating. "I'd say a glass of wine, but in my present state, that just might put me out."

She agreed, but kept that to herself. "How about a beer? That might relax you."

He vaguely remembered that he'd put a few bottles of beer into his refrigerator not all that long ago, although he couldn't remember exactly when. "Not a bad idea," he agreed.

As he watched, Becky took out a bottle, opened it and set it beside his plate. She looked as if she was ready to leave.

"Take a seat," he urged.

Becky pulled out a chair and sat down, but it seemed as if she expected it to slip out from under her at any moment. He caught himself wondering if he made her nervous for some reason. If he did, he certainly didn't mean to.

"So," he said, after taking another few bites of the pork loin she'd made, then washing it down with a couple of sips of beer, "you really have a degree in aerospace engineering?" It was obvious that he found the information astonishing, not because he didn't believe her but because she was working for him in the capacity of a housekeeper. It just didn't compute, not after all the effort it took to graduate with that degree.

"Yes," Becky answered with a smile, "I really do."

He shook his head in amazement. "Then why would

you want to work for a quarter of what you could make in the field?"

"Well, for one thing, I used to come home feeling just the way you looked when you came in through the door. Not at first," she qualified, "but after about a year in the field. I worked really, really hard on the projects they assigned to me, doing my best not just to get them finished, but under budget and ahead of schedule."

"They must have loved you," he commented.

"I'm not sure about that," she replied. "Whenever I finished a project, my only reward was being given another project to do." She sighed as she remembered those days. "I didn't feel as if what I did actually mattered. I mean, it mattered in the scheme of things," she was quick to explain, "but on a one-to-one basis, I really felt that it didn't.

"Yesterday, when Stephanie finally trusted me enough to tell me what was wrong, when I *finally* got through to her, it was as if there were a happy little parade going on in my head." Her tone changed as she added, "There were no parades in the company I worked for."

"I suppose I can understand that," Steve admitted, knowing how he felt at times. "And what I can also say is that I'm glad you feel that way about your breakthrough with my daughter." He paused for a moment. "Would it be violating some sacred trust if you told me what yesterday morning was all about?"

He saw the expression on her face. He could tell she was debating the pros and cons of telling him. Steve thought of what Chris had told him in the office yesterday. Watching her eyes, he asked, “It *is* about a boy, isn’t it?”

“No,” Becky answered, “I promise you it’s not. It might be someday,” she allowed, thinking ahead, “but not now.”

“Then what was it?” He found that he really wanted to know. “Stevi was practically throwing a tantrum yesterday morning. I admit that she’s been standoffish and distant lately, but she’s never done that before, not even when she was a little kid.”

Becky continued to watch him as he spoke. “And you haven’t figured it out yet?”

“If I had, I wouldn’t be asking you right now,” he pointed out.

He was right. Becky paused, searching for a way to delicately tell Steve something he might not welcome hearing. It meant his having to let go, at least to some extent, of the little girl Stevi had been up until now.

But he was Stephanie’s father and he did deserve to know. Becky made her decision. “Your daughter became a woman yesterday.”

“Became a woman?” he repeated, confused. “What is that supposed to—”

And then his eyes widened just as he was about to take his last swig of beer. Putting the bottle back down on the table, he stared at Becky in bewildered disbelief.

“No,” Steve cried, finding himself in complete denial. “It can’t be that. She’s just ten years old,” he protested.

“Almost eleven, according to Stephanie,” she reminded him.

Steve paled then as the full import of what was

being said hit him. Hard. "Oh Lord, there will be boys, won't there?"

Becky wasn't going to try to lie about it. "Probably. Eventually," she added. "But what you have going for you is that Stephanie is very smart and she takes after you. She's not going to become some wild party child overnight—or probably at all."

"But there will be boys coming around," Steve lamented, unable to get past that thought. After all, he'd been one of those boys at one time, excited to be alive and testing new ground.

"Not for a while," Becky calmly assured him. She smiled at him. "So you don't have to start digging that moat around the house to isolate her from the world just yet." Rising from the table, she patted Steve's arm. "Stephanie has common sense, Mr. Holder. She's going to be fine."

"She has common sense and you, right?" he asked, looking up at the woman as if she was his last bastion of hope.

"Well, yes," she allowed. As long as she was here, she'd be here for Stevi—and for him. However, things did have a way of changing. "But—"

He didn't hear her protest. He only heard his own thoughts forming. "And you're a woman."

Becky smiled. "You noticed."

Oh, he had more than noticed. And if she wasn't his housekeeper, he might be tempted to show her just how much he noticed. But right now, he couldn't do anything that might risk scaring the woman off.

Despite the fact that he found her attractive in a way that he hadn't found any other woman since he'd lost Cindy, that was just something he wasn't going to allow to surface as long as he needed Becky's help with Stevi. His daughter was the most important person in the world to him.

He cleared his throat and tried again. "What I mean to say is that you know what she's going through. You understand what it feels like to be an intelligent preteen who has all these emotions running amok all through you—"

"Well, I wouldn't exactly say amok," Becky replied.

Words were failing him and he knew it. But then, he'd never felt as if there was this much at stake before. "Whatever you want to call it, you've been there and can explain it to her a lot better than I can." His eyes were practically begging her for her continuing help. "You can be her guide through all this."

Becky sat back down, scrutinizing him more closely. "This really does scare you, doesn't it, Mr. Holder?"

"More than you can possibly guess," Steve confessed, although it wasn't easy. If this wasn't about Stevi, he would have just let the matter go. But it *was* about his daughter and he wasn't ashamed to make this plea. "I need help, Becky. I thought so before today and now I think so more than ever. You came into my life—our lives," he corrected, "just in time."

She felt a warmth pass over her, embracing her from top to bottom. Humor entered her eyes. "So you're not letting me go?"

For just a moment, at the start of this, until she'd realized otherwise, she'd honestly thought that the conversation had been heading in that inevitable direction.

"Letting you go?" He stared at her as if she'd lost

her mind. "No. Why in the world would I do that?" Steve asked. "You're the first housekeeper whose cooking didn't make me reach for a bottle of antacids, and more importantly, you're the first housekeeper that Stevi really likes."

"Stephanie," Becky quietly corrected.

"Right. Stephanie. See, you even remember to use the name that she wants me to use. That's really tough, you know," he confided. "She's been Stevi to me for so long."

Becky nodded. "I totally understand," she told him sympathetically. "But for whatever reason, your daughter likes to be called Stephanie. She probably thinks it makes her seem more like an adult." She could see that he needed more of an incentive to use the name than that. "You calling her by that name shows your daughter that you respect her choice and that you respect her, really.

"To be honest," Becky said, "I like the name Stevi better myself, but it's not about what I like, or even what you like. This is about what *your daughter* wants. Right now, at this age, she's having just as much trouble figuring herself out as you are. You can show your support by listening to what she tells you when she talks—because there will be times that she won't talk at all and that will be even harder on you."

Steve listened intently. He was clearly impressed. He loved his daughter and he didn't want them to become strangers.

"You really did go through all this yourself, didn't you?" he marveled. He knew he'd assumed it, but it was only now really hitting home.

"Adolescence is a really hard time," Becky admitted. "Don't you remember going through that yourself? That uncertainty, that confusion?"

Steve's laugh was self-deprecating as he shook his head. "To be honest, I really don't think I remember any of it."

"Another handy device to use—total denial. A lot of adults have no recollection of ever being adolescents. Others, like me, have *total* recall of those years."

"All I can say is that it's lucky for Stev—Stephanie that you do," he said.

"A for effort," she told Steve with a grin, for correcting himself before she did. "Now, if you're willing to listen to a little more of my advice..."

"Sure," he said, thinking she was going to say something more about Stevi.

"You look like you really should go to bed."

"What?" He gazed at her, startled because she had said something that dovetailed with a stray thought that had insisted on drifting through his mind. It definitely involved going to bed, but not for the sake of sleep.

"Bed," Becky repeated. "Unless the fate of the world depends on you burning the midnight oil again, I think you really should get yourself into bed. If I can be honest with you..."

"Don't stop now," he told her.

She wasn't sure if he was being sarcastic, but she continued nonetheless. "You look like your batteries could really stand to be recharged."

"I guess they do," he agreed. He smiled at her as he rose from the table. "You know, this might be a totally selfish thing to say, but I'm glad you decided to turn your back on the aerospace world."

She laughed, shaking her head. "Could I get you to put that in writing?"

He thought that was rather an odd thing for her to say. "Why?"

"For my mother," she answered. "She's very disappointed in me. I know that she feels like I've bailed out. The funny thing was," she went on, taking his plate to the sink, "when I was growing up, I think I made her uncomfortable. I'd catch her looking at me at times like I was some sort of anomaly of nature because I studied so much."

"Anyone who graduates from MIT at age eighteen is not a run-of-the-mill kid," Steve pointed out. "She was probably having trouble coming to grips with the idea that her daughter was less than half her age and at least twice as smart as she was."

"Is that how you feel about Stephanie?" Becky asked him.

"Only because I wish there were more times when she would stop studying and just enjoy being a kid—the way she used to." He sighed, thinking back to less complicated times. "She has so much time to be an adult and so little time to enjoy being a child. I guess that was what I was trying to get across to her."

"Give her a little time. She just might surprise you and come around again," Becky told him.

She saw the sadness in his eyes as he said, "I wish I could believe that."

She thought for a minute. "Tell you what. Stephanie's summer school classes are over with in another few weeks. Why don't you plan to take her on a two-day trip doing whatever it was that the two of you used to do when you went away? Maybe she'd even welcome it."

He really wanted to believe her, but he needed something more to hang on to. "Now, what makes you think that?"

"Because, for one thing, Stephanie's just as scared of becoming an adult as you are of having her become one. Even as she's straining at the bit, trying to break away, there's a part of her that's secretly pleased that you're still holding on to the reins, trying to keep her in check."

"You know what you said earlier tonight about being afraid that I was thinking about letting you go as a housekeeper?"

She was back to studying him, wondering if he'd changed his mind again. "Yes?"

"I think that what you should really be afraid of is that I'm *not* going to let you go even if you wanted me to."

Becky blinked, confused. "Excuse me?"

"In plain English, then," he said, trying again. "You, Rebecca Reynolds, have a job here for life—or for as long as you want it, at any rate. Because I need you to help me navigate some very choppy waters."

Becky smiled. There was nothing like being needed. She really loved the feeling. "I'd be happy to, Mr. Holder."

"Steve," he corrected. "'Mr. Holder' makes me feel ancient."

Becky inclined her head. "Steve. Now get to bed."

He forced himself not to allow her words to mess with his brain, and refused to allow his imagination to run wild. He didn't need any more complications in his life than he already had.

"With pleasure," he answered, moving quickly toward the stairs.

Chapter Ten

It took Becky less time to get used to the routine than she had anticipated.

She had lived by herself these last few years, so it did take her a little while to adapt to living in a house with other people. But oddly enough, it didn't take her nearly as long as she'd thought it would. Moreover, it hadn't really occurred to her that she was lonely until she didn't find herself alone anymore. The emptiness that she had been living with dissipated because it became filled.

And it no longer was the sound of her own voice that occasionally broke up the stillness. Instead, it was Stephanie calling out to her, asking her for help with a particularly taxing problem that involved schoolwork. Other times, although admittedly that occurred less often, it was Steve who called to her, wanting to use her as a sounding board for some concept he wanted to bounce off her.

In his case it was never anything specific—she understood that he couldn't deal in specifics with someone who wasn't cleared to be read into the program. But it was just vague enough for her to be able to offer suggestions. Not because Steve found himself stumped, but because he enjoyed being able to discuss, however vaguely, what he was doing. He liked the fact that she could understand terms that would have had anyone else staring blankly at him.

And as Becky was acclimating herself to her new world and her new "family," the end of summer school kept growing closer.

"You know what that means," she said to Steve one evening.

Stevi had finally gone to bed and they were in the kitchen. He was nursing yet another cup of coffee—black—and she was finally getting around to the dinner dishes she'd left in the sink.

"No more school?" Steve guessed, tongue in cheek, even though he had a feeling that Becky wasn't going for that.

And she wasn't.

"And?" Becky coaxed.

Steve thought for a moment, trying to come up with another response, then shook his head. "Sorry, I've got nothing."

She rinsed off a large platter, putting it on the drying rack. "Your brain is full of numbers, so you're excused," she told him.

"From this conversation, or from the fact that I don't have an answer?" he asked, curious if she was dropping the matter or still determined to arrive at some sort of an answer to her question.

"The latter." She took pity on him and gave him a hint. "Does the word *camping* mean anything to you?"

A nostalgic smile curved the corners of his mouth as he thought back to happier times. "It used to," he told her. And then his smile faded somewhat. "But not anymore."

He had obviously forgotten what they'd discussed the first week she had come to live with his daughter and him. "Think again," she coaxed, waiting for the legendary light bulb to go off in his head.

He was about to profess that nothing was coming to him—and then it did.

Maybe.

"Stevi—" he began, and saw that Becky was giving him a look, one he had grown familiar with. He'd slipped again.

"Stephanie," he corrected. Becky smiled at him approvingly. He pretended not to notice. "Stephanie is willing to go on a camping trip?" he asked incredulously. He'd begun to think that maybe, after all this time, his daughter had lost her taste for "roughing it."

"Why don't you ask her?" Becky urged.

"You wouldn't be setting me up, would you? Because even rough and tough dads have feelings," he confessed to her. "I know most women don't believe it, because it goes against the image that we're trying to project, but we do."

Becky laughed. She'd never bought into that image. The man might appear rugged, and there was no arguing with the fact that he certainly was manly looking, but she had never had the impression that he was a steely tower of unapproachable maleness.

"I think that Stephanie would like to be asked to go on a camping trip," she told him.

Steve came to attention. "Did she say that?"

There was no missing the hopefulness in his voice. Still, she wasn't going to lie to the man. She wanted to be totally honest with him. Having him laboring under the wrong impression might destroy all the groundwork she had carefully laid out so far in her attempt to bring father and daughter closer and closer together.

She weighed her response. "Not exactly in so many words…"

"Then in what kind of words?"

Rinsing off a few more dishes, she placed those on the drying rack, too. "Well, Stephanie started to talk about the camping trips that you'd taken her on and I managed to coax a few stories out of her."

"And that's it?" he questioned. "Why would that make you think that she wants to go on a camping trip with me? The last time I mentioned taking one, she looked at me with that pitying, condescending look she'd learned to perfect and totally dismissed the mere suggestion of a camping trip as being, and I quote, 'lame.'"

Undaunted by his revelation, Becky was determined to push on. "That was undoubtedly during her initial discovery period."

"She's not a fledgling lawyer," Steve told her. "She's my daughter."

"I know that," Becky answered. "I was talking about her 'Stephanie discovery period.'" When he continued to look at her, completely unenlightened, Becky added, "She was just starting to figure out how she should act, who she was, that sort of thing..."

He thought back to when all of this self-exploration had begun in earnest. "That was, like, three months ago," he reminded her.

She waited for more. When it didn't come, she asked, "And your point is?"

"Three months," he repeated. "You're telling me that she's now 'found' herself?"

Steve would have loved to believe that was happening, but he was a realist. A person's behavior didn't change overnight.

"What I'm saying," Becky said patiently, "is that Stephanie's a little less lost now than she was then. A little less scared and threatened by all these changes, as well."

Steve knew he'd be better off just discounting the whole idea. But the possibility of doing something he used to love with his daughter was awfully tempting. And although he didn't want to get his hopes up too high, he had to concede that Becky did have a point. For the most part, the hostile flare-ups had decreased and at times Stephanie behaved almost like the girl he had loved for the last ten years.

"Maybe you're right," he agreed.

He noted that she didn't respond with "Of course I'm right." He liked the fact that Becky wasn't full of herself, but then, he had already seen enough examples to show him that she wasn't.

"Ask her if she wants to go camping with you after summer school's over," she suggested. "What do you have to lose?"

He gave her a dubious look. "You're really asking me that?"

She could understand his leeriness. "Okay, then how about this?" she proposed. "Concentrate on what you have to win if she says yes. You two might start really bonding again. I have a feeling that Stephanie's ready to do that."

He had to admit that it was more than tempting. "Okay."

"Just remember to call her Stephanie," Becky reminded him.

He knew she was right, even though his inclination was to ignore that part of the advice and just call her what he'd always called her.

Reluctantly, he agreed. "All right. Sure," he murmured.

Becky could tell by his tone that he wasn't nearly as hopeful about the success of this venture as she was. "Look, call her Dandelion if that's what she wants. The name doesn't matter, because under all that is the girl you taught how to ride a bike and cast a line and throw a curveball. And *that's* who you're trying to rebuild your relationship with, not her name."

He looked at Becky, stunned, when she named all the things that he and his daughter used to enjoy doing together. Apart from the learning to ride a bike part, they weren't exactly the first things that came to mind when thinking about what a father would do with his daughter.

"How do you know about all that?" he asked her.

Becky smiled. "It's not something I just happened to pull out of the air, if that's what you're asking," she told him. "Stephanie told me. Not all at once," she added, not wanting him to misunderstand. She hadn't pumped his daughter; she'd just let the girl do the talking. "But over the course of several different conversations. By the way, you fared very well in all of them. Whether you realize it or not, you still are her hero."

He shrugged his shoulders helplessly. "Well, she doesn't act like it."

It took effort for Becky not to laugh at him. "Stephanie is a preteen with warring hormones. She's not supposed to act like her dad's her hero, at least not when he's around."

Steve shook his head. "None of this makes any sense to me," he lamented.

Rather than commiserate with him, Becky just nodded knowingly. "Welcome to the confusing world of the preteen." Finished with the dishes, she dried off the counter, as well.

"I am not cut out for this," Steve complained.

She wasn't about to let him bail out, even if he was so inclined—which she doubted. "Sure you are. You can't fail her now."

"Fail her?" Steve repeated, puzzled. He didn't know what she was getting at.

"Yes," she insisted. "No matter what Stephanie says or doesn't say, deep down inside she's counting on you to be there for her through thick and thin. You're her *dad*. Her rock, and she depends on you. That really makes her one of the lucky ones," Becky went on. The words had just slipped out without her thinking about them. "She's as confident as she's able to be that if something goes wrong, you'll be her parachute."

He looked surprised at the unexpected imagery. "Never thought of myself as a parachute."

She shrugged, trying to be nonchalant. Deep down, she knew she'd made a mistake, and wished she hadn't said anything.

"Maybe you should start," she told him.

"Was your dad your parachute?" he asked, and then before she could say anything, he laughed. "I can't believe I just asked that. You certainly have changed things around here, Becky."

She didn't want him focusing on her; she wanted him to focus on Stephanie and rebuild his relationship with the girl.

"I'm just here to cook and clean and to watch over Stephanie when you're not home," she said, summing up her duties way too simply.

He looked at her for a long moment before saying, "You do a hell of a lot more than that."

When he gazed at her like that, she forgot to breathe. She needed to remember that this was all about Steve and his daughter, not about her.

"If you say so," she finally replied in a quiet voice that sounded almost deceptively subservient.

"By the way, you didn't answer me," he reminded her. He knew she was trying to divert him. He just didn't know if she'd done it because she was embarrassed about her father for some reason, or if she just didn't like talking about herself.

"Oh?" Becky asked way too innocently, wishing he would drop the matter.

"Yeah. I asked about your dad. *Was* he your parachute?"

How did she word this without sounding as if she

was feeling sorry for herself? She gave it a try. "Let's just say he never got a chance to be my parachute."

"And why's that?" Steve asked, puzzled. "Because you didn't need one?"

Anyone who graduated from college at eighteen most likely hadn't needed to be sheltered, he assumed. She'd probably been way too independent. If anything, he guessed, her father came to her for advice.

"My dad left when I was eight," she told him stoically. "He told my mother that he wasn't cut out to be a father and he just…left," she repeated simply.

Steve found himself struggling with the desire to take her into his arms and comfort her. But that would probably raise a lot of problems instead of resolving any, so he remained where he was and kept his hands at his sides.

"I'm sorry," he told her solemnly.

"Don't be," Becky said. "You didn't make him leave."

Steve wasn't someone who was normally into feelings, or at least he hadn't been until Becky had come into his life and opened his eyes, allowing him to view his daughter in a different light. He could sense now that Becky blamed herself for the fact that her father had taken off.

"Neither did you," he said, as he looked into her eyes.

She took a breath, distancing herself from the story, from the heartbroken girl she had once been. "Oh, I don't know about that. It's what he told my mother and what he believed."

"What did he tell *you*?" Steve asked, unable to understand a man could just abandon his flesh and blood like that. He was trying to move heaven and earth to get closer to his daughter. How could Becky's father have just turned his back on her?

"Nothing," she answered stoically. "Not even goodbye."

Her words echoed back to her and she suddenly realized what she was doing. Something she didn't believe in doing. Ever. She never indulged in talking about this part of her past. The last thing she wanted was sympathy from Steve. The only one who knew about this, other than her mother, was Mrs. Parnell. The woman's caring, motherly attitude had coaxed the story out of her.

She had found herself sharing the story with Mrs. Parnell one day after they had returned to her office after work. It was her father's birthday, and out of the blue, Becky had suddenly found herself feeling sad and hating the feeling.

But other than that incident, she'd managed to keep it together. What had happened with Steve was a slipup.

"I'm sorry—I didn't mean to go on about this," she said, turning away from him. She began tidying things that didn't need tidying.

"No, it was my fault," Steve insisted, apologizing. "I have no business digging into your life." He moved around her in order to see her face as he spoke. When he saw the tears, he felt twice as bad. Digging into his pocket, he pulled out a handkerchief and handed it to her. "I just keep making things worse. I'm sorry. I don't mean to."

"You have nothing to be sorry for," she insisted. After a moment, she used his handkerchief to wipe away the tears, then, taking a deep breath, handed it back to him. "You're a great dad and Stephanie knows it. Just don't give up on her when she makes life difficult for you, because she really doesn't mean to."

He was more concerned about the hurt he'd caused Becky by prodding her and causing her to dig up the past and bring it to the surface. Had he known what she'd gone through, he would have never pushed her the way he had.

"Is there anything I can do?" he asked, thinking there had to be some way to atone for inadvertently making her cry.

She looked at him for a long moment. "Yes, there is."

Surprised, he asked, "What?"

Steve was relieved to hear that there was something he could do to make up for stirring all this up for her. Since Becky had been here with them, he hadn't ever seen her look sad, much less in tears. To have brought up all these hurtful memories in her made him feel extremely guilty.

"You can ask Stephanie if she'd like to go camping with you like in the old days," she told Steve with a smile.

He'd say one thing for her: Becky didn't back off. "You really think she'll say yes?"

"Only one way to find out," she answered. Then because she sensed that he wanted reassurance, she said, "But yes, I do."

He nodded. It was worth a try. "Tell you what. If she does say yes, why don't you come with us?"

The invitation startled her. "What?"

"Come camping with us," he repeated.

"I don't think you'd really want me along. I've

never been camping and I have no idea what to do," she told him, trying to beg off.

"Then this'll be a first for you." He saw the resistance in her eyes. Normally, he wouldn't have pushed, but Becky just might be the very leverage he needed to get Stephanie to agree. "Having you along might be the very thing to encourage Stephanie to say yes."

She'd done this to herself, Becky thought. She'd helped him paint her right into a corner. Now she was stuck.

"Sure," she answered, resigned to her fate. "Why not?"

Chapter Eleven

"Are you excited that this is your last day of summer school?" Becky asked Stevi as she drove her to class that Friday morning.

The girl's expression was unreadable. "I don't know. I guess so," she replied with a careless shrug.

Becky knew that she should leave talking about the proposed camping trip to Steve, but she was aware of how tenuous the relationship between father and daughter was at the moment. If he asked her to go camping and she turned him down, Becky had a feeling they could wind up right back at square one. Who knew how long it would take to talk Steve into making another attempt this time around?

She decided that she wanted to warm the girl up to the idea. This way, when Steve asked Becky to go on that camping trip this weekend, the girl might still behave as if she was bored by the idea, but she'd go because she'd had time to think about it and, deep down inside, she wanted to go.

"Well, your dad's really excited about it," Becky told her.

Stephanie looked at her as if she'd just declared that she was a Martian here on vacation. "Yeah, sure he is."

"Well, he is," Becky insisted.

Stevi made a disparaging sound of disbelief under her breath. "My dad doesn't even *know* it's my last day at summer school," she retorted. "I didn't see him come home last night and I didn't see him this morning, which means he left for work early—or he didn't come home from the office last night."

There was concern in Stevi's eyes. For a moment, she wasn't the bored, blasé preteen she kept trying to project. She was Steve Holder's little girl.

"He *did* come home last night, right, Becky?"

Becky was quick to assuage her fears. "Yes, your dad did—"

The annoyed, disinterested expression returned to Stevi's face. "I knew it. He just can't wait to go back to work." She blew out an angry breath. "He doesn't even know I'm alive."

Rather than arguing with the girl, Becky just gave her the facts. "Your dad stayed late last night and left early this morning so that he could finish a project that's due on Monday—without having to spend the weekend working on it." She sent the girl a long look as they waited at a red light. "Your father wants to spend the weekend with you, going camping and fishing."

"Camping?" Stevi echoed. She waved her hand dismissively. "We don't go camping anymore."

"That's because you haven't wanted to," Becky pointed out. "Your dad told me that he misses those camping trips and he'd like to go camping and fishing with you again—if you're willing to go," she added, watching Stevi's reaction.

"That stuff's for kids—and old people," she protested, turning her nose up at the idea.

They had arrived at the school. Rather than pull the car up to the curb and let her out, Becky drove into the parking lot just beyond the school building.

Stevi looked startled. "What are you doing? The door's over there," she cried, pointing toward the entrance.

"I just want to talk to you for a second," Becky stated. "Don't worry. I won't make you late," she promised, seeing the frown on the girl's face. What she was about to do was out-and-out interfering, but Stevi had left her no other option. "I think you should go camping with your father."

The frown deepened. "Why?" she asked defiantly.

"Because pretty soon you'll be going away to college and there won't be any time for camping or fishing, or doing any of those things that you and your father used to love doing together. You'll be sorry that you missed this opportunity just because you were trying to prove a point."

Stevi glared at her, daring Becky to convince her. "What point?"

She met the young girl's eyes. "That you were just too cool to spend time doing things with your father. Stephanie, it's hard for him to watch you grow up—"

"Yeah, don't I know it," Stevi muttered dismissively.

But Becky pressed on. "Your dad feels sad about losing his little girl and you really can't blame him for feeling that way."

Stevi tossed her head. "Sure I can. Look, I've gotta go—" She began to reach for the door, but Becky stopped her.

"Stephanie," she said, her voice low, "you have no idea how lucky you are to have a father who *wants* to spend time with you. I didn't."

"You didn't?" Stevi questioned. It was obvious that she was trying hard not to sound as if she was interested—but she clearly was.

"No," Becky replied quietly. Every word was costing her, but this was for a worthy cause. "I didn't. My dad didn't want to spend time with me. Didn't want to so much that he left."

"For how long?" Stevi asked suspiciously, not ready to believe what Becky was attempting to tell her. She thought she was making it up.

"Forever," Becky told her simply, as if making the admission didn't still cut her up inside. "Do you want my advice?"

Stevi shrugged, her small shoulders rising and falling. "I guess."

"If your dad slips and calls you 'Stevi' once in a while, don't get mad. Let him. And if and when he asks you to go on that camping trip with him, go," Becky urged. She saw students hurrying in through the school's front doors. It was almost time for classes to start. "Now get in there," she told her.

It was as if Stevi suddenly came to. "Oh. Yeah. I don't want to be late."

Opening the car door, she jumped out of the passenger seat and hurried over to the double doors.

Becky turned in her seat, watching Stevi disappear into the school. She wondered if she had done more harm than good, telling her about the camping trip. There was a lot of rebellion there. But she had to believe that beneath all that bravado, Stevi really wanted to spend some time with her father, doing what they used to do before her hormones had made her feel that it wasn't cool.

Becky had been listening for the sound of a car pulling up into the driveway for the last half hour. She'd been afraid that despite all his good intentions, Steve had either lost track of time or gotten bogged down in the project because, as she recalled, something always went wrong at the last minute, necessitating more time being devoted to correcting the problem.

So when she finally heard Steve's engine in the drive, five minutes before dinner was ready, she let go of the breath she'd been holding all this time. Stevi was in her room, playing the new video game Becky had given her as a "happy summer school graduation" gift.

With Stevi busy, that gave her enough time to waylay Steve before he came in.

Grabbing the card she'd bought for him to sign, she quickly and quietly slipped out the front door—and wound up walking right into him.

They would have collided had he not reacted quickly

and grabbed her shoulders to prevent a crash. But not quickly enough to prevent the momentary full body contact, with all the accompanying electricity that was created.

Catching his breath—and ignoring the way that his heart was suddenly racing—Steve looked down into her face. A face he'd caught himself thinking about more than he should.

"Whoa," he cried. "Something wrong?"

Her whole body was tingling. It took Becky several seconds to clear her brain and regain her composure, not to mention the use of her tongue.

"Um, no." She took a step back, away from him. Her body still felt as if it was heating up. "I just wanted to catch you before you came in so I could give you the card that I bought for you to give Stephanie."

"A card?" he asked, trying to understand why she would be giving him a card to hand to his daughter. She hadn't mentioned anything about it.

"Yes, a card," Becky verified. "To celebrate the end of her summer school classes."

His eyebrows drew together in confusion. "They have cards for that?"

Spoken like a man who hadn't been to a card store lately. Patiently, she explained, "They have cards acknowledging completing something important, which summer school was to Stephanie." She could see that he was still a little mystified by all this. That was the engineer in him. "Don't ask questions, Steve, just sign, okay? It'll make her happy. She might not show it," Becky added, "but it will."

He had a pragmatic question for her. "If she doesn't show it, how do you know it matters to her?"

"It does," Becky insisted. "Trust me. Now sign the card before you come in," she instructed, handing him a pen, as well, and then slipping back into the house.

Becky was back in the kitchen, getting dinner on the table, when she heard the front door opening.

"Stephanie, your father's home!" she called out toward the girl's bedroom. "See? I told you he'd be home in time for dinner."

Within a couple of minutes, Stevi walked in, making a show of being totally unhurried. "Did they run out of work for you to do?" she asked him as she came into the room.

"No, there's still work," Steve assured her. "I just told them I had to go because my daughter graduated from summer school today and I wanted to come home to give her this." He underscored his statement by handing her the card that Becky had just given him to sign.

Stevi was clearly caught off guard. "You're giving me a card?"

Steve smiled at his daughter. "Sure looks that way, doesn't it?"

For a second, from the way he worded his response, Becky was afraid that he was going to tell his daughter where the card had actually come from. But he didn't, and fortunately, his statement didn't raise any red flags for Stevi.

Trying to act nonchalant, she tore open the envelope and pulled the card out. She read it immediately. Twice, it seemed, given the length of time it took before she looked up at him.

Stevi stared at her father intently. “You really bought this for me?”

Becky quickly stepped in, giving Steve time to compose his answer. “I told you that your dad was a thoughtful man.”

Stevi tried not to look as if she was affected by this gesture, but it was obvious she was.

“It’s nice,” she finally said. “Really nice,” she added, her voice thick with emotion.

Becky could see that Steve was uncomfortable lying to his daughter. But if he said anything about it, any territory that had been gained would be lost, possibly permanently. So she stepped in again. “Dinner’s going to get cold,” she warned, ushering both of them to the table.

If Stevi was going to say anything further about the card, she forgot about it the second she saw what was waiting there. “You made tamales,” she exclaimed. “And quesadillas!” She was the picture of surprise as she turned toward Becky. “How did you know these were my favorites?”

Becky’s smile would have made the Mona Lisa envious. “I always believe in doing my research, even when it comes to something simple like food. Now eat,” she urged both father and daughter as she sat down to join them. “These things taste much better warm than cold.”

“Wow, I am *really* full. I shouldn’t have eaten so much,” Steve confided. He was seriously considering loosening his belt, but refrained.

“Overindulging once in a while never hurt anyone," Becky told him. "Do you have room for dessert?"

Steve responded with a groan.

"All right, moving on. How about you, Stephanie? Any room for dessert?" Before the girl answered, Becky delivered the crowning argument. "I bought *helado*."

Her eyes grew huge. "Really? You did?"

"I did," Becky answered proudly. Finding the dessert had taken effort.

"Sure!" Stephanie cried.

Steve looked at her, puzzled. He had no idea what Becky and his daughter were talking about. "What's—whatever you just said?" he asked.

"It's ice cream, Dad. Mexican ice cream," Stephanie clarified. Her eyes sparkled as she looked at the housekeeper. "Becky, you're the greatest!" she cried with enthusiasm, no longer trying to maintain a facade. "Isn't she, Dad?"

Steve responded with a smile. As far as he was concerned, Becky was a lifesaver—and she had given him back his daughter, however temporarily. "You'll get no argument from me," he replied, looking at Becky.

Becky could feel herself blushing, and struggled to bank down her response. She rose quickly from the table before either one of them could take note of the fact that her complexion had reddened. Red was not her best color.

"Well, you two are certainly easily bought," she quipped.

Taking the large container out of the freezer, she placed it on the counter next to three bowls. Using an ice cream scoop, she doled out servings for each of them, then brought them to the table.

Steve watched her balance all three bowls and then distribute them. “That’s a pretty neat trick,” he commented, clearly impressed.

“Oh, this is nothing,” Becky said, shrugging off the compliment. “I worked as a waitress part-time while I was in school.”

Stephanie looked up at her, confused. “I thought you said you had a scholarship.”

“I did,” she replied. “The scholarship paid for all my classes, but I still needed to earn spending money for incidentals. Being a waitress was good training.”

“You, Rebecca Reynolds, are an endless source of surprises,” Steve told her.

The comment pleased her as she took her seat at the table with them.

“I’m glad you think so,” she murmured. Then, because she didn’t want too much attention focused on her, especially today, since it belonged to Stephanie, she glanced at Steve and said, “Didn’t you say that you wanted to ask Stephanie something?”

“Right. I did,” he agreed. He looked at his daughter. “Stephanie, how would you feel about going camping this weekend?”

Stephanie’s spoon halted in midmotion. “With you?”

“Yogi Bear was busy, so yes, with me.” The corner of his mouth curved in amusement. “So is that okay with you?”

She raised her chin defensively. “Aren’t you going to be working?”

“No. I cleared my schedule,” he said. “I told them

that someone else was going to have to handle the emergencies." He smiled at his daughter. "I had some memories to recapture with my daughter—and hopefully, maybe a fish or two while we were at it. What do you say?"

Stephanie appeared to be thinking her answer over. She looked toward Becky. "Can Becky come with us?"

Alarms went off in Becky's head as she tried to beg off. "Oh no, this is father-daughter time. I really don't think I should intrude."

"You wouldn't be intruding, Becky. Would she, Dad?" Stephanie asked, turning toward her father for backup.

"Not at all," Steve said. "As a matter of fact, I think it might be fun."

Becky shook her head. "Oh no, I'm not fun outside, really," she insisted. "I don't know the first thing about camping."

"We'll teach you," Stephanie declared. "Won't we, Dad?" she asked, her enthusiasm growing with each word she uttered.

"We sure will," Steve told his daughter. "By the time we finish, Becky will be a seasoned camper. I guarantee it," he said, looking at her with a big grin on his face.

"So how about it?" Stephanie asked her eagerly. "Will you come?"

There was no getting out of this. She had a feeling that if she protested too hard, she could throw a wrench into this whole setup. She couldn't take that chance, even though she knew nothing about camping, and the idea of sleeping on the hard ground was definitely not enticing.

Becky could only sigh and force a smile to her lips as she answered, "Sure."

Chapter Twelve

This was a bad idea.

A *really* bad idea.

The sentence played itself over and over again in Becky's brain, mocking her. If she had any sense at all, she should make her apologies and beg off.

Actually, if she had any real backbone—the way she always thought she had—Becky felt that she should just declare that she didn't want to go on this camping trip and be done with it. After all, she had never been an outdoor person, never harbored the desire to be one with nature or fall asleep looking up at the stars, unless they were the kind that were artificially imposed onto her ceiling. Moreover, bathrooms were a very big part of her basic survival requirements, followed by accessible running water.

The only running water here at the campground

Steve had brought them to could be found in the stream where they would be fishing.

What she had signed up for didn't fully sink in until Steve turned off the engine and then announced, for her benefit, that they were "here." Then he and Stephanie got out of the car, and he urged Becky to follow suit.

She climbed out of the vehicle, moving like a person who was sleepwalking.

"We're leaving the car?" Becky asked, holding on to the passenger door. A wave of panic threatened to overtake her. Her knees actually felt wobbly. "Are you sure we should do that?"

"Cars aren't allowed where we're going to be camping," Steve explained. "Don't worry. It'll be fine right here."

She stared at what was her last connection to civilization. "It's not the car that I was worried about," she murmured under her breath.

"What?" Steve tilted his head slightly. "I didn't catch that."

"Nothing," she said, dismissing her words. "I'm just mumbling." Concern creased her brow. "Do you know where we're going?"

"Stephanie and I used to come out here all the time," he recalled fondly. "She could even lead the way without any trouble. It's really not that far," he assured Becky.

Becky gazed down at all the gear he was pulling out of the trunk and spreading on the ground around them. In her estimation it looked as if they were going to build a small city.

"How are we going to get all this stuff over to the campground without a car?" she asked.

"That's simple," Stephanie piped up. "We'll backpack it."

Becky looked at everything that had been taken out, and felt overwhelmed. "All this?"

"It's really lighter than it looks," Steve told her matter-of-factly.

It would have to be, Becky thought. She watched, all but speechless, as Steve began putting the packs together. "And this is what you used to do for fun," she said incredulously.

Working swiftly, Steve nodded and grinned. "We sure did." He glanced over his shoulder toward his daughter. "Right, Stephanie?"

Becky realized that her temporary lapse about the wisdom of her coming along on this trip might backfire and ultimately have an effect on the girl.

This wasn't about her, Becky upbraided herself. This was about Stephanie and her father. If they wanted her along, they obviously thought that she would enjoy this—although she had no idea how. If she gave in to her doubts and uncertainties, voicing them, she would wind up making them feel guilty about making her come along, which would in turn have a depressive effect on the whole weekend.

She needed to get a grip.

She pushed her fears out of her head. It was just a couple of days. She could get through this.

"Well then," she said, clearing her throat and pushing aside her massive self-doubts, "let's get started having fun." Becky began shoving the things next to her pack into it. She saw Steve exchange looks with his daughter. "What?"

"I think you'll be able to take more with you if you pack right," he tactfully suggested.

"I'm doing it wrong." It wasn't a question, but a conclusion. She tried not to give in to a sense of growing defeat.

"Don't worry. I'll show you," Stephanie cried, abandoning her own backpack and coming over to her. "Dad had to show me how to do it the first couple of times, too," she promised.

"With the right teacher, I'll catch on," Becky answered, smiling at the girl.

The backpack, once Stephanie was finished filling it for her, felt as if it weighed a ton. Becky tried not to show her surprise when she lifted it.

Steve helped slide the straps onto her shoulders and she had to concentrate really hard not to topple backward.

She looked at him, trying to hold in her alarm. "You don't expect me to run with this, do you?"

"Only if you're being chased by a bear," Steve answered drily. He saw the flash of fear that entered Becky's blue eyes. "Don't worry. There aren't any bears here."

"As far as you know," she said, not at all convinced of the fact.

"I suppose that the park rangers could have always missed one when they went over the area," Steve agreed for the sake of argument, "but the bear would probably be more afraid of us than we are of it."

"I *really* doubt that," Becky murmured.

"C'mon, people, we're losing daylight here," Stephanie cried, speaking up.

"Well, someone's eager to get going," Steve happily noted.

That makes one of us, Becky thought, even as she pasted a wide smile on her lips and said, "She's right. Let's get this show on the road. The sooner we can get to the campsite and set up, the sooner you two can show me how I'm supposed to bait a hook."

She couldn't believe she'd actually said that, and congratulated herself for doing so without shivering or making a face.

Stephanie, wearing her backpack and walking ahead of her, turned around and stared. "You don't know how to bait a hook?"

"Never needed to," Becky replied. "I get my fish from the supermarket."

The momentary look of pity passed from the girl's face. "Don't worry," Stephanie told her. "Dad'll show you how it's done. Right, Dad?"

Turning to look at Becky, Steve smiled. "It'll be my pleasure."

That wouldn't be her definition of *pleasure*. "I wouldn't count on that if I were you, Steve," Becky responded.

He laughed at her tone. And then he noticed her rather unsteady gait as she made her way up the trail. It was obvious that the backpack was weighing her down.

"You want me to take some of the things in your pack for you?" he offered. He began to reach for it.

"No." Becky waved his hands away. Stephanie's pack had to be around the same weight as hers. If the ten-year-old could manage it, she was determined to do the same. "Just promise me if I fall on my face, you won't laugh."

His eyes sparkled with humor. "I promise."

Becky found she had to bite her tongue not to voice the eternal question: *Are we there yet?* Even though she wanted to ask it with every plodding step she took.

And then, finally, when she was just about to give up, she saw it. Saw the area that was obviously the campsite Steve and his daughter were heading toward. The spot appeared to be about fifty feet from the lake.

Stephanie saw it at the same time. "We're here!" she declared happily.

Becky thought she'd never seen anything so beautiful in her life.

"Can I take this pack off now?" she asked, sounding a bit breathless.

Steve struggled to keep from laughing. He had a feeling that Becky wouldn't be too pleased with him if he did, and he really didn't want to hurt her feelings. She was trying so hard.

"Absolutely," he told her.

"I'll help you set up the tent, Dad," Stephanie volunteered. She looked at Becky. "You wanna help, too?"

What she really wanted to do was drop to the ground and just rest, but she knew that wasn't the response that Stephanie was after.

"Sure. I want the full camping experience," Becky answered.

Pleased, Stephanie took charge. Her father obligingly stepped back and let her take the lead. "Okay, this is how we put up the stakes..."

Becky listened intently. She did her best to follow instructions and was pleased to find that the result she achieved was better than she'd anticipated.

She had to admit she was surprised as well as impressed that none of them wound up getting in each other's way, especially since part of the time she felt as if she was flying by the seat of her pants.

"You're a natural," Steve told her, once they had finished putting up the tent.

"A natural klutz?" Becky asked, having no illusions about her outdoor abilities.

"No, a natural camper," he corrected. "You're way too hard on yourself, you know." Steve brushed off his hands. "You want to rest for a while?"

More than anything in the world, Becky thought. Every bone in her body cried "Yes" in response to his question, but technically, she knew they hadn't even gotten started yet.

Neither Steve nor his daughter appeared the least bit tired, and earlier Stephanie had said something about wanting to get setting up camp out of the way so they could *really* "get started." So she knew if she said yes and took Steve up on his offer to rest, she'd be letting Stephanie down.

"No," Becky answered, with as much energy as she was able to summon. "I want to fish. That's part of the reason we're out here, right?"

"Right!" Stephanie exclaimed, excitement dancing in her eyes.

Steve leaned over so that only Becky could hear

what he was about to say. "Thank you for this," he whispered into her ear.

His breath created warm ripples that spread to every part of her body, temporarily short-circuiting her brain. It took her a couple of seconds to get hold of herself enough to answer, "Sure. Don't mention it."

It took a few more minutes for her pulse to get back to normal.

"So, ready for your lesson?" Steve asked, taking out two of the poles.

Becky looked at him blankly for a moment, then realized what he was referring to. "Oh. Fishing." She struggled not to come across like a simpleton. "Right. Sure. Let's do this."

If either Steve or his daughter had noticed her verbal stumbling, they gave no indication, earning her eternal gratitude.

With Steve carrying the fishing poles and Stephanie the bucket of bait, they all went to the edge of the lake.

The girl got right down to business like a pro. Baiting her hook, she cast out the line with one smooth motion. In Becky's eyes, the execution was a thing of beauty.

She felt guilty about being the reason that Steve had to hang back. "Look, if you want to join your daughter, I can just sit here and watch the two of you do the hard work."

"Can't catch anything just by watching," he told her. "You said you wanted to fish."

"Yes, I did," she responded, wishing with all her heart that she hadn't.

"All right," Steve said, beginning her lesson.

"Some people like to use fancy lures. I've seen people spend hours working over just one. But Stephanie and I are down-to-earth. We like to use worms."

"Real worms?" Somehow, Becky had hoped that this part would never come. She heard Stephanie laugh at her question. "I take it that means yes."

"Real ones work better," he stated. He reached for the bucket Stephanie had been carrying, which Becky hadn't paid all that much attention to until now.

She looked into it and wasn't overly thrilled with what she saw. "They're alive," she declared.

"Tell you what," Steve volunteered. "I'll bait the hook for you."

Becky really wanted to say yes, but felt she couldn't shirk this part of it. Not when Stephanie was able to handle it so easily.

"No, I'll do it," she told him, manning up to the task. "Just show me how. I've never impaled a live worm before."

This time he did laugh, because she looked so cute despite her obvious aversion to all this. The fact that she was doing it meant a great deal.

"Nothing to it," he assured her. "Here, I'll show you."

Standing right behind her, Steve placed his hands over hers, and together, they succeeded in baiting the hook.

They also made a connection that neither of them had counted on. Having him standing so close like that, guiding her hands as she threaded the worm on the hook, made her infinitely aware of him. Aware of his slightly musky scent and of the fact that it had been an extremely long time since she had had any sort of relationship with a man.

As for Steve, he was almost startled to feel the very strong pull weaving through his body, the kind a man experienced when he found himself yearning for a woman.

That sort of thing hadn't happened to him since Cindy had died. Six whole years had passed and he hadn't even entertained the notion of going out with a woman, of becoming close to one.

And now this.

Standing here at the edge of the water, concentrating on helping Becky bait a damn hook, he found the notion flying at him, out of the blue. And while it captivated him, making him remember how things could be, it also disturbed him.

It made him feel as if he was being disloyal.

"Why aren't you showing her how to cast, Dad?" Stephanie asked, looking over toward the duo. "She's all set with a worm on the hook."

His daughter's voice managed to shatter the moment and break up the mood. It forced him to focus his attention on the subject at hand.

"That she is, Stephanie. Time for lesson number two," he told Becky. "Casting."

Again he went through the motions, keeping his hand on top of hers and showing her how to cast the baited line into the water as far as she was able.

The first few times were failures, partially due to the fact that his presence interfered with her ability to concentrate. Becky forced herself to focus harder. Eventually, after several more attempts, she was able to perform a successful cast.

It was silly, she knew, but she felt proud of herself.

* * *

"That had to be the best fish I ever had," Stephanie announced, as she set down her empty tin plate and beamed at Becky. "How about you? How did it feel catching your first fish? Did you feel good?"

"I have to admit," Becky said, "after I got over wanting to set it free, I was kind of proud that I actually got one."

"The *biggest* one," Steve pointed out. "You sure you've never been fishing before?"

"*Very* sure," Becky answered. She knew he was just being kind, but she appreciated it.

"We've got to bring you out again the next time we go," Stephanie said.

Becky turned toward her. Steve was sitting right next to his daughter and he mouthed *"Thank you"* to her just before she acknowledged the invitation.

"Sure—I'd love to come. Count me in." She looked around the campfire area. "Well, now that we finished eating, what do we do next?"

"Now," Stephanie declared, sounding every bit like a ten-year-old rather than the cool teenager she had been attempting to project, "we roast marshmallows!"

She said it with such gusto, Becky knew that this had to be another treasured tradition. "Sounds great to me," she agreed. "Let's get the sticks."

It was surprising how fast Stephanie could move when she wanted to.

Chapter Thirteen

After they had roasted enough marshmallows to stuff a small mattress, while nostalgically reliving previous camping trips, it was finally time to call an end to the first day of the trip and go to bed.

"No, not yet," Stephanie protested, as she struggled to stifle the yawns that were coming with more and more frequency. "C'mon, Dad," she pleaded, "bed-time rules don't apply to camping trips."

"You're right—they don't," Steve agreed. "Because if they did, you would have been in that sleeping bag of yours almost two hours ago."

Stephanie turned toward her ally for help. "Becky?"

Becky was torn, but in the end, she had to side with Steve. "I've got to call it the way I see it, Stephanie. Your eyelids are definitely drooping."

"No, they're not," Stephanie protested indignantly.

Then, because both adults were looking at her knowingly, she was forced to amend her statement. "Well, maybe they are just a little." And then she glanced up at her father. "Ten more minutes, Dad?"

Because this trip had turned out so well and was, in reality, like a precious, unexpected gift, Steve allowed her the extra time she was begging for. "Okay, ten more minutes."

Stephanie's grin was practically blinding.

But by the time the ten minutes were up, despite her efforts not to, Stephanie had dozed off. She was still sitting by the campfire, but was leaning her head against Becky's shoulder.

Becky looked toward Steve. "I think she's ready to go to bed," she whispered.

He glanced at his daughter's face. "Gee, how can you tell?" he deadpanned.

"I have this sixth sense," Becky quipped. She looked at Stephanie again. "Think we can get her into her sleeping bag without waking her?"

At first, Steve thought she was kidding. But then he realized that she was perfectly serious. "You don't know how a sleeping bag works, do you?"

If she said that she didn't, she knew he would think she was inept. But even so, she went with the truth.

"Haven't a clue," Becky confessed. "I really am a city kid."

His expression told her that he'd thought as much. "Okay, let me leave her with you for a little longer while I get her sleeping bag ready." And then he slipped inside the tent.

Becky felt almost maternal, sitting there with the

sleeping ten-year-old leaning against her as if she was totally comfortable doing so.

Maybe someday, Becky told herself.

"Okay, all set up," Steve announced as he returned. He nodded as he looked at his daughter. "And she's still asleep. Good."

Becky's arm and shoulder were beginning to ache a little. "I haven't moved an inch," she whispered.

"Well, we'll soon fix that." Steve bent over and scooped his daughter into his arms. "Okay, Stevi, time for bed," he murmured. Glancing toward Becky as he rose to his feet, he said, "She's asleep and can't hear me. I can call her Stevi when she's sleeping."

"I didn't say anything," Becky responded, spreading her hands innocently.

"Maybe not out loud," he allowed. "But you were thinking it."

The corners of her eyes crinkled just a little bit. "I'll never tell."

Moving ahead of him, she held back the tent flap, allowing Steve to walk in first.

Becky saw that he had spread out the sleeping bag in the middle of the tent, unzipped. As she watched, he laid his daughter down, then slowly zipped the bag up around her until she was snuggly sealed inside.

Becky felt a little foolish. "So that's how it's done," she murmured.

"That's how it's done. Another mystery of life solved," Steve chuckled.

"Not a mystery," she responded defensively, thinking he was having fun at her expense. Shrugging, she admitted, "I just thought you crawled into the sleeping bag. Obviously, I was wrong."

Steve chose to let the matter go. He wasn't looking to embarrass her. "You know, it is getting late, and knowing Stephanie, she's probably going to want to get an early start in the morning." His eyes met Becky's. "What do you say we turn in?"

"We?" she repeated.

Concerned with everything else, she hadn't thought about the sleeping arrangements until now. The tent had seemed so huge when they were putting it up, but now it suddenly felt a lot smaller and more intimate.

"Yes," Steve answered. "You and me and the sleeping bags. I thought you could take that side." He pointed to the left of Stephanie. "And I'd take the other side—unless you would rather reverse that order…"

His voice trailed off, as he left the decision up to her.

"No, no, that side's fine," Becky quickly assured him, her voice going up just a wee bit too high, even to her own ears.

"I can help you zip up your sleeping bag if you need help," Steve offered, nodding at it.

Right now, she thought it best if she maintained space between them. The man was just too tempting for her own good.

"No need," she answered quickly. "I can manage."

"There's no reason for you to be nervous," he told her quietly.

She looked at him with wide eyes, thinking that he was telling her he was going to be a gentleman. That he wasn't going to try anything.

"I'm not nervous," she stated, even though she could feel her pulse accelerating.

"Good, because there is nothing to be afraid of,"

he assured her. "The tent is secure and there really are no bears in this area."

She watched him and suddenly realized that he was talking about her being safe camping out here, not safe from him. The latter apparently hadn't even entered his mind.

Becky turned away and slowly let out a long breath. She really had to stop letting her imagination run away with her. Steve wasn't interested in her, and he certainly couldn't help being good-looking.

"You're sure about that?" she asked him, letting him think she was worried about their safety from the wildlife out here.

There wasn't a trace of doubt in his voice. "Absolutely."

The fact was, now that she thought about it, she *was* worried about being out here in the wilderness, and she gave voice to that. "I'm still going to think that every sound I hear is some bear, looking for a late-night snack."

"Well, we can stay up and talk if that'll make you feel better," he offered. He sat down, leaving his sleeping bag unzipped. "I'm not really sleepy."

He didn't fool her. "Yes, you are." She inclined her head. She was just going to have to be brave about this. "Thank you, but I am not going to be the reason for you missing out on your sleep."

Little did she realize that she already was, Steve couldn't help thinking. But that was something he needed to deal with and resolve on his own, without bringing her into it.

"Why don't you let me worry about that?" Steve said, amused.

Her eyes met his and she made her decision. "Okay," she said, sitting down.

They talked for a while. He told her about the project he was working on, carefully editing his words before speaking and leaving several crucial things out. Very quickly he found it fascinating that she could not only keep up with what he was saying, but had a few pertinent, interesting observations to make about the project.

Stimulated, Steve went on talking for a lot longer than he'd originally intended. But eventually, sleep finally overtook Becky.

"I think I'd better say good-night before I wind up falling asleep midword," she told him.

"Good night," he said. He doubted that she even heard him. Relieved that she'd fallen asleep, he was asleep himself within five minutes.

The second day of camping was a reenactment of the first and yet it felt different, somehow more intimate and comfortable than the first had to Becky. Stephanie was totally relaxed, having let the last remnants of her defensive guard down. She appeared to be in her element.

When they went on a hike, Stephanie enjoyed pointing things out along the route. And when they got down to fishing again, Becky was no longer the total novice she'd been the day before.

They caught a few more fish, and this time around, Becky felt confident enough to ask if she could clean them.

"You sure you want to do that?" Steve asked. "You

know you're still technically our guest and can beg off from having to do chores like that."

But she didn't want to beg off. "Being waited on was never really my thing," she confided to him. "I watched you yesterday and it didn't look as if it was all that hard."

"It's not hard. It's just messy and tedious," he told her. He thought for a moment, secretly pleased that she'd offered to clean the fish. "Tell you what. If it'll make you happy, we'll split up the catch. You can clean half of them."

"I think you're crazy," Stephanie declared, shaking her head. It was obvious that cleaning fish was not high on her list of fun things to do. "Is this going to take long?" she added, looking from her father to Becky and then at the bucket filled with fish. "I'm getting really hungry."

"Don't worry. We'll work as fast as we can," Becky promised.

"Unless you want to pitch in," Steve suggested with a straight face.

Stephanie held her hands up in the air. "I'll wait," she told them.

"I can't believe the time went by so fast," Becky remarked several hours later. The fish had been cleaned, fried, then eaten, and were now being happily digested by all of them.

"Do we really have to go home tonight?" Stephanie asked her father. With summer school over, Monday was wide open for her.

But not for Steve. "I wish we didn't, but I'm afraid so. I've got to be at work in the morning, honey."

Stephanie pouted. "They work you too hard, Dad."

Steve laughed at the face she made. Sitting at the campfire, he put his arm around her shoulders and pulled her closer.

"No argument here," he told her.

"Then stay an extra day," Stephanie pleaded. She looked up at him. "You deserve it."

"Tell you what. Why don't we make plans to do this again really soon?" Steve suggested.

Suspicion was already entering the girl's eyes. She was bracing herself for disappointment. "How soon?"

Eager not to let this opportunity slip away, and worried that Stephanie would change her mind, Becky was quick to step in.

"How about a week from next Saturday?" she asked, looking at Steve. "Does that work for you?"

He thought of his schedule for the next month. Work was being ramped up in order to make sure that they didn't miss their next deadline. But thanks in part to Becky, he had managed to recapture a little of the time he used to enjoy spending with his daughter. He wanted to hold on to that for as long as possible.

He might have to put in extra long hours during the week, but it would be worth it if it allowed him to spend another weekend with his daughter and this woman who seemed to have a knack for making things happen.

"That absolutely works for me," he said. "How about you, Stephanie? Does that work for you?"

"Yes!" She paused for a moment, biting her lower lip as she chewed on a thought. "And, Dad?"

"Yes?"

"It's okay if you want to call me Stevi when it's just the two of us—and Becky," she added, glancing her way. "Just don't do it when there are other people around." She raised her eyes to her father's. "All right?"

"Okay," he agreed, smiling at her so widely that his lips felt in danger of splitting. Again he shifted his eyes toward Becky.

But he didn't have to say anything to her. She knew what he was thinking.

Becky smiled back.

Her backpack felt even heavier as they made their way back to the car.

Maybe because they didn't want to leave, Becky thought. She had to admit that she had never been exactly enthralled with Mother Nature, but the camping trip had done its trick. It had brought Stephanie and her father closer together. And because it had, Becky felt as if she had accomplished something herself, and that felt good.

The fact that she had sustained a number of bug bites this weekend and was trying very hard not to scratch her skin off was a small price to pay for this success. And because this weekend had been so successful, she wasn't entirely dreading the camping weekend that was looming on the horizon—even though she *still* would have been just as content spending the weekend in some hotel with room service and a large TV screen where she could view films about nature if she was so inclined.

"You're awfully quiet," Steve noted. They were very close to home now. The drive had lulled Stephanie to sleep, ending most of the conversation. "Are you tired?"

"No, I just don't want to take a chance on waking Stephanie," Becky answered. She turned in her seat to make sure that the girl was still sleeping.

"I think we could probably have an explosion go off and she wouldn't wake up. All that fresh air got to her," Steve explained. "Nothing like the great outdoors to make you sleep like a baby."

Becky smiled, amused. "You'd better not let Stephanie hear you make that baby reference."

"She knows that I don't mean to imply she's a baby," Steve answered.

But Becky wasn't nearly as sure about that as he was. "Better to err on the side of caution," she told him.

He thought about it for a moment. "Yeah, you're probably right. I guess it's a good thing I have you around to keep me straight. By the way, thanks for all this."

Becky shrugged, dismissing his thanks. "You're the one who drove us out here. I didn't really do anything," she protested.

"The hell you didn't," he contradicted. "If it wasn't for you, Stephanie and I would still be totally alienated." His mouth curved fondly. "And I wouldn't be able to call her Stevi again."

"Only in private," Becky reminded him, as they pulled up in the driveway.

"Hey, better than nothing," Steve said. "A *lot* better than nothing."

After getting out, he made his way around to the rear passenger seat. He opened the door and gently drew his daughter into his arms. Since she was still sound asleep, he didn't attempt to wake her, but began to carry her toward the house.

"I'll get the door open," Becky volunteered.

"Take the keys." He still had them in his hand, even though he was holding Stephanie in his arms, and turned so that Becky could take them from him.

"Thanks." She hurried to open the door.

Chapter Fourteen

Moving quickly, Becky went up the stairs just ahead of Stephanie's father so she could open the girl's bedroom door. Going in, she pulled back the covers on her bed so Stephanie could be tucked in.

"Do you think I should get her out of her clothes?" she asked Steve as she looked at the sleeping girl.

"Don't worry about it," he said. "She slept in them while she was out camping. One more night's not going to hurt." He smiled as he gazed at his daughter.

When Becky thought about it, she did tend to agree with Steve, but it was hard to shake off the teachings of her childhood.

"My mother was always very big on following all the rules." She spread just the sheet over Stephanie and backed out of the room. "I think that was probably her way of trying to maintain some kind of control over me, since the rest of the time, I had the feeling that she felt I was way out of her league."

It wasn't that Becky felt superior to her mother; she just viewed things differently and was able to grasp so much more than her mother did.

At times she was certain that her mother felt they came from two very different worlds.

"Doesn't sound like you had a very easy childhood," Steve observed as he slipped out of his daughter's room and closed the door.

"It had its moments. And don't get me wrong, my mother did try." Becky changed the subject to something lighter. "Well, you have an early day tomorrow, so I'll let you get to bed. Thank you for including me."

She was surprised when she heard him laugh in response. "I had the feeling that you came under duress."

She couldn't tell him that he was imagining things, because he wasn't. "I have to admit that the thought of going camping wasn't exactly appealing to me at first. But it got better," she said quickly. "To be honest, I even wound up liking it." And then she looked at him ruefully. "Everything but the bug bites."

"I noticed you were scratching," Steve admitted, his mouth curving in a smile. "You do realize that the more you scratch, the itchier those bites feel."

Becky exhaled loudly in frustration. "I know, I know," she cried. "But they're driving me crazy."

He made a quick decision. "Why don't you come with me?" he suggested. "I think I've got something in my medicine cabinet that'll help. A friend of mine concocted this salve. It's a homemade remedy," he explained. "It's not overly pretty, but it really does work."

Becky followed him to the master bathroom, feeling a little uneasy. This could all be very innocent, and yet it might not be.

She debated for a moment, then finally said, "All right, I'm putting my fate in your hands."

He nodded, acknowledging that he understood. "Then I promise to be gentle. Where are the bites?"

"Mostly on my back," she told him. Hesitating, she finally turned around to let him see.

It took everything for him not to release a low whistle. Rather than a bite or two, her back looked as if it was a veritable feasting area for mosquitoes.

"Wow, you weren't kidding," he marveled.

She let go of a breath, doing her best not to reach behind her and scratch. "That bad, huh?"

Rather than answer, he told her, "Stay there for a minute." He opened the medicine cabinet and quickly scanned its contents. Finding what he was looking for, he took out a jar and placed it on the counter, then turned the faucets on and washed his hands. "I'm going to put this on you," he told her as he dried them.

"Will it sting?" Becky asked. Then, so Steve wouldn't think she was afraid of incurring a little discomfort, she said, "I just want to know what to expect."

"It's a little cold," he told her. "I guess it feels like having a mixture of whipping cream and honey spread on your skin."

She laughed drily. "Sounds like you're turning me into a dessert."

Now, there's a thought, Steve thought, smiling to

himself. He was grateful that Becky had her back to him and couldn't read his expression.

"Ready?" he asked.

Becky braced herself. The urge to scratch was becoming really difficult for her to resist. Anything had to feel better than this.

"I guess," she replied.

She drew in her breath as Steve began to slowly spread the homemade salve across the red welts that had formed on her back the more she scratched.

He frowned as he looked at them. "Why didn't you say anything earlier?"

"I thought I could grin and bear it," she told him. "I've had mosquito bites before, just not en masse like this."

Right now, the bites were exceptionally itchy, but beyond that, she could feel Steve's strong, capable fingers slowly spreading the homemade paste across her skin. She could feel herself growing progressively warmer.

It was crazy, but she could swear that his fingers gliding along her back—despite the welts and the paste—were creating a feeling within her that she couldn't seem to block.

One of deep, aroused longing. Becky did her best to struggle against it.

"This should do the trick," she heard Steve telling her.

That depends on the kind of trick you're looking for, Becky couldn't help thinking.

And then she heard him ask, "How does it feel?"

Like heaven.

She cleared her throat, as if that would keep him from reading her mind. "Less itchy," she reported.

"That's good," he said, satisfied. "I can leave this with you in case you find more bites." He put the jar down and washed off his fingers. "You know, sometimes insects are just drawn to one person more than to another. It makes no sense, but that would explain why you were bitten and Stevi and I weren't."

"Wonderful," Becky murmured, turning around to face him. "I'm a bug magnet."

Steve laughed. "I wouldn't exactly put it that way." He dried his hands and nodded toward the jar. "I hope that helps a little."

"Actually," Becky said, as she paused to take stock of the situation, "it does." She looked at him in wonder. "I'm not itchy anymore."

"Told you," Steve said, as pleased as she was that his remedy had worked.

She was more than just pleased; she was relieved. Very relieved.

"Thank you," Becky cried, feeling so grateful that she threw her arms around Steve's neck and kissed him.

And then opened her eyes wide in horror as she realized what she'd just impulsively done.

Her arms dropped to her sides. "Oh, I didn't mean to do that. I'm so sorry," she declared, feeling totally chagrined.

The expression on her face got to him. "Don't be," he told her. "I'm not."

To be honest, she'd stirred something within him and he was really, really tempted to kiss her back. It had been so long since he'd kissed any woman other than his wife. For one brief moment, he realized that he missed the human contact, the warm feeling of connecting with a woman in that very distinct, special way that only a man and woman could.

"You're not?" Becky whispered.

Something in her eyes drew him in, seemed to guide him through the next steps. Before he knew it, he was framing her face with his hands and bringing his mouth down to hers.

Heat exploded within Becky's chest.

The kiss was everything she'd known it would be and more. It was beyond exquisite.

This despite the fact that she had nothing to compare it to. Most of the men she'd dealt with in her life had either treated her as if she was some sort of an anomaly or were intimidated by her, even though she had never once knowingly tried to make anyone feel inferior to her.

That was something they were responsible for doing to themselves. But whatever the cause, Becky found herself suffering from the resulting fallout whether or not it was deemed intentional. Consequently, when she was working in aerospace, men shied away from her despite her looks.

And after she had changed her vocation and gone to work for Celia, there was never an occasion for her to actually meet men unless they were the husbands of women whose homes she cleaned. There was no future in that and Becky wasn't the type to go out with a married man even if there had been the opportunity.

The bachelors whose homes she occasionally cleaned were few and far between. Most of the time they weren't home, and anyway, Celia was the one who dealt with them whenever matters needed attending to.

Because she wasn't the type to turn to an internet dating service, Becky had resigned herself to leading a solitary existence.

This, however, was a very unique situation. A delicious, unique situation, and she could feel her whole body wildly celebrating as she lost herself in Steve's kiss.

Steve could feel his pulse racing. He felt things stirring within him that had remained dormant for so long, he was convinced that they had died and that he wasn't capable of feeling anymore. Not in *that* way.

But this was beyond the small tingle that had caught his attention whenever he'd taken note of Becky, or felt attracted to her.

This was something a great deal more intense than that.

The next moment, the wave of emotion he was experiencing ushered in a sense of guilt. It hit him hard, making him pull away.

"I'm sorry—I didn't mean to do that," he said, practically stuttering as he backed away from her. Conflicting feelings were butting heads within him. He needed distance. "I'll see you in the morning," he told her stiffly.

She held up the jar he had given her. "Thank you for the…whatever this is," she finally said.

"Don't mention it." And then he disappeared back into his room, closing the door.

For a moment, Becky wasn't sure what to do.

The kiss had been pure heaven. She could still feel

her lips throbbing from the feel of his against them. But kissing her had been an obviously impulsive, spur-of-the-moment thing. Anyone could see that he was feeling extremely guilty over it, perhaps because he had stepped over some imaginary employee-employer boundary—or maybe it was something else, she suddenly thought.

Maybe Steve felt guilty kissing her because he thought that it somehow made him disloyal to the memory of his wife. She wasn't trying to take the woman's place, but if she said as much, it would sound as if she was just making empty denials.

This was all too complicated for her to attempt to untangle tonight. She was way too exhausted to even think straight and make sense out of all this.

What she needed, she told herself, was to go to bed, and tomorrow, unless some magnificent idea occurred to her, she was just going to pretend that nothing had happened between them tonight. That way he could stop being embarrassed and continue as if it was business as usual.

Even though it really wasn't.

Steve went through the motions of getting ready the next morning, all the while searching for the right approach to take with Becky.

He had no idea what had come over him. Granted, he hadn't gone out with a woman since he'd lost Cindy, but he definitely had been in contact with them, for heaven's sake. There were a few women who worked in his department and he found himself interacting with them all the time. He'd never been tempted to kiss any of them.

What had come over him last night? This wasn't like him.

Okay, he didn't date, but he wasn't exactly a hermit. He'd just never felt the inclination to interact with any of those women socially, never wanted to move on to a higher plateau with any of them.

So why now?

And how was he supposed to conduct himself?

Well, he couldn't just hide in his room until she went out, Steve thought, upbraiding himself. For one thing, he needed to be at work early if he hoped to make good on his promise to Stevi of a repeat camping trip next week.

Coming out of his room, Steve glanced downstairs. The house was quiet, which was understandable, given how early it was. With luck, he could get out the door without running into Becky. In all probability, she was still in bed.

With each step he took as he made his way down the stairs, he felt a little closer to victory. The door was in his sight when, suddenly, Becky seemed to appear out of nowhere.

And she was blocking his way.

"I thought you'd be up early," she said cheerfully. "I have your breakfast all ready."

His heart sank, right along with his stomach. Still, he tried to dissuade her. "I was just going to get some coffee at a drive-through."

Her expression told him what she thought of that idea. "Well, 'drive' yourself right this way," she urged. "No need to go out of your way to buy coffee that you can probably use to repave the driveway." Her smile was inviting. "Breakfast is waiting. Come. I promise it'll be painless."

He dutifully followed her to the kitchen and slid into his seat. The tempting aromas swirled around him. "That smells good," he had to agree.

Her eyes crinkled in a grin. "Tastes even better," she told him. "Now eat your breakfast so you can get to work."

He still couldn't get over the feeling that he was waiting for the other shoe to drop, but it was becoming a little less probable.

Steve looked around. "Where's Stevi?"

Becky poured him a glass of orange juice, then placed it next to his plate. "She's still asleep. It is six thirty, you know."

"Oh. Right." He looked at her suspiciously. "What are you doing up?"

"Making you breakfast," she answered simply. "I had a feeling that you'd be leaving super early, and with all the work you're going to be putting in, I felt you needed to have a good breakfast in your stomach."

It all sounded logical, but he was still uneasy about the situation. "You didn't have to do this."

"Maybe not," Becky allowed. She took a sip of her own orange juice. "But I wanted to."

Steve took a few more bites of his scrambled eggs and toast. And then, unable to put up with the way he felt about his actions last night, he cleared his throat and tried to apologize.

"Um, about last night, Becky…"

"Last night?" she repeated, looking at him with

wide eyes and a confused expression on her face. "Nothing happened last night."

He eyed her uncertainly. "Don't you remember?"

"Remember?" she echoed. Since he was finished, she cleared away his plate and put it into the sink, then ran water over it. "Remember what?" she asked him innocently. "I don't remember anything."

"But—"

"If you don't get on the road soon, you're going to find yourself stuck in Monday morning traffic and you know how bad that can be. Getting a late start negates the whole idea of getting ready so early. Why don't you get going now?" she suggested. "And we'll talk later tonight—if you still feel you need to."

He paused for a moment, just watching her. He knew what she was doing—deliberately washing away his guilt. Somehow, she'd figured it out, realized that he had suddenly found himself dealing with a sense of remorse over behaving like a normal male, because in his heart he was still married to Stevi's mother. Apparently, Becky had not only figured it out, but had decided to absolve him of it.

"Thank you," he told her.

"Nothing to thank me for," she replied. "Making breakfast is part of my job description. Now please get going. You know what Mondays are like."

"You know you're the best," he said.

Her eyes crinkled again. "Maybe not the best, but at least in the top ten."

And then Becky deliberately turned her back, signaling that their conversation was at an end and that he should get moving.

She smiled to herself when she heard the door finally close.

Chapter Fifteen

On the home front, things went along smoothly for another several weeks. The same, Steve felt, couldn't be said on the work front. Because there were setbacks to the current project due to a failure in one of the missile's firing pins, he had to put in long hours at the office, working on the redesign. It was a relief knowing that Becky was there at home to pick up the slack and take care of Stephanie. With some rearranging, Steve even managed to pull off two more camping trips with her and Becky that month.

It dawned on him—though he tried not to dwell on it for fear of jinxing it—that he had not been this happy in a long, long time. Stephanie was still a mystery to him at times, but she was also more like her old self a great deal of the time, and that helped put everything into perspective.

As for Becky, because of her, a weight had been lifted off his shoulders. He didn't have to worry and feel guilty about having to leave his daughter alone so much, because she *wasn't* really alone in any sense of the word. Becky was always there for her and Becky was a decent, responsible person who his daughter enjoyed spending time with.

A person who, Stephanie had confided to him once in a rare moment of sharing, treated her like an equal, not like some little kid. "I like Becky. She's cool," she told him.

"Cool, huh?" he said, trying to understand just what that meant in "Stevi-speak."

"Yeah. Cool," Stephanie repeated. "Maybe if you weren't so busy being away all the time, you would have noticed that."

"I'm not always busy and I'm definitely not always away," Steve told his daughter seriously.

Stephanie didn't surrender easily. "Sure feels that way."

Overhearing their slightly raised voices, Becky walked in—just in time, she felt, to rescue Steve.

"C'mon, Stephanie. Be fair. If your dad was *always* as busy as you just said he was, he wouldn't have been able to take you on those camping trips, would he?"

The girl frowned and looked away with a deep sigh. "I guess not."

Becky grinned. "That's better. Okay, you two," she said, taking off her apron, "dinner's on the table. Come and eat."

"You know," Steve said to Becky, lowering his voice as his daughter made a beeline for the kitchen, "she was telling me how cool she thought you were."

Becky knew she and the girl were getting along, but this was news to her. She smiled. "Cool, huh?" she repeated, savoring the word.

"Yes, that's what she said." He smiled back. "She also told me that I needed to notice that."

"Maybe you do," Becky agreed, just before she walked into the kitchen ahead of him.

The thing of it was, Steve thought as he sat down at the table, he *did* notice. Perhaps a little too much. He was actually trying hard *not* to notice, but wasn't having all that much luck with that. Moreover, his rate of success was getting smaller every time he was in the same room with her.

He didn't know if he should be alarmed over that, or happy that he was finally coming out of his emotional coma.

It was easier just to take the whole thing moment by moment and concentrate predominantly on how his daughter was faring, not him. There was no denying that Stephanie was blossoming. No matter how much he wanted to hold that at bay, his little girl really was growing up.

But her questions, the ones that had until recently confounded him, no longer came his way. He assumed that Becky was handling that end of it, supplying answers that would have embarrassed him—and possibly Stephanie—no end if he'd had to supply them.

His workdays were long, often stretching on into the evening. One night he had to stay at the office until almost ten o'clock. When he came dragging home, all he could think of was making it into bed.

But Becky had other ideas.

As had become her habit, she had dinner waiting for him and insisted that Steve have at least a little of it before going to sleep.

"You can't be Super Dad unless you keep your strength up," she told him. "So c'mon, please eat at least some of it."

He knew this wasn't an argument he was slated to win, and the thought of having someone actually worrying about him was heartening in its own way.

"Okay," he agreed reluctantly, looking at her. "As long as you keep me company."

As far as Becky was concerned, he didn't have to ask twice. Taking a seat at the table, she asked, "How's the project going?"

He sighed. "Flowing like molasses in January." He took a few bites, then said what had been playing hide-and-seek through his mind for the last couple of days. "Is everything okay with you and Stephanie?"

"Never better." She studied him for a moment, wondering what had prompted him to ask that out of the blue. "Why?"

He shrugged. "I was just wondering if she still confided in you or if she's decided to fly solo these days."

Was he fishing, or just concerned in general? "If you're going to ask me something specific, I'm afraid I can't answer you. There are things that she tells me in confidence."

He looked at her sharply as his father radar caused alarms to go off in his head. "What kind of things?"

She could see what he was thinking. "Not those kind of things," she was happy to assure him. "Nothing's going on that's bad for her or remotely dangerous. Trust me, I'd be the first one leading the charge to get her to stop if that was the case.

"No, these are 'secret' things, 'girl' things that we're talking about. What I *can* tell you is that you have a normal daughter who's experiencing all the same ambivalent, confusing feelings that have haunted adolescents, no matter how intelligent, since the very beginning of time." She smiled at him. "Now I have a question. Why did you ask me if she still talked to me?"

He shrugged again, addressing his food rather than her. "Because she doesn't really talk to me anymore."

"Sure she does," Becky contradicted. "She just doesn't ask you about the embarrassing stuff—for which I think you're actually very grateful, since that was why you went looking for help in the first place. Right?" she asked, peering into his face.

He raised his head and looked into her eyes. "Yeah, you're right. It's just that I do want Stevi to know that I am there for her even if the subject is embarrassing. I want her to feel that I'm her dad in good times and bad."

Steve suddenly realized that he'd gotten so wound up in the conversation, he hadn't noticed that he'd finished eating. His plate was empty. He had to admit that he felt better now with a full stomach—and a relieved mind.

"Have I ever told you how happy I am that you came to work for me?" he asked her.

Becky pretended to think for a moment, although she knew what the answer to that was right off the top of her head. "No, I don't believe that you have."

"Well, I am," Steve told her seriously. "I'm very happy."

She managed to keep a straight face as she asked, "Does that mean you're going to give me a good review on Yelp?"

"Yelp?" he repeated. His world didn't touch on social media or anything that went beyond research. "Is that a thing?" he asked, slightly confused.

Becky laughed. "Never mind. I'm just pulling your leg. Oh, before I forget, Stephanie was invited for a sleepover." She beamed as she told him about what was, for the girl, a major event. "Her very first, from what I gather."

"Oh." The word was uttered without any emotion. And when Steve didn't say anything further, Becky looked at him expectantly.

"Well?" she asked, taking his plate and glass to the sink.

"Well what?" He had no idea what she was waiting for him to say.

Becky turned away from the sink. "Can she go?"

The idea of a sleepover had never been raised. To his recollection, Stephanie had never mentioned wanting to sleep over at anyone else's house. The whole idea seemed almost out of character for her.

Finally, he asked, "Does she want to go to this sleepover thing?"

"Absolutely," Becky said with conviction. "She's rather excited that she was asked. Between the two of us, I think this makes her feel like a normal girl."

A thought suddenly occurred to him. "There won't be any boys at this thing, will there?" he asked, his imagination already beginning to run wild.

Was he serious? After all, Stephanie was ten years

old and a sleepover involved supervision from the hosting girl's parents.

Keeping all that to herself, Becky treated his question as if it had been voiced in earnest. "Well, I think the girl's father will be somewhere in the house during the sleepover, but most likely he'll be with the girl's mother."

Steve got the message she was trying to convey. Relieved, he had a few more questions. "What do you think about this?"

"I think that it'll be good for Stephanie. It'll help her learn how to interact with other girls. Up until this point, she's been a bit of a loner," Becky tactfully pointed out.

He knew that. He supposed he was just worried about her being hurt. "Do you have the name of the girl who's having this sleepover and the name of her parents?" he asked.

Becky found it hard not to laugh at him. It was either that or take offense at what was implied, and she chose the easier route.

"Yes, I have their names." Since he was looking at her expectantly, she paused to write them on a pad, then gave it to him.

As he studied the names, she could almost see the thoughts forming in his head. "You're going to run a background check on those people as soon as you get into work tomorrow, aren't you?" she asked knowingly.

Steve raised his eyes to hers. For just a second, he thought of denying her supposition. But then he decided that if he lied to her and she found out, rebuilding that trust would take time and would be difficult.

Besides, she seemed to be able to see right through him. It would have been unnerving if he wasn't rooting for her to succeed. No way around it—he *liked* this woman.

No, he corrected himself, he *more* than liked her.

"Yes, I am," he answered simply. "You don't think I should?"

Becky wasn't about to tell him not to. He was Stephanie's father, and this was something new for the girl. She didn't have overly developed people skills and Becky could see why he'd worry.

"I think that you should do whatever makes you happy," she told him.

The problem was, what would make him happy had nothing to do with a background check on the Alexanders.

"You didn't answer my question," Becky said as Steve began to leave the room. When he turned around to look at her, she elaborated, "Can Stephanie go to the sleepover?"

He wanted to say yes, but years of caution had him stating, "I'll get back to you on that."

"It's tomorrow."

He nodded. Still, he had to do it his way. Just faster. "I'll get back to you quickly on that," he amended.

"Or," she interjected, raising her voice a little because he'd begun to walk out again, "you could trust my instincts and say yes," she told him, addressing her comment to his back.

He turned to her once more. "I'm her dad, Becky," he pointed out. "I need to know who I'm entrusting with my daughter."

"Do you honestly think I'd just send Stephanie

off without looking into the matter myself?" Becky asked him. For the first time since she'd come to work for Steve, she found herself feeling hurt. "In case I haven't made myself clear before, Stephanie isn't just a 'job' to me. She's someone whose welfare is very important to me. I wouldn't just let her go off with a pack of wolves—even if they were very attractive wolves and that was what she wanted to do."

"I didn't mean to insult you."

"No, but you did," Becky told him, wanting to get her point across. And then she took a breath, willing herself to calm down. "Never mind. I'm not the one who's important here," she said, rethinking the matter. "Stephanie is and I understand that you're just trying to make sure she's safe. These people are very nice, upstanding folks, and Stephanie is going to be fine over there. If all the parents wind up saying yes to the invitation, there'll be seven girls at the sleepover. Seven's a good number. Not big enough to be overwhelming, not so small that it might turn into some kind of a clique."

He looked at her, confused. "I don't know what you just said there."

She smiled. "You don't have to. You're a guy and this is a girl thing. And I really think she needs to go. It'll broaden her horizons. So do your 'background check' on these people and get back to me by noon."

Steve shook his head. "I don't have to."

"Yes, you do. She needs to tell her friend if she's coming by then," Becky stated.

"No, you don't understand. I don't have to tell you by then because I've changed my mind," Steve told her, smiling. "I'm saying yes."

She'd been so geared up to argue him down that it took her a second to absorb his answer. And then she smiled back at him.

"She's going to be really happy to hear that," Becky told him. "Although between you and me, I think if you weren't going to let her go, she might have had her first experience with out-and-out rebellion by climbing out of her window and down that old tree that's right outside of it."

"I really wish you hadn't put that image in my head," Steve muttered. "Now that's what I'm going to worry about her doing if I tell Stevi she can't do something or go somewhere."

"Why? You're the one who took her camping."

He didn't see the connection. "What does that have to do with anything?"

"You taught her how to be self-sufficient and improvise."

"All I did was teach her how to pitch a tent and how to fish," he argued.

Sometimes, the man was just too linear. "Extrapolate on that," she encouraged.

"Extrapolate?" he repeated, puzzled. And then, just like that, it suddenly dawned on him what she was saying. "I guess I've got no one to blame but myself," he said with a sigh.

"I wouldn't use the word *blame*," Becky commented. "What you did was equip her with skills that she will need to survive in this world. If anything, Steve, you should be commended and applauded."

He laughed, shaking his head. "You do have a way of turning a phrase."

"If I do, it's a holdover from my engineering days.

I learned that no matter how bad something might be at the time, there was always a way to present it in a better light." She could see that he was visibly fading. "Now, I believe you were going to bed before we got caught up in this debate."

"Right." Even as he was saying the word, he had to stop himself from yawning. "See you in the morning, Becky."

"Count on it," she called after him.

The thing was, he realized that he did.

Chapter Sixteen

The quiet hit him the very moment he walked into the house.

Not that Stevi ever created a high level of noise when she was home or listened to loud music. It was more a feeling than anything, like knowing that something was missing.

This was probably the way it was going to be when Stevi moved away to college, Steve thought. He would have to get used to being alone.

Still, with any luck, he'd have another seven years before he'd have to face that situation. Unless Stevi turned out to be some sort of a prodigy like Becky.

No, he wasn't going to go there. That was something he would tuck away for the time being. He didn't want to have to deal with any of that right now.

Aside from the quiet, he noticed that the enticing

aroma of cooked food didn't greet him the way it had all the other evenings recently. Even when he was late, he could detect the lingering smell of food that had been prepared for him.

But this time there was nothing. There was no meal warming on the stove.

Undoubtedly, Becky had taken advantage of the fact that Stevi was gone and had decided to go out. Not that he could blame her. To his recollection, since she'd started working as his housekeeper, Becky hadn't taken any official days off, even though she was definitely entitled to them. The most she'd done was take a few hours off while Stevi was attending summer school.

Instead of behaving like an employee, she was acting more like a member of the family.

The other glaring thing that hit him, although he tried not to think about it, was that he found himself missing Becky. He was just accustomed to her being here to greet him and insist on his having at least part of his dinner.

After throwing his jacket over the back of one of the kitchen chairs, he loosened his tie and opened the refrigerator door. He peered inside. Just as he'd thought, Becky hadn't left anything prepared for him. Although he knew it was unreasonable, he couldn't help feeling the sting of disappointment.

No, this was good for him, Steve silently insisted.

It just served to remind him that he shouldn't become dependent on anyone, least of all this woman. Becky was his housekeeper, for heaven's sake, not someone he had an emotional bond with. There was no reason in the world for her to have left dinner waiting for him. That she'd done so consistently in the past was a fluke, a bonus, not a requirement. All this did was serve to remind him that she had a life of her own, and she certainly didn't owe him explanations or—

The sound of the front door closing had him quickly shutting the refrigerator door and looking up. The next minute, Becky walked into the kitchen carrying a large, flat square box.

Something smelled good, he thought—something aside from her.

"You're home earlier than I thought you'd be," she was saying. "I just dropped Stephanie off at her friend's house for the sleepover. I've never seen her this excited before."

She put the box on the table and he noticed that the logo of a popular pizza restaurant was splashed across the top.

He looked at her in surprise. "You bought pizza."

"You noticed, huh?" Becky quipped. And then she went on to explain, "I thought that since this was Stephanie's first night away from home, you might be a little antsy and might want to be distracted." As she spoke, she took out some napkins and a couple of plates. "There's a home game on tonight with the Angels playing against the Mets, so I thought a pizza and some beer might be in order. We can watch and have dinner in front of the TV—or I could just let you watch the game alone if you'd prefer doing that instead."

If he wanted to be distracted, having Becky around would do a far better job than either the pizza or the game would.

"Why would I prefer to watch alone?" he asked, puzzled.

"Because I know that sometimes I have a tendency to take over and tell people what to do, and maybe you'd rather be alone tonight—to concentrate on the game."

"Tell people what to do? I hadn't noticed," Steve deadpanned. And then his face split into a grin. "See, I can make a joke, too."

"I see. C'mon," she urged. "Game's already started. I can set everything up in the family room."

"We can set it up together," he told her. He saw the slight uncertain look in her eyes. "You do realize that you are entitled to some time off, don't you?"

"I know," she told him. "This *is* my time off."

Steve decided not to argue with that. Otherwise, she might change her mind and decide to do something else. He found himself wanting to spend this time with her.

He brought in the pizza while she handled the plates, napkins and two bottles of beer. Fortunately, Steve had an old-fashioned, oversize coffee table that more than accommodated everything and then some.

She went to turn on the TV before she sat down. "I didn't know you liked baseball," he commented once the game came on.

"I do," she assured him.

"I never saw you watching a game," he pointed out.

"That's because I usually just follow the scores during the season unless it starts to look like one of my teams is actually headed for the playoffs," she confessed. "And even then I don't always watch, because I get too nervous for them. I hate seeing them lose.

"But tonight, as I was dropping Stephanie off, she told me that you like the Angels, so I thought you might like watching them play while you eat."

"As a matter of fact, I would," he told her. Leaning over, he took out a slice of pizza and put it on his plate. Looking at her, he shook his head and marveled. "You know, you're not a housekeeper. You're more like my own personal genie."

"If that were the case," she said, as she took a slice for herself, "I could only grant you three wishes and then poof! I'd be gone. I think having me as your housekeeper might be the better deal."

"You might have a point there," he chuckled. "I certainly wouldn't want you to disappear."

I wouldn't, either, Becky thought, although she did her best not to show it.

"You know, I wound up eating more than half of this pizza." It was as much an apology as an observation as he looked into the box sometime later.

"You were probably hungrier than I was," she said. "Besides, you got caught up watching some of those close plays. I don't think you were even aware of the fact that you were chewing until after you'd finished the slice—and maybe not even then." As if by agreement, they both got up and cleared the coffee table of the empty box, the dirty plates and the crumpled napkins. "It was a pretty exciting game."

"It was, wasn't it?" he commented. "I'm glad I had a chance to catch it. If it wasn't for you, I probably wouldn't have remembered that there was a game on until after it was over."

He paused for a moment after they walked back

into the kitchen and he threw the box into the recycle bin. His eyes met hers. "Thanks for this," Steve added after a moment.

"I thought you might like to do something a bit different tonight, since Stephanie was doing something different." Becky flushed a little, thinking that maybe she was saying too much. "Like I said earlier, I have this tendency to just take charge—unless someone actually stops me."

"Doing something different is good," he told her. "Although, if I was really looking to do something different..."

Realizing where he was going with this, Steve stopped himself before he got in too deep and said something he couldn't take back.

But Becky was still waiting for him to complete his thought. "Yes?" she asked.

Steve turned toward her, his common sense warring with his desire, causing him to grind to a complete standstill as each side fought to come out on top.

He looked into her eyes, warning himself not to get lost there even though it would be so easy for him to do that.

"I think you can probably figure it out," he murmured.

Silence hung between them like a lethal live wire, giving off sparks.

She caught her breath. This was where she took the reprieve, held on to it with both hands and gracefully backed away.

Or ran.

But she didn't want to back away, gracefully or otherwise, and definitely didn't want to run, even though, in her heart, she knew she should. Because taking that route only led to more of the same, while the other way promised to lead to something a great deal more exciting.

The thought tempted her.

As it grew and took on a life of its own, she could feel her heart slamming against her chest, threatening to give her away at any moment.

She could hardly breathe.

"Do I get a hint?" Becky asked in a low voice.

He was losing this battle.

Damn it, why did she have to look so appealing? He wanted to tell himself that it was the lighting, but it wasn't. She would have looked just as appealing if she'd been standing in a forest during a moonless night at midnight.

And he wanted her.

Heaven help him, he wanted her even though he knew that there would be a very heavy price to pay for all this.

But he didn't care about some price that would have to be paid somewhere down the line. Didn't care about anything except this overwhelming need that was eating away at his gut, pleading with him to at least assuage that need just a little if he didn't want to lose his mind.

So, even though every fiber of what made him a logical engineer ordered him to back away from this woman now, before he found himself getting in so deep that he couldn't find his way out again, Steve allowed himself to move on his instincts.

He framed her face with his hands and he kissed

her. Kissed her with a force that took *both* their breaths away.

And when he finally drew back, trying desperately to grab on to the last shreds of sanity, Becky murmured, “I think I’m going to need a bigger hint.”

And just like that, Steve was lost.

Lost because he didn’t want to back away. Lost because it had been too long since he’d felt that overwhelming, gut-warming glow of wanting to connect with a woman he both liked *and* desired.

It was a combination far rarer than it sounded.

He didn’t have the will to talk himself out of it, or to think through his actions. There was only here, only now, and this gnawing, insatiable longing that was completely undoing him like a runaway spool of thread.

Becky couldn’t put a name to what she was feeling because she had never felt it before. All she knew was that it was ravaging her, reducing her to a pulsating ember whose fire would consume her.

But before it did, she wanted to make the most of it, the most of this feeling comprised of wild, earth-shaking ecstasy that had taken possession of her.

That owned her.

It was as if she’d suddenly been born again. Everything was new for her. Everything that was happening just created larger and larger needs within her, sweeping her up to the next plateau, and then the next one.

Becky found herself doing things she’d never dreamed of doing. For every stitch of clothing he pulled away from her, she did the same with him. She was undressing him in a frenzy of wild, uncoordinated movements. Desire was dictating everything she did.

She had the uncontrollable urge to draw her palms along his taut chest muscles, absorbing the feel of his body through her skin even as he was exploring hers, claiming her with every hot, demanding kiss that he branded her with.

Her head kept swirling, making her brain play hide-and-seek with reality.

Because she had never felt this way about a man, had never been this close to one before—until now. Never made love with one before.

Now she wanted to experience everything at once, to touch and be touched, to kiss and be kissed, and most of all, she wanted to go where this achingly hot desire was leading her.

Her skin was soft, pliant, and the more he kissed her, the more he wanted her. She was like a feast and he couldn't seem to get enough of her. He attributed it to his long, self-enforced celibacy, but in the back of his mind, he sensed that there was more to it than that. However, right now he couldn't think, couldn't reason things out. All he wanted to do was to feel, to savor this delicious, wildly erotic woman.

It just showed him that he could *not* tell a book by its cover. To look at her was to look at a woman who was every inch a lady. But then she had all but exploded in his arms and she was a wildcat, and the thought of having her gave him a rush the likes of which he had never experienced before.

Wanting to satisfy her, he forced himself to take

his time. To draw the process out even though all he wanted to do was to take her now, this moment.

So he made love to every part of her, exciting himself in the process. Slowly drawing his lips along every inch of her, lingering, causing her to twist and turn beneath him and look up at him with complete awe.

And then, because he couldn't hold out a second longer, he drew his hard body along hers until they were totally aligned and more than ready for the last step that would create one out of two.

His eyes on hers, Steve moved her legs apart with his knee and then began to enter her.

In no way had he anticipated the resistance he encountered.

Chapter Seventeen

Steve was going to stop.

She could sense it. Just like that, he was going to stop. The very thought caused a tidal wave of regret to fill up the spaces inside her. She'd come too far, wanted him too much to have him just draw back. The initial thrust had brought pain, but there would be so much more pain if he backed away from her right now.

She *needed* him not to back away.

So Becky tightened her arms around his neck and arched her body higher against his, shattering the last of his self-control and blowing it apart.

The pain that had scissored through her subsided as the tantalizing rhythm of their bodies increased. Fiery heat and passion swallowed her again.

Every movement he made she emulated and then

surpassed, until suddenly, the very sky exploded, raining ecstasy down all around her.

All around them.

Making her want to hold on to this precious moment forever.

But after a few moments, the intensity that had seized her began to slowly fade, taking with it the euphoria that had colored her world in such exquisite, blazing hues.

The adrenaline that had sped up her heart began to slip away, as well, taking with it her feeling of well-being.

Steve rolled off her, lying instead at her side.

Silence slowly seeped into the room where only a few minutes before, the sound of heavy breathing had permeated the very air.

Becky braced herself for what she knew, in her heart, was coming.

She didn't have long to wait.

"Why didn't you tell me?" Steve asked.

She ran the tip of her tongue along lips that had gone completely dry. She willed her heart to settle down. "Tell you what?" she asked in a stilted voice.

He looked at her in disbelief. "That you were a virgin!"

His voice sounded accusing, sharp. Was he really angry? Or was that disappointment she heard in his voice? She couldn't tell.

"I must have missed filling in that line on my résumé," she said, staring up at the darkened ceiling.

"This isn't a joke, Rebecca," he told her, his guilt getting the better of him.

She turned toward him. "And exactly *when* was I supposed to tell you?"

"I don't know," he answered, feeling helpless, guilty and a host of other things he couldn't even name. *"Sometime,"* he stressed. Raising himself up on his elbow, he looked down at her incredulously. "And how is it even possible that you've never…you've never… You're twenty-seven, right?"

"What does that have to do with it?" she asked. Grabbing the edge of the comforter, she pulled it up against her, covering her nudity. "There's no expiration date for being a virgin." Her voice lowered to sound like a voice-over announcer. "'Do it by twenty-one or you're automatically not a virgin anymore'?"

"I didn't mean that." He dragged his hand through his hair, frustrated, searching for the right words to use. "Hell, Becky, you're beautiful. I would have thought any number of guys would have tried to get you into bed by now."

Didn't he get it yet? "It doesn't matter what they might have tried. I'm not that easy to get," she informed him.

Her meaning was beginning to dawn on him. "You mean you never wanted to do this before?" he questioned, astonished.

She pulled the comforter closer as she sat up. Tears stung her eyes and she blinked them back. "Look, I'm sorry if you were disappointed—"

"Disappointed?" he echoed, dumbfounded. "What the hell are you talking about? You're the one who should be disappointed!"

Now this was *really* not making any sense. She stared at Steve, totally bewildered.

"Were you *there* just now?" she questioned. "That was the singularly most wonderful experience of my life, so why in the world would I be disappointed?"

"Because," he stressed, "your first time should have been special."

"Again, *were* you just there with me?" she asked him incredulously. "It was beyond special. I can give you a written recommendation if you want—of course, I would be sorely tempted to kill the woman who accepted the recommendation, but that's my problem, not yours."

Steve slowly moved the comforter she was holding aside and pulled her to him as he lay back down.

"You have no problem," he told her, just before he kissed her again.

She could feel her body heating once more as she melted into his arms. There was still something unresolved between them. A large something. She could sense it. But for now, all she wanted to do was capture the tail of the fiery comet one more time before she retreated from the field.

Throwing her arms around his neck, she silently let him know that she wanted to make love with him all over again.

And he was there for her.

In all honesty, Steve thought he would feel guilty, but he hadn't expected the guilt to be this oppressive, to weigh him down so heavily that he had to concentrate in order to breathe. Making love with Becky had been a wild, rejuvenating experience, and for the space of time while it was happening, he felt glad to be alive again.

But after the euphoria passed and the dust settled, the feeling of disloyalty reared its head again. Left unchallenged, it flourished, creating strong waves of oppressive, soul-crushing guilt. Guilt he found he couldn't deal with.

Faced with this, Steve did the only thing he could do. He retreated. Getting up the minute he opened his eyes, he decided that he was going to go in to work even though it was Saturday.

"You're going to work?" Becky questioned as she placed the breakfast she had barely finished making before him.

Something had made her get up while he was still sleeping. Perhaps she'd sensed that he wasn't quite ready to wake up to the sight of her when he first opened his eyes. Unable to get back to sleep, she'd headed to the kitchen.

By the time she'd finished preparing his breakfast, Steve was up and walking toward the door. Moving fast, she'd managed to waylay him.

"Aren't you going to have breakfast?" she'd asked him.

Since she'd gone through the trouble, he reluctantly sat down at the table and had breakfast, but not before telling her that he had to go in. That was when she'd stared at him, stunned, and asked if he was serious.

"Yes." Steve said the word to his plate as he quickly finished what was on it.

She didn't understand. "I thought you said you had the weekend free."

"Yes, well, something came up," he told her, avoiding her eyes again.

Becky looked at him for a long moment. He'd

scared himself, she realized. He'd felt something last night and he was frightened. She would bet anything on it. "I'm picking Stephanie up from the Alexander house in an hour," she told him, watching his face for some sign that she was getting through. "She's going to be disappointed not to find you home."

Guilt ate another little piece of him. He didn't want to disappoint his daughter, but he couldn't deal with this right now. He shrugged, then let his shoulders drop.

"Can't be helped. She'll understand. She's used to it," he stated. Standing up, he drained the last of his coffee from his cup.

"She'll most likely want to tell you about the sleepover," Becky reminded him.

She could see that her words stopped him for a moment.

Torn, he gave the matter some more thought. But he really needed to be able to sort things out in his head and he couldn't do that if he stayed here right now. He felt as if there was a war going on inside him.

He felt awful about it, but for everyone's sake, he had to get away now. "Tell Stevi she can tell me all about it when I get home."

"And when will that be?" Becky asked.

Steve had reached the door at this point. He knew if he turned around to answer her, something in her eyes would tempt him to stay and he couldn't do that. Not yet. Not until he was able to figure some things out and put this uneasiness permanently aside.

"I'm not sure yet" was all he was able to say before he left.

Becky stood there, staring at the closed door, a

numbness descending over her. She'd waited twenty-seven years to give her heart to someone, only to have it lobbed right back at her as if it didn't matter.

Now what? she asked herself.

Feeling like someone who was sleepwalking, she picked up the empty plate and coffee cup from the table and brought it to the sink.

She didn't remember turning on the water, or reaching for the soap, but suddenly found herself washing the dishes over and over.

She couldn't think about this now.

She had to pick up Stephanie from the other girl's house. More important than that, she had to come up with a plausible excuse for why Steve wasn't home, eagerly waiting to hear all about this milestone that had just occurred in his daughter's life.

Becky sighed.

This wasn't going to be easy.

Becky went to pick up Stephanie. She did what she could to keep the girl entertained and distracted, directing her attention elsewhere. Not just for the moment, but for the duration of the afternoon.

They went to a matinee and took in a fantasy action movie that Stephanie had expressed an interest in seeing. After the film let out, Becky took the girl to a jungle theme restaurant for a late lunch as an added treat.

Between the sleepover, the movie and the restaurant, Stephanie had more than enough to talk about for the remainder of the day. And if she felt disappointed that her father wasn't there to share any of this with her, she gave no indication.

By the time Stephanie went to bed, Becky felt she had successfully shielded the girl's feelings. Her own feelings as far as Steve went, however, were in shambles.

Steve continued to leave the house in the wee hours of the morning and didn't get back until really late. He kept this up for the entire week, including the following Saturday and Sunday.

When it began to look as if he was going to continue playing hide-and-seek indefinitely, Becky decided something had to be done. She wasn't happy about it, but she had no other choice.

It was after ten o'clock when he came home.

Although she'd left the light on for him in the kitchen, Becky wasn't anywhere in the vicinity. He assumed that she'd gone to bed, and for once, he was disappointed that she had. He'd finally managed to work things out in his head and he was anxious to tell her about it.

This entire week he'd been struggling to reconcile what he felt for Becky with the guilt he felt because he was moving on. Moving on when obviously Cindy couldn't. Couldn't move on, couldn't feel, couldn't do anything. But he'd realized that Cindy wouldn't have wanted him to withdraw into himself. She would have wanted him to be happy—and Becky made him happy. He admitted that to himself now and accepted it.

Now what he needed to do was to tell Becky.

About to go upstairs to see if she was in her room, Steve stopped dead when he saw Celia sitting in the living room. The woman was reading a book when he entered, but looked up the moment he appeared.

"Mrs. Parnell, what are you doing here? Is something wrong?" he asked. "Where's Becky? Is Stevi all right?" His mind started going in all directions at once.

"Catch your breath, dear," Celia advised. "Your daughter's fine. She's asleep upstairs. I don't think she even knows I'm here. She's a very peaceful sleeper," the woman commented.

He could feel uneasiness beginning to scramble within him. "Please don't take this the wrong way, Mrs. Parnell, but *why* are you here?"

She offered him a serene smile. "Becky called me and asked me to stay here with Stephanie until you came home."

"I don't understand. Why would she do that?" he said. "Isn't Becky here?"

"No, she's not," Celia replied quietly. "She told me that she was handing in her notice and she wanted me to find a replacement as soon as possible. She specified that she wanted to make sure that Stephanie liked the new housekeeper before she was hired."

None of this was making any sense to him. "But why would she do that? Becky's quitting?" he questioned. "Why? When did this happen?"

"She didn't say anything to you?" Celia asked, although her manner seemed to convey that she already knew the answer to that.

"No, she didn't," Steve insisted, and then belatedly added, "I haven't been around lately..."

"Work?" Celia asked politely.

"Yes, something like that," he muttered. His mind was racing. "She's really handing in her notice?"

Celia nodded. "That's what she said."

"But she can't do that," he cried, suddenly coming to life like a man who found himself waking up out of a prolonged coma.

"I'm afraid that she has," Celia told him. Opening her purse, she produced a folded piece of paper and handed it to him.

Steve could feel his stomach knotting and then sinking even before he took the note and scanned it.

"Dear Mr. Holder,

I've asked Mrs. Parnell to find another housekeeper for you. Stephanie needs you home and you no longer seem to be comfortable here as long as I'm under the same roof. I'm taking myself out of the equation so you don't need to keep finding reasons not to be here.

Remember to keep working on your relationship with Stephanie. Don't just back off when things don't go smoothly. She's a wonderful girl, but she needs your guidance now more than ever.

It's been a pleasure knowing both of you and I wish you the best of everything.

Sincerely,
Rebecca Reynolds."

It sounded so removed, so *sensible*. Well, what did he expect after the way he'd treated her? he thought, mentally berating himself.

He looked up at Celia. "She really quit."

"I'm afraid it looks that way, dear. I'll come by in the morning myself until I can find someone to fill in as your housekeeper..." She stopped to look at the expression on his face. He wasn't paying attention. "Mr. Holder? Did you hear what I just said?"

His mind was still racing. He had to get her back. *Now*, before he lost her forever.

"Where does she live?" he asked the woman suddenly. "Becky—where does she live?"

"She wanted me to sublet her apartment for her, but I haven't managed to arrange that yet."

Celia was making it up as she went along because so far she hadn't gotten around to having Maizie sublet the apartment for Becky. She'd wanted to make sure this pairing was going to work out. If it didn't for some reason, she'd wanted Becky to have somewhere to come back to.

When Becky had called her this afternoon, Celia had thought it was all over. But now, apparently, there seemed to be hope, and she felt her heart warm.

"What's the address?" Steve asked.

When Celia gave it to him, he took her hands in his, squeezing them.

The ambivalent feelings he'd been warring with for over a week had all vanished. Hearing that Becky was gone solidified his convictions. He knew what he needed to do. Beg for forgiveness.

"I have to impose on you a little longer, Mrs. Parnell," he told her. "I know it's a lot to ask, but could you stay with my daughter until I get back?"

Yes! Celia thought. "Of course I will," she said out loud. Then she innocently asked, "Where are you going, dear?"

He was already at the door. "I've got to go tell someone that I've been an absolute idiot."

Celia smiled in approval. "Humbleness is always

a good trait, dear," she told him. And then she waved him off. "Go, do what you need to do. I'll stay here until you get back."

He was gone before she stopped speaking.

Celia crossed her fingers, then picked up her book again.

Chapter Eighteen

It didn't feel like home anymore.

Actually, Becky thought, her apartment never really did feel like it was "home." She hadn't been inside it for over a month and now it almost felt alien to her. Alien and cold, but she'd get used to it again, she told herself.

At best, it had been a place where she came to shower and change, to eat and sleep. Occasionally, she'd watch something on TV, but it hadn't been a place she thought of fondly and it certainly didn't feel all that welcoming to her.

But now it was going to have to be all those things, she told herself. Because this was where she was going to regroup and start all over again.

Maybe she'd even go back to engineering…

No, she couldn't do that, Becky thought. She didn't like that world anymore. Though she knew her mother thought it was beneath her, given her education, she really liked working for Celia.

Besides, engineering reminded her of Steve and right now she really couldn't handle that. The wound he'd left was still too fresh.

After what had ultimately been the very best night of her life, she had been forced to face a morning that registered in at less than zero. That had been followed by possibly the worst week she could ever remember and that was saying a great deal, given the ridicule, verbal abuse and bullying she'd had to endure at times as a child because she was considered "different."

She'd thought that was all finally behind her, and in a way it was. However, what she'd gone through this last week, trying to muster on without allowing Stephanie to see or even suspect that something was wrong, that she was hurting, had been much harder than she'd expected.

Her mind turned to Steve's daughter.

It bothered her that she had left Stephanie without explaining why she was going. She'd made up a flimsy excuse, then quickly left. Anything more and she would have broken down, telling the girl why she was really going. Despite what Steve had done to her heart, she didn't want Stephanie being upset with her dad. Right now the relationship between father and daughter was a delicate one, and for Stephanie's sake, it needed to continue unmarred.

Becky looked around the dark apartment. She hadn't turned on the light when she came in. Somehow, having the place lit up would seem almost too cheerful, given what she was feeling. So she left it the way it was, bathed in darkness.

She didn't know what to do with herself.

It had been so long since every moment of her waking hours hadn't been accounted for that to be sitting here now with nothing demanding her time felt really, really strange. Lack of having something to do made her feel restless, not to mention lonely.

Maybe she'd give her mother a call tomorrow. It had been a while now since she had gotten together with her mom. And right now, she needed to be fussed over and treated like someone's child.

Needed to feel as if she mattered to someone.

Who are you kidding? Fussed over and treated like someone's child? You know you'd hate that. It's just your insecurity talking. Get a grip, Becky. You're still you. So you fell for a guy who's not able to commit—you think you're the first one to ever do that? Puh-lease, just grow up.

But that was exactly what she had done, and if this was what it meant to grow up, maybe this whole "grown up" thing was highly overrated.

She was better off not being attracted to anyone, not even if—

The doorbell rang, catching her entirely off guard. The first thing she thought of was that it had to be her mom. As far as she knew, no one else ever came by.

"Oh God, Mother, not now," she murmured. She debated just sitting here in the dark, not making any noise and waiting for her to go away.

But then the doorbell rang again, more insistently this time. She knew her mother wasn't going anywhere. The woman would stand outside her door, ringing the bell forever—until she answered.

With a sigh, Becky got up and moved to the door like a condemned prisoner walking her last mile.

"Mom," she said, even as she began opening the door, "I think I'm coming down with something. I'm really not up to having any company right now."

She stopped dead when she saw who it was.

"I'm not company. I'm the jerk who's come to beg you for forgiveness," Steve told her as he crossed her threshold. He looked around in surprise. "You don't have any lights on. Did you pay your electricity bill?"

"I paid it," she told him. "I just felt like sitting in the dark." Since he was obviously staying, she closed the door behind him. "You were saying something about being a jerk."

"I was." About to launch into an apology, he paused. "Do you mind if I turn on a light? I want to be able to see you when I say this."

"I thought that was the whole point of you being at work all the time," she said. "So you *wouldn't* have to see me."

He wasn't about to dispute that. Turning on the light, he just began explaining things. "I needed some time to work a few things out."

When she began to move away, Steve caught Becky's wrist and made her look at him. He felt as if he had just one chance to make this right and he was not about to mess things up.

"Becky, it doesn't take a rocket scientist to know that you are the best thing that's happened to me in a long, long time. You are the first woman I've been attracted to since Cindy died and I felt guilty as hell that I was moving on, even *thinking* of making a new life for myself, when Cindy couldn't." He looked at her helplessly. "Maybe that sounds crazy to you—"

"Actually, it doesn't," Becky answered.

Her words surprised him and he stared at her, relieved.

"Another reason to love you," he said, without realizing that he had voiced his thoughts out loud. "Anyway, you need to know that I had been in love with Cindy since the fourth grade. There'd never *been* anyone else except Cindy. Ever. I never sowed any wild oats, never did anything wild and unpredictable. Nothing," he insisted. "There was just puberty and then there was Cindy.

"The day she died, it was because she was in the wrong place at the wrong time. I was working overtime—again," he confessed in a husky voice. "And I asked her to run an errand for me. She did, and she wound up walking in on a robbery. If I hadn't been working, if I'd run my own damn errand," he said, with barely controlled emotion, "I would have been the one to walk in on that robbery. I would have been the one to get shot and die, not her." He took a shaky breath. "I can't begin to describe the kind of guilt I felt over that.

"And then you came along, and without meaning to, I somehow found myself falling in love with you without even being aware of it. When I realized what was going on, all that guilt came flooding back, almost drowning me. So I ran," he concluded. "I just ran."

Overwhelmed, Becky found it took her a moment to speak. "That's why I left. I didn't want to be the reason you felt you couldn't come home. Stephanie needs you to be there," she insisted. "You're her dad and she needs you."

He knew that. But he also knew something else now. "She needs you, too."

That wasn't necessarily true, Becky thought. She was just a place holder. "Stephanie needed someone to listen to her for a little while as she untangled some of the things she was going through." Becky smiled at him. "But now that the hard part's over, you can do that, too."

It sounded as if she was about to tell him to leave, but he wasn't finished yet. He needed her to know something.

"While I was hiding out at work," he continued, "using it as an excuse not to come home, I figured out something." His eyes met hers. "I figured out that Cindy wouldn't want me living like a hermit. Or a monk. That she would want me to be happy, just like, if the tables had been turned and she was the one who had lived, I would have wanted her to go on with her life and be happy. I was so busy being guilty that she wasn't here, I'd forgotten what Cindy was like when she *was* here." He searched Becky's face, trying to see if he was getting through to her. Hoping that he had.

"It sounds like she was a wonderful person," Becky murmured.

"She was," he agreed. "Just like you're a wonderful person. Becky, it's taken me almost seven years to find someone I'm attracted to. Someone I want to be with. Not just for a day, or a week, but for the rest of my life."

She looked at him, not sure what she was hearing. "What are you saying?"

He'd thought he was clear. Obviously not. He tried again. "That I love you, Becky, and I want to be with you."

She wanted to believe him, but she was afraid to. Afraid to unlock the door to her heart again after he'd slammed it so hard.

"You scarcely know me," she protested.

"I know you better than you think," Steve told her. When Becky began to protest again, he started to enumerate all the different things.

"I know you understand Boolean algebra. That you respect that I can't always share things with you because the information I have is deemed classified. I know that I can talk to you about the things that aren't classified and be confident that you understand what I'm saying. I also know that you put up with going camping and fishing with me because those things are important to Stevi, as well," he allowed. "I know that my daughter is crazy about you, and trust me, that is no small thing.

"And most of all, I know that the thought of holding you in my arms makes me go weak in the knees."

Please don't do this. Please don't make me put my guard down again. "Maybe you're just allergic to the shampoo I use," she told him.

"Oh no, you're not going to get out of this that easily," he said. "I honestly didn't think I'd ever love another woman after Cindy died. I felt that there was room in my heart only for Stevi and that I would never let anyone else in. But I was wrong," he said, his eyes pleading his case to her. "I love you, Rebecca Reynolds, and I want you in my life."

Becky paused, wrestling with herself, afraid of what lay ahead. But she had no choice. She knew that.

"All right," she told him. "If you feel that strongly, I'll come back to work for you. We can leave now if you want. I couldn't get myself to tell Stephanie why I was leaving. That means I don't have to explain anything to her when she sees me in the morning. She doesn't have to know anything about this."

Steve let her say her piece, and then he shook his head. "I don't want you to come back to work for me."

Well, that hadn't taken long, she thought. He'd shot her down. "Then I don't understand what this is all about."

"I don't want you to work for me," he repeated. "I want you to marry me."

Stunned, she could only stare at him, momentarily speechless. And then she finally found her tongue. "You want me to what?" she asked, certain that she'd either heard him wrong or that for some reason he was having fun at her expense.

Maybe this was how he was making her pay for having left him without any notice.

Rather than repeat what he'd just said, Steve took her hand and right in front of her astonished eyes got down on one knee. "Rebecca Reynolds, I know I don't have the right to ask you this after the way I've treated you, but will you marry me and make me the happiest man on earth?"

Because of the doubts he'd had earlier, she didn't think it would be fair of her to say yes, the way she ached to do. Instead, Becky looked into his eyes and asked, "Are you really sure about this? Sure that you want to marry me?"

Rather than answering her, he crossed over to the front door of her garden apartment. Opening it, he loudly announced, “From the bottom of my soul, I want to ask Rebecca Reynolds to marry me.”

Within moments, several doors and windows in the immediate area opened.

“So do it already!” one man shouted back.

“Ask her to marry you!” another yelled.

A woman joined in. “If she won’t, I will.”

“Say yes so he’ll shut up! I’m missing my program!” another woman cried.

Smiling, Steve closed the door and turned back toward Becky. “I believe the consensus is ‘yes.’ Your neighbors want you to marry me.”

“You know, I never went along with public opinion,” Becky told him, placing her hands on his chest. Then she grinned as she added, “Until now.”

Steve pulled her into his arms. “Finally!” he cried. “Remind me never to do anything stupid again. Atoning for it is way too hard.” His arms tightened around her. “You had me worried there for a while.”

“Right back at you,” she said, thinking of the emptiness she’d felt when she’d believed he wanted to get away from her. “Well, now that that’s settled, we’d better be getting back to your house. I’m sure Mrs. Parnell wants to go home.”

“She told me that she’d stay with Stephanie until I returned, and she didn’t seem to be in any particular hurry to go anywhere,” he told her.

Becky had her own theory about that. “That’s because Mrs. Parnell is nothing if not polite. That woman wouldn’t tell you to hurry up even though she’d want you to.”

"No, I'm pretty sure that my interpretation is right," Steve stated. "Besides, I don't intend to keep you here much longer. I just want to seal this with a kiss." He fitted her snugly against him. "Did you know that engagements aren't considered legitimate until the official engagement kiss takes place?"

"I did not know that," she responded, her eyes sparkling.

"It's true," he told her solemnly. "I saw it written in a book of rules somewhere. You want this to be an official engagement, don't you?"

"Oh, absolutely," Becky responded, weaving her arms around his neck.

"That's what I thought," he said, just before he lowered his mouth to hers.

And to make sure that there was never going to be any question in her mind about just how official her engagement was, Steve kissed her until they both finally had to break away in order to draw in some air.

But that didn't happen for a long, long time.

Epilogue

"I don't know how to thank you," Bonnie Reynolds gushed, clutching Celia's hand as ushers in black tuxedos moved up and down the aisles, seating wedding guests in the church. "You've produced nothing short of a miracle."

"The miracle was your doing, Bonnie," Celia corrected. "You're the one who gave birth to Becky, and who worked hard to single-handedly provide for her while she focused on her studies."

"Celia, I'm talking about this wedding," Bonnie told her. "I never thought I'd actually be the mother of the bride."

"It was all leading up to this, trust me," Celia assured her, putting her hand over her friend's and squeezing it.

"And there's more good news," Bonnie told her.

"Do you know that Rebecca's even talking about going back to engineering? Part-time for now, but that's better than turning her back on her education altogether. Steve said they had an opening in his company that she was perfect for. And I even get a granddaughter!" Bonnie cried, her heart swelling with utter joy. "I really don't know how I'm ever going to be able to pay you back for what you've done."

"It was my pleasure, Bonnie. *Our* pleasure," Celia amended, glancing at her friends Maizie and Theresa, who were already seated in a pew on the bride's side. "And right now, I think you'd better take your seat up front. Something tells me the ceremony's about to start."

"You're right," Bonnie exclaimed. She began to walk toward the front of the church. However, she turned back long enough to give Celia a quick kiss on the cheek and murmur, "Thank you again!" before she hurried up the aisle.

Celia slipped into the pew with her friends. The look of satisfaction on her face was telling. "Well, ladies, chalk up another one," she whispered.

Leaning in, Maizie commented, "You carried this one all by yourself, Celia. You came up with both the potential bride and her groom, so the credit is all yours."

"Technically," Celia agreed. "But I wouldn't have been able to do this without you two for inspiration." The music began to swell and she turned toward the rear of the church just as the doors parted. "Oh, look, there she is. Isn't she beautiful?" she sighed.

"All brides look beautiful," Maizie told her friends. "I think it's an unspoken rule."

The music grew louder and all eyes turned to watch Becky slowly move up the aisle, walking behind Stephanie, who was her flower girl.

Stephanie appeared to be beaming as she scattered white rose petals in front of the woman who was in a matter of minutes going to become her stepmother.

Stephanie was down to the last two petals as she reached the altar. Winking at her father, she stepped aside and went to stand by her new stepgrandmother.

When Becky joined Steve at the altar and turned to face the priest who was officiating the ceremony, her groom leaned over and whispered, "I was afraid that at the last minute you'd change your mind and not come."

"And miss showing off this dress?" she teased in an equally low voice. "Not a chance," she whispered back. Her eyes danced as she smiled up at him. "Let's do this," she said, her heart bursting with happiness.

Steve more than happily concurred.

* * * * *

MILLS & BOON

Coming next month

THE MILLION POUND MARRIAGE DEAL
Michelle Douglas

Sophie had had good sex before, but what she shared with Will wasn't just good. It was *spectacular*. She hadn't known it could be like this.

Not that she said that to Will, of course. It smacked too much of a neediness that would send him running for the hills. She didn't want him running for the hills. Not yet.

Not that they spent all their time in bed. They spent hours riding Magnus and Annabelle as he showed her all the places he'd loved when he was young. They explored the glens and the hills, traversed lochs and cantered through crystal-clear streams. They spent hours playing board games and watching musicals with Carol Ann.

But when they retired to their room each night — they made love as if they never wanted to stop. Not just once, but again and again. As if they couldn't get enough of each other. As if they were addicted.

It wasn't until Thursday, though, that Sophie finally realised how much trouble she was in. When Will told her he had to go back to London the next day. The depth of the protest that rose through her had her clutching the wedding folder she held to her chest. As casually as she could, she leant a shoulder against the bedroom doorframe to counter the sensation of falling, of dizziness. Loss, anguish and despair all pounded through her.

Will sat on the side of the bed, his back to her, pulling on his shoes, so she allowed herself precisely three seconds to close her eyes and drag in a breath, to pull herself together. 'No rest for the wicked?' she forced herself to ask, with award-winning composure.

He didn't move and she tried to paste what she hoped was a cheeky grin into place. 'I suppose I should be focusing on the wedding anyway. Nine days, Will. The month has flown!'

He turned, a frown in his eyes. 'Do you want to back out?'

'Of course not.' It was just… She hadn't known when she'd agreed to this paper marriage that she'd be marrying the man she *loved*. 'Do you?'